THE
WORLD
THAT WE
KNEW

ALICE HOFFMAN

SIMON & SCHUSTER PAPERBACKS

NEW YORK   LONDON   TORONTO   SYDNEY   NEW DELHI

Simon & Schuster Paperbacks
An Imprint of Simon & Schuster, Inc.
1230 Avenue of the Americas
New York, NY 10020

This Simon & Schuster Canadian export edition September 2019

SIMON & SCHUSTER PAPERBACKS and colophon are registered trademarks of Simon & Schuster, Inc.

For information about special discounts for bulk purchases, please contact Simon & Schuster Special Sales at 1-866-506-1949 or business@simonandschuster.com.

The Simon & Schuster Speakers Bureau can bring authors to your live event. For more information or to book an event, contact the Simon & Schuster Speakers Bureau at 1-866-248-3049 or visit our website at www.simonspeakers.com.

Interior design by Carly Loman

Manufactured in the United States of America

10   9   8   7   6   5   4   3   2   1

Library of Congress Cataloging-in-Publication Data

Names: Hoffman, Alice, author.
Title: The world that we knew : a novel / Alice Hoffman.
Description: First Simon & Schuster hardcover edition. | New York : Simon & Schuster, 2019.
Identifiers: LCCN 2018057681| ISBN 9781501137570 (hardcover) | ISBN 9781501137587 (trade paperback) | ISBN 9781501137594 (ebook)
Subjects: LCSH: Paris (France)—History—1940–1944—Fiction. | Holocaust, Jewish (1939–1945)—Fiction. | Jews—France—Paris—Fiction. | Jewish Children—Fiction.
Classification: LCC PS3558.O3447 W67 2019 | DDC 813/.54—dc23
LC record available at https://lccn.loc.gov/2018057681

ISBN 978-1-9821-3626-0
ISBN 978-1-5011-3759-4 (ebook)

"Can you tell me the way then, and I will seek you . . ."

"Yes, you may do that," said he; "but there is no way thither. It lies east of the sun, and west of the moon, and never would you find your way there."

"East of the Sun, West of the Moon"

The strangers in your midst shall be to you as the native-born, for you know the stranger's heart, for you were strangers in the land of Egypt.

Exodus 23:9

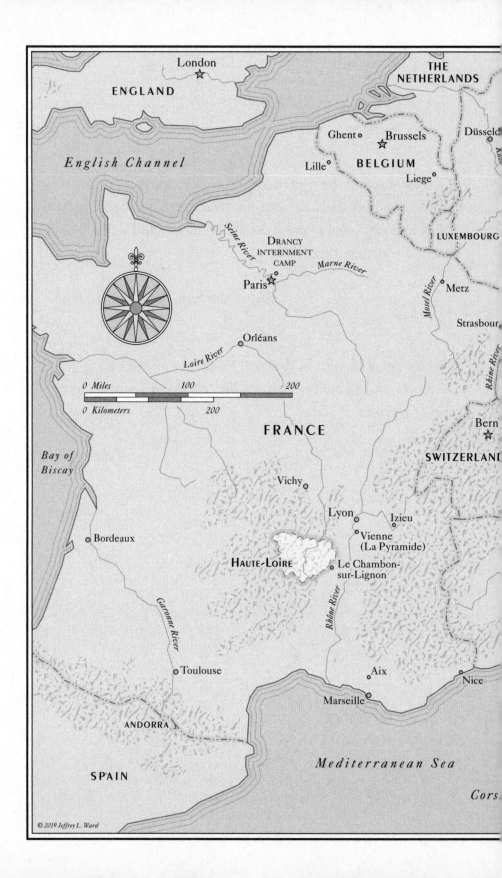

London ☆

ENGLAND

English Channel

THE
NETHERLANDS

Ghent ○   Brussels ☆   Düsseld○

Lille ○   BELGIUM

Liege ○

LUXEMBOURG

Seine River   DRANCY
INTERNMENT
CAMP

Marne River

Mosel River

Metz ○

Paris ☆

Strasbour○

Orléans ○

Loire River

Rhine River

0 *Miles*   100   200

0 *Kilometers*   200

FRANCE

Bern ☆

SWITZERLAND

*Bay of
Biscay*

Vichy ○

Lyon ○   Izieu ○

Vienne ○
(La Pyramide)

Bordeaux ○

HAUTE-LOIRE   Le Chambon-
sur-Lignon ○

Garonne River

Rhône River

Toulouse ○

Aix ○

Nice ○

ANDORRA

Marseille ○

Mediterranean Sea

SPAIN

Cors

© 2019 Jeffrey L. Ward

PART ONE

1941–42

CHAPTER ONE

EAST OF THE SUN

BERLIN, SPRING 1941

IF YOU DO NOT BELIEVE IN EVIL, YOU ARE DOOMED TO LIVE IN a world you will never understand. But if you do believe, you may see it everywhere, in every cellar, in every tree, along streets you know and streets you've never been on before. In the world that we knew, Hanni Kohn saw what was before her. She would do whatever she must to save those she loved, whether it was right or wrong, permitted or forbidden. Her husband, Simon, was murdered on a winter afternoon during a riot outside the Jewish Hospital on Iranische Strasse, which was miraculously still functioning despite the laws against the Jews. He had spent the afternoon saving two patients' lives by correcting the flow of blood to their hearts, then at a little past four, as a light snow was falling, he was killed by a gang of thugs. They stole the wedding ring from his finger and the boots from his feet. His wife was not allowed to go to the cemetery and bury him, instead his remains were used for animal feed. Hanni tore at her clothes, as tradition dictated; she covered the mirrors in their apartment and sat in mourning with her mother and daughter for seven days. During his time as a doctor Simon Kohn had saved 720 souls. Perhaps on the day that he left *Olam HaZeh*, the world that we walk through each living day, those who had been saved were waiting for him in *Olam HaBa*, the World to Come. Perhaps his treatment there, under the eyes of God, was that which he truly deserved. As for Hanni, there was not enough room in the world for the grief that she felt.

In Berlin evil came to them slowly and then all at once. The rules changed by the hour, the punishments grew worse, and the angel in the black coat wrote down so many names in his Book of Death there was no room for the newly departed. Each morning people needed to check the ever-changing list of procedures to see what they were allowed to do. Jews were not allowed to have pets or own radios or telephones. Representatives from the Jewish community center had recently gone through the neighborhood asking people to fill out forms with their names and addresses, along with a list of all of their belongings, including their underwear, their pots and pans, their silverware, the paintings on the walls, the nightgowns in their bureau drawers, their pillows, the rings on their fingers. The government said they must do so in order for proper records of valuables to be made during a time of reorganization under the Nazi regime, but this was not the reason. It was easy to lie to people who still believed in the truth. Only days afterward, each person who had filled out this list was deported to a death camp.

As the months passed, the world became smaller, no larger than one's own home. If you were lucky, a couch, a chair, a room became the world. Now, as spring approached, Jewish women were no longer allowed on the street except for the hour between four and five in the afternoon. They filed out of their houses all at once, stars sewn to their coats, searching for food in a world where there was no food, with no money to buy anything, and yet they lingered in the blue air, startled by the new leaves on the trees, stunned to discover that in this dark world spring had come again.

On this day, Hanni was among them. But she was not looking to buy anything. That was not where fate had led her. In a matter of months, Hanni had become a thief. She was fairly certain that her crimes wouldn't stop there, and if people wished to judge her, let them. She had a mother who was unable to leave her bed due to paralysis and a twelve-year-old daughter named Lea, who was too smart for her age, as many children now were. She looked out the window and saw there were demons in the trees. The stories Hanni's mother had told her as a child had now been told to Lea. They were tales to tell when children needed to know not all stories ended with happiness. Girls were buried in the earth by evil men and their teeth rose up through the mud and became white roses on branches of thorns. Children were lost and could never find their way home and their souls wandered through the forest, crying for their mothers.

Grandmother was called Bobeshi. She had been born in Russia and in her stories wolves ruled the snowy forests, they knew how to escape from the men on horseback who carried rifles and shot at anything that moved, even the angels. Lea was a shy, intelligent girl, always at the top of her class when school had been in session and Jews were allowed to attend. She sat close to Bobeshi while the old woman told how as a girl she had walked alone to a great, rushing river to get water each morning. Once a black wolf had approached her, coming so close she could feel his breath. They had stared at each other, and in that moment she'd felt that she knew him and that he knew her in return. In stories a wolf might have torn her to shreds, but this one ran back through the trees, a beautiful black shadow with a beating heart. A wolf will seldom attack, Bobeshi always said, only when it is wounded or starving. Only when it must survive.

Hanni Kohn was not the sort of person to give in to demons, although she knew they now roamed the streets. Everywhere there were *ruach ra'ah*, evil spirits, and *malache habbala*, angels of destruction. Her husband had saved so many people she refused to believe his life had meant nothing. It would mean, she had decided, that no matter what, their daughter would live. Lea would live and she would save more souls, and so it would go, on and on, until there was more good in the world than there was evil. They could not let it end this way. Hanni had no choice but to survive until their daughter was safe. She found ruined gardens and dug in the earth for young onions and shallots, from which she fashioned a family recipe called Hardship Soup, made from cabbage and water, a food that sustained them while others were starving, She went out after curfew to cut branches from bushes in the park so they might have wood to burn in their stove even though the smoke was bitter. Dressed all in black so that she would be nearly invisible, she ventured into the muck of the river Spree, where she caught fish with her bare hands, even though doing so was a serious offense punishable by lashings and prison and deportation. The fish sighed in her hands, and she apologized for taking their lives, but she had no choice, and she fried them for dinner. She was a wolf, from a family of wolves, and they were starving.

Her plan was to steal from the tailor's shop where she had once worked. In the last years of her husband's life, Jewish doctors had been paid nothing, and she had become a seamstress to support the family. It was a talent that came to her naturally. She had always sewn clothes for her mother and daughter, all made with tiny miraculous stitches that were barely visible to the naked eye. But now the Jewish shops had all been destroyed or given over to Aryan owners. The only work for Jews was forced labor in factories or camps; one had to hide from the roundups when the soldiers came in search of able-bodied people, for this kind of work was meant to grind workers into dust. In a time such as this it wasn't difficult to become a thief, all you needed was hunger and nerve. Hanni had decided to bring her daughter along. Lea was tall and looked older than her age; she would be a good student when it came to thievery. She understood her grandmother's stories. Demons were on the streets. They wore brown uniforms, they took whatever they wanted, they were cold-blooded, even though they looked like young men. This is why Lea must learn how to survive. She was to remain in the alleyway while Hanni went to search for anything left behind by looters. If anyone came near she was to call out so that her mother could flee the shop and avoid arrest. She held her mother's hand, and then she let go. Lea was only a girl, but that didn't matter anymore. She knew that. *Be a wolf,* her grandmother had told her.

7

She was waiting for her mother, standing on broken glass, hidden in the shadows as Hanni rummaged through the shop. Hanni knew where tins of tea and beans were stored for the employees' lunch, and where the best satin ribbon was kept, and, if they hadn't yet been stolen, where the shop owner hid a few silver teaspoons inherited from a great-aunt.

Lea heard footsteps. The alley seemed darker and she had the urge to flee even though she'd been told to stay where she was. Should she call for her mother? Should she whistle or shout? She had a bleak shivery feeling, as if she had fallen through time to find herself in Bobeshi's village. Before she could decide whether or not to run, he was looming there, a man in his twenties, a soldier in the German army. His eyes flicked over her and she shrank from his gaze. In his presence Lea immediately lost the power of speech. He was a demon and he took her voice from her and held it in his hand. He grinned, as though he'd picked up the scent of something delicious, something he wasn't about to let get away. No one wants to be the rabbit, standing motionless in an alley, ready to be devoured.

"Beweg dich nicht," he told her. *Don't move.*

She was only a girl, but the soldier saw her not just for who she was, but for who she would be. For him, that was more than enough. He ran a hand over her long blond hair. Right then and there, she belonged to him. He didn't have to tell anyone else, or share her, or even think what he would do with her after. *This was what it was like,* she thought. *This was the trap.*

"Schön," he told her as he petted her. *Beautiful.*

One touch and he changed her. This was the way dark enchantments worked, without logic, without cause. You are one thing and then the world pitches and you are something else entirely. A bitter fear was rising inside of Lea. Without knowing anything about what men and women did, she knew what came next. She'd felt it when he touched her. Ownership and desire.

When the soldier signaled for her to follow him down the alley, she knew she should not go. She was shivering, and her throat was burning, as if she had swallowed fire. It's not easy for a girl to face a demon, but she forced herself to speak.

"My mother said to wait."

The soldier grabbed Lea and shook her by the shoulders. He shook her so hard her teeth hurt and her heart ached. She thought about her father opening people's hearts and putting them back together again.

"I don't give a damn what your mother said," the soldier told her.

He dragged her to the end of the alley and shoved her against the wall. She felt something break. It was her tooth, cracked in her mouth. The soldier had a gun under his jacket. If she called out, she was afraid he might shoot her mother. He might tear them both apart. She thought she saw a handsome man on the rooftop in a black jacket. She could call out to him, but what if he was a Nazi? Then she realized he was Azriel, the Angel of Death, whom a mortal is said to see only once in her life.

Before Lea could think of what to do, the soldier was reaching beneath her skirt, pulling at her undergarments. Her heart was shredding inside her chest. He covered her mouth with his, and for a moment she saw nothing and felt nothing, not even dread. The world went black. She thought perhaps this was how her life would end. She would walk into the World to Come in darkness, a sob in her throat. Then something rose up inside her.

She braced herself, arching away from him, nearly slipping from his grasp. He didn't want a girl who fought back. He didn't find it amusing in the least. He covered her mouth with his hand and told her she could scream if she liked, but there was no one to hear her, so she had best shut up or he would shut her up. She belonged to him now.

"Du wirst nie entkommen." *You can never get away.*

That was when she bit him. She was the wolf in her grandmother's stories, she was the girl who rose out of the darkness, the flower on a stem of thorns.

He shook her off, then clutched at her more roughly, kissing her harder, biting at her lips so she would know she was nothing more than his dinner. He felt her body as an owner would, going at her until she wept. Everything was moving too fast; a whirlwind had descended upon them and the air smelled like fire, burning up all around them. This happens when the Angel of Death is near, the one who is so brilliant he is difficult to look upon.

Lea thought it would never end, but the soldier suddenly lurched forward, falling onto her with all of his weight, so heavy she thought she might collapse. But before he could topple them both onto the ground, her mother pulled her away. Then he dropped like a stone in a stream, sprawled out on the cement. It was his blood that smelled like fire. There was so much that it covered the pavement, spilling over their shoes. The angel on the roof had gotten what he came for and had disappeared like a cloud above them.

Hanni had known exactly what she must do when she left the store and saw the soldier with Lea. She didn't think twice. "Don't look," she told Lea.

Lea always did as her mother instructed, but not on this day, not now. She was another person. The one he had changed her into.

She saw her mother pull out a pair of shears she had stabbed into the soldier's back. His shirt was turning black with blood and his eyes had changed color. In stories, it is possible to tell who is human and who is not. But here, in their city, it was impossible to tell them apart. A demon could look like a man; a man could do unthinkable things.

Lea and her mother ran hand in hand, disappearing into the crowds of women who were so intent on finding food for their families they didn't notice the blood on the hem of Hanni's skirt or the slick black liquid on their shoes. They left footprints at first, but the blood grew thinner and more transparent, and then disappeared. When they reached their apartment building, they ducked inside, still trying to catch their breaths. There were families sleeping in the hallways, displaced from grander neighborhoods where their homes had been stolen by Germans. At night people knocked at their door to plead for food. Hanni made Hardship Soup once a week and left bowls out in the corridor for those in need, but there was never enough.

They went up three flights of stairs, stepping over strangers, hurrying as best they could. Once inside their apartment, Hanni locked the door, and the spell of the night was broken. She had murdered someone and her daughter had been a witness. She quickly slipped off her bloodied skirt, then took up the sharp scissors to cut the cloth into tiny pieces, which she burned in the stove. Lea couldn't help but think of the way the soldier had grabbed her, so fiercely she thought her ribs would shatter. She hoped that somewhere in the alley her tooth would grow into a rosebush and that every man who tried to pick one of the flowers would be left with a handful of thorns.

Out of her mother's sight, Lea took the scissors, then went along the hall to the linen closet. She sat on the floor in the dark as if she were hovering between worlds, her heart still aching. If she had died she would have been with her father, but instead she was here. It had felt so good to bite the demon. She wished she had torn him in two. She heard her mother call her name, but she didn't answer. By now Lea was certain that everything that had happened was her fault. Her long blond hair had made him notice her. She held her hair in one hand and with the bloody scissors, she began to cut. She should have been invisible, she should have never been there, she should have called out to her mother, she should have murdered him herself, she should have recognized him as a demon.

Her mother was outside the closet.

"My darling girl," she called, but Lea didn't answer. By now her hair was uneven, as short as a boy's. When Hanni opened the door to see what her daughter had done, she gasped. The floor was layered with strands of hair, brilliant in the dark.

Hanni came to sit beside her daughter.

"This is their doing, not ours," she told Lea.

His eyes had been blue, then blood had filled them, then he was gone. Now he was among the demons who sat in the trees, waiting to scoop up the innocent and carry them away.

"He liked my hair."

"That was not the reason it happened. It was because of who he was, not who you are."

Lea didn't answer, but she knew the truth. *Who I used to be.*

Hanni held her daughter's hand, grateful that God had allowed her to enter the alley with the shears in her hand. But what would have happened if he hadn't been so kind, and what would happen next time? Every day there were arrests, and by the following autumn men and women and children would be taken to the remote Grunewald freight station, where they would board the trains that would bring them to killing camps in the East.

Hanni collected the strands of hair littering the floor. Later she would place them on the windowsill for the birds to weave into their nests. But as it turned out, there were no birds in the trees. This was the day when they had all risen into the sky in a shining band of light, abandoning the city. There was nothing here for anyone anymore. Bobeshi could not leave her bed, let alone flee from Berlin, and Hanni intended to honor the fifth commandment. She could not leave her mother. The problem was time. There was so little of it. Each day groups of people were taken to Grosse Hamburger Strasse, where they were kept, without knowledge of their future, in a former old people's home, and would soon be sent to their deaths on trains that were leaving to resettle Jews in the East.

All Hanni knew was that someone among them must be saved.

Then and there she decided to send her daughter away.

CHAPTER TWO

THE MAGICIAN'S ASSISTANT

BERLIN, SPRING 1941

TANTE RUTH HAD LIVED FOR OVER A HUNDRED YEARS. SHE was so old that everyone she had ever loved had died. Now she wished to join them. Every day she set out a cup of tea for the Angel of Death, but Azriel never appeared, even though sooner or later he must walk through her door. She could not live forever, despite her talents as a seer and a healer. People believed her wisdom was inherited. Her father had been a rabbi in Russia who was so learned he was called The Magician, and her husband, also a rabbi, had been named The Magician's Assistant. These men studied the Zohar, The Book of Splendour, which delved into the holy mysteries. Since the time of Solomon, sorcery had been attributed to the Jews, although the Torah condemned sorcery, except for a certain type of magic, permitted from the start, which used the mystical names of God and the angels. Access to such studies was denied to women, but Ruth had managed to learn quite a bit as she'd sewn the men's garments, and cooked their dinners, and listened to their debates.

Ruth covered her hair with a black scarf she had worn ever since she'd lost her husband. His ghost was beside her each night in her small bed, but every time she reached for him, he disappeared. This was how life was, tragic and unexplainable. When you were young you were afraid of ghosts, and when you were aged you called them to you. She knew it was impossible to completely understand the world God had created, but she had lived with two men who knew the seventy-two kinds of wisdom that were contained within God's seventy-two names. Despite everything she had witnessed and all she had lost, she still believed in miracles.

Her father, The Magician, and her husband, his Assistant, had access to books from Spain that revealed the inner workings of the known world through sacred geometry. The circle, for instance, was a perfect shape that possessed the power to ward off evil. In the first century B.C.E. a miracle worker named Honi Ha-Me'agel stood in a circle to call down rain upon the parched earth. Even now, on a couple's wedding day, a bride must circle a groom, as mourners must circle the graves of the pious with thread. Numbers and shapes revealed the mysteries of the universe and the sacred name of God, which numerically represented the divine, and was present in all of His creations, including the mathematical equation of *pi*. Therefore it was through the purity of numbers that the rabbis attempted to understand God's miracles. It was believed that all creation came from thought, language, and mathematics.

When Hanni knocked on the door, Ruth drew her distraught neighbor into her tiny apartment and listened as Hanni wept, insisting she must send her daughter away. Ruth didn't need magic to see the blood under her neighbor's fingernails. It was indeed a terrible time.

As Ruth made tea she thought over Hanni's predicament. Ruth knew what evil could befall a young girl traveling alone, especially now, when there were demons dressed in army uniforms on every corner. Ruth knew of them as *mazikin*, terrible creatures whose work was the misery of humankind. They had accomplished their work in Berlin. Her neighbors hadn't listened to Ruth when Nazi policy first began to separate Jews from the rest of the population. She had seen children and their mothers standing in the snow, begging for food, while the newspapers printed captions beneath photographs of Jewish businessmen and lawyers and professors. *Here are the animals. Do you know this Beast?*

That was how evil spoke. It made its own corrupt sense; it swore that the good were evil, and that evil had come to save mankind. It brought up ancient fears and scattered them on the street like pearls. To fight what was wicked, magic and faith were needed. This was what one must turn to when there was no other option.

"My father once told me of a creature." Ruth lowered her voice as she poured the tea. "The golem."

She went on to explain that this monstrous entity was made of earth, but imbued with life by God's allowance and man's practice. A golem was created by use of the twenty-two letters of the Hebrew alphabet. First mentioned in the Book of Psalms, it had no soul, only *ruach*, the life and breath of animals. The Talmud stated that Adam himself was a golem until God gave him a soul, for a soul is said to be what divides us from all others.

"What good would such a thing be to me?" Hanni wanted to know.

"Have you no idea of what a golem can do? It can use the language of birds and of fish, tell time without a clock, and leap from a roof like a bat. It can see the future, commune with the dead, overcome demons. It can tell the day and hour of a person's death. It can speak to angels and live among them. It cannot be stopped from any act unless it is held ten cubits above the ground, for at that height it is powerless. It continues to grow stronger each day, so much so that it can become too dangerous to keep. This creature has protected our people since the beginning of time. For one girl, it is likely this cannot be done. But one never knows what might be possible. With a golem beside her, your girl would be safe."

Ruth gave Hanni the address of a rabbi who was famous for his knowledge of spirits and magic.

"The rabbi will refuse to talk to you," Tante Ruth warned. "He will not even be in a room with a woman other than his wife. So you must go to her. Perhaps she will understand you, woman to woman. She brings babies into the world, so she may have a tender heart. But in case she doesn't, bring something valuable with you. Perhaps, if she has knowledge, the wife can be bought. If you want a champion to protect your daughter, one who will follow her to the ends of the earth and never abandon her, a golem is the only answer. And only the most learned person can use the seventy-two names of God to bring forth the creature."

Hanni went to Bobeshi and sat beside her in bed. Whole families were disappearing every day. From her window, Bobeshi could see people using mirrors to communicate with their neighbors in code as they planned to flee.

"We saved our treasure for a desperate time," Hanni told her mother. "Now that time has come."

Bobeshi immediately gave her blessing.

There was a small suitcase beneath the bed. In the lining was a slit no one could see, although Hanni knew where it was, even in the dark. She had made the cut, then sewn the seam closed with tiny, miraculous stitches that were nearly invisible. Her husband always said that if times had been different, she might have been a surgeon herself.

She reached inside for the jewels they had brought with them from Russia. A poor man, Lea's grandfather had come across a stranger in the woods who was being attacked by wolves. Lea's grandfather shot each wolf, not knowing who it was he had saved. He cursed himself upon seeing it was the landowner and berated himself for the beautiful, wild lives he had taken; he had always felt they were his brothers. Still, he carried the master over his shoulder all the way home. In return for what he'd done the landowner's wife had taken off her diamond ring and emerald earrings and placed them in his hand as he stood outside in the snow. *Never sell these jewels for profit*, he told his wife and his daughter. *When the time comes, and you need them, know the wolves were the ones who saved us.*

CHAPTER THREE

THE RABBI'S DAUGHTER

BERLIN, SPRING 1941

IT WAS PAST NINE AND THEREFORE ILLEGAL TO BE IN THE street, but Hanni couldn't think about what would happen if the authorities discovered her. She went quickly, wearing a cape Ruth had sprinkled with herbs that would make her invisible, if the night was dark enough, and the soldiers' eyes were bad. Soon she had passed the community's poorhouse, behind the synagogue on Pestalozzistrasse. The air was sweet with the scent of new leaves, despite the garbage that had been dumped on the streets. It was a soft March night filled with promise. Fortunately, there was no moon.

The house was a squat stone structure that had once been a stable and appeared to have been abandoned. No lights burned. The rabbi and his family lived in small austere rooms, like mice in the dark, dependent on handouts from their community. When it was time for prayers, dozens of somber men in black hats had come to pray and to look to the rabbi for guidance in all matters of scholarship. Jewish men were no longer allowed to shave, so that they would stand out as enemies of the Reich, and the young men appeared to be as old as grandfathers, and the grandfathers seemed so ancient they might have been entering the World to Come, *Olam HaBa*, and had already left the world that we walked through and knew so well.

The men had once praised God three times a day in their long, black coats, but now, there was only one prayer meeting a day, held secretly at dawn, when the men of the community dared to leave their homes to assemble in the rabbi's kitchen, which served as their shul. It would be a death sentence if they ever were found out.

The first stars were sprinkled across the sky by the time Hanni reached the rabbi's door. She shrank against the building as she knocked, softly at first, and then, when no one answered, with more urgency. It was late to be calling, a perilous hour, and she feared her presence would be ignored after the risks she'd taken to come here. But to her joy, the door opened at last and a bright-eyed young woman of seventeen stood on the threshold. She had pale red hair and a narrow face that was sparked with intelligence. She spoke in Yiddish, asking Hanni to come in without any questions. The stone hallway was dim, lit by a single candle on the wall. It was so cold in the house the girl wore a jacket and, underneath that, a hand-knit sweater. It was the time of year when one day was spring, and the next was winter, when birds in their nests often froze to death, and roses bloomed in the snow.

"I need your mother's help," Hanni told the girl. By now she was so nervous her head was spinning. How she hoped that the rabbi's wife would have compassion for her situation. "Please! I must speak to her."

"My mother has gone to bed." The girl's name was Ettie, and it was she, not her mother, who had the tender heart, although she was careful to hide it, for such things were bound to cause only grief. All the same, she was naturally curious, so she brought Hanni into the kitchen and gave her a drink of water. The kitchen was large and cold, with a fireplace in which to cook and a rusty iron sink. The place was a hovel, really, with no electricity. An old-fashioned lantern sputtered black smoke that singed the plaster ceiling.

It was said that Ettie was too clever for her own good, and perhaps this was true. She was ambitious and often wished she had been born a boy and could do as she pleased. Her mother had taught her to keep her eyes downcast, unless someone addressed her directly. Then she could not stop herself from speaking bluntly and honestly. She had a heart-shaped face and a lovely body, but no one was bold enough to court her, although many considered doing so. Young men her age feared her contempt, which flared easily when she thought someone was a fool. She could always tell when a caller was desperate, as this visitor certainly was, for people in need often came to this house in search of help. Wanderers, widows, those without family or food, all begged for what they needed. Whenever possible and practical, Ettie's mother did what she could to help, not out of the goodness of her heart, but because it was her duty. If she'd ever had a tender heart it had been locked away long ago. She had too many children and too many responsibilities to be tender, a quality that was weakness in her eyes.

Now the rabbi's wife had been awoken by the murmur of voices. She came into the kitchen in her nightgown, her shorn hair covered with a kerchief called a *tichel,* her face worried and drawn. There was danger everywhere, but it wasn't her place to speak about such things. She had given birth to ten children and five of them had lived. Among the five, Ettie was her favorite, not that the rabbi's wife let it show. What good did it do to have a favorite in a world that was so cruel?

"What have you done?" she asked Ettie when she spied a stranger in her kitchen. She was not so foolish that she didn't see that her favorite child had her flaws. The girl was too open and modern and much too smart, all qualities that led to nothing but trouble. "It's too late to invite anyone in. The children are sleeping." She gave Ettie a dark look that conveyed what was really meant: *Your father cannot be disturbed.*

Ettie loved and respected her mother, and was wise enough to defer to her. They both had strong characters, but Ettie's mother could be won over when she was convinced that God's will was being upheld. "I thought the Almighty would want me to offer kindness to a neighbor," Ettie said in a solemn voice.

"She's not my neighbor," Ettie's mother told her daughter. "I've never seen her before."

"We are all neighbors in God's eyes," Ettie responded.

Her mother nodded, a smile on her lips despite herself. Truly, she had never seen a more intelligent girl, one she loved beyond all reason.

Mother and daughter were so focused on one another, they seemed to have forgotten Hanni entirely. Without waiting any longer, she went directly to the rabbi's wife and sank to her knees. What she wanted, she must ask for now.

"I have no one else to ask for help, so I am here. I beg of you, please don't turn me away."

Embarrassed, the rabbi's wife pulled Hanni to her feet. "I am nothing more than a woman. Get up!"

But it was precisely because she was a woman that she took pity on Hanni. What would make a woman venture out when breaking the curfew could mean prison or death? There was only one cause. This woman was someone's mother. The rabbi's wife understood this. Her gaze lingered on her own daughter, who was watching her with shining eyes. For no reason other than her fierce love for her own child, she gave in and signaled Hanni to join her at an old table that was riddled with indentations left in the wood by cleavers and knives used for preparing meals. Women came here when it was time to give birth, and it was here that life came into the world. Countless children had been born on her table, while the rabbi slept or studied in his chambers. Afterward, the wood was always cleaned with salt and prayers were said. No child was safe during the eight days after birth, and circumcision and naming could not occur before that time. Birth was the ultimate gift and the ultimate sacrifice, the time when malevolent forces in the natural and supernatural worlds conspired to claim both the baby's life and the mother's. To suffer so for another, from the moment of existence, marked a person forever. In The Book of Light it had been written that true compassion and true love existed only among children and for children.

"I want to send my daughter to France. I have a cousin there."

"France!" The rabbi's wife was contemptuous. "The Nazis are eating France in one bite."

"When they do, she'll move on to someplace safer."

"Are you a fool?" the rabbi's wife said. "Those safe places won't take in Jews."

Boats of refugees were being turned away, in New York and Cuba and England. Still, there were people who managed to forge papers, and those with relatives in another country had a better chance of finding asylum.

"It's a beginning," Hanni insisted. "What would you have me do? Let my child stay here, where she will certainly perish?"

The rabbi's wife and daughter exchanged a look. When the rabbi left Russia, he had decided he would never run again. Their people were being arrested every day; still he had not changed his mind. Half of the Jews in their village in Russia had been murdered in a single day, and the survivors continued to dream of crimson-streaked snow and children who would never grow up to be men and women. The rabbi vowed never again to be chased from his home by tyrants. He refused to leave Berlin despite his wife's pleas.

"This is not a discussion for us to have," the rabbi's wife declared, though she herself had begged her husband to take them to Eretz Israel. Did he not see that soon there would be no escape other than to be raised up into the World to Come? Did she herself not have children whose lives were in danger?

In another room the youngest son whimpered in his sleep. After that the women lowered their voices. Sound echoed here, and should the rabbi wake to see them he would be furious. If their visitor called attention to them, the entire congregation would be in danger.

"Be quick. What is it that you want?" The rabbi's wife observed Hanni, carefully taking in her wide expressive mouth and black liquid eyes. Her clothes were plain and worn. A brown cotton dress, black stockings, a shawl that covered her hair. She had been beautiful, but she no longer cared about her appearance.

"I need protection for my daughter when she travels."

"Go with her if you want to protect her," the rabbi's wife suggested.

"My mother is too ill to go and I can't leave her behind." Surely, everyone understood the commandment to honor one's parent. Hanni took the rabbi's wife's hand in her own, and for a moment the room seemed to float. "My daughter is too beautiful and innocent to be on her own. I need someone who will never leave her side and will fight every enemy on her behalf." She took a breath so that she would have the courage to ask for what she wanted. "Someone that is created."

"Created?" The rabbi's wife pulled her hand away. Her voice was brittle. Now she understood what the stranger wanted. Magic and darkness that could only lead to tragedy. "You're a fool to think such things can be done easily, and to satisfy a mother's whim! Do you think you're the only one with a beautiful daughter? All over this city daughters are being murdered. What of my children? What of the children next door?"

"I would do what I could for them, had I the means."

"What you want, you cannot have," the rabbi's wife said. "If it can be done at all, and I'm not saying it can be, educated scholars must do the deed, men of God who know the mysteries of life, not a woman who knows only how to bring babies into the world." She stood, smacking her palms on the table. "This conversation is over. It is likely a sin to speak of these matters! You are asking for a creature that is little more than an animal, a beast one step above the world of demons and spirits. We have no business with such things!"

27

Hanni took a leather purse from her pocket. Inside there was a diamond ring and a pair of emerald earrings, her mother's treasure from Russia. These jewels were all they had, a payment worth thousands of Reichsmarks, but if anything, the offer further outraged the rabbi's wife.

"The act of creation is holy! One must have read from The Book of Concealed Mysteries and make a covenant with the Almighty. Who are you to ask for this? You think you can pay for what is God's to give! No, I'm sorry, you must look elsewhere for another kind of help."

Hanni was beside herself. She could feel her daughter's chance slipping away. "You're a mother! I thought you would understand!"

"I understand that we must adhere to God's will. You're looking into things you have no right to know about. Go home to your mother and your child! Leave us alone."

Ettie was told to usher their guest out. The rabbi's wife must return to bed before her husband woke and took note of her absence. She was nothing, a wife and a mother, not a magician. "Don't come here again," she told Hanni, whose face was now streaked with tears. "If you think I don't understand, I do. But I am smart enough to know that sometimes you have to give up and leave things in the hands of the Almighty."

Ettie led Hanni from the kitchen. Perhaps the rabbi's daughter knew how broken she was, for as they walked the red-haired girl leaned in close to whisper. She smelled of cloves and lamp oil.

"I can help you. I know how to do it."

Hanni stopped, her heart hitting against her chest. The two were huddled in a corner by the door.

"How do you know?" Was it possible that someone so young could be party to anything concerning this sort of business? Tante Ruth had said only men could bring a golem to life.

The rabbi's daughter shrugged and was evasive. "Trust me, I know." The girl had almond-shaped eyes and skin dusted with freckles. A line of worry crossed her forehead as she gazed over her shoulder to make certain her mother wouldn't appear before she spoke further.

"Why should I believe you?" Hanni asked.

"I've watched them," Ettie told her. "My father and his students gathered not long ago. It was an experiment to see if such a being could be created again, as it was in Russia. It was accomplished, here in this house. I sat outside the door and I can memorize whatever I hear. It's a gift I have. I can recall what my father said, word for word."

Hanni was damp with sweat. If the impossible was possible, who was to say a girl could not perform magic? "Are you sure? The results will be correct?"

The rabbi's wife had gone back to bed, and the house was utterly still. All the family, including Ettie's favorite sister, Marta, were asleep in one cold bedchamber. Hanni and Ettie continued to whisper.

"When you deal with spirits," the girl went on, "you don't know exactly what you will get. A golem can be like a dog, following at your heels, or it can be more, perceptive, intelligent really. I have heard my father teach about such a thing. It may look human, but it has no soul. It is pure and elemental and it has a single goal, to protect. I saw the one they made, a huge man. I looked through a crack in the door with one eye, but one eye was all I needed. It came to life naked and eager to do their bidding. But my father made an error, which can happen even to the wisest of scholars, and the creature was too strong. It was growling, and when it grabbed a lantern it didn't even notice its fingers were aflame. It might have burned the house down. I heard them say it was uncontrollable. If they didn't act, nothing would be able to stop it from doing as it pleased. So they did away with it. They hadn't used the right ingredients. They dug soil from our yard, but it wasn't pure enough. Clay that has never been used for any purpose must be found. My father and his students laid the creature back to rest; they reversed what they had done. They walked backward in a circle, erased what they must, and let him become the dust he had been before he'd been called up."

"So just like that, they disposed of it?"

"You must understand one thing. It cannot have a long life span. There is danger in letting it exist for too long. My father taught about what could happen, and often the maker of the creature is its first target. All things yearn to be free, even a monster wants that for itself. But for the time you need it, it will complete its duties. But of course, you must earn such an undertaking."

"What must *I* do to earn it?" If she must be free of sin, then surely Hanni would fail whatever test the Almighty might place before her. "I'm a woman who has done as I must."

All at once Ettie noticed the blood under Hanni's fingernails, which she could not wash away. "I don't care what you've done. In this situation, we both have to share the burden."

Ettie was prettier than she'd first appeared, or perhaps it was the strength of her inner spirit that was reflected outward. Many young men had fallen in love with her and discussed marriage with her father, but he always told them, *You would be happier with someone else,* and after a while no one asked anymore. They saw that she wanted things no woman should want.

"If we go forward," Ettie went on, "I would be putting myself at great personal risk. If I recite anything incorrectly I will immediately die. And if I make my father's mistake, the thing could be strong enough to kill me. I will be its maker, responsible for what it does in the world. You must wonder what would make me take this chance?" The girl met Hanni's gaze. "There is something I must have as surely as you must have your golem. I don't plan to stay here because my father is too filled with pride to run away. I will do what anyone with any sense is doing and leave Berlin. And I'll take my sister." Her plan was forming as she spoke. They would go first to France, then to New York, where they had cousins. "Identity papers are expensive, and so is the passage."

It was now clear to Hanni. The girl didn't care about any sins Hanni might have committed. She wanted the jewels.

The moon had come from behind the clouds and shone through the window. In that illuminated moment they understood their fates were intertwined, and that one was impossible without the other.

"So we have a bargain?" Ettie said.

"You're sure? You're not too afraid?" Hanni asked. The rabbi's daughter was only a few years older than her own child.

"Do I appear to be afraid? Look closely. You'll see exactly who I am."

Hanni saw a girl who was willing to do anything to save herself and her sister. "Fine," she agreed. "We go forward."

Ettie put out her hand for payment, but Hanni shook her

head. Bobeshi had always told her to wait and see what is revealed before you walk through a door. There might be demons waiting on the other side. As always, she followed her mother's advice.

"You'll have it when I get what I want." Hanni was sure of herself. And why not? This was a forbidden bargain they were making, one sinner to another.

Though Ettie was still a girl, and had rarely ventured from this house, she had the confidence of an experienced woman. "Fine. Those are reasonable terms. But if I die doing your business, then the jewels go to my sister. Someone should profit from what is attempted here whether or not it succeeds. And I want two tickets on the night train to Paris."

As the eldest of the children, Ettie hadn't felt young in some time. She had a special bond with her sister, and had cared for Marta when she was little more than a baby herself and her mother was too busy with the children that followed. She had decided upon Paris because even though France had surrendered, no one believed that the city would fall for long. From there, the world would be open to them. Ettie had already resolved that she and her sister would leave together, for what good is it to rescue yourself if you leave behind the person you love most?

"How can I get the tickets?" Hanni couldn't simply pick them up. Jews were not allowed in the streets, much less the Pulitzerstrasse Station.

"Pay a Christian to do it for you. Someone willing to take a risk for a price. Use one of the emeralds." When Hanni seemed as if she might argue this point, Ettie gave her a good reason to find such a fool. "And be sure he buys two tickets for your daughter and her companion."

Hanni would send Thomas, the janitor, a drunkard who slept in the cellar of their building, to the Pulitzerstrasse Station. For a bit of cash, he could obtain the tickets to Paris from a porter who was willing to exchange four seats on the night train for an emerald.

Now that they were in agreement, Ettie was ready to go forward with the preparations. "When is your birthday?" she asked.

"March first."

That fell in the current Hebrew month of Adar, an auspicious time for what was needed.

"You were born under the sign of water. I was born under the sign of fire. All we need is a third party born under the sign of air. Luckily, my sister is such a person. Combined with the earth we dig, we'll have the four elements. That is the way we begin. We must act without fear and without regret."

"I can do that." Hanni cared about nothing else.

"Then we have an agreement."

From now on they were partners in bringing forth life.

CHAPTER FOUR

WATER, FIRE, EARTH, AND SKY

BERLIN, SPRING 1941

HANNI SLIPPED OUT BEFORE DAWN. IN THE HALLWAY, SHE sprinkled the last of Ruth's invisibility mixture over her coat, then made her way through the dark morning. Her heart was already beginning to break, but she was a seamstress and she stitched herself together well enough so that she could go forward. She felt light-headed as she raced along the quiet street, fearing that the rabbi's daughter would change her mind. It was a relief to spy Ettie and her sister at the arranged meeting spot on the bank of the river Spree. Marta was a quiet, dark girl of fifteen, only three years older than Lea, not a pretty girl, but kindhearted and willing to do whatever her beloved sister insisted she must. Of the two, Marta had always been a follower, a shy, dreamy girl who had rarely been away from their household.

She had her father's large distinctive features, and she wished that she looked more like Ettie, with red hair and light eyes. Now, on the muddy banks of the river, she shivered and wished she were home in bed. It was so early the air was a silvery mist and the calm surface of the water reflected a pale gray. They must use soil that had never been plowed, the damper the better. That had been the rabbi's mistake, one his daughter was not about to repeat. That is why they had come to the river, despite the danger.

The world was a marvel and, if you didn't remember what the day would bring, achingly beautiful. The sisters didn't spy Hanni until she was upon them. She realized how young the girls were; she was old enough to be their mother. But they had come together with a single purpose, firm in their resolve to do what they must. All three wore black dresses and head scarves to hide their long, plaited hair. They walked until they were knee-deep in mud. The sisters had brought along their mother's large wicker baskets, and were silent as they dug up mounds of damp clay, their backs soon aching with the weight of the wet soil. Marta paused to take a breath. In the past, her sister had done all of the hard work, but this day was different. There was more than enough work for three. Beneath the clotted clouds, there was already a pale band of light in the sky as time spun around them.

"Don't stop," Ettie urged. She was working with such ferocity she had sweated through her dress. Her hair was wet as well, and her head scarf soaked through. Last night she'd had a terrible dream that she herself was a bird whose feathers were plucked until she was bleeding and bare. She had wings, but they did her no good. She had a voice, but no one could hear her call. She feared the Almighty's punishment for what she was about to do. But a bargain was a bargain, and what was promised would be granted.

Her father was a great rabbi, but she was the one who had a true talent. For the thousandth time she wished she were a boy. She had no interest in marriage or babies, only in the world of scholars, from which she was prohibited. She could taste the bitter dirt as they finished digging, and she nearly choked on it. It occurred to her that once she broke the rules of her family and her faith, there would be no going back. But on this morning, all she knew was that she wanted to live. She nodded to her sister, and Marta nodded in return. They were in this together.

Before long there would be light and soldiers would be posted on the streets. The air was gauzy, a haze that was filmy and oppressive. But perhaps the Almighty was looking over them; the horizon remained dark, which allowed them to walk in the shadows. The deed they were attempting must be accomplished before dawn, and the rabbi's followers would be at the door soon after for their secret prayer gathering, rocking back and forth in praise of God as the sun rose. This was the end, this was the beginning, and they had no time for doubt.

The women slipped into the doorway, then went along the dark corridor until they had reached a small wooden door leading to the cellar. It was kept locked, but Ettie had taken the key from her father's key chain. They had dug a pile of sopping earth that was three cubits long, an ancient measurement that was varied, for a cubit stretched the length from elbow to fingertips, a different length for each man or woman who had measured, approximately eighteen inches. Ettie began to cast clods of earth onto the cold, dank floor. The mound of clay was frightening, a mountain of gloomy darkness. The room itself was foul, a place where the rabbi's wife kept potatoes and onions in barrels. Some of the rabbi's most precious belongings were stored on a wooden shelf, for no one would think to look here. Ettie went to fetch a flask of pure water, collected in a rain barrel, kept for ritual cleansings. She poured it over the mud, then kneaded the sacred water until the mud became clay. The mixture looked less dreadful then, ready to be shaped.

Quickly, Ettie bent to smooth out the clay, forming legs and a torso, arms and a head. Each limb corresponded with a letter in the Hebrew alphabet; with the formation of the body there was a combination of four letters of the Tetragram of God's name. Ettie went back in her mind to all she had overheard about opening the 221 gates that led to God's knowledge. If she did so incorrectly, the mud on the floor would remain lifeless and hollow. If she erred in a way that was an affront to God, she herself might burst into flames. There were dangers abounding, and yet she felt oddly composed as she began to chant. This was her calling, what she had always been meant to do, had she not been a woman, barred from such holy endeavors. Ever since she was a small child she had been discreetly eavesdropping to learn all she could, her ear set against the door where her father taught his lessons. Now her memory served her well. She could actually see the words she was to say, as if they had been written inside her mind.

In the Sefer Yetzirah, The Book of Formation, the individual must take the letters of the Hebrew alphabet through each of the gates of both the mind and the spirit. *Bereshit bara.* In the beginning. He created. But could *she*? Was a mortal woman allowed to be so brave? The clay suddenly seemed monstrous, and Ettie hesitated, unsure if it was even possible for a woman to have the power of creation. She had been a sinner all her life, refusing to do as she was told, holding on to dreams that were improper for someone of her age and sex.

"Perhaps my mother is right," she wondered aloud. "It may be that women are not meant to bring such a creature to life or to walk through the gates of knowledge."

"Of course it's possible," Hanni said in a reasonable tone. "Women create life, and therefore shouldn't those gates open all the more easily to us?" She knelt beside Ettie. Their arms were smeared with slick black mud. "Make certain it is able to have a voice."

"You want it to speak? Are you positive?" Golems were not meant to have the ability to talk back or argue.

But Hanni nodded, sure of herself. What good would a silent, lurking monster be? The creature that protected her daughter must be able to speak up on her behalf, as a mother would do. Ettie went on to make an indentation for a mouth, then moved the clay to form eyes and a nose as well. But there was more that Hanni desired for her daughter's guardian. From an inner pocket of her jacket, she brought forth a garment she had been sewing. She had made a simple but perfectly tailored dress, gray with white buttons. Leaning close she whispered, "Make certain it's a woman."

Ettie turned pale. There had been tales of female golems, made secretly for depraved personal use, for housework or slavery or sex, but most legends spoke of male creatures. "My father said a golem must be created as Adam was. All that I know, I learned from hearing what he did. I wouldn't know how to create a female." By now the rabbi's daughter was trembling. Brave as she was, she feared the punishment that awaited anyone who tried and failed to create life out of dust.

"As a woman you can form the creature in your image." If such an undertaking was blasphemy, then wasn't every act they were committing on this night directly opposed to the expected conduct for women, who themselves were made of a man's rib? Hanni was not about to trust a male monster with her daughter. It must be a woman. A mother figure who would feel not a forced duty, but real, tangible love. To make sure of this she had saved a vial of her tears, which she now poured over the creature's eyes. *See as I see. Do as I would have. Be who I might have become.*

Ettie's face had a somber expression. Perhaps it was wrong to create a woman, but the creature belonged to Hanni and this was her choice. Ettie did as she was asked, fashioning clay breasts and an indentation to serve as the being's sex. When she observed what had been wrought, she was disappointed to see the clay being looked neither male nor female.

"Do you have your monthly bleeding?" Hanni asked. "If we add blood perhaps that will let the creature know what she is and God will not be offended by what we do."

"We?" Ettie said with a frown, for she knew full well where the Almighty's fury would be placed should an unforgivable error be made. She would be the one to burn for all eternity. Still, what she had begun, she must finish. She turned to her sister. "You have yours."

Marta had been half-asleep, exhausted from digging at the river, but she instantly was wide awake, shocked when she was instructed to reach inside her underthings and bring forth her monthly blood. She was modest and this aspect of being a woman brought her shame, even when it was private.

"I won't!" she cried. Bleary-eyed, she appeared younger than her age, but her discomfort didn't deter her older sister. Getting out of Berlin was the only thing on Ettie's mind, and no shame would stop her.

"You'll do it right now," she said, intent on their success. "Or I'll do it for you!"

Marta wept, not that it mattered. What they needed was blood, and although she seemed like a young girl, she was a woman. At last Marta turned from them and did as she was told, reaching into her undergarments.

"Place the blood inside the creature," Ettie urged, bossy at the best of times, insistent now. When Marta balked again, Ettie tugged on her arm. "Do you want to live? We have no time to be ashamed."

The younger girl did as she was instructed, whimpering as she smeared the blood into the indentation her sister had made in the clay figure.

Now they must circle the body they were creating. The circle would protect and complete the ritual. As they did so, Ettie recited the secret names of God she had heard her father and his students utter. She had spoken these words along with the men from her hiding place outside her father's chambers, and she knew how intense such a recitation was. The name had seventy-two parts and was so holy that each section of the name scalded the speaker's lips. Ettie had coated her lips with cooking oil to ease the burning. Everything she was doing was a sin and she knew it, but even angels, who had no inclination to evil, were imperfect, and she was nothing compared to them, only a girl who wanted to live.

"Forgive me," she said to the Almighty, in the hope that He would hear her one small voice.

If she were a boy, perhaps her father would have heeded her words, and they might have created a golem to protect their family and his students and their neighbors and all of the Jews in the city. But of course her father would never have listened to her. Had he known of the existence of a golem, he would have destroyed it immediately. His own experience had made him distrust such creatures, whom he considered to be little more than demons. But perhaps a demon was needed to fight demons. Perhaps some sins were prayers sent up to the Almighty.

With a final effort that left her panting, Ettie opened the gates with her prayers. To her amazement she saw the letters of the illuminated Hebrew alphabet hanging in midair. Before there were numbers, there had been letters, so ancient and intricate they were used for both counting and speech. Ettie's awe of the Almighty and His wonders intensified. She felt a web of power in the room. Beads of sweat formed on her burning lips as she continued her recitation. The incantation felt hot and sweet in her mouth. She seemed no longer attached to the ground; everything was equal, earth, fire, water, sky. The other women opened their minds as well. Marta, who was so chaste, imagined a corridor filled with doors. Behind every one there was one of the seraphim, the angels that did God's bidding and were so close to men it was sometimes possible to see them brush by in the shadows. It was happening now. An angel had appeared in the corner of the dim cellar. He was crouched down, his eyes aflame as he watched, but of course they could not see him, for he was the beautiful and fearsome Azriel, called from his slumbers when the door to the World to Come was flung open, as it was now, ready to take whoever might be chosen to go with him.

It was then the clay figure began to glow, as if burning with human emotion. Its veins turned densely black, before becoming the color of ink. The sisters and Hanni continued to keep their minds open, their thoughts so deep it was as if they had fallen into the center of the earth. The air in the room grew stifling, as it does before a birth. And then it was so. In that instant there was only *Olam HaZeh*, the world that they lived in, and one more creature entering that world. All three gasped in disbelief at what was before them. The figure had cooled into the shape of a woman. She was tall, with long legs and a well-proportioned body. Her hair was flowing and dark, the color of damp soil. The form had been given *ruach*, the breath of bones, the life force that animates every creature on earth. Its lack of a soul would allow it to perceive the spiritual aspects of the world that no human could ever know or see. Good and evil appeared in their truest forms to a golem, death was easy to perceive and the spirits of the dead could be summoned. It was possible for a golem to see the angel in the corner, its bare feet dusted with soil, as it took in this miracle.

Ettie marveled at what she had wrought. The mystery of creation hung in the air, a thick, deep curtain that carried the odor of blood and of the future and of all the lives that had come before this one. The creature's eyes were closed.

Hanni was in knots, terrified they had failed and that her daughter would have no protector. Perhaps the creature had been stillborn. Without thinking, Hanni reached out. Its skin was warm beneath her touch, but it had no reaction. "Why isn't it moving?"

"It has to be activated," Ettie told her. "That is the last step."

She rushed upstairs to her father's study to search for his pen and a vial of ink that had been sanctified for the use of creating sacred scrolls. She had never been allowed to enter this room, and now grew light-headed at the thought of all she had done. She could hear the youngest of the children rustling under their blankets, and her father groaning as he began to wake. The day was moving too fast, like a spoke in a wheel that would not stop spinning. What was done was done, and so it must be completed. Ettie returned to the cellar, taking the steps two at a time. She had peered through the keyhole during the making of her father's golem, and she knew the last step. Her father had written the word *emet* on the creature's arm. Now she carefully did the same. The word meant truth.

She put down the pen and took the golem's hand, which tightened in her grasp. It was then its eyes flew open. They were deep gray, the color of the river at the hour when they had assembled on the bank to dig for clay.

"Is it alive?" Marta asked, her voice hoarse from fear.

Ettie hushed her sister. "You can walk among us," she told the golem. "Sit up."

As the creature did so, Hanni was overcome with tears when she saw the expression of mute trust in its eyes.

Ettie sat back on her heels, a strange feeling in the pit of her stomach. There was an intense connection, as if the four were one. The very air was smoky and foul.

"She should have a name," Marta whispered, for the clay was now clearly alive.

"Don't be silly. The other one wasn't named." The men had called it "you" and "it" before they had destroyed it. Ettie doubted that a naming was proper.

But Marta was unyielding. Her blood had helped bring it to life. They could not treat it like a slave with no identity. "She must be named."

Ettie was reluctant to treat a monster as if it were human, but her sister was so insistent that in the end she relented. What difference would a name make? Dogs were named, and that was not an affront to God. They decided to call the thing Ava, reminiscent of *Chava*, the Hebrew word for life. They hadn't expected her to be beautiful or young, but she was both, appearing to be no more than twenty-five. When they began to clean up the mud and muck, the creature quickly took over, sweeping the floor, cleaning out the basket in which they'd carried the clay that had made her. Then she clapped her hands together so that any remnants of soil were dispersed. She was given the dress Hanni had sewn, which fitted her perfectly. The sisters offered up a pair of the rabbi's old boots, for the creature's hands and feet were as large as a man's. She was strong, they could see that, and, they could tell, she was learning more about their world every second. She cocked her head and listened to their conversation.

"Do you understand us?" Ettie inquired.

The golem stared at her, then nodded.

"I believe you do," Ettie told her creation. "You should know from the beginning you do not have a heart or a soul and can never be a woman."

The creature nodded again, acknowledging what she'd been told. Ettie took Hanni aside, out of the golem's hearing, and out of Marta's hearing as well. There were rules when one fashioned a golem, some of which Ettie believed her sister was too sensitive to hear. It concerned the creature's extermination, which Ettie now revealed was as important as her creation. Everything had an appointed season and there was a time for every matter under heaven.

Hanni gazed at the innocent creature with compassion when she was told of the last step.

"You must understand," Ettie confided. "It doesn't matter that she looks like us. She is not human. If she lasts too long, and gathers too much strength, she will be uncontrollable, and will no longer do as she's told. As in all things, there is a beginning and an end. This is what my father told his students, and this is what I must tell you."

When they came back to address the golem, Ettie informed the creature of what her task would be, from this time forward. "You'll do as this woman tells you. You'll care for her daughter at all costs. You cannot abandon her or leave her on her own. She is the only one who matters to you." The golem nodded, having understood.

Now that the deed was done, Hanni gave the rabbi's daughter the packet of jewels and two tickets to Paris on the night train. She was a thief and a murderess, but she paid her debts and she knew how to love someone. In this brief time, she had come to love this serious red-haired girl. In a moment of raw emotion, she threw her arms around Ettie. "You would have been a great rabbi," she told her. It was likely a sin to say such a thing, but what was one more sin after what she had already been party to?

For so long, that had been Ettie's secret wish, the reason she had yearned to have been born a boy. But that was no longer her desire. She didn't ask to be a scholar or a student or even to earn her father's respect. The most she dared to wish for now was to live long enough to become a woman.

CHAPTER FIVE

THE FOLLOWER

BERLIN, SPRING 1941

THE GOLEM MADE CERTAIN TO KEEP TEN PACES BEHIND Hanni. She understood both her purpose and her place from the moment she was brought into this world. She was tall, nearly six feet, made even taller by wearing the rabbi's heavy winter boots. She didn't feel cold or heat or wind or rain, but as they walked into the sunlight that was breaking through the foggy morning sky, the light fell upon her for the first time, and she was amazed. The marvel of all she saw was staggering. *He has made everything beautiful in its time.* She understood her time was now. What had been clay had become flesh.

Every now and then, Hanni glanced behind her, fearing that the golem might disappear, rise into the air and float away or disperse into dust. Or perhaps she herself would wake in bed to discover that everything that had transpired in the cellar had been a dream. But no, there was the golem, calmly following, her long dark hair flowing down her back, her eyes raised to the sky as if looking for the Almighty, who had allowed her to breathe and walk and speak.

She may be like a dog, or she may have thoughts and desires.

This one seemed more like a dog, stopping a few steps behind Hanni each time Hanni paused to find her way. At last they came to an address Ruth had given her, an apartment house not far from Grosse Hamburger Strasse, near the oldest Jewish cemetery in the city, in use from 1672. Everyone in the neighborhood had been taken away to Judenhäuser, overcrowded housing. A single squatter remained, moving from flat to flat. The forger. He had been an artist and a printmaker, and Ruth had assured Hanni that he created false documents so well made no authority would dare to question them. Hanni had one treasure left. On their wedding day her husband had presented her with a gold necklace. Now, in exchange for the necklace, she acquired visas to France and identity papers under the names Lillie and Ava Perrin. Each visa cost ten thousand Reichsmarks, but the forger was delighted to have gold instead. Currency changed; gold never lost its value.

While the golem waited in the courtyard, she let herself rest, perching on a stone bench. She was good at mimicking human behavior, to ensure that she wouldn't stand out, and when Hanni emerged from the forger's apartment, she had to remind herself it was not another woman who was waiting for her. She assumed the smile on Ava's face was meant for her, but, in fact, Ava was astounded by all she saw. The green leaves of the trees. The brightening of the mottled clouds. A bird wheeling across the gleaming sky. *Fly away*, it said to her in a beautiful language that she immediately understood. But she couldn't listen to the bird's counsel. She had a duty to uphold.

When they passed the river, she found herself drawn to the water. She could hear the fish calling to her in cool, silvery voices as they warned her to keep herself far from mortal life. But she had no choice. She had come to life with a single purpose, to watch over a girl of twelve who was waiting in a small apartment, on the third floor, half a mile away.

Ava was not sure what sort of being she was. She knew she was not a bird or a fish; she hadn't that sort of freedom to go where she pleased and do as she wished. As they walked along, she spied a black dog in a fenced yard. She gazed into its eyes. Was this what she was? A beast such as this? The dog was chained, and when it barked plaintively Ava felt something inside her chest tighten. They must do as they were told. They were bound to humans, but humans were not bound to them.

"Hurry," Hanni called when Ava lingered at the fence listening to what the dog had to say, a litany filled with loyalty and despair.

Do what they say, but don't think they will ever hear you in return.

The sun had already risen when they entered the courtyard. At last they were safely off the street. There was a measured pause while Hanni stopped to draw a deep breath. The enormity of what they had done and what was still to come overwhelmed her. She was overtaken by emotion when she imagined sending her daughter away. Until the incident in the alleyway, she would have said nothing could be worse than being separated from her child, but now she could think of far more terrible possibilities.

When Ava saw that her companion was crying, she couldn't help but be curious. This was her first encounter with human sorrow.

Hanni wiped her eyes with her hands. She noticed the golem staring. Clearly, her daughter's guardian was not a monster, and so she confided in Ava as if she were a woman. "I beg you for one thing. Love her as if she were your own."

What Hanni spoke of was the deepest human mystery, which could not be understood by mortals or angels. All the same Ava nodded. "Whatever you say I will do." Her German was already perfect. She was a very quick learner, and she knew exactly what Hanni wished her to say.

They were beneath a beautiful, old oak tree whose branches had been cut down for bonfires for those newly homeless Jews who slept on benches and in doorways. Only a few green leaves remained on the ancient tree. Hanni took the golem's hand, warm in her own.

"I want you to feel what I feel. Do you understand what I mean? Real love. That is what I feel for my daughter, and what I will always feel for her, no matter what happens. Even when I am no longer here."

"I will see no other," Ava assured her. Her eyes were strangely hot and wet.

"Yes." Hanni was relieved that the golem had understood. "We should go in now. They'll be worrying."

Lea had been awake for hours. Once she'd found that her mother was gone, she stationed herself at the window, in a panic. She had been changed into a girl who expected the worst. She thought of the fierce look on her mother's face in the alleyway, and worried what Hanni might do next. Perhaps there was some evidence against her that had come to light, an eyewitness to what had happened in the alleyway had come forth, or some neighbor willing to turn her in, in order to save himself.

When Hanni appeared in the dim courtyard, Lea called out to her grandmother. "She's come home!"

And not alone, it seemed, for a tall, dark young woman followed her into the building. As soon as Bobeshi spied Ava from her window, she knew the miracle had been accomplished. It was an amazing achievement, but it brought its own sorrow. The time for Lea to leave had arrived.

"Pack up anything that matters," Bobeshi told her granddaughter. "The suitcase is under the bed."

"I'm not going anywhere," Lea insisted. But when she saw her grandmother's dark expression she did not dare to argue.

By now Hanni had unlocked the apartment, and Lea ran to embrace her mother. She had a strange feeling in the pit of her stomach. "Bobeshi said I should pack."

"You should," Hanni said. "Right now."

"And when will you pack?" Lea asked.

Hanni turned to the woman lingering in the doorway. "Come in. Come in," Hanni told her before turning back to Lea. "Here is your cousin, Ava. Say hello."

In time Lea would forget how suspicious and angry she was and would come to remember the details of this day as if a light had poured over them. She would forget the way she glared at the stranger, and how she had taken a step back, as if ready to run and hide. Instead she would recall the blue pot of soup on the stove, the ticking of the clock on the mantel, the way Bobeshi covered her face so no one would see her cry, the stranger's heavy boots, more suited to a man than to a young, pretty woman, her mother's dark hair swept up with tortoise-shell combs, the sadness in her eyes, the gauzy curtains that made it seem as if the world was still the same, if you narrowed your eyes, if you didn't look too closely, if you managed to still have hope in the world.

"I didn't know we had cousins." Lea was cautious. Too much was happening all at once. The world was turned upside down and nothing made sense.

"You have many," Hanni insisted. "You've just never met them. You'll be visiting cousins who live in Paris."

Hanni turned away so that her daughter wouldn't see her eyes brimming with tears. It didn't matter. Lea saw her mother as she was, fierce as always, but broken inside.

"Where will you be?" Lea asked.

"I'll be here, taking care of Bobeshi."

Bright tears burned in Lea's eyes. "Then I will be, too."

"No," Hanni said. "You must honor your mother, as I honor mine. This is not a choice. You must do as I say."

"You'll send me away alone?"

"Of course not. You'll be safe with Ava. She will follow you to the ends of the earth. And she's stronger than a hundred horse-men. What you ask her to do, she will do without question."

"I won't go," Lea cried. "You can't make me."

Without thinking Hanni slapped her daughter, the love of her life, the child she would have done anything for. Lea put a palm to her cheek, confused by her own feelings.

Hanni sank to her knees, reaching to take the girl's face in her hands. "I need you to do as I say."

Perhaps her mother blamed her for what had happened with the soldier and this was her punishment, to be sent away.

"When you travel you will no longer be yourself," Hanni told her.

She would be Lillie Perrin, a Catholic accompanied by her cousin Ava. Jews were no longer issued visas or allowed to travel outside the country, and if asked she must remember an unfamiliar prayer to prove her identity.

Glory be to the Father, and to the Son, and to the Holy Spirit, as it was in the beginning, is now, and ever shall be, world without end. Amen.

That evening they shared the last pot of Hardship Soup. It was made only of cabbage and water, for there were no longer any spices. Ava lifted Bobeshi from bed and carried her so she could sit at the table, something she hadn't been able to do for more than two years.

Bobeshi kissed Ava in gratitude. The kiss was sweet and pure. "She is the one," Bobeshi declared.

"Why is she so strong?" Lea asked her mother.

"Because she needs to be," Hanni told her daughter.

In the midst of the heartbreak of what was to be their last dinner, Hanni took out a small paper box. Inside was a gift she'd planned to give her daughter on her thirteenth birthday. Now she understood that they would not be together on that day.

Hanni had considered this gift carefully, ordering it before the Jewish jewelry stores had been closed down, forced to turn over their gold and silver to the government. The charm she'd had fashioned was a silver triangle marked with Lea's birth date and three Jewish stars. On the back there was the mystical letter *hey*, the most mysterious symbol in the Hebrew alphabet, which in the ancient world could mean thread or window or fence or behold. It was made up of three lines to represent the three aspects of humanity: the physical world, the spoken word, and the soul. It was one of the names of God. It was protection, it was love, it was a secret, it was the beginning, it was the end.

Hanni clasped the necklace at her daughter's throat. She must keep it hidden to ensure that no one noticed the Hebrew letter, but one day, when she was at last safe, when there were no more soldiers on the streets or murderers knocking at the doors, she must unlatch the necklace, open the charm, and do exactly as she was instructed.

"You cannot debate or make up your own mind. You must do what I've written. Do you understand me?"

Lea didn't understand the way the soldier had touched her, or the demons in the trees, or why the dark-haired woman sat at their table. She didn't understand why her mother would give her such a beautiful gift when Lea had caused Hanni to become a murderess. There was still blood on their shoes. Their visitor had taken it upon herself to clean them, wiping the leather with warm water, then using a stiff wire brush to get rid of the last of the stains.

"My dearest," Hanni said. *Mein Kind, mein Schatz. Heart of my heart, love of my life, the one loss I will never survive.* "Make me this single promise and I will never ask you for anything else."

"Yes," Lea said. She had decided not to cry, but that didn't mean she wasn't broken inside. "I will do as you say."

To say goodbye is a terrible thing, made even worse when you don't know why you are being sent away.

"We can't give up," Bobeshi whispered as she hugged Lea. "We have to save the next generation so that one day you can rescue people, as your father did. We love you more than we love our own lives."

Their embrace lasted a long time, long enough for Bobeshi to tell Lea the story of the last wolf in her village. It was the middle of winter, when the whole world was white, and a wolf and her cub had been chased as far as they could go. There was no escape, at least not for both. When the mother wolf ran to attack the hunters, all they saw were her claws and her fangs. While they shot her, the cub disappeared into the snow. That was the moment when its coat turned from black to white so that it was forever after invisible to hunters.

"That is the way a mother triumphs," Bobeshi said. "All you have to do to is survive and your mother lives through you."

Lea kissed her mother, nothing more. She did none of the things she wanted to do. She did not lock herself in the closet or throw the suitcase across the room.

"I will always love you," her mother told her. "Wherever you are."

Lea knew this was true, but Bobeshi had told her a harder truth. The wolf turned white in the snow. It managed to live, but it went on alone.

She was in the hallway with the stranger, her suitcase in hand. It was difficult to take a breath because something inside her chest was burning, but she went down the stairs and she didn't look back.

Do not cry, do not weep, do not beg, do not demand, do not ask why, do not hold on to her waist, do not throw yourself upon the floor, or hide beneath the bed, or lock yourself in the closet, and spit out words you will regret. Pack your bag and kiss your mother and know what she has done, she has done for you. Kiss her again, that is fine, and tell her you will miss her, you can do that, too, and then turn around and walk out, even if you hear her crying, even if your heart is telling you not to go. Her triumph depends on this. Her triumph is you.

In the courtyard, Tante Ruth was collecting weeds to boil into a mixture even more bitter than Hardship Soup. The weeds were poisonous and she had been waiting for the right time to pick them. She was ready for the World to Come, and had already lived too long, so she had decided to take matters into her own hands. This was the day. She had the cooking pot on the stove and the water was boiling. When she saw Hanni's daughter and the golem, she was grateful to have lived long enough to see a last miracle. The old woman's gaze fell upon Ava with compassion, and with something that was as close as she could get to love on the last day of her life, when Azriel was waiting beside her bed with the book he always carried, at last opened to her name.

As they walked to the station, Ava reached for the suitcase; it was her duty to do such things, but Lea wouldn't let go of it. She didn't trust the stranger, and what was more, she didn't trust herself. She had the scissors in her pocket. She remembered what it felt like to bite down on the soldier's hand, and when she ran her tongue over her broken tooth she felt a chill. All she had witnessed in the past days had left something sharp inside of her. She kept one hand on the scissors in her coat pocket. She could feel the wind on the back of her neck.

"I should help you," the golem said. "The suitcase is heavy."

Lea didn't answer. If she had to hate someone, it might as well be Ava. The hatred tasted sweet in her mouth. She rolled it over her tongue and her broken tooth.

Ava had been given directions to the Pulitzerstrasse Station, but she had no need of them. She instinctively knew which route would keep Lea safe. She saw the path they must take as a crow sees the earth, from a distance but with complete accuracy. At the station, she kept one hand on the girl's wrist as they made their way through the crowds. Lea's pulse was racing.

"Let go of me," she said.

She had been between girlhood and womanhood, looking forward to her thirteenth birthday. Now she was nothing, a changeling, half of each and nothing of either. Tall and awkward, someone who had been beautiful until she told herself that being beautiful was a crime. Now she was a pale, gawky girl. She did her best to pull away, but her mother had told her that Ava was strong and she was right. There was no possibility of eluding her grasp, not unless Lea wanted to reveal herself for the wolf that she was. That could wait until the time was right.

No Jews were allowed out at this hour, still the station was mayhem with so many Germans leaving the city. The crowds opened for Ava, perhaps because of the way her gaze settled onto people, as if she could see inside of them. Some wept when she drew near, some stopped speaking, some realized they had forgotten how to love. Some, like the girl she was with, were frightened of her for reasons they didn't quite understand.

As they walked along the platform, Lea had a vision of her mother weeping behind the apartment door, and of Bobeshi, in her bed, blaming herself for splitting the family apart because she could not walk. It was possible that she would never see them again. A wave of panic set in. She didn't think she could contain herself and keep going, pretending nothing was wrong. If she turned and ran right now, perhaps she could find her way home through the unfamiliar streets around the station.

"Don't think about that." Ava could read her thoughts now that they were linked together. One breathed in, the other breathed out, like it or not. "Everything your mother has done is to ensure your escape. We will do as she says."

Lea glared at her companion. *You are nothing to me and everything I care about is here.* "You don't know what I'm thinking," she said in a bleak bitter voice.

"You're thinking I am nothing to you." Ava gave the girl a sidelong glance, finding herself pleased that she had been able to shock her. It was strange to have such a feeling when she was made to be clay.

"You're not my cousin," Lea said.

"If your mother says I am, it must be so."

They stared at each other with cold eyes. Both must do as Hanni had instructed.

The conductor checked their tickets, then allowed them to board. Those who had not managed to get onto the train soon began to shout and strike their fists against the doors, but it did them no good. Soldiers were called in, and the riot was stopped as quickly as it had begun. The last people to board were the rabbi's daughters. Marta's dress was torn when a man grabbed for her ticket.

"Keep your ticket hidden," Ettie told her. "Everyone wants to steal."

The sisters had nearly missed the train. There had been so much to do before their departure. First they bought packets of hair dye to turn Marta's dark hair blond so she would appear more Aryan. Both girls had rid themselves of their head scarves and cut their waist-length hair, which had never before been shorn. It was shoulder-length, with a fringe of bangs, so they might look like ordinary Germans. They had fled through the window above the sink, landing in a patch of their mother's herbs. Now they both smelled like rosemary, the scent of remembrance.

They'd found themselves lost in the narrow cobbled streets near the station for more than an hour as they searched for the shuttered storefront where they were to purchase their visas. Before this night they'd barely been out of their house, and Berlin was a mystery. Despite Ettie's harsh manner, she was innocent in the ways of the world, and now realized they had been taken in by a charlatan. Hanni had given her an address where they could buy their visas, but that man charged too much and instead they'd gone to what people called the Street of Forgers. In her haste she'd chosen an amateur, a painter from the art school who was new to the task and not terribly adept. Once she'd handed over the second emerald, Ettie had no choice but to go forward with his flawed work and hope for the best. They were now sisters called Karin and Margrit Beck, although it was difficult to make out the forger's messy print. Marta's fingers had turned blue from the running ink.

As the sisters approached their compartment, Ettie was dismayed to discover they would not be traveling alone. When they slid the door open, Marta gasped. "What is she doing here?"

"It's not a problem," Ettie assured her sister. "It's safer this way." Ettie seemed confident, but in truth she was nervous to come face-to-face with the golem, although quite amazed by how utterly human her creation appeared to be. Ettie's first thought was that the monster might take the opportunity of their meeting to harm her, for it was well known that golems often destroyed their makers.

Ava had seen the girls through the glass and had immediately risen to her feet, her face rapt, her shining dark hair flowing down her back like a river. She fell to her knees in gratitude, for her maker was right in front of her, the giver of life, whom she'd believed she would never see again. Ava bowed her head, praying that Ettie would see fit to grant her the continuation of breath and life.

"Stand up!" Mortified, Ettie peered over her shoulder to make sure no one had noticed Ava's behavior. "You mustn't call attention to yourself," she told the creature. "You're a woman like any other."

Lea watched this encounter with great interest. What would make Ava get on her knees to a girl not many years older than Lea herself was? Something was amiss, she knew that much. She had the shivery feeling she'd had right before the incident with the soldier. A warning bell inside her that told her this meeting was not what it seemed.

Ava did as she was told, but she took Ettie's hand and kissed it before Ettie could pull away and throw the creature a dark, irritated look. They hadn't thought to teach her what it meant to be a woman. Now, if they weren't careful, she would give them all away. "That's not necessary. Just sit down. Follow what everyone else does and don't make a scene."

"Of course." Ava was learning human behavior by the minute, although as far as she could tell there was no logic involved.

Ettie glanced at Lea. "I assume this is the daughter." When Ava nodded, Ettie said, "Make sure she behaves."

Lea took an instant dislike to the red-haired girl, whose face was pale with anxiety despite her domineering manner. As for Ettie, she ignored Lea completely. All she could think about were the shoddy visas she and Marta carried. Marta, on the other hand, was more than ready to befriend Lea. There were only a few years between them, and Marta was so unworldly and childlike that she seemed younger than the angry twelve-year-old who shared their compartment. Ever since they'd left home, Marta had been crying on and off as she thought of how their mother would react when she discovered they had climbed out the kitchen window. It was a relief to talk to someone else who had left her home behind.

"We know your mother," she told Lea.

Lea narrowed her eyes. *What was this?*

"We hardly know her at all," Ettie interrupted. She wished she'd thought to tell Hanni to get them tickets in different compartments. There was no need for Lea to know the truth of her situation.

"You seem to know Ava." Lea did her best to figure out what was being hidden from her. There was a secret, one that everyone, including her mother, had been privy to, except for her. "She certainly knows you."

"She's my maker," Ava said simply.

Ettie gave the creature a scathing look. She hadn't thought the golem would come to life as an idiot. "Stop talking," she told Ava.

"Does she answer to you?" Lea asked Ettie. "Because she told me she answered to my mother and no one else."

"We all answer to God, don't we?" Ettie said.

It was a difficult statement to dispute. Ettie was tricky that way. She knew how to answer a question with a question. Still, Lea knew something was amiss. When the train began to move, she took hold of her suitcase. She should not be here. She should be with her mother. They'd held hands, they'd run with blood on their shoes, they'd slept in the same bed when there were thunderstorms, they'd celebrated Passover with a single apple and no matzoh, reading from a Haggadah, though to own such a book was a crime. Everything was a crime in their world, but she must return to where she belonged. If her mother and Bobeshi were arrested, she would go with them. She could save them; she knew that she could if only she had the chance. The train was still going slowly. It had to be now. Lea could leap onto the platform and then find her way home. She stood up, suitcase in hand, but the train was moving faster than she'd initially thought, and she stumbled. Ava reached out to stop her fall.

"We must do as we're told," Ava reminded her. "We will honor your mother and follow her instructions."

"Because she is your maker?" Lea asked, her heart breaking.

Ava shook her head. "Because she is yours."

Once they had left the outskirts of the city, Ava gazed out the window. She could see the world beyond men's eyes. There were angels in the canopy of the trees that lined the train tracks. Melahel, angel of safe travel and healing. Haiel, angel of courage. Ornael, the angel of patience who guards against sorrow.

Each time someone was born, three angels were sent to watch over her for a lifetime, and these angels were Lea's. Seventy-two angels guided humanity, but men and women couldn't see them and, on those rare occasions when the angels spoke, they couldn't hear. But Ava observed their world as easily as she did the world of human beings. She spied Azriel, the angel that could be seen by human eyes in the final instants of a life. He was following the train, for his work was never done. He came to peer in their window, and Ava held Lea's hand. She wasn't about to let him come anywhere near Hanni's daughter.

Lea pulled away. "I won't run," she said.

At least not yet, not until she was ready, not until she had a plan. She looked out the window, but all she saw was her own reflection in the glass. Lea was someone completely different than the person she'd been before her grandmother told her to pack up her suitcase. She was the tall, resentful girl who'd once had a mother and a grandmother and a father, who went to school and was the best student in her class, who always followed rules, who had never been kissed, not a real kiss, not one she wanted, who did as she was told, who had no idea there were angels above them.

All through the night they could hear the wheels of the train; the sound soothed them and made them forget everything that had happened. Berlin was far away, it was slipping into the darkness, a tiger of a city filled with soot and ashes, where glass was never swept up, and fires were burned in the hallways of apartment houses, and people disappeared without a trace, and shoes littered the streets, left behind by those who had struggled. The sisters fell asleep in each other's arms and dreamed of their mother's kitchen and the babies that had been born there. Lea curled up with her head against the glass. She still had her hand wrapped around the scissors, and in her sleep she saw flowers blooming in their yard, each grown from a murdered girl's tooth, on a stalk of thorns.

Heart of my heart, love of my life, the one loss I will never survive.

Ava felt something dark approaching, a black cloud of angels. Angel of destiny, angel of confusion, angel of crimes and of discovery, angel of rage, angel of the wicked, angel of the fallen. It happened at dawn, just before they reached the French border. The train suddenly stopped, so unexpectedly people were thrown from their seats, roughly awakened from their dreams. In the thin blue light of morning, they could see German army trucks. Soldiers were shouting orders. It was nearly April but frost was still on the ground. Passengers with suspect papers, or those who had what were considered Jewish features, were pulled from the train and led into the field, clinging to their suitcases, their eyes squinting in the new light. Some wore coats, others had their shoes off and were in their socks as they walked through the tall grass. Women and children were separated, and panicked mothers called out the names of their daughters and sons. Men suspected of being Jews were forced to pull down their pants to reveal whether or not they had been circumcised. A woman argued with a soldier, insisting she wasn't a Jew. In an instant she was knocked to the ground, where she lay sprawled and unmoving, disappearing into the tall grass. A shot rang out. After that, no one in the lineup argued.

There was a hush as soldiers boarded to go through the rest of the cars, demanding to look at visas and examine faces and identity papers. Ettie reached for their papers only to find the ink had now smeared completely. Her face was hot and she muttered a curse she had never said aloud before. *Zum Teufel mit allem*. To hell with it all.

Ava felt the darkness enveloping them. She could see the future as if it were happening in front of her eyes. It was a good thing men and women could not foresee their fates. Even without a heart, without a soul, Ava could scarcely bear to know what was to come.

"No matter what, do not leave this train," she told Ettie. She was nothing, mere clay, and her maker was everything, the giver of life and breath, but Ava understood that Ettie was also a headstrong girl. "If you stay I can protect you, but if you leave, I cannot follow."

"You're not made to protect me." She nodded at Lea. "You're here for her. That was the bargain." Ettie grabbed her sister's hand to pull her into the corridor. "We're not safe here."

"Why? We have our tickets and identity papers."

"With running ink and your fingers turning blue? They're clearly forged."

Marta looked behind her, frightened. She had her father's profile, the sharp nose and high cheekbones. "But the golem said not to leave."

Lea was paying attention.

"She's a dumb creature," Ettie told her sister. "We can't listen to her."

They made their way toward the rear of the train. They didn't speak, they didn't run, and they didn't look back at Ava, who'd come to stand in the corridor. She could go no farther, she was born to keep Lea safe. She wanted to cry out her maker's name, but it was impossible; she had not been made to do as she pleased or come to her own conclusions. There were more gunshots outside. Soldiers went from car to car, asking questions. *What church did you attend in Berlin? Recite the Lord's Prayer. Tell me your address. Your pastor's name.*

They were not easily satisfied. There were suspicions even when the answers were correct. They looked for dark hair, dark eyes, sharp features, a nervous demeanor.

Juden müssen die erste Tür benützen, um den Zug zu verlassen.

Jews have to leave through the first door.

"Keep walking," Ettie urged her sister. They went in the opposite direction of the crowd, to the far exit. But when they reached the rear door, a porter was there.

"My sister is sick. We need some air," Ettie told him.

The porter looked them over. He had girls of his own, so he opened the door and told them to be quick about it.

There was no other way, really, no matter what the golem had said. When they leapt from the train there was a rush of cool air. They could not go backward now. The sisters held each other's hands as they jumped. The grass was even taller here, and for a moment they were startled as they landed in a pool of mud. There were gnats in the air and swallows rose and fell in the sky. Ettie helped her sister to her feet and they ran. It was like flying as the blades of grass hit against them. They heard shouts from the rear of the train; they were commanded to halt. It was a rough voice, shouting from a distance. But when you are flying, you can't stop. You don't dare. Ettie ran so fast she feared her heart would burst. She could hear her sister right behind her, breathing hard, so hard it seemed as if she were crying.

A story their mother had told flashed through Ettie's mind. There was a beggar who prayed every day for God to stop his sorrows. He believed no one had a more terrible life and greater losses, and he would do anything, please God, to make them stop. One day the east wind carried him away and dumped him into the sea, where he drowned. Then he had no more problems. *So think over what you are complaining about before you do so and be careful,* their mother always said. *You may look into the world, you may wish you were there, but what if you were? You have no idea of what you might have to face.* Their mother, who was so strict, so exacting, so sure of what was right and what was wrong, who loved them so, in some deep place she could never reveal, who loved them now and always.

Ettie wished for the east wind as they ran from the train. If only they could rise into the air and not come down until they reached Paris. A few more steps was all it would take. The forest was before them, a dark bower of pines. They simply needed to keep their eyes open and not look back. They must run, say farewell to everything they had ever known. They were racing so fast they lifted into the blue air. It was a miracle, it was more than anyone could ask for. They were nearly to the woods and the horizon shimmered. France was in the distance, in that pale horizon.

And then it happened. Ettie stopped in her tracks when the shot rang out, but her sister had already entered into the World to Come. It was not a miracle, it happened every day, it was the rising of a soul. That was how quickly a life could be lost, in the time it took to breathe in and breathe out. All that was left was the beautiful husk of who she had been, crumpled in the grass.

Ava could not follow them into the field with a slingshot or an ax. Instead, she had jammed down the window and called to the birds in their language, inspiring a band of crows to fly directly at the soldier who fired his gun in the girls' direction. He got off one shot, then ducked to avoid the crows' attack. The soldier cursed and shot again, squinting in the sun, but the other girl was gone. It was as if she had never existed, so he fired into the mass of crows that had ruined his aim, striking nothing but the sky.

Ettie was in the woods by then, stuffing down her sobs as if there was a bird in her mouth. She swallowed the bird of sorrow and it sang a mourning song inside of her. It was too late to turn back, too late to climb back through the kitchen window and find themselves in bed, alive and warm in each other's arms as their mother called for them to see to their chores and start breakfast. It was too late to stop the angel in the black coat from writing down Marta's name in small black script as he walked among the trees. Some things hold on to you forevermore: the sharp crack of sound, the whirl of insects rising from the grass, the birds disappearing into the trees, their feathers falling to the ground like black rain. Afterward, Ettie would recall the moment when her sister fell again and again, each and every night at the same blue hour. She would never forget her sister's face or her mother sitting beside her on winter nights; she wouldn't forget the morning when they dug earth from the river, or the tall grass that reached almost to her waist as she ran, faster and faster, into the forest, her heart hitting against the cage of her ribs, until she found the east wind and at last disappeared, wondering how she would ever find a reason to live.

Through the window Lea saw one sister fall and the other run into the forest. She saw the cloud of crows and heard a strange rustling as Ava leaned out the window to call to the birds in a language that was too mysterious and beautiful for mortals to understand. Lea had heard what the younger sister had said. She had called Ava a golem. She had no idea what that might mean, but the word stayed with her.

Do not worry about who she is, but know she will always protect you. That is all I want and all I ever wanted.

Those detained in the field were being led to waiting trucks. Lea and Ava could hear women weeping as their children were taken away. A young soldier came to their compartment to examine their papers. He was impatient and he snapped his fingers at them. He looked like the one in the alleyway. His eyes were pale blue, but Lea was certain that it was just a matter of time before they turned red. She slipped her hand into her pocket to feel for the scissors. When the soldier asked her name, she could not remember what she was supposed to say. Again, she was unable to speak. She gazed into his eyes. If she had to, she would stab him in the neck or the heart. She would have to do it quickly, reaching upward, he was so very tall.

"What's wrong with you?" The soldier wanted an answer when he spoke to someone, and when she was silent, his eyes began to change. He grabbed Lea and pulled her toward him, but all she could do was stammer. The scissors were cold against her fingers. She jerked away so that she could attack him, and when she did the clasp of her necklace unfastened and her birthday charm fell to the floor. The engraved Jewish symbols were there for him to see should he look down.

Ava was between them now, visas and tickets in hand. She

was as tall as the soldier and for some reason he couldn't look away. It wasn't her long black hair or her wide beautiful mouth that mesmerized him. It was her gray eyes; he fell into them, unable to resist. He was drowning, silent, confused by his own reaction.

"We have all the necessary documents," Ava told him.

Lea went down on her hands and knees. The locket lay open, and a slip of paper had fallen out. Lea was not meant to read the message. She had been told not to open the locket until the war was over and she was safe. But as she collected the message to return it to its proper place, she was drawn to her mother's familiar handwriting. Without thinking she read the inscription. *Do what I tell you, do what you must, all things that begin must end, all things that you know, you cannot unknow.*

Lea's heart hurt, as it had in the alley, before life had changed forever. She stuffed the folded paper back into the charm and slipped the chain around her neck. Lea could barely breathe. She knew she would never be herself again. That girl was gone.

The soldier was satisfied that nothing was amiss with their papers. He nodded and moved on, although clearly he wished to stay.

"Will you be back in Berlin?" he asked Ava.

"Perhaps," she said, though the answer was no, she had learned not to say too much. Her maker had taught her this lesson.

When they were at last alone in the compartment, Ava turned to Lea. "Give me the weapon," she said.

"There is no weapon."

Ava held out her hand. "I speak to you as if I were your mother."

"You're not, and you won't ever be."

Lea had no idea why she was crying. Ava was not like other women; she likely didn't even have feelings. Why fight with her?

Ava reached into Lea's pocket and brought forth the scissors. "That's not how you kill a soldier."

Lea was interested despite herself. "How would you do it?"

"Quietly. Without blood."

Lea scowled. She'd seen a murder. "There has to be blood," she said knowingly.

"Sometimes yes, sometimes no."

Ava was becoming more fascinating all the time. Lea felt the silver locket, cold against her chest. She didn't understand Ava, yet she felt comforted by her presence. "What will happen to the girl who ran away?"

To that there was only one answer. "Whatever is meant to happen."

"And do you know what that is?"

"Can anyone know?"

"I think maybe you can."

"It's best to get some sleep," Ava advised, for this is what Lea's mother would have said.

"And what will happen to me?" Lea ventured to ask.

The train lurched forward. They were leaving behind scores of people in the tall grass. Some were living, some were dead, some would be arrested, some would do anything in order to survive, and one was in the forest, running toward the blue mountains. Ava looked out to where her maker had disappeared. She saw the souls of the lost in the trees, side by side with the angels. She saw the future, but the future could change at the angels' commands.

"We must hope for the best," she told the girl.

She might have said more if she'd had the freedom to speak her mind, but in her formation she hadn't been given the choice to confide what she felt. If she could do so there would have been much she would have said: how green the verdant countryside was, how bright the light had become, how grateful she was to her maker each and every minute, how the birds in the treetops could be heard even when the train rumbled by, how the first of the season's bees hit against the windowpanes as if searching for flowers, how absolutely marvelous it was to be in the world.

CHAPTER SIX

IN ANOTHER COUNTRY

PARIS, SPRING 1941

THE FRENCH COUSINS LIVED IN A TALL STUCCO HOUSE THAT
had been in the family for three generations. There were two
yellow brick chimneys, a wrought-iron fence, green shutters on
every window, and an enormous garden, now in ruins. No one
had time to take care of a garden, for there was no help and
no money to pay the gardener, a fellow named Edgar, who had
worked for the family for over a decade. France had declared
war on Germany in September 1939, and by June 1940, the Germans had entered Paris. By that time two million Parisians had
fled, and those who stayed saw the city grow dark and silent,
with food shortages. Of the 150,000 Jews in Paris, a third were
foreign refugees, but soon enough that number dropped by two
thirds. Many people fled or were arrested. For those who re-

mained, there was no fuel or coffee or soap or shoes, and the increasing fear and hatred of the Nazis was expressed behind closed shutters.

This past winter the Lévis had been forced to cut down the lime trees to burn in the fireplace. There was no coal, and bundles of wood were no longer sold on the streets. Even in spring the world was surrounded by gloom. Markets were closed, people didn't venture outside, parks were empty.

The Lévis had not been among the hordes of people who left the city when a radio announcement was made by the government that accepted France's collusion with Germany. The local politicians knew Professor André Lévi and made an allowance, permitting him to keep his house and go on with his work, which might be useful to the military. Many residents went west and south, many to Toulouse, where the archbishop, Monsignor Jules-Gérard Saliège, was one of the first Catholic priests to speak out against the treatment of foreign-born Jews. The government itself had moved to the center of France in the city of Vichy, which they promised would remain an unoccupied area. Yet people wondered what that freedom meant. Free to do as they were told? Newspapers were censored, a curfew was put down, and residents were lifted off the street and never seen again.

For three generations, the Lévis had never thought of themselves as anything but French. Their tall house had a fish pond and, until they had recently been cut down, the oldest lime trees in Paris, and was hidden away on a tiny street on the Left Bank. The third Monsieur Lévi, André, was a mathematician who had been a child prodigy in the field of rational numbers and algebraic geometry and for two decades had been an eminent professor at the École Polytechnique, until Jews were asked to leave. He thought the next few years under the Germans must be navigated as a maze would be, and at this he was expert. There was a small maze of hedges in the garden, and it was here the professor first taught his son Julien about spatial analysis. He had often brought him to the garden at the Château de Villandry, where a Renaissance maze signified the progression of life. He would blindfold Julien so that the boy could *feel* the geography and learn to visualize spatial relationships. In time Julien became astoundingly good at running the maze without stumbling over the hedges, excellent practice for a mathematician who must be willing to believe there is a logic to all things.

In his everyday life, André Lévi continued to think of number theory, the study of whole numbers that traced back to the Babylonians. His special professional interest was the speed with which the universe was expanding, in part by refining the use of Cepheid stars as yardsticks. For him the world was divided, and because of this he often didn't see human beings, not even those he knew intimately, whether they were his wife or his two sons, Julien and Victor, or the young housemaid, Marianne. Professor Lévi had managed to keep the house by paying off a local magistrate. Each week more of their belongings were sold in order to do so, first the paintings off the walls, then silverware from the table, then the cameos in Madame Claire's mirrored jewelry box.

The professor did his best to continue with his life's work, published in several groundbreaking papers in France and Germany, coauthored with several renowned German mathematicians who were working on Fermat's last theorem, proposed by Pierre Fermat in 1637, the most famous but not yet proven theorem in number theory. But now his wife had come to his study to tell him two strangers claiming to be cousins had arrived, interrupting his thoughts about the length of the solar system. It often seemed that his wife, Claire, was speaking an entirely different language, one in which household details played a great part. There was so little food to be had that she had begun a vegetable patch in the garden, tearing out the bellflowers and vivid pink roses in order to plant leeks and cabbages and escarole. She let the rest of it go to seed, and the wilder sections of the garden near the old and beautiful greenhouse, where jasmine and all manner of exotic plants once grew, had become home to *glis glis,* large dormice that were usually only to be found in the countryside. Madame was practical at all times. She had come to prefer a scraggly plant laden with tomatoes to a fragrant peony, and a mouse to a rat. But cousins were another matter entirely.

"They can't stay here," Madame Lévi told her husband. "We'll be the ones to pay if they're caught."

Foreign Jews had begun to be arrested, and now the cousins had come from Berlin, presumably with falsified identity papers. You could tell they were refugees with one look: the battered suitcase, the exhaustion in the girl's eyes and her short, ragged haircut, the set of the young woman's mouth, as if nothing they said or did could make her go. Madame Lévi had always managed the household despite the circumstance, but cousins appearing out of the blue, like beggars at their door, was too much. The young woman was especially strange. Although she spoke flawless French, she possessed a shifty look, taking in every detail with her pale gray eyes. She wore a plain dress and heavy boots fit more for a man than a woman, a style that was definitely not French. It was impossible to gauge what her emotions were, let alone her intent. The girl was well mannered, but something was off there, too. She first called herself Lea, then stammered and asked to be called Lillie, as if confused by her own name. Were they thieves or impostors? Was their plan to steal what little the Lévis had left? The professor's wife resolved to have her husband's help in the matter despite her vow never to interrupt him while he worked.

"When I asked them to leave they refused," Claire complained. "They sat down in the hallway and there they are!"

"It's all a mistake," André assured her with a grimace. He had been measuring algebraic curves and barely knew what his wife was talking about. He had on a white shirt and black pants held up with suspenders. He wore his father's gold watch, a family treasure, but in fact time meant little to him; in his opinion, it was an untrustworthy measure of the universe. All the same, the real world he had always avoided had slowly been creeping into his calm office for weeks. His sons had been dismissed from school, a senseless measure, for the family had supported their elite private school near the Place Voltaire for three generations. But perhaps in this new world it made sense. Jewish professors, himself included, had been asked to leave the university. Still, he remained convinced that life would eventually assume its natural course.

"Well, if it's a mistake, go talk to them," said his wife, still agitated.

He had no choice but to go. No matter what was happening in the country, between husband and wife, a truce must be achieved at all costs.

The visitors in the front hallway were amazed by their surroundings. Here, it was almost possible to forget the homeless men sleeping in tents along the river and in the Bois de Boulogne, refugees camped out beneath the bridges that crossed the Seine, soldiers collecting such people in mass arrests of undesirables. The entranceway floor of the Lévis' house was patterned with black and white marble, and the walls were Italian plaster mixed with cinnabar-colored paint. There were pale pink peonies in a tall vase, the last from the garden, and stray petals had drifted over their shoes.

The Lévis' younger son, Julien, came downstairs, surprised to see guests seated on the bench beneath the portrait of his grandfather, the war hero. He stopped dead in his tracks. If he wasn't mistaken they were refugees, something his mother was particularly suspicious about, insisting that foreign Jews would only bring trouble upon them.

Julien was fourteen, tall, lanky, darkly handsome, and completely unaware of his good looks. Lately, he was in a constant state of fury. Apparently, no one cared what he thought or felt or wanted. It was expected he would become a mathematician, like his father, but he had other ideas. He had always wished to be a painter, but since the German occupation, all he could think of was joining the Resistance. His mother had thrown a fit at the very idea. He was too young, and, anyway, he was needed at home. *To do what?* he wondered resentfully. Chase the mice in the garden, collect plums from their fruit tree, study the universe from the confines of his grandfather's library? He pretended to be who he wasn't to appease his mother, as he had since he was a small child, for she took his good behavior for granted, not knowing his rebel soul resented every minute.

His brother, Victor, called him a mama's boy and an *enfant gâté*, a spoiled child.

"And you?" Julien had snapped at Victor, who was seventeen and did little but sit around the house in a state of gloomy rage, forced to hide in the attic whenever anyone came to the door, because his mother feared he would be taken to a forced labor camp. "What makes you more of a man?"

They'd almost come to blows then, but fortunately Victor, afraid he might hurt his brother if they had it out, stalked away. "She'll always tell you what to do, until you refuse to listen. That's when you'll know you're a man."

Julien watched the visitors from the corridor, glad that Victor wasn't here to take over, as he so often did. There was something about the girl that struck Julien immediately, her long legs, her short cropped hair, her luminous, intelligent face, the immense sadness in her eyes. He had no idea who she or her companion might be, but at least something interesting was happening. Something that might wake up this sleepwalking household in which they were not to discuss burning bridges, or the convoys of soldiers, or the signs on restaurants that declared *No admittance to Jews*.

Julien ducked into the kitchen, where he grabbed a handful of plums meant for that evening's dessert. His mother was not yet aware that their housemaid, Marianne, had vacated her position that morning, leaving notes for Julien and Victor. She had been deeply attached to the household, and to the boys in particular, for she wasn't much older than Victor, four or five years at most. Her destination was the Protestant village of Le Chambon-sur-Lignon, near the farm where her elderly father lived alone. Before going, she had scrubbed the stove in the kitchen and made up the beds with fresh linens. *You should leave*, she had written to both boys. *It's not safe here anymore.*

When Julien found the nerve to introduce himself to the strangers, the young woman gave him a dark look that was so off-putting he took a step back. The girl studied him with a re-served gaze. However, when they realized he was offering food, they quickly turned their attention to devouring the plums. It was the first fruit Ava had eaten, glorious and delicious, grown in the Lévis' garden on an old twisted tree. Lea was starving, hav-ing barely eaten since leaving Berlin, and she ate two, one after the other, before spitting the pits into the palm of her hand. Julien was pleased that his offering was appreciated, and even more pleased when the girl threw him a grudging smile. She had a chipped tooth that made her look enchanting. Everything changed when she smiled.

"We've been traveling," she blurted. She'd been told by Ava to say nothing at all, but her stomach was growling. "There's been nothing to eat. Is there anything more?" The young woman elbowed the girl, who immediately stopped talking, but not before glaring at her companion resentfully.

When the young woman shifted her gaze to look down the hall, Julien nodded to the girl and rolled his eyes conspirato-rially. Lea covered her mouth, so as not to laugh aloud. They looked at each other with a tacit understanding, for then and there they made a secret pact against adults, especially the ones who told them what to do.

Julien was often arrogant and standoffish, always the smartest in his class, a far better student than his older brother, but in the past year he had changed. His emotions had been raw ever since he'd been requested to leave school, as all Jews were. As a further injury his closest friend, Bernard, had stopped speaking to him, and instead passed him on the street as though he were a stranger.

He's showing his true colors, Victor had said. He'd never liked Bernard anyway. *You're better off without him.*

But Julien had suffered after the dissolution of the friendship. He'd gone to speak to Bernard at his home, thinking it only right that he be granted an explanation. For years they'd been inseparable, but when Julien came to call, he was not allowed in the house. They'd stood in the street in the fading light and Bernard had seemed jittery, fearing they might be seen together. *I don't associate with criminals,* he'd finally blurted.

How am I a criminal? Julien knew he sounded even more arrogant than usual, ready for a fight, but Bernard had shrugged, unfazed.

A Jew, a criminal, same thing.

He'd struck Bernard, not once but several times, ignoring his friend's protests, drawing blood before he knew what he'd done. It was so unlike Julien to be violent, even when provoked, that he ran off afterward, mortified by his own actions, feeling he had somehow proved Bernard right. He had a dark soul, he was bitter and betrayed, and he knew something horrible was coming. He'd been more agitated with himself than with Bernard. For days afterward he couldn't sleep and was woken by his frantic heart, which served as a reminder of who he might become if he let himself go.

The world was falling apart around them, a dire situation Julien's parents continued to ignore. Did they not know that at the conference in Evian as far back as 1938, thirty-two countries in the League of Nations had voted not to help Jewish refugees fleeing Germany? Even America had refused to accept 20,000 endangered refugee children. The professor's head was in the clouds, he was so busy with his work that he never read a newspaper, and their mother was concerned with very little beyond their home and garden. In the minds of the elder Lévis, France would always prevail.

When the professor arrived in the hallway, the visitors rose to their feet, as if they were servants.

"Thank you for having us to your home," the girl said politely.

"There's been a misunderstanding," Professor Lévi began in response, but Ava was quick to interrupt, as if she had no common courtesy.

"You are Madame Kohn's cousin. That's why we're here."

"Well, yes. But a distant cousin. Hardly related, really. We've never actually met."

"Nothing is misunderstood. You have room. We'll stay here."

Ava looked at him in a way that sent a chill down his spine. He knew what was happening in Paris, he wasn't a fool, after all. Refugees were registered, and many were taken away to labor camps. He simply wanted to protect his family from a fate that was likely impossible to stop.

"Father, they're our cousins," Julien reminded him. "No matter how distant."

There was an expression on Julien's face the professor didn't recognize, as if he were the teacher, rather than his own father, the one who knew right from wrong. Professor Lévi felt that if he erred here he might lose his son's respect entirely. "Of course, then you must be our guests," he was obliged to say.

Claire had come to stand beside her husband. Immediately, he felt her annoyance, as people do when they've been married for many years. Certainly, his wife was exasperated with him. He had agreed to allow refugees into their home, people she didn't even know. On top of the unwanted visitors, Madame Lévi had discovered the housemaid was missing. When she pursued the matter, she found Marianne's room was neatly made up, her four gray uniforms pressed and hanging in the wardrobe.

"Can you cook?" Madame asked Ava now that she'd realized they were without help. Above all else, she was practical. Perhaps the current situation could serve them both.

"I can as well as anyone else," Ava responded.

Pleased by this news, the professor's wife changed her mind. "They can have the maid's room." *At least for now* was not said aloud but her meaning was clear.

"But where will Marianne be?" the professor asked, confused.

"Marianne has deserted us," Madame Lévi informed her husband. She turned to Ava. "So it's up to you to keep us fed while you're here."

Ava learned new skills in the blink of an eye. She began to cut up cabbage for Bobeshi's Hardship Soup, an easy recipe that took ingenuity and little else. Lea looked for spices in the cabinets, then chopped up celery discovered in the larder. She continued to dwell on what a strange companion she had. Her hatred had been replaced by curiosity and mistrust. "Do you really know how to cook?" she asked Ava.

"It's simple enough."

Still, Lea was wary as she thought of Ava sinking to her knees, kissing the hand of the girl she had called her maker. Why would her mother send her away with such a person? "Have you ever cooked before?" she asked.

"Having done something doesn't mean you're good at it."

Lea touched the locket she wore. She suddenly felt as though she were a little girl, abandoned on a street corner or in a marketplace, straining to see through the crowds so she could find her mother. She heard her mother's voice inside of her.

Heart of my heart, love of my life, the one loss I will never survive.

"You've stopped working," Ava said, motioning to Lea. "Carrots are next."

Lea rinsed a bunch of small carrots and began to chop. The red-haired girl on the train had told Ava to act like any other woman. Lea gazed at Ava now, who tasted a pinch of salt, her mouth puckering slightly, before she spat the salt into the sink. She did not seem like any other woman.

Julien was leaning in the doorway, his face thoughtful. How could he not take note of the girl? There was something beneath Lea's reserved demeanor he thought he understood. He was that way himself, hiding his true nature, in his case with bravado and sarcasm. Ava caught him watching Lea. She didn't like what she saw inside him, a wild, reckless heart that spelled trouble. "You can go," she told him.

"This is his house, not ours. Of course he can stay, although I don't know why he'd want to," Lea said with feigned indifference. The truth was, she had noticed him as well.

Julien came to sprawl in a kitchen chair, his long legs extended so that Ava and Lea had to dodge around him. "I can't cook a thing," he confided to Lea.

"Why are you proud of that?" Ava said as she cast a wary eye on him. It was difficult to read this boy as she could most people; his thoughts were such a jumble, but his interest in Lea was evident.

"Oh, I'm not," Julien said. "I just admire anyone who can."

There was some flour in a canister, which Ava mixed with water, doing her best to make a crust without butter. Trying to charm her was pointless. He had better watch his step if he knew what was good for him. "You might as well be useful," she told him, suggesting he cut the fruit in thin slices.

Julien seemed pleased to be asked. It was a good excuse to stand beside Lea at the counter. They looked at one another and laughed in a way Ava didn't understand. Nothing was funny, but such was the behavior of mortals. *Illogical, impractical, emotional.*

That was how it began.

CHAPTER SEVEN

ARRIVAL

VIENNE, SPRING 1941

THE RABBI'S DAUGHTER FOUND HERSELF IN THE OUTSKIRTS of the small city of Vienne in the Rhône-Alpes region, a little more than twenty kilometers from Lyon. This was the city where Hannibal had arrived and the Romans held chariot races around La Pyramide, an ancient obelisk, an artifact that some local people vowed contained the bones of Pontius Pilate. Ettie was someone else now. She had named herself Nicole Duval, with no proof but her word, for her smudged papers had been worthless, and she'd tossed them away.

She had been traveling from place to place, always going toward Vichy, though she had discovered the so-called free zone was in the hands of a government collaborating with the Germans. At first she had lived hand to mouth, searching for food in trash bins behind markets, sleeping in the woods. When she hitched a ride she always climbed into the truck bed, or, if she had no choice and had to sit beside the driver, she kept a hand on the door handle in case she was forced to jump out at a turn in the road. She had discovered that men often felt a young woman traveling alone was a target for unwanted advances. Whenever she came to a new town she searched for a bakery that was open, in the hope they would throw out baguettes no longer fit to be sold, whether they were moldy or stale made no difference to her. She slept in barns, and looked for chicken houses where she could steal eggs. On a few occasions she had given up a kiss or two in exchange for dinner, but not more than that. Her French was decent, although she was quiet and kept to herself. She had not left for America, as she had planned. She had other plans now.

For a while she had worked as a laundress in a small hotel, fleeing when her employer began to come at night to her door, which she kept bolted at all times. When he tried to attack her in a hallway, she immediately left and stumbled upon the café, where she worked in exchange for shelter and a meal taken at midday. She slept on a cot that had only a thin blanket, no sheets or pillow, but it didn't matter. Only her body was curled up there; her spirit was elsewhere. As soon as she closed her eyes she was in the tall grass with her sister. After a while she didn't even have to close her eyes. She could be in two places at once at all times, both inside and outside of her body. She was with her sister while she was waiting on customers or washing dishes, out in the field in a haze of pollen, but in her fantasies no shots rang out and they ducked into the woods together, through the dark pools of shadow. The past was simply where she lived now, crossing over from one world to the other with such ease it was becoming more difficult to remain in the here and now. Sometimes she felt the heat of her sister's body next to hers. She felt her heart beating, her whispered voice. Once she thought a young woman who walked into the café was Marta, she had the same lively dark hair and slight figure. She'd grabbed the stranger's hand, wildly, without thinking twice. The woman had pulled away from her, startled, and Ettie had stuttered an apology. There was no Marta, she knew that, and when her shift was over she went out behind the café and wept, then returned to splash water on her face and went back to work. She could not afford to let her emotions get the best of her.

After her sister's death, Ettie had torn her clothes, but she hadn't upheld the traditional mourning period of shiva, which lasts for seven days. She hadn't wanted prayers or consolation. In the time after a loved one's passing, mourners must not bathe or brush their hair or wear leather shoes, they must cover mirrors so as not to look at their appearance, for their own needs do not matter, and their grief is all-consuming. But Ettie's grief had turned white-hot, burning inside of her. She wished to do more than mourn. She remembered the story of Esther, who had been called the Morning Star by her people, the Jewish queen who had lived in exile in Persia and used her beauty to beguile a king, disguising her brilliant mind, causing the king to save her people and her nation. Clearly, a woman could engage in battle. That was when her plan came into focus.

Ettie had heard rumors of underground groups that rescued foreign Jews, young people, and children and fought against the

Germans, creating as much chaos as possible, destroying roads and train tracks with homemade bombs made of cheap ingredients, match heads, gunpowder, old nails and tacks, as they did their best to remove the most evil players among the Nazis stationed in their cities and towns. To prove that she, too, was ready to take radical action, Ettie challenged herself. There were days when she didn't eat or drink, merely to toughen herself, and when she had time she often did push-ups of the sort her little brothers used to do, to keep her body in shape. One evening she took a sharp knife from the kitchen. In the shed where she slept, she cut an *M* into her arm in memory of her sister so that she would always remember what she was fighting for. In her faith she was never to cut herself, not in service of an idol or in the throes of grief, but Ettie's faith was gone, and that command no longer mattered. She remembered Queen Esther's cry to God. *Why did you leave me? I call out to You in the day and You don't answer.*

Ettie was no longer the Orthodox girl who did as she was told. She was someone else entirely. To prove this to herself, she broke every rule she could. She worked on Friday nights, she ate pork, she let her hair loose and didn't cover her head, she spoke with men she didn't know while she served them their dinner, she didn't burn candles or respect the Sabbath. God had forsaken her, and in turn she had forsaken His ways and His word. People barely glanced at her; she was thin and unkempt, with a haunted look in her eyes, no one worth looking at. This was the way she wanted it. Let her be invisible, a shadow who was overlooked. It was easier to pick up information if she went unnoticed, and plain girls always went unnoticed. She knew that thousands of young men and women, both French and Jewish, had escaped forced labor to disappear into the forests or safe houses in villages and towns in order to fight back against the Germans.

This was what Ettie wished for. A way to fight back.

In the café, she had overheard people speak about a local priest in soft, respectful tones. He was a supporter of France at all costs, and had already been interviewed by the police. Father Varnier was so beloved in the village that he had not been detained, as most prisoners would have been, only briefly questioned about his parishioners. Did he know where there were hidden Jews? Had he heard of convents taking in foreign children? Where were the members of the Resistance and their girlfriends and families, anyone who might be imprisoned and tortured for information? He knew nothing and spat out that they should be ashamed of themselves to mistrust a man of God. They let him go and wished him luck, but behind his back they laughed at him. What good would God do him if they decided to arrest him again?

Ettie made her way to the church, an ancient stone building in the middle of town, passing by the even more ancient relic of the obelisk. This part of France had been a Roman stronghold, and there were memorials to that time everywhere, with the past and the present threaded together. It was a land of martyrs, of those who had been betrayed and those who had betrayed them. Perhaps the one matter of faith that was most important, at least to Ettie, was that she must still find it in her heart to trust someone. That person was Father Varnier. It was dark in the church when she entered, and she felt a fluttering of nerves. She had never been inside a Christian house of worship. All she knew was her father's study, which had served as a shul, a room that became crowded with his followers, who prayed with such enthusiasm the floor often shook. Here in the chapel, dozens of lit candles flickered and the stained-glass windows let through blue and rose light that left patterns on the stone walls. As she took a seat in one of the carved wooden pews where the faithful had prayed since the 1300s, Ettie was someone new, someone she had never expected to be. She saw the world in the light of the Morning Star, Queen Esther, for she, too, had been in exile when she had managed to save her people.

Ettie sat alone in the church for so long that the woman who swept up noticed her and went to Father Varnier, who soon enough came to see if Ettie was all right. He asked if she would like to pray with him, and she said no, she wished to do more than pray. She was so slight, hardly more than a girl, not especially pretty, except to those who had loved her, but she looked fierce, with a brittle sort of determination. She was pale beneath her freckled skin, and her eyes were luminous and damp. The priest didn't need further evidence to know what she meant. He had ties to both the French who were loyal to Charles de Gaulle and to the Jewish Resistance. Still, he was cautious even when speaking with a girl of seventeen. This is what had happened to their people, a division that would take decades to heal. When Ettie greeted him, he took note of her faint German accent, and was aware that she was a refugee, a most dangerous thing to be. He told her she was taking a foolish chance speaking to a stranger. She responded that the same was true of him, but after all, weren't fools the ones who were willing to do what others would not? Wasn't this the true meaning of faith?

"I work in the café," she told the priest. "Send whatever fool you know to find me. I'm willing to do anything."

She didn't flinch under his gaze, something the priest couldn't help but notice. She shook his hand, quickly pulling her sleeve down so he wouldn't notice the letter she'd carved into her skin. But he did, and he knew she was serious about matters; she had her own war to wage.

Ettie left and went through the old streets of Vienne. She took her time walking back to the café. She went to work, as she always did, but every morning and every night she was waiting for whatever was meant to happen next.

CHAPTER EIGHT

THE GIRL IN THE COUNTRY

HAUTE-LOIRE, SUMMER 1941

MARIANNE FÉLIX HAD LIVED IN PARIS AS THE LÉVIS' em-
ployee for five years, but she was a country girl, and was still
able to find her way in the dark. It was a talent she'd learned
during childhood on her father's farm, a place he called Maison
de la Ruche, Beehive House. In the dusky evenings she would
go into the woods to look for the cows let out into the pastures.
At first she had stumbled over bramble bushes and the twisted
roots of oak trees, but after a time she realized night fell in different textures of black and blue. Some things turned the color
of ink, some became ebony. It was easy enough to find the cows,
gathered together in the soft darkness, and to go home she followed a trail of white wildflowers.

All the while she was growing up, each morning before

daybreak, Marianne would awake to fetch eggs from the henhouse. She moved swiftly as she bent to reach under the hens, all of which complained when they were disturbed. The eggs were brown and blue and spotted, warm to the touch. She then helped with the bees, dressing in white with a net over her head. Sometimes she dreamed of the hum of their buzzing when they surrounded her on summer days, their feet dusted with pollen so that they left traces of yellow and green on her shoulders and arms.

Her mother had died when she was very young, and Marianne's father depended on her. By the time she was seventeen, most other local girls had married, and the boys who once teased her fell away; soon they had families, and merely nodded when they saw her, as if they had never begged for a kiss. Every day was like the one before, not bad, merely the same. When she sat outside in the evenings to gaze at the stars pricking the darkness, she was filled with longing. Fate was waiting for her, she just didn't know where.

Their village was secluded and blizzards of snow fell. Sleds or snowshoes were needed to get anywhere, and for months the snow was too deep for cars; even horses and carts were useless. They were cut off from the rest of the world. It was possible to hear wolves from across the mountains in Italy. In the highlands there were wild mountain goats, called *chamois*, and little nocturnal animals called genets, which kept their distance from human beings. Occasionally, if one was very lucky, perhaps once in a lifetime, it was possible to spy a lynx. In summer, the forests were so thick a person could disappear into the mossy glens and never be found.

The villages and the farms for miles around were populated

by Huguenots, hardworking men and women who were used to the deep silence of the mountains. In their world, churches were plain but forests were holy. Louis XIV had been brutal in forcing the Huguenots to convert or flee, and they were without the rights of citizens until 1789, after the Edict of Toleration was signed. Only a tiny fraction of Huguenots had remained in France and most of those were in the villages nearby. They were French, but they held themselves apart from all others, for they had been treated as outsiders, disrespected and imprisoned and murdered. One didn't forget such mistreatment; it was in the blood, as much as these mountains were, for these mountains, impassable in winter, had saved their lives.

When Marianne was eighteen, she went to the market to sell eggs and a shock wave went through her. It happened for no reason and every reason. She looked at the road she had never taken any farther than town. She thought of all the things she would never see or do. Marianne was still young but life already seemed ordinary. It was the time of year when the chirping *cri-cri* bugs called and Osiris blue butterflies flitted along the hedges. Instead of going home that day, Marianne walked in the other direction. She trekked on until she came to a small town she had never been to before. She went to have a coffee at a café, and since she had her egg money she ordered a small cake as well. It was the first time she had eaten a cake that she herself hadn't baked. It was made with apricots and sweet cheese and it was delicious.

Marianne still thought she was going home and had simply taken a detour. She would be back to look for the cows in the gloaming dark, and close the goats into their pens, and check her father's beehives to see if there were enough honeycombs to sell. But instead she lingered until the proprietor asked if she was waiting for someone. And then quite suddenly she realized that she was and that she wanted something larger than the world that she knew. When she asked if there was any work she was told there was an organization in Lyon that found work in Paris for farm girls such as herself.

Marianne caught a ride to Lyon and sat in an office filling out a questionnaire. She didn't think she did a very good job; she didn't have much to say about herself, after all. It was too late to return and collect the cows, and she assumed her father was furious as he stumbled through the dark. She slept on a cot in a shabby room of the office, where country girls like herself came to search for work. Soon enough Professor Lévi sent her a train ticket and a cash payment for the organization's fee. Before she knew it there she was, in the professor's house. She couldn't tell which was the dream, her life before Paris or this other life, wherein she planted the garden and watered the rosebushes. She pretended everything that bloomed was hers, every rose and peony, flowers she wouldn't have had time to bother with had she been on the farm, for her father expected everything they did to serve a purpose and a rose had no purpose other than its own beauty.

She appreciated her life with the Lévis, her lovely pressed uniforms, her new coat and boots, a bureau filled with undergarments and scarves the lady of the house had offered when she'd grown tired of them. A girl who had had only cows for company had come to reside in the most beautiful city in the world. She spent hours walking in the Jardin des Tuileries and along the boulevards with their heavenly shops, buying ice cream on summer evenings and eating all manner of cakes, all more delicious than any of the ones she had ever baked. Sometimes she forgot that the house where she worked was not her own. Nothing was, really, not the kitchen, or her clothes, or the boys she had come to care for, perhaps, in Victor's case, too much. In the last year, when she'd realized he'd become a man, it was awkward to be with him, especially when she noticed the way he looked at her. Perhaps her thoughts of leaving began then.

Or perhaps it was on the day she heard the professor's wife speaking about her. Madame had called Marianne *la fille*, the girl, as if she had no name, and all at once she realized that, indeed, she had nothing of her own. Hadn't that been why she'd left her father's farm in the first place? To find something that belonged to her and her alone? That hadn't happened here, and what was worse, the city had gone dark, all of the initial light she had been so amazed by disappearing day by day.

The Lévis did not understand their slow disenfranchisement and the erosion of their rights, but Marianne came from a line of people who had been persecuted by the Catholic majority; she'd grown up sitting in the town hall, hearing stories of mistreatments and murders. The residents of this region knew that people must seek protection before it was too late, and Marianne began to sense it was too late for the Jews. She heard what people were saying in the markets and was privy to displays of hatred that would have stunned the Lévis. All Jews were refugees, people said, even those whose parents and grandparents considered themselves French and had fought in the Great War. None were truly French, and all should be deported to Germany and Poland. Jews weren't really people, they baked blood into their loaves of bread; their children were brought up to be thieves. No one wanted the Germans in Paris, but surely they would not be marching on France if not for the Jews.

Marianne hadn't seen her father for five years, although they'd written letters all this time. Now, with the Germans on the streets of Paris, the guilt of leaving home struck her. Perhaps she had thrown the last few years away, dreaming. Certainly, she'd left her father with the work she herself should be doing to spare him a miserable old age.

Marianne had enough money for the train to Lyon, so she left, without speaking to Victor, who always got his way, to ensure she couldn't be talked out of her decision. She had left behind notes for the boys. She wrote to Julien she would always be proud of him. Victor's message took more thought, for he would be far more hurt when he found her gone. Marianne had told him stories about her father's farm, the bees he kept, the road that was impassable in winter, the stars she gazed at each night. She wanted to say what she felt, she wanted to give away her feelings, but she told herself it was wrong.

In the end she wrote a single sentence.

Always remember me, as I remember you.

She took the train to Lyon, a bustling city that seemed even more crowded than she remembered. There was then a smaller train to the station in the center of Le Chambon-sur-Lignon. She still had to walk several miles in the hilly terrain. Theirs was an isolated community and the farm was even more isolated. It had been so long since she had been in the countryside that blisters formed on her feet. The weather was hot for the time of year, and there were bees buzzing in the air. Her father would likely be wondering what had happened to this week's letter. He had never reprimanded her or asked why she'd left. Perhaps he understood she had reached a marriageable age and still was at home and that she wanted more. He often wrote about his bees, how much honey had been produced, how much he had sold at the market. When she thought of him she imagined him in his beekeeping attire, the frothy netting, the white cloak. He never wore gloves as she did; he said he needed his hands so that the bees would see he was indeed human and not a monster in their midst.

When Marianne arrived at the farm, her father was standing in the yard with his favorite goat, Bluebell. When he saw his daughter it was as if she had never been away. In an uncharacteristic display of emotion this rough-hewn man embraced her, then he wiped his eyes, and told her she was in time for dinner.

She settled in quickly. In less than a week, Bluebell became used to her when it was time for milking, and the chickens returned to be fed grain every evening when she called to them. Only the bees never became accustomed to her. As a girl she would let them hover near to perch on her arms. Now she had been stung several times.

"Bees are the least forgiving creatures on earth," her father told her. She understood this was his way of letting her know that he forgave her for leaving, and that, all this time later, although he never said so and though he never would, he was overjoyed that she had come back at last.

CHAPTER NINE

THE REALM OF THE SHADOW

PARIS, SUMMER 1941

LEA HELPED AVA WITH CHORES IN THE MORNINGS, BUT HER afternoons were spent in the library with Julien. They were in a world of their own. Easy enough, as Victor ignored them. He had been in a foul mood ever since Marianne left, and had never had an interest in reading, even though the selection of books was quite incredible. The first Monsieur Lévi had been a collector of Greek and Hebrew texts, and the second Monsieur Lévi had followed suit, although he favored mythology, folktales, and novels. Lea and Julien read for hours, stretched out on the floor, each extremely aware of the other's presence, though they both pretended not to be. What they held in common was their aloneness, and in time, thrown together, with no world other than their own, they grew close. Often they could finish each other's sentences, and then they would laugh, embarrassed, lying on the floor, side by side, feeling the heat of one another's body.

Lea read novels, one after the other, and then science books, texts about the natural world, psychology, and the miracle of the human body. In the mornings, Julien took lessons with his father. He was already ahead of most students his age, at the university level due to his father's tutoring and his own innate ability to problem-solve. But he had very little interest in mathematics, a fact he had yet to reveal to his father. He preferred a blank notebook so that he could sketch. He could mimic most things found in nature with ease: a rose, a bird, a single leaf. It might be their own garden that inspired him one day, then the plane trees in the Jardin des Tuileries, or the imaginary landscapes he conjured, islands that were made of rock, rivers that were green as glass. Lea was the first person to whom he showed his work, and her reaction was all he could have wished for. She sat for him so that he could sketch her portrait, and in those hours a door opened for both of them, insight into one another, a close bond.

When Lea looked at the finished product of Julien's sketch, however, she laughed.

"I don't look like that!" The girl in the drawing was beautiful, and she hadn't been that girl since she'd chopped off her hair in Berlin. He had even made her chipped tooth look attractive, when she was well aware of how horrible it was.

As far as Julien was concerned, he'd captured her completely. "Of course you do," he said.

He knew she was homesick. He'd stood outside her door at night and heard her crying. One night Ava came up behind him, surprising him. Julien felt a shiver go through him. She was so quiet, even wearing those heavy boots of hers. There was something vaguely off about her. She had stood there glowering at him, as if he were a criminal.

"I'm not doing anything wrong," Julien told her. Then why did he feel *caught*?

"Why would you be?" Ava said, her silver eyes narrowed.

"I wouldn't be."

"If you ever do, you will regret it." That she had no expression on her face made her threat all the more chilling.

"What do you consider wrong?" Julien asked.

Ava shrugged. "You'll know when I consider it to be so. So be careful."

"Your cousin is very protective," he told Lea after his encounter with Ava. "She reminds me of a guard dog."

Lea had often thought of the name one of the sisters had used for Ava on the train. A golem. One morning, she sneaked into the library before anyone was awake. There was a book she had spied days earlier, one she had been waiting to get her hands on. It was an ancient book of Jewish magic the second Monsieur Lévi had bought from a famed French kabbalist. She found the passage referring to a creature noted as a golem in Psalm 139, verses fifteen and sixteen, praising God. *My frame was not hidden from you, when I was made in secret, intricately woven in the depths of the earth. Your eyes beheld my unformed substance.*

She read on, shocked to discover that a golem came to life after an elaborate and secret ritual, wherein the maker must have a deep understanding of the spiritual and physical manifestations of the Hebrew alphabet. The creature was activated by magical incantations. It might look human, but it was a sort of changeling, stronger and more fearless and imbued with supernatural abilities, to speak with birds and angels, to see dreams and predict the future. More than anything, it was a warrior. Its goal was to protect the Jewish people, yet it was said not to have a soul, or even a heart.

Lea stored the book back in its proper place. *She will follow you to the ends of the earth*, her mother had told her. *What you ask her to do, she will do without question, as I would if I could be there with you today and the next day and the day after that.*

As it turned out, it wasn't only Ava who disapproved of Lea and Julien's friendship.

"Stay away from the girl," Madame Claire told her son. The strangers had been with them for more than three months. Far too long, in Madame's opinion, particularly when it came to the girl. She had seen her with Julien in the garden, speaking with their heads close together. Something Julien said had sent Lea into gales of laughter. That was when Claire knew. She'd seen it before. She herself had been a girl of twelve when she'd first become infatuated with a neighbor, and it had not turned out well. Young love could be harmful, and the best thing to do was nip it in the bud. "I don't want you in the same room when no one else is there."

"Why would you say that?" Julien asked his mother.

"I have your best interest at heart," Madame Lévi told him. It was not a time to form attachments or venture into *amour de jeunesse*, foolish puppy love. "It doesn't matter if you understand. Just do as I say."

From then on, they were carefully watched. Still, they managed to leave notes for each other in the first Monsieur Lévi's desk drawer in the library.

Hidden candies on the third shelf of the library. Not very good. Caramel.

Have you read Kafka? You should. You must. The Castle *is on the fourth shelf. Don't let my mother see you reading it. Of course, she disapproves of him.*

Are you a hunter or a wolf?

Trick question?

Tricky question.

Wolf.

Agreed. Always.

I want to show you Paris.

I want to be shown.

We'll be in trouble.

Good. Let's.

Meet me at noon.

This past May, Jewish men, most of whom were foreign, between the ages of eighteen and forty had been called up to present themselves to the Paris police. All had received a green postcard, and so the wave of arrests of five thousand men that followed was called *billet vert*. Almost all had been Polish refugees. Even if French Jews had been included, Julien and Victor had been too young, and Professor Lévi, at forty-six, was too old. Still, Madame Lévi worried more than ever. She instructed both of her sons that they were not to leave the property. Both boys nodded and didn't argue, but the boys knew they would disobey her. They could not sit still and let the world pass them by. Victor often went out his window at night, leaping down to the garden, to meet with his friends. Julien planned to show Lea Paris, no matter what he had promised his mother.

On the day Julien took her to see the city, his hair was slicked back and he wore a pressed white shirt. Lea hadn't seen any more of the city than she had during her initial walk from the train station. The neighborhood was a maze of tiny streets and alleyways, a maze Julien knew so well, he could be blindfolded and still find his way. He backtracked through the small cobbled streets that took them to a bridge that crossed to the Île Saint-Louis. They waited until the bridge was empty, then dashed across and quickly took the flight of steps to the river so they could walk along the Seine in the wilting, green heat. There was such a hush it was as though they'd entered a dream. They went on in a trance, as Julien described the places where they walked as they'd been before the war, the crowds on summer days, the ice cream shops, the boats on the river, the fishermen underneath the bridges who caught salmon, carp, and eel.

Lea didn't know where to begin when he questioned her about herself. What could she say, that she'd witnessed a murder, that there was still blood on her shoes even though Ava had cleaned them so well, that her mother had sent her away and her grandmother was trapped in their apartment with no means of escape, that she kept a secret close to her heart that she could never divulge?

The best she could do was shrug off his interest. It was probably a bad idea to become attached to someone when she had no idea how long she would stay. "I like to keep my thoughts to myself," she told him.

She gave him a keen glance that made him uncomfortable. Suddenly, he felt awkward, and somewhat in her power. Without his shield of charm, he was vulnerable and easily wounded.

"Maybe you'll share them with me," he said.

Lea laughed and made a face. "Please don't count on it."

Julien grinned, his self-assurance regained. At least he had made her laugh.

He watched what he said for the rest of the morning, for fear he might ruin everything by trying to rush her into taking him into her confidence. They were both half-dazed as they went along the river, from the heat and from the intensity of their time together; every moment was one they stole, free from the gaze of adults with their never-ending rules. Both were unaware they were not alone. Ava had tagged after them, so quiet not even the birds in the hedges took note as she passed by. She knew it was unsafe in Paris, and she was not the only one who had spied them. Two German soldiers rounded the corner, one elbowing the other when he caught sight of Julien and Lea, now on their way back home, hoping they could sneak over the garden wall before Madame Claire awoke from her nap.

"Halt," one of the soldiers called. "Komm jetzt her." *Come here now.*

They stopped, both thinking the same thing. Could they dare to run?

"Ich gebe euch eine Minute Zeit."

They had one minute to turn and walk forward. They had been speaking of foolish, childish things. How they would sneak out their windows one evening so Madame wouldn't know, how

Julien might convince his mother to allow him to have a dog, which she had always denied him before. Now their hearts were beating in rhythm, in terror. He could push Lea aside so perhaps she could escape. She could go forward and be arrested for being a foreign Jew so he might flee. They could stand together or run together.

"Schicke nur das Mädchen," one of the soldiers called, and both men laughed. *Just send the girl.*

Julien muttered a string of curses under his breath. He felt the way he had when he'd beaten Bernard, a rising fury he was afraid he wouldn't be able to control.

"Don't say anything," Lea said in a whisper. She had spoken only French since her arrival, and the German of the soldiers sounded strange to her now.

"Bist du taub?" Julien was now asked. *Are you deaf?*

One of the soldiers had a grasp on his rifle as he muttered to his friend and began to approach. That was when Ava appeared from a doorway, her black hair falling down her back, her face serene. Lea hadn't realized how beautiful she was; in the kitchen she looked so plain with her hair tied back, wearing those horrible boots. But now, she was illuminated. *Supernatural,* Lea thought, her breathing ragged and uneven. *A magical creature formed from a different substance.* She thought of her mother. *I'm still here every time she looks at you. She sees you as I would.*

The soldiers held their hands over their eyes to shield themselves from the brightness that filled the street; they tried to make out what caused the brilliance, but they would never know that Ava was accompanied by the light of the three angels sent to watch over Lea. Melahel, and Ornael, and Haiel, the angels of safe travel, patience, and courage.

"Was machst du hier?" one of the soldiers called to her. *What are you doing here?*

She was here to see to her duty, her burden, her obligation, her child. In this street that is what she felt and what she knew. Hanni had placed her own tears in Ava's eyes before they had opened to the world. Perhaps that was why at this moment she felt what she should have not felt, a rising panic. She heard the wind and it told her what to do. *Do what you must, do the most not the least, make certain, save her at any cost.*

"Come close," she said in the first human language she had learned. *Komm näher.*

She was stronger than a hundred horsemen. She would follow her burden to the end of the earth. She glanced at Lea and, with no words, let her know she should run. Lea grabbed Julien's hand the moment the soldiers' attention was diverted. They dashed around the corner, over the cobblestones, their hearts pounding, flying along alleyways, throwing open the garden gate, then sinking down behind the greenhouse, their backs against the wall, as they did their best to breathe.

"We left her there," Julien said, furious with himself. Just as he suspected, he was a coward. His brother had been right. He was not a man.

"She can take care of herself," Lea told him. "More than we ever could."

"It's not right. I'm getting my grandfather's rifle and going back."

Lea took Julien's arm. She leaned close to whisper. "She's not like other women. You don't have to rescue her."

He recognized the truth in this. He had seen Ava at work in the garden; in her hands a spindly tomato plant was suddenly laden with fruit, a wilting rose could be plucked and bloom again. Once, he had spied her in a tree with a dove in her hand, speaking to it before it flew away.

"What is she, then?" When Lea was silent, Julien grew concerned. "If you trust me you'll tell me."

"You wouldn't believe me if I did. But she can take care of herself. I can't tell you more."

"Ever?"

"When the war is over."

Julien laughed and said, "I'll hold you to that."

Lea nodded, but the truth was, *Maybe not even then.*

Ava left the soldiers in a doorway, so no one would see. She should feel nothing, but there was something strange inside her, some raw emotion she couldn't name. Was it the shock in their eyes, the way their spirits lifted from them, the presence of the angel in the black coat there beside her even before she had made a decision, as if he had known what she was destined to do?

She felt called to the water and clay from which she'd come. She wanted the cold current and she wanted to wash off the deaths. There was the river, only steps away. For the first time Ava wanted something for herself, that river, that water, that clay. Without thinking, she stripped off her dress, folded it on the bank, then took off her boots. She went barefoot, quickening her pace, the mud between her toes. When she plunged in, the water was delicious and familiar, as if she had come home.

A lone heron stood at the edge of the river. Ava could tell this one was in mourning, for herons were always in pairs. His heron wife had been shot by a farmer who believed the flesh of a heron brought good fortune and courage. It was an old story, fashioned out of a lie, but people believe lies if they're told often enough. In ancient Rome, this was the bird of divination. Its hollow bones tossed onto the floor would form an augury used to predict the future, and its bold call warned men of wars and famine. In Greece, herons were messengers, for both mortals and gods.

Herons were usually no more than three feet tall, but this one stood nearly as tall as a man. His plumes were ash gray, and his head was blue-black; his wings were ink and ash combined. A bird's heart is larger than a man's. It sees colors no human has ever seen, it can gather more light, hunt in the darkness, hear the wind on the other side of the city. This one saw Ava for who she was. A creature like no other. The heron walked to her and she to him. This is how it began, out of water, out of clay, out of air, when it was not expected, when it should have never happened, when no one else understood who she was.

CHAPTER TEN

THE DISAPPEARANCE

PARIS, AUTUMN 1941

BY NOW EVERYTHING THEY HAD COULD BE TAKEN AWAY. YOU couldn't influence a magistrate when you had nothing to offer in exchange for his favor. You couldn't put yourself above others when the soldiers who came to question you helped themselves to coats and jackets from the wardrobe in the hall. Madame Lévi sold the rare books for next to nothing to an underground dealer, then used the money for food. The locust trees had been cut down for firewood, and the rosebushes came next, their branches tossed into the fireplace for a flame that barely flickered with pale green smoke. Two professors of mathematics from Berlin, coauthors of academic papers with André Lévi, had moved into the third floor, along with their wives and children, all of whom had been taught to conceal themselves in the cupboards should the police arrive. André Lévi had answered when they came to the door. Two brilliant colleagues who were now wearing rags, carrying their children on their backs, thinking of starvation rather than algebra. They called what was happening in Berlin The Destruction. All Jews would be relocated, and then exterminated. The professor let his colleagues in without a second thought and asked Ava to make a pot of her soup. Claire was no longer speaking to her husband. She worried about her sons, fearing what lay in wait for them outside the garden gates. She had begun to keep certain treasures in a bag she carried around her waist, beneath her skirt. A few gold coins, her favorite earrings, her children's baby teeth in a small glass jar.

Victor seemed especially lost. He'd never been a good student, for he'd always been a person of action. He'd wanted to join the French army, but he'd been too young. Soon he would be eighteen, and would likely be arrested. He kept a packed rucksack hidden beneath his bed, ready for the time when he would have the opportunity to leave and do his duty for his country and his people.

It happened one cold night when the sky was filled with clouds and ice coated the streets. There was a commotion on the other side of the river and he slipped out of the house without his parents' knowledge and quickly made his way to the Marais. There was a curfew, but on this night groups of young men and boys had collected in protest. Among them was a fellow Victor had been chummy with in his younger days, Claude Gotlib. They'd been in the Jewish Scouts together and had spent weekends and holidays in the forest, learning the practical skills needed to survive in such circumstances. Claude motioned to him so they might speak privately as they surveyed the boys and young men who were rallying and demanding their rights. Many had mothers or girlfriends who had followed them and were now weeping, begging for them to come home. Before too long, the Germans would send soldiers to contain the crowd and many who were alive and protesting would be shot down.

"They can riot all they want," Claude said sadly. "They can't fight the Third Reich in the streets of Paris. The Germans have the soldiers, the weapons, the tanks, all of it."

"So we do nothing?"

Claude shook his head. "There's another way."

Victor looked at his old friend.

"The Scouts are still functioning. Only now, we're not playing." Bands of young Jewish renegades, later to be called La Sixième, lived in the woods and did their best to help others escape and work against the Nazis. These young people were fearless and wild and felt they had nothing to lose. "Have you ever shot a gun?" Claude asked.

As a child, Victor had often been taken into the countryside by his grandfather. He'd been perhaps six or seven, too small to hold a proper rifle, so his grandfather had one made especially for him, the correct weight and size. They'd shot at birds, although it seemed a crime to do so; Victor had cried the first time they'd gathered the doves they shot, piled into a white sheet to carry home. Later, he had been given a full-size rifle, and as it turned out, he had perfect vision and excellent aim. Perhaps it had all been for a reason, his embarrassment at having cried in front of the old man on that first hunting trip, the rain of gray feathers that fell from the sky, the fact that he had learned to be so good at something that repelled him. Now it all made sense, as if his fate had been preordained the moment he walked out into the field with his grandfather and picked up the gun he hadn't wanted to touch.

"Quite a number of times," he told his friend.

At the hour when night was disappearing, Claire Lévi discovered that her elder son was not in his bed. She looked through the house, then searched the icy street, out in her nightclothes, in a panic, not bothering to think of the curfew that kept Jews inside at night.

When she failed to find Victor, she went to sit in the garden on a stone bench, a shawl wrapped around her shoulders. She had not thought this was what her life would come to, but now she saw that it had. The professor noticed Claire wasn't in bed, and when he found her in her nightgown, crying, he sat beside her.

There had been an early storm and the branches on the trees crackled with a sheen of ice. All of the rabbits that had once lived here had been caught and cooked by the neighbors, and the dormice had taken over the empty garden house, where bulbs and cuttings had once been stored under the glass dome of a ceiling. It was silent and dark, and Claire was hopeless. What a fool she'd been to think the world would not touch her or those she loved. André took her hand. For once he was truly beside her, not thinking of anything other than the moment they were in as she told him their son was gone.

"He'll come back," the professor insisted.

Claire shook her head. She knew how fearless and headstrong young men were; she just hadn't realized that Victor was anything more than a boy.

"Of course he will," her husband insisted. "He'll be home by morning."

But when the sun had risen, Victor hadn't returned and they had no choice but to go inside and lock the door. That day the professor did not go to his study, but instead walked through the neighborhood and crossed the Seine at the appointed hour when Jews could shop, hoping to catch sight of Victor. He had always avoided the Marais, and had felt more connected to the academic Left Bank. Now as he went along Rue des Rosiers, past the bookshops and markets, and along the cobblestones of Rue des Barres, he realized how cut off he'd been.

When he'd had no luck finding Victor, the professor went to see the rabbi, although he hadn't been to services for a dozen or more years. Neither of his sons had been bar mitzvah, and in the last few years they hadn't celebrated Passover. He'd considered himself French through and through, but now here he was knocking at doors, asking if anyone had seen Victor. But no one could help him. Sons were missing all throughout Paris. He could search the world over, but when a young man wanted to fight for what was right, there was no holding him back.

CHAPTER ELEVEN

RUNAWAYS

VIENNE, WINTER 1941

ETTIE CAREFULLY OBSERVED EVERY CUSTOMER, HOPING someone would signal to her, but no one came for her. No strangers waited for her, no notes were dropped beside a table, no customers making eye contact. The only person who seemed to notice that she was alive was the beastly owner of the café, Monsieur Favre, who liked to stand too close while he put his hands on her waist, insisting she was too pretty to be a waitress. She knew he was a liar as soon as he said that. Not wanting to be dismissed, she swallowed her fierce dislike of Monsieur Favre and forced a thin smile onto her face.

"Your wife is much prettier," Ettie said, even thought Madame Favre was a dumpy, ill-tempered woman.

The café owner backed off once his wife was mentioned,

for Madame Favre was working not ten feet away. Still, from then on, Ettie slept with a knife in her cot. You couldn't trust anyone, really, especially when you yourself were living a lie. Weeks passed and no one contacted her. She began to think Father Varnier had decided she wasn't worthy of becoming a fighter.

Then one evening she left soon after the dinner hour to take a walk and everything changed. By then winter was closing in. She washed dishes for so long every day that her hands were raw from the harsh soap they used. "Don't use too much," Monsieur Favre always told her. He was cheap and preferred dirty dishes to the cost of soap.

Ettie felt free whenever she was away from the café. She often took long walks so she could practice her French with no one near to overhear her mistakes. The night was cold, and she hadn't a coat, so she walked quickly, quicker still when she heard someone behind her. The more speedily she walked, the closer they followed. She'd left her knife in her cot and was defenseless. She had the urge to run, but on this evening she was Nicole, her alter ego, a French girl who had a perfect right to walk the streets of Vienne, who was as good as anyone, who had no fear of strange men, who had faith and said her prayers, who was convinced that God was looking after her and was there to protect her.

She turned to face her follower. They were stopped on a dark corner. He was more a boy than a man, tall and lanky, and she only saw a glimpse of his large, handsome features. He had a strong physique, although his shoulders were hunched, as though he were deep in thought and didn't wish to be disturbed. He slipped his arm through hers and softly said, "Just keep walking."

To anyone watching, they appeared to be a couple taking a stroll after dinner. They were similar in age and demeanor. They didn't speak, but that was not so unusual. Couples often had little to say at the end of the day, yet were happy enough to be together in silence. They got into a car that had been parked not far from the church. The key was hidden under the seat. The car had been stolen in Nice and driven here to use until the time came to ditch it and find another.

"Are you old enough to drive?" Ettie had always been one to challenge boys her age.

"I'm the best driver you'll ever meet." He took out a blindfold, pleased to have the upper hand when he saw the shock on her face. "It's better for you not to know where we're going. Then you can't divulge the address."

Ettie felt a sort of terror slide under her skin, yet she didn't flinch when he blindfolded her. She thought of the Morning Star, Esther, and how she had rescued a nation when no man could have done so, and as she imagined this heroine, Ettie's nerves died down. In the car the young man told her about the underground movement of young Jews who resisted in every way they could, trying to rescue the next generation. They had learned to make explosive devices, most often pipe bombs that would stop German convoys or trains. When they could, they procured papers for families or children, whom they transported to *passeurs*, local people who were lifelong residents of the small villages who knew this wild, mountainous countryside, and could see Jewish refugees to the border. The organization was divided into small groups, cells that worked together, who often didn't know the names or locations of the other cells so they would have less information, for the good of all.

"I deliver you, and then, after they train you, if you're any good, you'll be my partner," the young man said.

"Good at what?"

"What do you think?" her companion said. "You went to the priest."

"I'd like to destroy the people who killed my sister."

"How do you plan to do that?" he asked.

She had no idea. A knife in her hands would do little.

When she didn't answer he said, "We'll show you."

She turned her head so he would not see that beneath her blindfold she was crying, tears streaming down her face. Whatever she did could never bring her sister back. Perhaps the boy felt for her. "I'm Victor," he told her despite the rule to keep his identity secret. "From Paris."

"I'm called Nicole here," she said. "My family called me Ettie."

They drove for quite some time, Ettie in the passenger seat as they barreled down the roads at a high speed. She couldn't see through the blindfold, but she knew they were headed into the countryside, for the roads were now bumpy and steep. They stopped once and the back door was wrenched open. A man got in and sank heavily into the backseat. He stank of cigarette smoke and he brought the cold inside with him. Ettie felt a wave of panic. She didn't like the idea of being outnumbered. The driver must have sensed her fear.

"Don't worry," he told her. "He's one of us."

So that was it, she was one of them now, and she didn't even know who they were. They were simply fools the priest had sent for her, who she hoped knew how to do battle. They drove for perhaps an hour. She learned that the fellow in the backseat was Claude. At last the car turned down a rutted road filled with puddles the tires splashed through, coming to a stop in a half-cleared spot in the woods where the parked car would not be seen. Victor got out and came around to help Ettie from the passenger seat. When he took off her blindfold, she saw they had come to a small abandoned house. They walked past it, into the woods. It was nearly midnight now. Ettie knew the café owner would find her empty cot, and the knife she kept there, and curse her. Let him. She was never going back. She had leapt from a cliff and now all she could do was wait to see where she fell.

There were two more young men, and a young woman. Jean and Arno and Bettina. They greeted her, and gave her supper, then asked what she knew about fighting. She knew how to hate, nothing more, so she shrugged. The others were not impressed.

"She'll be fine," Victor said. "All she needs is a teacher."

They laughed because Bettina had been an art teacher in Paris.

"If you're ready, so am I," Bettina said.

Ettie nodded, her face glowing. Someone had come for her.

When the snow began to fall, Victor and Claude and the other men piled into the car and took off, saying nothing of where they were going or what their mission was.

"We don't discuss such things," Bettina told Ettie. "It's safer for all of us that way. If one of us is caught, we know that no one can resist torture, and the less you have to say the better."

The women moved into the old house. The snow was so high it was impossible for a car to get down the dirt road. No one could come after them or blunder upon them. They felt they would be safe, at least for as long as the snowdrifts covered the roads and the fields. There was a fireplace and some wood, as well as a pile of onions and potatoes in the cellar, gnawed on by field rats, but perfectly edible. As it turned out, Bettina was a forger, and soon enough Ettie was in training, her hands blue with ink at the end of the day. Bettina's knowledge of printing techniques as an artist allowed her to produce a variety of identifications used by the Resistance to help smuggle Jews to the countryside or to the border. Visas, driver's licenses, baptismal certificates, ration cards, anything that allowed Jews to move about the country or make their way into Spain or Switzerland or begin the journey to find a Jewish state. She had access to ink and paper in Lyon from a sympathetic French owner of a poster factory that was no longer in service.

A few weeks after the men had departed, Ettie stumbled over some loose floorboards. She knelt down and lifted a board. Hidden there was a cache of gunpowder and batteries.

"I think you could tell me something of what we're doing here," Ettie said while she and Bettina worked one afternoon. By then the snowfall was over the windows, and they were eating rice and fried onions. There had been days when Ettie imagined they would starve to death before the men came back or the snow began to melt.

"Our boys interrupt convoys to Montluc Prison and what we

do here in this kitchen allows those who escape to have the proper documents."

"Interrupt?" Ettie said.

Bettina shrugged. "Bomb."

Ettie wished she were out with the men. She had spent most of her life in a kitchen, and now here she was again. They had been gone for so long, both she and Bettina were anxious. More than a month had passed. It might be possible for the women to hike to a village, or to a safe house Bettina knew about that belonged to a doctor on the other side of the mountain. But it was rough terrain, where people said wolves still roamed.

At dusk Ettie often went outside. She wore a heavy coat and her shoes were stuffed with paper to keep her feet from freezing. She had dug a small path to a stream, and once there had broken through the ice. Ettie crouched down and concentrated, then dipped her hand in the water, ignoring the cold. She caught a fish that was asleep in the frigid water. She carried him up the path into the house and placed him in front of Bettina. Bettina stood up, stunned by the fish flopping about on the table, then she laughed and couldn't stop.

"This is a miracle," she declared.

Bettina cooked the fish for dinner, and after they'd eaten the two women felt they had been saved. Every day Ettie went fishing in the mornings, and most days she caught something. She was a better fisherman than she was a forger. The fish swam directly into her hands. She was coming back from the stream one afternoon when an unfamiliar car pulled up the road. Ettie stopped behind a tree, in a panic, until she recognized Arno. She ran through the snow to meet him. She was about to ask if he had thought to bring food with him, until she saw the look on his face. She knew that something had gone wrong. He grabbed his rucksack and they went up to the house. The snow was turning blue. Soon it would begin to melt. Arno had indeed brought food, and he unpacked some bread and cheese and sausage. Bettina was there, her hands covered with ink, and when she saw him she burst into tears. There was no easy way to say what had happened, an explosion gone wrong, the bomb in Jean's hands. Claude was fine, but Victor had been badly burned and after a doctor had seen to his wounds, he'd insisted on being taken to a farm near a village about an hour away.

"They'll come back," Arno said.

"Of course," Bettina agreed.

Ettie made dinner that night, she was as good a cook as any of them. Afterward she went outside as she always did. Arno came out as well.

"We'll have to move back into the woods soon," he said.

He'd been nearby when the bomb had gone off and had seen what it had done to his friend. He now had ringing in his ears, but more than that, he seemed changed. He had a gun that he played with, as if he could never be ready enough for an attack. He'd brought in some rifles from the trunk of the car.

"All of those people on the convoy we couldn't stop will die because we made a mistake," he said. "I made the mistake. It was my plan."

"We all make mistakes," Ettie told him. It was better to make a mistake than to do nothing. "I think you should teach me some things."

He looked at her, confused. "Bettina is teaching you to be a printer."

"That's not what I want to be."

He took her in, then handed her the gun.

Vengeance was just beneath her skin, a shadow self, her true self, the one who had been holding her sister's hand, the one who ran into the woods, who wanted to learn everything she could be taught, starting now.

CHAPTER TWELVE

THE HERON

PARIS, SPRING 1942

THE HERON HAD GONE TO SPAIN AND THEN TO AFRICA. HE simply couldn't tolerate the cold; his bones were hollow and he needed light and food. But at last he came back for her and one warm night he called to her. Ava heard his voice and she could feel his cry echo inside of her. When she knew Lea was safely asleep, she rose from the blanket on the floor, which served as her bed. She went out the window, through the garden that was covered with blue squill, and then climbed over the garden gate Madame Lévi kept locked. She ran to the river, her breath coming hard. This was what freedom felt like, escaping the bonds that tied her, doing as she pleased, if only for a few hours. It was wrong, and she knew it, but she could not deny herself this one pleasure. She spied the heron in the shallows, in the place where she most wanted to be. Every night she went there, at the same hour, and every morning she returned with her hair streaming down her back, wet from the river.

One night, Lea woke to find Ava gone. Lea had been dreaming of her mother, and when she had such dreams it was as if she'd had a visitation, as if the dream was real and her waking life was imagined. In her dream, they'd sat together on a bench in their courtyard, and Hanni had leaned close to whisper. *She is not who she thinks she is, she was made to love you, but she doesn't know that yet. Every time she looks at you, I see you. Every time she embraces you, you are in my arms.*

This spring Jews in Paris had been made to buy yellow stars to be sewn onto their clothing. They had been given food cards imprinted with the word *Jew*. All public places were now forbidden.

Lea went into the garden to wait for Ava. She felt as though her mother had woken her for a reason. She thought of all her mother had done for her and all she had sacrificed.

If what she'd read was true, Ava would not refuse her one wish.

At last, near dawn, the golem returned with mud on her bare feet and her hair wringing wet. She leapt over the wall as if she were a deer and landed in an overgrown bed of ivy. When she saw Lea, she was embarrassed to appear as a wild creature, hands patchy with river silt, nearly flying into the garden. She came to sit beside Lea on the bench. The hem of her dress was wet; it was the same dress the housemaid had worn before she'd run away, but Marianne had kept her clothes starched and pressed, and now the fabric was streaked with mud.

"You should be asleep," Ava told Lea.

"So should you."

"But here we are."

"I won't ask you where you've been," Lea said.

Good. Ava was surprised by her own thoughts. *I won't tell you.*

"But I need you to save my mother," Lea went on. "We must go back to Berlin."

It was impossible. Ava was made to do as she was told and she had been told to keep Lea safe. "I must do as your mother instructed."

"Would you do anything my mother told you?"

"I'm here to keep you safe" was all Ava would say.

Here because you have to be, Lea thought. *Because you are a slave and I am your burden. I am your duty and nothing more. We are yoked together and we'd best not speak about it, or look into each other's eyes, in case we find that nothing at all is there.*

The golem knew that Lea's neighborhood in Berlin had been emptied of Jewish residents. Thousands had been sent east to Poland to the killing camps, Hanni Kohn among them. Soon after they had left for France, on an ordinary afternoon, the soldiers came. Bobeshi had been shot as she lay in her bed; she'd been too infirm to be taken from the apartment, too much trouble, too unimportant, not a person, not a soul, not a woman who spoke to God as she was murdered, turning to the angel in the black coat when he came to offer her comfort and take her in his arms.

"There's nothing to go back to," Ava said.

It was a dark dream, Hanni whispered in her daughter's ear. Lea did not need to be asleep to hear her mother's voice. *It was nothing like the world that we knew. Stones, murder, lice, greed, horror, birds falling from the sky, the grave you made for others, the grave you made for yourself. There were more demons every day, so many, there was no longer any room for them in the trees or on the window ledges. They walked through the streets as if they were men, ready to own the world. And where were the angels, the ones who walked so near to mortals you could sometimes feel them beside you? There was only one angel left in all of Berlin, the one with the black coat and the book of names. There were as many names as there were demons. The book was filled in a matter of days. There was another book needed, and then another, until there were three hundred, and then three thousand, and then the books were piled upon each other until they reached to heaven.*

Keep her safe.

That was her last thought as she stood in the cavernous hole she had been forced to dig, in a country where she didn't belong. Those were the words Ava had heard at the moment Hanni arose into the World to Come. Those were the words Lea heard now.

Lea went to hide behind the greenhouse. She was there crying when Julien found her. The whole city of Paris was crying, but hers was the only voice he heard.

"I want to go home," she told him.

"All right."

"But I can't. I can never."

"Of course you can. I'll go with you." When she gave him a look, Julien insisted. "Why not? Who's to stop us?"

But Lea knew that Ava was right. Hers was a wish that could never be granted. It was too late, it was over; there was no home to go back to. When you have lost your mother you have lost the world. You can sit in the garden and see nothing at all, not the woman on the garden bench watching over you, not the boy who refuses to leave you, even when you tell him to go.

Your grief won't go away; it's not a door you can close, or a book you can put back on the shelf, or a kiss you can give back once it is given. This is the way the world is now. Keep the worst things to yourself, like a bone in your throat.

He will do the same, he will blurt out everything, but not the fact that his father cries in his study because he knows that the only numbers that matter now are the numbers of the dead. This is how it begins and how it ends, this is your weakness and your strength, when you are alone, you are not alone, when you have lost the world, you have found each other. After a while it doesn't matter if the garden is ruined and the trees are all cut down. It doesn't matter if there is ice over your heart. He knows who you are.

In the midst of dinner there was knocking at the door. The professors from Germany and their wives and children had been served bowls of Hardship Soup, but they now ran upstairs and hid in the cabinets, holding knives in their hands. When André Lévi went to open the door, it was only their neighbor, Monsieur Oches, who'd come to call. But he was frantic as he reported that people were fleeing, not just the foreign born, but their own neighbors, French citizens, even those who had fought in the previous war and were decorated veterans. People were leaving for Lyon or Toulouse, where life was somewhat better for them, or to the border of Italy or Switzerland. Anyone with a relative in America or England had already left. There was talk of a roundup to come when no one would be saved, not women, not children, not the sick, not the elderly.

"It won't happen at dinner," the professor said. "Go home and be with your family."

"Don't think I'm exaggerating!" Monsieur Oches said. "We'll all be murdered before long!"

Professor Lévi thanked his neighbor and led him to the door so the family could finish their dinner. Claire Lévi had worried that these cousins of her husband would call trouble to them, and now they had an attic full of unwanted guests. When she and her husband were at last alone at the table, she told him their guests must leave. "We can't have refugees here."

"Not tonight." There was strange resolve in the professor's voice. He had realized his wife did not yet understand what was happening. They were all the same now, whether they were refugees or French born. This was not their city anymore.

After dinner the professor took a box of their most valued possessions out to the yard and had Julien dig a hole underneath the oak tree. Julien's shirt was soon soiled, as if he was a gravedigger, but he kept going until his father told him to stop. Into this trench went what was left of the silverware that had belonged to Julien's great-grandmother, along with the professor's studies packed into a leather case and a box of family photographs. If they were forced to leave, they could later return for these things.

Lea stopped at the doorway when she saw the Lévi family gathered in the garden. During the time she'd been their houseguest, the professor and his wife had mostly ignored her, but now Professor Lévi gestured to her.

"Join us. Perhaps you have a treasure to bury?"

"Don't be ridiculous," Claire said. "What on earth would this girl have?"

Lea touched the charm around her neck. Her only treasure, and she yearned to be rid of it. Julien was watching her with his fierce dark eyes that were flecked with gold. His white shirt was streaked with dirt, and he couldn't seem to look away from her. Lea met his glance and hesitated, until Madame Lévi urged him to hurry, and then it was too late for Lea to be rid of the locket. Not that it mattered. She had memorized her mother's instructions. She knew what she must do, whether or not she had the charm.

Shovels of dirt were tossed over the trench, and a frozen rosebush was planted above the buried treasure. The one thing of value the professor kept was his watch. It had belonged to his father, and, though he had paid no attention to time in the past, he thought he must now do so. He asked his son to bring out a bottle of cognac, the last they had. The German professors and their wives came to join them. Julien returned with the bottle and a tray of small glasses. The glasses were green and fragile and would all be broken before long. It was the first time Lea had tasted alcohol and she felt grown up and reckless. Ava came to look for her and immediately noticed that she was standing too close to Julien. She gave him a look, but it was too late. He was sick of being told what to do. They might be considered children, but it was possible they would not be alive long enough to become adults.

Out of sight, Julien took Lea's hand.

Out of sight, she let him.

"Now they'll know where our valuables are," the professor's wife whispered once their belongings were in the ground. She threw a look over her shoulder. There was Ava, glaring back with cold gray eyes. "Who's to say that woman's not a thief?"

"She's not, but even if she was, it wouldn't matter," her husband responded. "We no longer have anything to steal."

Ava heard the call outside the window at an hour when no birds sang. It was the call of a messenger to warn of a battle to come. The gray heron was in the garden. He looked at the world as a map, in shades of blue and green, but now the colors were murky and there were black clouds everywhere, so that it was nearly impossible to see. Already, huge flocks of birds had taken to the sky, fleeing the city as if escaping from a fire. The darkness was caused by the descent of the angels. There were angels of confusion and of destruction and fear, and accusing angels who did their work in the darkness, so men and women never knew when they'd been marked. This world was shattering. Ava could see where it was breaking, a fine white line that revealed what had already passed and what was to come. She shook Lea awake.

In her groggy state, Lea didn't think to be defiant when Ava said they must leave. She dressed quickly, while Ava tossed the suitcase out the window, then they both climbed out. There was a stream of pale moonlight, like the moonlight in a dream. It was already spring. The world was green and pulsing and beautiful.

"Hurry," Ava told Lea, who lagged behind.

Lea now stopped on the path, refusing to go any further. "I don't have to listen to you. You're not my mother."

Ava was not made to have emotions, but the remark hurt, as if she had pricked her finger on glass.

"You're nothing to me," Lea went on, furious with Ava ever since her refusal to go back to Berlin. "You go! Leave me here."

Ava put down the suitcase. "I may not be your mother, but I act on her behalf. Do as I say."

Lea's eyes were blazing. "I won't. I don't want to go because I don't want to be with you!" she cried.

"You can come with me," Ava said, "or I can take you with me."

"How? With a rope around my neck?"

"If I need to, yes."

Their breath came hard in the cool, foggy night. Ava seemed even taller in her black boots.

"There is no rope," Lea said uncertainly. "And, anyway, you wouldn't dare."

Ava nodded at the shrubbery that was covered with burlap, tied with heavy rope. It was a lilac and the leaves were growing right through the burlap. The rope was slack.

Lea knew what her mother would say if she had been there. *She has been sent to you to save your life. Don't throw everything away.*

"Fine," Lea said grudgingly. "But first I say goodbye."

The heron was waiting in what had once been a sapling the first Monsieur Lévi had planted, a cutting from the oldest locust tree in Paris, which had stood on the Rive Gauche for more than four hundred years at an ancient Roman crossroad. It was said that good luck would belong to anyone who ran their hand over the locust's bark, but Ava could see demons massing in trees all over Paris, in the cherry trees that surrounded Notre-Dame, the sequoia brought from California that stood in the Parc des Buttes-Chaumont, the huge ginkgo biloba planted in the Parc Monceau in 1879.

Ava let Lea have the one thing she wanted, such a small request, really, when she would lose everything else. Their time here was over, it was already in the past, and they both knew it.

Lea rushed to take some pebbles from the ground to toss against Julien's window. He woke and looked out, rumpled with sleep. When he saw her, he knew. Julien pulled on his clothes and took the stairs two at a time. He brought his rucksack with him. He had decided that if they should leave, he would go with them and had already written a note for his parents, wherein he did his best to explain his disappearance. But when he reached the kitchen, there was his mother, waiting for him. Since Victor had vanished she hadn't once slept through the night. Now she'd heard stones flung up to his window.

"What are you doing?" she asked him. "Do you think you're going somewhere?"

"Mama," Julien said. He could see that her hands were shaking. "I must."

"And do what your brother did? Abandon us?"

He came to sit beside her. She was brokenhearted. He had never seen her cry before, and now tears streamed down her face. "It's not like that."

"It's that girl," Claire said.

"Not at all."

She gave a short bitter laugh. "You're too young for such things anyway. You're a baby."

"It's time to go. You know it's true."

"When your father says it's time, it's time!" Claire's expression was set, her eyes bright with hurt. If she lost her children she lost everything. The house and all the time she'd spent on keeping up appearances meant nothing. This was her heart, sitting beside her, the boy who looked anxiously through the window, so ready to leave. "Go on," she said. "Go! But you tell your father, not me. Wake him up and tell him. Look at his face while you do so. Then you can leave."

Julien thought of the look on his father's face as he'd buried his papers. Most likely all of his writings would rot in the ground before anyone could dig them up again. He was well aware that his father cried late at night, alone in the library. There were hardly any books left, and the empty shelves haunted him.

"Tell him right now!" Julien's mother said. "And then you can break my heart because we will never see each other again."

Because he could not do that to her, Julien left his rucksack on the chair and went into the garden. As soon as Lea saw his expression she knew he wasn't going.

"My parents," he said. "My mother."

His mother was in the doorway now, watching. Even from a distance Lea could tell she was crying.

"I'll write to you," Lea told Julien.

Julien smiled, a weary look on his face. She could tell he didn't believe her, but he was wrong. She would find a way. Julien was so tall Lea was forced to stand on tiptoe as she leaned closer. There was only one thing he had to do and they would surely see each other again.

"Stay alive," she told him.

CHAPTER THIRTEEN

THE FARAWAY PLACE

HAUTE-LOIRE, SPRING 1942

THE SOLDIERS ARRIVED WHEN MARIANNE WAS IN THE WOODS, looking for the chickens that had run off into the underbrush. She'd been distracted when she noticed a *milan royal,* the red kite that was so fierce and beautiful only members of the royal family in France had been allowed to fly it in the practice of falconry. She'd climbed along a ravine to watch, then stretched out on the hill, sprawled in the grass. She was thinking about Victor, though she probably shouldn't. The shadows grew long and she realized it was late. She began the trek home, embarrassed that she'd failed to find the chickens. When she saw the trucks, she ducked into the underbrush. By then the soldiers were taking the cows, which lowed as they were forced into trucks and pulled against the thick ropes looped around their necks. A cow had been shot in the pasture, an act of thoughtless savagery. Flies buzzed over the blackened blood. Marianne's father came out with a shotgun, and one of the soldiers grabbed the gun and hit him over his skull. When he was on the ground several of the soldiers kicked him with their heavy boots until he stopped moving.

"Don't be a fool, old man," one told him. "Next time we'll shoot you instead of the cow."

Marianne sank down behind the hedges with one hand over her mouth so she wouldn't cry out. She was shattered by what she saw, but knew it would do no good to run into the fray and be beaten herself, perhaps raped and murdered in a failed attempt to help her father. Still, her inaction stung. She pinched herself, hard, until her nails drew blood.

When the trucks pulled away they'd left very little behind, only Bluebell, who'd wandered into the woods, and the bee-hives teeming with bees, and of course, her father, lying prone, bloodied and broken. She ran to help him up, then brought him to the house, and escorted him up to bed, nearly carrying his full weight. She saw to his wounds with a damp cloth, then nursed him with herbal remedies, nettle tea and a poultice composed of mint and leaves of rosemary. Marianne should have cleaned the blood from her dress with salt, but she was too agitated about her father's condition to do so.

For three days she thought her father would die, but she dared not go to the village for help, fearing the Germans would be there. When finally her father could speak he said, "Are you my daughter?" She said she was and he then said, "You have saved me," and he wept. They never discussed this exchange afterward. He was a tough old gentleman who didn't wish to take help from anyone.

Marianne realized she must find a doctor to see to his broken leg or he wouldn't walk again. There was a physician on the other side of the mountain who her father said was a decent fellow, often seeing patients for free. She went to the neighboring farm and used the telephone, thanking her neighbor, Monsieur Cazales, a taciturn farmer who was too polite to ask why she had blood on her dress.

The doctor came to set Marianne's father's broken leg. He had a dusty Renault that managed to take the rutted road quite nicely. He was tall, and well dressed, and he asked only medical questions. Marianne's father allowed himself to be examined, although he suggested that the doctor be quick about it. The leg was promptly and simply set against a splint. Marianne's father cursed while the procedure was taking place, then thanked the doctor for his efforts.

The doctor left some pain pills, which the farmer would not take as a matter of principle, and he recommended that the old man stay off his feet for three weeks, then use crutches, continuing to keep the weight off his leg for another three.

As Marianne walked the doctor out, they blinked in the bright sunlight.

"They could come back," the doctor said.

"We'll have faith that they won't," Marianne responded.

They agreed on that and shook hands.

Marianne saw to her chores when the doctor had gone, cleaning out the barn, milking the goat, gathering the geese, and finally chasing after the chickens that had scattered into the woods. She supposed they had saved her, for surely if she had not gone to chase after them she would have been the one the soldiers had turned on, and perhaps her enraged father would have been shot point-blank. She made a vow not to eat chicken again, only their eggs, and not to be as impatient with them as she usually was.

As for the slaughtered cow, she butchered it and burned the bones on a bonfire. Someone had once told her that when you return to a location from your past, it is never the same, and perhaps this was true. She had left an ordinary place, and had come back to something quite different, somewhere where anything could happen.

When Monsieur Félix was well enough to come downstairs on his crutches, they went out to the barn, where Marianne helped him put on the white cheesecloth veil so he could see to the honey. In the distance there were spikes of purple and pink lupines, a riot of color. The honeycombs were rich and golden, and later that week Marianne would bring the honey to the market to sell. People took note of Marianne now that she was back, but she rarely ventured into town, and no one was rude enough to mention her long absence, although the pastor came to speak to her as she was leaving for home. She remembered going to see him when she was an unhappy, sulky girl. He hadn't understood what she'd wanted, but of course she hadn't known herself. A different life, a chance at love, a larger world, buried desires that seemed silly now that she was back. Pastor Durand had aged and was wearing a black coat. He walked Marianne home down the same road she had taken when she left. At first they politely spoke about the weather. But clearly there was more to discuss. The pastor glanced at her.

"You may have noticed," he said, "everything has changed."

Of course it had. Everything did, even she herself. Still, she wanted to hear what he had to say that was so important he was huffing and puffing as they walked on at a quick pace, for Marianne was not one to dawdle, especially when she had what her father called the "bee money" in her pocket.

"We have many children at the school at the top of the hill," Pastor Durand told her. "They're not from here. They're refugees." The road from the village careened steeply, ending in fields of greenery where there were half a dozen buildings, including classrooms and dormitories. From the corner of his eye he gauged Marianne's reaction. The boarding school sheltered Jewish children, and the ministers André Trocme and Edouard Theis had arranged for thousands of Jewish children to be hidden with families in town and in the countryside, and Daniel Trocme, the principal of the school, accepted as many Jewish children as possible.

"I should give you some honey for the schoolchildren," Marianne said. "They'd enjoy it."

It took two hours to hike from the village to the farm, but the pastor didn't seem to mind even though it meant he would be journeying back in the dark. Marianne had a newfound respect for him. He came into the house and shook hands with Monsieur Félix, then he slipped off his black coat, under which he had been carrying a rifle. He placed it on the table and winked at Marianne's father. Monsieur Félix brightened then. The Germans had taken his rifle and he liked the look of this one.

The pastor knew the old man's gun had been stolen. As it turned out, Monsieur Cazales had told the pastor about the blood on Marianne's dress. From the hilltop that abutted their properties the neighbor could see for himself that the cows were gone. When he added these facts together, there was only one reason why this should be.

Marianne's father now had a long scar down one side of his scalp, and he limped. When asked about it, the old man avoided complaining.

"Something may have happened." Monsieur Félix shrugged.

"We refuse to bow to anyone," the pastor said. "We never have and never will."

Marianne's father nodded in agreement. Fifty years earlier there had been a movement called le Réveil, the Awakening, a period in which Huguenots were asked to remember their mistreatment by the Catholic majority to remind them they must never let persecution happen again. They were pacifists who believed in the greater good, a philosophy they began to act upon in 1939, when they accepted Spanish war refugees into their community, taking them into their houses and barns. Later it was the sick children of workers, for the mountain air was thought to cure their ailments. Now it was the Jews. Monsieur Félix had never met a Jew, but that didn't matter to him.

"We will hide anyone in need as we were forced to hide," he told the pastor.

The men shook hands on it. The entire village had agreed to stand up to the Germans and would, by the time they were through, rescue between three thousand and five thousand Jews. There would be a messenger coming by, the pastor said, with identity papers that must be hidden so that children could

cross the border into Switzerland. Other members of the Resistance would later come to claim the papers. Would this be
a problem? Monsieur Félix laughed. He so rarely did so that
both the pastor and Marianne were surprised. Then they found
themselves laughing with him. No, it was not a problem; it was
a blessing to rebel against tyranny, as their grandfathers had
done.

Marianne served tea with their own honey. Everyone said it
was the best on earth, and the pastor agreed. He asked if Marianne still knew the mountains as well as she had when she was
a girl, and she said that indeed she did, even after her time away.
She still had the talent of finding her way in the dark.

Would she be willing to take children across the border? She
would be a *passeur,* a local resident who knew the topography,
as well as the times of the patrols, and could manage to get those
who were fleeing through the barbed-wire barriers. She would be
assisted by the OSE, who provided for as many escapes as could
be arranged into neutral Switzerland. The Œuvre de Secours aux
Enfants was a Jewish organization begun in Russia and Berlin,
whose goal was to rescue the next generation. The organization
placed refugee children in châteaus the government allowed to
be designated as schools.

Marianne thought over this request as she went to collect
some speckled eggs from the hens to send home with the pastor. Her heart jolted against her chest and she noticed how sweet
the air was. When she returned she said that yes, she would indeed be a guide.

"I can't promise her safety," Pastor Durand said to Monsieur
Félix.

Marianne looked at her father, who nodded, but she made

certain to answer for herself. "No one has to promise me any-thing."

Marianne's father was a man who was always willing to try to do what was right. If he was not a warrior or an angel, if he rarely spoke and never asked her what she thought or what she felt when she was young, he had always tried to do God's will and act with faith. Now it seemed his daughter was the same, and he was filled with a raw pride. Guiding people across the border was dangerous. Several people had been detained at a crossing place known as the *plaine du loup*, the Wolf's Plain. If Marianne were apprehended, she would be on her own. Monsieur Félix gazed at her and thought about Jeanne d'Arc, the girl warrior. Perhaps his daughter was stronger than he'd thought.

"Are you sure you want to help the pastor?" he asked.

"Oh, yes," Marianne said. She had always wished to accomplish something, and, as it turned out, this is what she had been waiting for all along.

She went the first time with a man from the village, Albert, with whom she had gone to school and who now had a wife and five children. They shook hands and he told her to take the lead, even though he was a practiced *passeur*, to see if she still knew her way through the mountains. It took them close to a week, and then they got a ride back from another *passeur* from Annecy. Marianne felt exhausted and enthralled. She had remembered everything, and was as good a hiker as anyone. She walked from town thinking of the faces of the children who had been rescued. When she got to the house she was surprised to hear voices inside. She went to the barn for a hatchet, fearing another incident with the Germans, but when she returned her father opened the door to tell her they had a visitor, a young man who was a friend of hers.

"I don't have any friends." Marianne kept the hatchet in her hand as she walked inside, but dropped it the moment she saw Victor at the table, where he'd been having lunch with Monsieur Félix. Victor looked completely different, thinner and tougher, with his dark hair shaggy and long enough to bother him so that he kept flinging one hand through it, pushing it back. There were fresh burns on his hands and face that showed clearly he had been in an accident.

"Isn't he your friend?" her father said, confused.

"Yes of course," Marianne said, her heart lifting. Victor rose so quickly from his chair that it tipped back and fell with a clatter. He came to embrace her, and in his arms she rose off the floor. She was surprised when he stole a kiss, and even more surprised that the kiss burned. That was how it had begun.

He explained he had been living in the forest with a small group of Jewish resisters, and there had been an accident, a bomb had gone wrong. They'd scattered for a while. Victor had been hurt, his face and hands had been scorched. "You need to heal or you'll be no use to anyone," his friend Claude had told him.

Victor had seen a doctor known for helping their people. After that, the one place he could think to go was Beehive House.

"I remembered everything you ever told me about your home," he told Marianne. "That's how I found you."

Marianne insisted he put her down. She sat to join them for lunch. She was starving, but it didn't matter. She couldn't take her eyes off him. Even before the dishes were done, she melted beeswax in a pan, then added olive oil and lavender as an herbal salve. Victor grinned at her as she saw to his burns. When he leaned forward to whisper he was much too close. "It was always you," he told her.

"Quiet," she said, glancing at her father. "That's nonsense."

But it wasn't nonsense, at least not for her. She let him kiss her again, but only once, when her father was outside with Bluebell, the goat. "That's enough," she said, but of course it wasn't. She made up a bed for him in the parlor, and he went to sleep immediately, grateful and exhausted. Victor was beautiful and young. But he wasn't a boy anymore; he was a fighter. Marianne's head was spinning to think he was here, in their house. When her father asked if she'd like to look at the stars, she was happy to do so.

"That boy seems to know you well," her father said in an offhand way as he lit a small cigar, one of a few that he rationed for special occasions.

"Well, of course. We shared a house for five years."

"Were you happy when you were away?" For all those years he had wondered what his daughter's life was like in Paris. He thought she might come home with a family, a husband and perhaps some sons, but that was not the case.

"I was happy," Marianne said. "He made me happy," she admitted. "But I missed this place."

The stars were falling from the sky as they climbed up the hill, he on his crutches, she with a ready arm to guide him. She made her father a promise that nothing would happen under his roof.

"Whatever happens, you're my daughter," he said.

She nodded, content to be here with him to gaze at the constellations that were so familiar from her childhood. You couldn't see a trail of stars covering the entire sky in Paris. You had to be here in the countryside on a clear night. She thought of Victor asleep in the parlor, and the powder burns on his face and hands. He was here for now, and that was enough. Everything might disappear, but not these stars. Her father should not have the strength to climb this hillock, but he did it anyway, and he trusted her to do what was best. He was who he was, after all, and had loved her even while she was gone. Standing beside him, she felt fortunate to have found her way home.

CHAPTER FOURTEEN

BLESSING

RHÔNE VALLEY, JUNE 1942

THE SISTERS HAD BEEN THE RESIDENTS OF A TALL STONE convent where there was a boarding school for girls for nearly three hundred years. The spires reached to heaven. The gravel paths were worn down from those who walked there daily as they recited their prayers. In the woods near the convent, Ava could hear the rise and fall of voices from inside. The nuns at prayer, the students at the dinner table, and then, the faintest voices of all, five Jewish girls in the attic who were well cared for, but who still wept at night, longing for their mothers. More and more children had been separated from their parents when the Vichy government decided to arrest Jews, except for children under the age of sixteen. Many of these children, who were now on their own, were living in châteaus and schools run by the OSE, who turned to convents such as this, and to the homes of those good neighbors who believed a child's life was worth more than adhering to arbitrary laws.

The sisters had originally been lacemakers, but during the Reign of Terror many were beheaded by guillotine or thrown into prison. For the next twenty years they were in hiding, until they could at last be free to live and work as their faith decreed. During the Revolution, when they would not sign documents stating their first allegiance was to France, rather than to God, the congregation was outlawed until 1807. The sisters understood what it was to be persecuted and arrested and murdered, for a crime no worse than faith.

The convent and its grounds were elegant and lush, thanks to several wealthy women who, over the convent's long history, had joined the order and brought their wealth with them. In their legendary garden grew roses of every color: *rouge; noire; blanche; feu,* the color of fire; *cerise,* the shade of cherries; *argent,* silver; and *or,* gold. Some varieties had first names and surnames, as though they were elegant women shrouded in vivid color standing between the hedges in silk dresses: Madame Isaac Pereire, created in 1881, Madame Ernest Calvat, first grown in 1888, Bourbon Roses and tea roses of every hue and tone, all grown by the grace of God.

The mother superior, Sister Marie, had grown up in a château outside Paris and recalled the bliss of the garden of her childhood. She'd been delighted to come to the convent as a young woman to find the leggy, half-remembered, and utterly neglected planting of roses. From the start, she vowed to bring the garden back to its former glory. Her first act as mother superior was to hire a landscaper who would teach the sisters to garden.

Sister Marie had been orphaned young and left with a huge inheritance. Her aunt, a grudging and disagreeable caretaker, had initially disapproved when the child yearned for convent life, but when someone is convinced she has a path, it is not easy to dissuade her, and in the end it was a relief for the family to have her safe and sound, outside of their orbit. Sister Marie had been very single-minded even when she'd been Madeleine de Masson, a shy girl who, nevertheless, possessed a fierce independent streak. It was no surprise that she had dedicated her life to teaching. Nor was it a surprise that she didn't need to think twice when the Archbishop of Nice, Monsignor Paul Rémond, asked her to enroll Jewish girls who had been brought to them by the OSE.

The new girl was discovered camped on the front steps. Lea had barely spoken a word to the sisters; perhaps the convent looked like a prison with its tall spires and weathered gargoyles that seemed neither beast nor man. There was a stone fountain, and green water poured from the beak of a pelican, the bird that signified Jesus, for as pelicans were said to pluck their feathers to feed their young with their own blood, so, too, did Christ sacrifice himself for mankind. Lea felt a chill when the tall woman in a black habit came along the gravel path. Fewer questions would be asked if Lea came to the convent alone, and so Ava would wait a day or two before presenting herself and asking to work in the kitchen. As soon as Ava suggested this plan, Lea suspected she would not return. What would keep her from disappearing, following the heron to the far reaches of the world? And who was to say it would not be best for them both if she did? They would be free of each other, and of the burdens they carried, and of the fate that awaited them.

Sister Marie came to greet the new girl, who was clearly troubled, as so many of these motherless children were. Perhaps this girl, who kept her hands folded in her lap, and her eyes lowered, would like to help in the garden. It soothed the soul to do so and it might serve to remind her of the beauty of the world.

She asked the girl for her name.

"Lillie Perrin, Madame."

The girl's eyes were lowered, which led the mother superior to believe this was not the truth.

"Lillie is your given name?"

Lea had been given it, surely, by her own dear mother before leaving Berlin, so perhaps when she said yes it was not truly a lie. Lea had heard that Catholics confessed their sins to one another rather than to God, and she worried she would be expected to do the same. Her greatest sin would be committed in the future, and it was one for which she could never be forgiven.

"And you are Catholic?" the mother superior asked.

"It says so on my papers, Madame."

They exchanged an open gaze. A lie was a lie, papers or not. The mother superior understood that the girl was Jewish, carrying a false name and identity. "We're glad to have you with us, Lillie," she said warmly. "We ask only that you obey the rules and pay attention to your studies." Usually, Sister Marie was told a bit of background, where the child had previously resided, perhaps, or the fate of her parents, but this girl had come on her own and her arrival was a bit of a mystery. Still, they turned no one away. They'd made that decision after the monsignor had first come to talk to them. Every child was equal in their eyes. "I'm sure you will learn the prayers easily."

"My mother taught me several already," Lea told the sister.

"Then I think your mother would approve of you being here. She would be happy to have you safe in our midst."

Lea was given a uniform consisting of a navy blue dress, black stockings, and a pair of laced shoes. There were new under-garments and a nightgown as well. A younger girl called Pauline had been asked to show her the dormitory. It was a special sec-tion for the Jewish girls, hidden in the attic behind a wrought-iron gate and a heavy wooden door. The room was guarded by an old nun, Sister Félicité, a very deep sleeper who snored quite loudly. The sister slept with a broom in her lap, there to defend herself and her girls if the need arose. She claimed to be fierce, but she was nearly eighty and walked with a limp and she didn't even manage to scare her own students when she threatened they would have to clean the stone floors with a scrub brush if they didn't behave.

Pauline, also from Berlin, was to bring Lea to their room. She was eager to show off her French.

"The sisters practiced with me until I lost my accent. It's best to do as they say."

Remember your own room, the blue rug on the floor, the way the light came in through the curtains in the morning, the sound of my voice as I called to you in the park, my darling, my girl, light of my life, come here and give me a hug, eat this apple, sit on this bench, watch the birds above us, and the sky that's so bright, take the love that I have for you that will never end.

Lea quickly dressed in her new uniform. She did her best

not to think, she pushed away dark thoughts until they were folded into a tiny corner of her mind, behind a locked door. At night the heron came to Lea's window and stood on the ledge, so close she could feel his heart beating. She knew that Ava had told him to watch over her. *She is nothing to me*, Lea told herself. *She is not my mother, she is not my cousin, she may not even be a woman. She is here because she has to be, because she was made to be, because she cannot make her own decisions or cast her own fate.*

Lea found her way along the confusing corridors of the convent, but her stomach twisted with nerves. She had already decided; Julien would be her only friend. She needed no others. *Tu me connais,* she would have told him if she could. You alone know me.

At lunch, Lea was so famished she could barely restrain herself from reaching for the hard heels of bread until all of the prayers were recited. Then the other girls chattered away about the baker who had left; there'd been nothing to eat but old bread all week, although they knew they should be grateful. After lunch had been served Sister Marie stood to announce there was a new student. Lea had no choice but to stand as well and be introduced as Lillie Perrin. Everyone greeted her in unison, in perfect French, except for a petite, dark girl called Renée, a recent arrival from Berlin who refused to speak anything but German. She had been rescued, fortunate to have been among a group who had managed to escape when being moved from one camp to another. She had a tattooed number on her arm that she rubbed at when she thought no one was looking and she never undressed in front of the others. The OSE brought her to France, and to this convent. Her name had been Rachel. Her mother, father, uncles, aunts, grandparents, sisters, and brothers had all been on the trains. She was older than Lea, perhaps already fifteen. In the attic, her bed was next to Lea's. That evening as they prepared for bed, Renée glared at Lea. She looked fragile, but there was a core of fire inside her. "Rühr mich nicht an," Renée said. *Never touch me.* "Und schau nie unter mein Bett." *And never look under my bed.*

It was difficult to follow the rules, much less understand them, and now, after Lea's encounter with Renée, she felt even more unsure of herself. No one dared to break the silence before going to chapel in the morning or at breakfast. There were scores of prayers to recite, many more than her mother had taught her. The sisters looked sterner than Sister Marie in their stiff black habits. She thought of biting the soldier in the alleyway, of the wolves in the snow, of the blood on their shoes, of how fast she had run. After a while she wasn't afraid, but she kept her eyes lowered when she greeted the sisters, and she stayed as far away from Renée as possible.

In class, she did her best to follow along as they studied the stories of the martyrs, including the Carmelite nuns of Compiègne, who went to the guillotine. She was imagining the death of the first and youngest sister to die, Sister Constance, who was said to face her fate with the grace of a queen, when in the midst of the lesson, she heard the heron on the roof call out with joy. Lea gazed out the window, and there was Ava, coming into the courtyard.

Lea raised her hand even though she was meant to be silent in class. When the sister approached, she asked to leave the room, claiming to have an upset stomach. She quickly took the stairs, making her way past several stained-glass panels representing scenes from the Bible in which angels climbed into a cobalt blue sky. She wanted to witness how Ava managed to get herself into the convent.

The young nun at the door was thanking Ava for her gift of wild berries. "I don't know if we need anyone in the kitchen," the nun said.

"We do," Lea said from her hiding place on the stair. "The baker has gone."

Ava and the nun both turned to her. "Aren't you supposed to be in class?" the sister asked.

"Yes, of course." Lea raced up the stairs to the classroom and went back to her seat, surprised to find herself comforted by Ava's presence.

She will follow you to the ends of the earth. When she looks at you I will see you, when she embraces you I will feel your heart beat. You can love her if you want to. It will not be a betrayal, because when you do, I will be there with you.

"Please take Ava in," Lea said softly as she faced a painting of Jesus, who was said to watch over them all. "Please save her."

Renée was sitting next to her, and now clucked her tongue. She understood French, but simply refused to speak it. "Niemand kann uns retten," she said in a whisper when she overheard Lea's pleas. *No one can rescue us.*

Ava asked for no payment, other than food and shelter, and it was true the baker had run off, taking a pair of silver candlesticks with her. Ava was taken on as the baker's replacement, who, as it turned out, had disappeared with the cook. Ava would take on both positions. She was brought to the huge stone kitchen, where there was an enormous woodstove and the stone sinks were large enough to bathe in. There she was given a cot in the scullery, along with two black dresses and a white apron. She was taller than any of the nuns, and because there were no shoes to fit her, she kept the rabbi's boots. She was comfortable in them by now, and they fitted her perfectly. Ava said she was an excellent cook and she wasn't in the least bit daunted by the baking. She came upon a pile of cookbooks in the pantry in which some of the recipes were three hundred years old and no longer practical. Blackbird pie, trout stuffed with pine and minced dove, hearts of ducks sautéed in brown butter and spice. She kept to simple fare for the nuns and their students, potato soup with leeks and what little butter they had, cheese pie, chicken stew that could feed fifty, with a gravy that tasted of chestnuts, rice fragrant with wild mint and fennel, apple tarte made with fruit she had collected in the woods, the crust formed from day-old bread.

Twice a month there was a delivery of wheat from a local shop owner. Ava's first order of business each morning was to bake the baguettes served at breakfast and dinner, a chore that soon became a pleasure. She hoped to learn more about human beings through the process of baking, for their hunger was a mystery to her. She loved to knead the dough, which she set out in tin bowls to rise under white dishtowels. She was quick in forming baguettes, and her loaves were perfectly even. Sonya, the old woman who had been the housemaid at the convent for two decades, came in on Ava's first morning in the kitchen and was dumbstruck by the new woman's abilities. The housemaid asked if Ava was a baker's daughter, but no, such things came naturally to her, she said.

In truth, she felt a kinship with bread and the way it was

made, the damp weight kneaded and shaped into proper form, heated until it was set. When she worked in the kitchen she kept her long dark hair swept up with pins, with a white cap on her head. In the afternoons, when Lea was in class, she went walking in the forest beyond the convent to the marshes alongside the river. She carried a basket and often found marvelous things to bring back to the kitchen: mushrooms, hazelnuts, wild blackberries, chervil, water cabbages.

There were no mirrors in the convent, but Lea could see her reflection in the shine of the silverware the girls were made to polish, and she didn't recognize the person looking back at her. Her hair had grown and was shoulder-length. Her features were so like her mother's, she had to look away or she might burst into tears. She had begun her monthly bleeding. "Jetzt bist du in Schwierigkeiten," Renée told her. *Now you're in trouble.* "Niemand möchte eine Frau sein." *No one wants to be a woman.*

Although Lea hadn't told Ava about her situation, Ava seemed to know. She left clean rags and new undergarments, and when Lea found them she sobbed. Her mother should be the one to instruct her. She would have told her that Renée was wrong, becoming a woman should not be considered a terrible fate, even though it meant you bled. It was life that you carried inside you, your own and the life of the future. *If you survive, I survive inside of you.*

By now Lea had looked beneath her roommate's bed. Renée hoarded food there, bread that was growing moldy, bits of cheese, fruit taken from the lunch table. Lea liked the quiet kitchen, with its stone floors and large windows, and helped Ava in the dark hours of morning before prayers and breakfast. She often filched a baguette, then ran upstairs and hid it beneath Renée's bed. Renée never thanked her, but her dark eyes would settle on Lea, as if she wished to tell her something. All the same, Lea was friendless and lost and she missed Julien. Ava tried to cheer her with treats. Some new apples, a bar of chocolate she'd found in a cabinet, but Lea couldn't even bring herself to smile. While the loaves were baking, she wrote notes that she kept in the back of her prayer book. Perhaps one day she would be able to send them to Julien.

"You're still thinking about him," Ava said.

"I'm not," Lea insisted. But she was and they both knew it.

There was no news from Paris, but she worried about Julien's fate. But there was nothing to do about it, or at least it seemed so until Ava sent Lea to pick up a basket of eggs from a neighbor. There she noticed a pigeon house near the chicken coops.

"You like birds?" the old woman who lived there asked. "These ones are smart. They can always find their way home." The neighbor wore a red coat that she'd had for thirty years, and a pair of black boots. She took out a pigeon and called him by his name, Étoile, which meant star, with extreme tenderness. "I send my sister in Lyon messages." All she needed to do was attach a tube to the pigeon's leg, clasped in place with a leather band. A rolled-up message to her sister was inserted into the tube. *All fine here. Come visit one week from Sunday. Don't miss our visit like you did last month.*

Lea watched as the neighbor lifted the bird into the bright

sky. They held their hands over their eyes, squinting, as he disappeared into the darkening horizon.

"He'll be back, don't you worry," the old woman said.

She smiled at Lea, unaware that she was speaking to a thief and a liar who had come up with a plan of her own. When the woman was about to go inside, Lea asked if it would be all right if she watched the pigeons for a while, and that is what she did, she watched them coo and peck at one another as she slipped one of the cylinders and a leather band into the pocket of her dress. She ran back to the convent in the falling dark. Ava was waiting for her at the edge of the lawn. From here she could see the neighbor's yard; she'd kept an eye on Lea. It had been her idea to send her there, after all.

"What were you doing for so long?" Ava asked, as if she didn't know. She couldn't abide seeing grief in Lea's eyes, not when there was a remedy.

Lea shrugged and bit her tongue. "Looking at birds" was all she would say.

"Nothing more?"

"Could you teach me their language?" When Ava hesitated, Lea added, "I know you can. I've heard you talk to the heron."

"It takes time to learn a language." Especially when it was complicated, with an ancient structure more complex than any human language. There were no numbers, no tenses, more syllables and vowels, and a series of clicks, all with ten or more meanings.

"I have time," Lea vowed. She knew she was asking for a favor from someone she had treated shabbily. "I promise, I'll be a good student."

They went to the garden so lessons could begin. They sat

facing each other. Everything else dropped away, everything changed between them, they were of one mind, and as they looked into each other's eyes neither had the desire to look away. *Think in blue, in green, in starlight, in song, in a blessing, in beauty, in gratitude.*

Inside the convent they could hear birdsong all through the dinner hour. Some of the girls began to cry and others laughed out loud. The sisters remembered things they had long forgotten, from a time when they were young and filled with faith. No one noticed that Lea was late, and that when she arrived she sat down beside Renée, as if they were friends and had always been so, and that beneath the table, out of sight, Lea handed her a chocolate bar she'd stolen from the kitchen.

When the time came for Lea to ask the heron for what she wanted, she brought a pan of bread and milk into the courtyard as an offering. She had practiced the phrases so often through the night that the girls in the attic thought she was singing them to sleep, and even Renée closed her eyes and dreamed of things she had never seen before, trees made of flowers, beaches of black sand, clouds that were spun out of rain.

The heron came down from the roof when Lea entered the courtyard. After he'd had his breakfast, she begged for a moment of his time. It was a poor attempt at speaking his language, but he gazed at her with his yellow eyes, doing his best to understand her. When he didn't immediately swoop away, she went on, hopeful he would help her. She asked politely for what she wanted, pleading for him to go back to the house in Paris.

Please find him for me.

She had no idea that Ava had already asked the heron to do this one kindness for her. And so he allowed her to tie the metal canister to his leg, though he was no one's servant, and looked the other way as she did so.

Her script was tiny and neat. She'd used pale blue ink she'd found in the mother superior's office when Ava sent her to deliver bread and jam and a pot of tea. She'd taken a pen as well, for she'd been taught to be a thief when the need arose.

I am fine, but no one knows me as you do. Please stay alive.

The heron returned a week later. He perched on the ledge and pushed the window open. The other girls in the attic thought they were dreaming, for what they saw was impossible, and so they went back to sleep. They thought that birds and mortals lived in the same world, but only the world of men mattered. Julien had thought the same thing when he found the heron in the yard in Paris. By now the military had taken over the house, and the family lived in the greenhouse with the domed skylight. When the rain fell it sounded as if rocks were falling. Julien and his father had been taken as forced labor. They cleaned the streets, scrubbing stones. They had blisters on their hands and they didn't speak to Madame Claire about their humiliation. They didn't have to. Claire now cleaned the house for the German captain who lived there. When she thought of Marianne and how she'd treated her, she closed herself in the linen closet and cried. The German professors and their families were still on the third floor, behind a brick wall, mice who no longer dared to speak. Where would they go if they left? Wasn't it best to hide in plain sight where no one would think to look? Claire brought them food whenever she could, the leavings from their own table or from the captain's dinner.

When Julien saw the metal cylinder attached to the heron's leg, he approached cautiously and untied it, then crouched behind the greenhouse to read Lea's message. His hands shook and he read it three times before he could make sense of it. He was grateful and confused. He told himself not to have hope for the future. The life that he knew had ended, and what else was there for him? He told himself he was part of a dream in which a huge gray bird allowed him to tie a message to its leg before rising into the sky. For an instant he remembered who he was. *I know exactly who you are*, he'd written back. *Je sais qui tu es.*

Je suis ici.

I'm here.

When the roses bloomed, the garden was a sea of silver. Before Ava knew it, summer would be gone. This is the way time moved in the human world. Slowly at first, and then much too fast. The heron still nested on the rooftop, but she knew that in a few months' time he would leave for Spain or Africa. She tried not to think about his parting, and she wondered if love was like that, and if all mortals needed to close their eyes against the future and what it might bring. Sister Marie, who went to prayers at four, noticed Ava on her way to the chapel. The younger nuns remained nervous in Ava's presence, and avoided her entirely. They said she never slept and some of the sisters believed she could read their thoughts. When she pressed their garments, the younger nuns swore that she gathered information about them. How else could she know their private thoughts and desires?

Why she had even made Sister Félicité a bread pudding for her birthday, when no one in the convent had known that date or had ever celebrated the sister's birthday before.

The mother superior paused in the courtyard in the dim light of morning to listen to Ava sing to the heron in a voice that brought tears to the sister's eyes. They danced in the courtyard, bowing and circling one another, singing as if their hearts would break. Spying this on her way to prayers, Sister Marie knew enough of the world to know what she was seeing.

When Lea received the note from Julien she went behind the kitchen to be alone to read it. She sank down near the old stone water troughs, for the kitchen had once been a large stable. There was chervil and mint growing wild, and the scent would ever after remind her of him. His message was brief, but she read it again and again. All she needed was a word or two. A young sister came and shouted at her to come in to her studies, and although she did so, she took her time so that she could savor his message. It didn't matter what anyone else thought or said or did.

He was there.

In class, they were studying Jeanne d'Arc, and during these lessons Lea often thought of Ava. The Maid of Orléans had been born to fight, chosen by God. Even though she was a woman, she looked upon war as another woman might rejoice on her wedding day. She was made for battle, and was so fierce that when the British captured her they had to burn her three times, for once was not enough. She had only been thirteen when she was visited by the archangel Michael in her father's garden, and nineteen when she was burned at the stake. The cinders and ashes from her burning were said to have been thrown into the Seine, although a vial was later discovered in a jar in the attic of an apothecary in Paris. They remained illuminated, as if sparked by fire. In class, they spoke her sainted name in low tones, as if her name had a power of its own.

After class, Lea and Renée sat on their beds in the attic and Lea helped her practice her French. "Not everyone can be Jeanne d'Arc. Sometimes you can't fight," Renée told Lea. "Sometimes they cut you open and do terrible things to you." She let Lea hug her even though she never wanted to be touched. "Nur einmal," she said. *Just once.*

They both wished their mothers had not been on trains. They wished there were happy endings. This was why Lea kept the note from Julien under her pillow. So she could dream about another world and another life. At school they were called Renée and Lillie, but when they were alone they called each other by their true names, Rachel and Lea, as in the Bible. *We'll escape,* they promised each other. *We'll start new lives,* they said. But neither one could look at her reflection, for if they did the girls they had once been might stare back at them, and those girls, they both agreed, were gone.

Ava spent late afternoons in the kitchen, before going out to see to the garden. Time was moving faster all the time. It was the season to clip back the roses. They must be carefully tended, for they wilted in hot weather. The plants had black, leathery leaves and dark thorny branches, and were especially difficult to cut back, not that that would be a problem. Ava was always a hard worker; the nuns commented to each other that she was tireless and could complete one task after another.

But on this day her thoughts were elsewhere, beyond the garden. She was experiencing emotions she wasn't made to have. She worried over Lea in a profound way that caught her by surprise, acting not out of duty but from someplace inside of her. Why this should be, she had no idea. She was so deep in thought she didn't notice when she caught her finger on a thorn as she cleared away a twisted, black branch. A single bead of blood formed, crimson in the early morning light. She stared at it, confused. Was she meant to have blood rather than water and clay?

Lea had been sprawled out on her bed, studying her lessons, but she had put down her book and she spied Ava from the window. She knew her caretaker was not like other women, but she marveled at how human she could seem, more so all the time. She had noticed Ava crying when the heron left to go fishing in distant lakes, an unwanted ability she had learned without trying. Lea wished Ava could turn herself into a heron, then she could leave and never return. She wished that she was an angel that couldn't be seen by mortal eyes and could disappear into the clouds. But here she was, at work in the garden. They were bound together. Where you found one, you would find the other. Every day Lea tried not to think about the moment when her locket fell open, when she read the message she wasn't yet meant to see. But it was too late then and it was too late now. She had read her mother's instructions. She knew exactly what she must do.

When the war is over, and you are safe, you must kill her.

CHAPTER FIFTEEN

THE GATHERED

PARIS, JULY 1942

In the middle of the month, on the sixteenth day of July, when the plane trees were a brilliant green, an ordinary day, the French police came knocking on doors. This past spring, Jews were made to wear yellow stars and were only allowed to ride in the last car of the Métro and were forbidden in restaurants. It was known that at least one synagogue had been converted into a brothel for Nazi soldiers. But now there were mass arrests. There was a sweep of Jews; refugees and French citizens alike were taken to the cycling stadium, Vélodrome d'Hiver, in the 15th arrondissement. The Nazi-planned event had the code name Opération Vent printanier, Operation Spring Breeze, meant to exterminate an entire population. In all, more than thirteen thousand Jews were rounded up over two days, four thousand of them children. Anyone under the age of fifteen would be handed over to the Union Générale des Israélites de France and sent to foundations and children's homes.

They found the professors and their families on the third floor behind the brick wall, the children in the wardrobe, the wives beneath the beds. All were immediately arrested, but the police considered the real criminals to be the Lévis. What argument could they offer for breaking the law? There was none to be given. Still, when the Lévis were told they must come with the police immediately, Claire was shocked. "We're French," she argued. She had known nothing good would come of having foreigners in their house. She'd never wanted them in the first place.

The professor quickly stepped in to calm his wife. Of course they would accompany the police and answer any questions. There was no harm in that. Tempers were high and it was best to do as they were told.

The whole family. Bring your son.

Madame Lévi looked at her husband through tears.

"It will be fine," he said, but the German professors and their families had already been led away. They had not been allowed to take their belongings or, in the case of the children, put on their shoes.

Julien was in the greenhouse when they called for him. He thought about scrambling over the garden wall. How this could be accomplished flashed through his mind—the lift into the air, the steep drop to the alley below. Victor had leapt from the roof of their house once, why couldn't Julien do the same now from the top of the wall? But when he spied his parents at the door with the police, he couldn't leave them. They didn't even look like his parents, they had become two older, confused people. His father had put on his hat, as if he were going to a meeting and must look his best. Julien went to the door and did as the police asked. The family took nothing with them. Already, a soldier had taken the purse his mother carried, stealing the gold coins and her favorite earrings, scattering the baby teeth she had saved on the ground.

Julien saw the heron in the sky above them, but he threw his arms into the air and warned him away. The note Lea had written to him would never be received, and the one he had written was crumpled in the grass.

There are almost none of us left in the city. If not for Hardship Soup we would have starved.

I know I will see you.

Please stay alive.

"It will all be fine," Julien heard his father tell his mother. Perhaps he was saying what they both most wished to believe. "We'll be back soon enough."

If it wasn't the end, what was it? They stood in the garden with no weapons and no defense against evil. The heron still circled, but it was too late. They were forced along the path near the new rosebush, which had taken to the soil and bloomed as if it had always been there, with large crimson flowers that hosted a few lazy bees. The German captain had two Jewish men who had been doctors in Poland come in to tend to the roses and clear out the ruined plants. They, also, had been arrested, though they'd been down on their knees in the garden beds, their hands covered with soil. They were all too slow, they were all too trusting, there were rifles pointed at them in the place where the lime trees had been planted a hundred years ago. It was the last time Professor Lévi and his wife would see the garden, although in their final hours they dreamed of it, they held hands and whispered the names of the plants that had grown there, *peony, coralbell, lavender,* as if such things could remind them of the beauty of the world.

At a corner, before they were herded onto buses, Julien again thought of running. There was panic, and people were frantic, especially those who had been separated from family members. It was the end of something, that much he knew, so why not run? He had been the fastest boy in his school and excelled at sports. Perhaps he could find Lea in her convent, but just then his father stumbled on a loose cobblestone. Julien put out an arm to steady him. He helped his parents onto the bus, and later this caused him to be unable to sleep, the fact that he hadn't insisted they flee, not that they could have outpaced the police with him, but perhaps they might have hidden in a doorway, shuddering, terrified, but invisible until nightfall. He made mistake after mistake, thinking of what to do, yet not acting quickly enough. He was in a dream, he was frozen, he was all his parents had left in the world, but now it was clearer. It was the end.

After a twenty-minute ride, the buses stopped, and those inside were herded into the street, then shepherded into the stadium, which was nearly full. Julien's ears began to ring. He shook his head, but the warning was still there.

"We shouldn't go in," he told his father.

The police gestured for them to go forward. Several sounded whistles.

"They'll let us go," the professor decided, always preferring order and logic, and assuring his family that the situation was temporary. But when he tried to explain they were French citizens, no one listened.

There was no food or water available and the weather was hot. It was a time when people used to get ready for their August holidays, but now they were here. Children over the age of three had been separated from their parents, and many were crying, completely disoriented, lost in a sea of people. Luckily, there were women who took in these children right away, treating them as if they were their own.

The horror of this place must be a temporary situation, the professor insisted. He spoke in a low, measured voice. *Keep calm. Don't panic.* This was Paris after all, and it was the police along with hired local people who guarded them, not German soldiers. "We'll stay a day, maybe overnight, then they'll let us out," the professor assured his wife and son.

"Do you not understand what's happening?" Julien had spied many people he knew from the neighborhood among the crowd. "We're like lambs, doing as we're told. Do you think they'll give you back your beautiful house? You'll never see it again. And all those treasures you buried? They'll rot."

By now guards had begun to collect wallets, jewelry, keys. Those who tried to keep such things were beaten, there in front of everyone. An old man was stomped upon when he refused to give up his wedding ring.

"Do you not see?" Julien pleaded.

At last, in that instant, as the old man begged for his ring, the professor understood everything that was happening and everything that was to come. He slipped the watch he always wore into his pocket. It was the one thing he had left that might be useful to them.

"Look," Madame Lévi said, grabbing her husband's arm. "Isn't that Edgar?"

It was indeed their gardener, only now he'd been hired as a guard at the stadium, steering people through the crowded entryway gate. The Lévis went to him, navigating through the crush of people. After all, Edgar had worked for them for more than ten years and had always been so punctual and polite before they could no longer afford him. The professor's wife had already lost her scarf in the chaos and she was light-headed, for she hadn't had a sip of water since early morning. There were older people doing their best to sit in the shade, yet some of them were seriously ill. People were evacuating right out in the open, for there were no toilets, and already there was a terrible stink. Madame Lévi lowered her gaze, feeling a chill. She had been right to panic this morning.

When they reached the gardener, the professor tapped his shoulder, so surprising Edgar that he turned to his employer with his stick in hand as if to strike him.

"Oh, Monsieur," he said when he recognized the professor. "I didn't know it was you."

The professor leaned toward the younger man. He sounded desperate, even to himself. "We're here by mistake." Soon enough there would be mass arrests of French Jews but for now the professor still had hope. "Can you let us out?"

Edgar looked around. He took in the sheer number of the police, let alone men such as himself who had been brought here as forced labor on a daily basis to contain the crowds. He shook his head. "Three people? It would be too noticeable.

They'd have my head. I have to do what I'm hired to do, you understand."

"Then my son," the professor urged. "Just him."

Claire linked her arm through her husband's. "Yes. Take Julien."

Edgar felt uncomfortable just talking to these people. They looked different to him, almost unrecognizable.

"He's no problem," the professor went on. "No one will notice one boy. And he's a fast runner. Look at the guards. They're not paying attention."

The gardener glimpsed a group of men who had been picked up by the German army to work here in the stifling heat. They were lounging by the gate, chatting with each other as the crowds of those arrested poured through.

Professor Lévi reached for his watch from his pocket, the gold one his father had given him. They would take it from him anyway. Better to get something in return.

"Here. It's yours," he told Edgar. They exchanged a look and the deal was done. He signaled for Julien to approach.

Julien came forward. He nodded to the gardener, already mistrusting him, before turning to his father. "What's going on?"

His father embraced him and his mother did likewise, then they hurriedly walked away.

"What are you doing?" Julien called after them. "You're not supposed to be here."

But life now depended upon luck, not reason. The sun was so bright Julien lifted a hand to shade his eyes. His parents seemed to have disappeared, swallowed up, lost in the light and the masses of people. It made no sense. His mother would not turn from him in such a way. Julien made a move to go after his parents, but Edgar stopped him.

"Walk backward, as if you were coming into the stadium rather than leaving. I will open the gate and you can lose yourself in the crush of people, only you will be walking away. Don't come back. These people are all being shipped off."

Julien stood there stunned. By now he was unable to see his parents in the chaos of the stadium. Or was that his father's jacket, the one he had worn to teach his classes?

"Go!" Edgar told him. "You don't have forever!"

Julien's head was ringing. He couldn't hear a word anyone said, least of all Edgar. But then he saw his grandfather's gold watch on the gardener's wrist and understood. His father had bought his freedom, and he knew then, although it broke his heart to do so, he wasn't going to throw it away.

He walked backward through the crush of people that was being pushed past him. Once he was at the edge of the crowd, he turned and ran, spiraling through the maze of city streets, tearing the buttons from his shirt to leave behind on street corners so he would be able to find his way back if necessary. By then it was dusk, the end of the first day of the roundup. He had to fight the urge to go home and seek out his familiar life; instead he went to a tunnel near the river, where he sat shivering, though it was a hot night.

He returned to the stadium in the morning, following the path he had taken, still hopeful that he could find his parents and get them out as well. It was the seventeenth and the raid was in its second day; twice as many people were now trapped inside. There was a full-fledged hysteria as people realized they had walked into a trap. This was not temporary, Paris was no longer their city, and there was no way out. German soldiers now patrolled the gates. Julien watched through the fence and saw things he never imagined he would see. There was still no food or water and some people had already died. There was no choice but to step over them, or to pile them up in the shade. He thought he saw his father among the jostling crowd, no longer wearing his jacket or his hat. He called out his name. The professor may have looked up, but if he saw his son, he acted as if he heard nothing at all. He disappeared into the crowd to ensure that Julien wouldn't call out for him again.

As for Julien, he had nothing to trade; even the so-called treasures they had buried in the garden were not enough to buy a life. He walked away, hardly able to breathe. That night he hid in an alley where groceries were delivered for the German officers, not far from his home, staying put until dusk, the blue hour, when he would be less noticed. Each time he heard sirens his blood raced, as if he were guilty of something, a common criminal, as his onetime friend Bernard had claimed. He realized he would never see his father's watch again, though it had been promised to him his entire life. Victor had never wanted it. *I'll only break it,* he had said. *Give it to Julien, he's the careful one. He's always on time.*

Time now meant nothing. He had betrayed his parents and left them behind. In a few days they would be sent to Auschwitz. He was a boy of fifteen who had lost everything. He looked at the stars, constellations whose names his father had taught him as they stood in the dark of their garden, not knowing they would never be there again.

He heard someone call out to him. Surely he imagined it, for he was alone. He leaned up against the wall, eyes closed.

"You," he heard now. A clear soft voice. "Julien."

There was a young, unkempt man, no more than eighteen, signaling. The fellow was Claude Gotlib, who had gone to school with Victor. "Your brother sent me. He was injured or he'd be here himself. I tried to get to your family before they were picked up."

"You're too late," Julien said.

"Not for you."

Julien hesitated. He didn't know Claude, and he didn't know why Victor himself hadn't come for him, all he knew was that his parents were still in the stadium.

"Come on." Claude was impatient. "Wait any longer and you'll land us both in trouble. Believe me, your brother will have my head if I don't get you out of here."

Julien heard train whistles and sirens. He was still shivering. Above them, the stars were burning bright. He could not think of his parents, his father without his good jacket, his mother, who was so elegant, searching for a place in the shade. All he knew was that he was alive. That was his promise to keep.

CHAPTER SIXTEEN

THE TWO BROTHERS

HAUTE-LOIRE, AUGUST 1942

JULIEN AND CLAUDE DIDN'T TALK MUCH AS THEY TRAVELED. They slept in the woods or in safe houses, where their hosts often didn't speak to them at all, for it was best not to know too much about those you had hidden. Some people graciously left dinner for them to share, and once they were given a bottle of wine, which they gulped down before falling deeply asleep. There were some stops along the way that seemed curious to Julien. He was told to wait outside, while Claude saw to his own private business. Afterward, Claude guarded the rucksack he carried and told Julien to keep his hands off it. "Don't even breathe near it," he was told.

One night, while Claude was asleep, Julien crept over to take a look. Once he had, he quickly backed away. Now he understood what Claude and Victor were up to. Claude was transporting gunpowder and sticks of dynamite.

The last night Julien and Claude were on the road together, they went to the stone church in Vienne, sleeping under the pews, grateful to be given warm milk and rolls in the morning by the old woman who did the cleaning.

"If you're ever in real trouble, come here," Claude told Julien. "They won't ask questions, and the priest will help as best he can."

The villages became smaller as they went on into the mountains, the lanes were cobbled, and rose trees grew up between the stones outside front doors that were painted pale blue, or green, or gray. Julien closed his eyes at night and replayed their journey, so he might remember his way back. To learn a maze it was best to leave something behind, to chart the path, as Hansel and Gretel had done in the tale of their escape from evil. Since he had no bread crumbs, and no more buttons on his shirt after leaving a trail to the stadium, he left a mark on a tree whenever they stopped. An *L,* for Lea. A letter he would be sure to notice.

They stayed out of sight during the day and traveled at night. But on the last day they went on until noon. They were near the Ardèche Mountains by then, only a few days' hike from Switzerland, and the Germans rarely came this far. At last they stopped in a field. The sun was strong. Julien's skin tanned rather than burned, but Claude, who was pale, was suffering with sunburn and was glad autumn would soon be upon them. Already there had been frosts in the hills, and snow could be seen in the mountains.

"Why are we here?" Julien wanted to know. There were

hawks above them and the clouds were moving fast. Everything was changing.

"You ask a lot of questions. Why don't you ask him?" Claude gestured to the road.

A speeding car had stopped and pulled over. Normally they would duck into the woods if anyone was nearby, making certain not to be seen, but Claude was relaxed, even when the driver got out and approached. Julien thought perhaps the man was a farmer from the look of his clothes and his long, shaggy hair. But the stranger grinned and waved. "It's me," the man called. "What idiot doesn't recognize his own brother?"

Victor was nearly unrecognizable; he had a beard and was angular and rough looking. His skin was puckered on the left side of his face from the burn he'd received, which was as healed as it would ever be, although the scar had only served to make him more handsome. The brothers embraced with grins on their faces.

"I would have come for you, but I had an accident," Victor explained. "It's taken a while to recover and I knew you'd be in good hands."

"He's the fireman," Claude said with pride in his friend. "Mr. Explosives."

Julien was surprised. "How did you learn to do that?"

"Science class."

They all laughed. Victor, the notoriously bad student, had apparently learned something in school. Claude gave Victor the rucksack and the two embraced before going their separate ways. "He's a good man," Victor said of his old school friend before hauling Julien into the car. The rucksack was on the floor in the back, wrapped up in an old wool blanket. Victor and Claude had been working with the Jewish Resistance, and now as they drove, Julien tried to convince his brother to let him join up as well. He would soon be sixteen, but Victor wouldn't hear of it.

"You know what our mother would think if I ever did that. Plus, you're still a kid."

They didn't speak for a while and Julien stared morosely out the window. They had never truly been close, and now Julien felt an old wave of resentment as they drove the bumpy back roads even further into the mountains. Twice they had to wait for goats to cross, the bells around the goats' necks ringing in the still, blue air. The light was brilliant here, so clear that as they drove along they could see the blue edges of the mountains of Switzerland. They stopped in a yellow field of flowering *genêts* to have lunch, some apples and cheese and meat, a feast in Julien's opinion. The clouds above them moved quickly, buoyed by the wind.

"I didn't even know you could drive," Julien said.

"Drive! I can drive through anything and get anywhere."

Victor was a puzzlement to Julien, a new person almost entirely. But some things were the same: the lopsided grin, the self-confidence, the daring.

"I'm going to Eretz Israel when it's all over," Victor told him. "We'd be fools if we hadn't learned our lesson. No country will let us in. No one will protect us. We need our own country." He took out a cigarette and lit it. "Bad habit." He grinned. "Only one of the many I've acquired." He squinted against the sunlight. "Maybe you'll come along."

Victor's wild life agreed with him and he looked happy. He'd never liked being caged up in polite society, made to do as their parents demanded. He was hardly the same person he had been in Paris, gloomy and often at odds with their father, who had wished him to be more studious. It was good to be together after so long, and to know that fate had led them here. And there was more, there was Marianne.

Victor stood and brushed the grass from his trousers, ready to get on the move.

"So now we go to Marianne's."

"You know where she is?"

"She talked about her farm and her village constantly, if you'd ever bothered to listen. I've been staying with her since I was hurt. I can never thank her enough for all she's done."

Julien noticed an odd expression on Victor's face as he spoke of the housemaid. "You and Marianne? Seriously?"

Victor shrugged, then signaled for his brother to get in the car. "Why not?"

"Our mother would have had a fit." True enough, even though Marianne was only five years older, she was older all the same, uneducated and not Jewish. Both brothers had mentioned their mother, which brought up fears Julien usually repressed. "Do you know what happened after they were taken?" he dared to ask.

Victor shook his head. Julien really was something of a fool if he still held out hope for their parents. "You must have figured it out. They went on the trains."

There was no more talk, and after a while they pulled down the long rutted road that led to the farm. Marianne was waiting on the porch. She ran to the car and hugged Julien and told him she would never have recognized him. He, too, had changed. He was tall and lanky, nearly a man.

"So this is where you came from," Julien said.

"It is." She looked around and threw her arms out and he could tell that she was glad to be back. He saw the way she looked at Victor, and the way Victor looked back at her.

Marianne's father was out at his beehives, dressed in his white beekeeper's suit, including a hat with white netting.

"He looks like a ghost, doesn't he?" Julien said.

"He's anything but," Victor said. He whistled and waved to the old man, and Monsieur Félix waved back. "You'll see when Marianne and I go off. He's a tough old bird."

"This is your brother?" Monsieur Félix said when he came in for dinner. The brothers had settled in, taking over the front parlor. Julien noticed that Victor stored his rucksack in an old wooden bureau.

"He's the one," Victor told Marianne's father.

Julien stood and shook his hand.

"I'll teach you about bees if I think you're smart enough to learn," Monsieur Félix said. "We'll keep you busy here."

The brothers slept on quilts in the parlor, but halfway through the night, Julien realized he was alone. Victor had made his way to Marianne's room and Julien could hear the sound of their voices and moans. It was a good thing the old man was half-deaf. Julien felt a sort of anger rise inside him as he lay on his back in a thin strip of moonlight that streamed through the window. He was fed up with being treated like a boy, while Victor did as he pleased.

The following day, Victor and Marianne both set off, Marianne to once again shepherd children to the border, and Victor to complete some business for the Armée Juive, a secret Jewish militia that he clearly didn't wish to discuss.

"Why can't you say where you're going?" Julien complained,

feeling left out, as if he were still a child when he was almost as tall and as strong as his brother.

Victor grabbed him in a rough embrace. "You don't need to know."

Privately, he believed he did know, and once Victor had gone, Julien searched the bureau. Sure enough, the rucksack was gone. He worried about his brother, driving like a madman with a bag full of explosives, but he envied him as well.

"Time for you to get to work," Monsieur Félix told him as he was moping around.

Julien was taught to do chores on the farm and took a liking to the little goat, Bluebell, who followed him around. He wasn't yet allowed to collect the honeycombs from the beehives.

"For that you need an experienced beekeeper," Félix told him. "You're not ready."

But Julien had the sort of fearlessness a person needed to tend bees, and soon he'd convinced Monsieur Félix to let him try his hand. As they worked, Félix explained what happened here at the farm. Identity documents would arrive with a man who traveled from town to town, the papers hidden in the frame of his bicycle. He was a postman, therefore no one thought to stop him as he made his rounds through the mountains. Monsieur Félix was to give the documents to Marianne to use in transporting children across the border.

The postman came, a quiet, skinny fellow who had no problem bicycling throughout this rough terrain. Julien saw him give Monsieur Félix an envelope before he rode on. Félix disappeared into the dusk. When Julien went outside to look for him, he was coming back from the barn. He asked about the papers, but the old man shrugged.

"Hidden away so no one would ever find them. I'm smarter than I look. The Germans could send a thousand soldiers, and search for a thousand days, they still wouldn't find them."

"Maybe you should tell me, in case you're not here and Marianne needs them."

"I'll always be here." The old man continued to limp after his encounter with the Germans, still he was fast, and Julien had to struggle to keep up with him when they went to collect the chickens, who were let free during the day. "Anyway," he went on as they walked, "I couldn't tell you. They could torture it out of you, but with me it's different. I'll never talk. I've done this transaction thirty-three times, which means thirty-three souls are alive." He slapped Julien on the back. "Now that you're my helper, the next soul who is saved can be yours."

CHAPTER SEVENTEEN

THE MESSAGE

ARDÈCHE, SEPTEMBER 1942

VICTOR ARRIVED AT THE SAFE HOUSE ONE BLUE EVENING, cutting his headlights before turning off the road. There were fields of white wildflowers that glowed in the dark. He had been gone for several months, working with the Armée Juive. When he and Marianne were together, he felt like a carefree boy, helping her father with chores, sneaking up to her room when the old man was safely asleep, not thinking of anything more than his bare skin against hers. But as soon as he left the farm he was someone else entirely, and a darkness lingered inside him. He had been party to acts he did not wish to discuss or even think about. Now he had returned to the house in the woods because he was in need of a partner.

He had brought a satchel of food and supplies from the Félix farm, and after he greeted his old cohorts, he set to helping with dinner. Watching Marianne, he had learned how to cook, and he prepared a vegetable stew that was surprisingly tasty. In the past weeks it had become clear that Arno was still reeling from the bombing that had taken his friend's life. It was decided it was best for him to stay and help guard Bettina and the forgery operation. It was Ettie who would be Victor's partner, and after dinner they walked out toward the little silver river to talk privately.

"I hear you can catch a fish in your hands," Victor said, amused. She was so slight and fierce he thought of her as a wild little sister.

"I'm even better with a gun," Ettie informed him.

"I'm not surprised. So tonight we move on from here."

Ettie had been waiting for this, the chance to fight, but she felt a tug inside her. She had grown close to Bettina, and it was difficult to say goodbye, and she worried about Arno, who suffered from nightmares and often gave them a scare when he disappeared into the woods and couldn't be found. Her feelings must have shown in her face, and Victor offered to get her belongings and say her goodbyes while she waited in the car.

"It's fine," Ettie said. "I have nothing and there's no need to say goodbye."

Victor shrugged; there she was, the fierce girl, her decision clearly made. Without a word to the others, they got into the car. Ettie was always a surprise, so much tougher than she looked. Being with her in the car, as she silently looked out the window, made him long for Marianne, who was so kindhearted and gentle that even when she was angry with him for some foolish thing he'd said or done, he felt her deep affection and love.

They drove for quite a while, over the mountains, on steep

narrow roads framed by thornbushes that hit against the car. After more than an hour they arrived at a small stone château painted a pale pink, with windows that were framed by dark green shutters. It was past twilight now and darkness was settling down into the woods. The trees were crisscrossed by vines, and something smelled sweet, a wildflower Ettie didn't recognize as she followed Victor along the path. There was a side entrance, a black iron door decorated with filigree. The house belonged to a doctor, and this path was the route his patients took to his office during the day. In the evening, it was shadowy, and a chestnut tree blocked the entryway from view. *Safe*, Ettie thought. *This is a safe house.*

Henri Girard had been the doctor in town for nearly twenty-five years. Before that, his father, also called Henri Girard, had been the local physician. Girard was a good-looking, tall man, very dignified. His grandfather had been a nobleman, and even though he was a country doctor, Girard's manners were very refined. He had been to school in Paris, and had taught at the medical school there for a while. But he had decided he preferred the relationships he had with his patients in this small village. People came from across the mountains to see him, sometimes traveling hours, and he had brought more than fifty souls into the world, most of whom he still saw as patients, though many were now grown men and women with families of their own. He had come to be known as someone who would help Jewish resisters, and his barn was often a stopping point for those on their way to the border.

The doctor shook Ettie's hand and welcomed her in the parlor where patients waited should the doctor be busy when they arrived. The furniture had belonged to the doctor's father and was still in perfect condition, with several chairs and a sofa covered in green mohair.

The doctor poured three drinks from a bottle of eau-de-vie to welcome them and offered Ettie a glass.

"Thank you, I don't drink," she said.

"But you must start," the doctor recommended, placing the glass in her hand. "It's good to be able to drink and remain sober. That is," he added, "if you really want to be part of this."

"This?" Ettie said. "Perhaps you'd like to explain."

"He's helping us out," Victor said. He had come to the doctor's when he'd been burned and they'd had a frank discussion of how to best be rid of those who were responsible for the local arrests.

Ettie shrugged and downed the liqueur all in one gulp, then gasped at the fiery nature of the drink. The doctor laughed. He realized how young she was, which was both a good and a bad thing.

Ettie placed her glass on a highly polished tabletop. "I don't like to be laughed at."

"Of course not," Dr. Girard allowed.

"I'm here for my murdered sister," Ettie said. "I'll do whatever needs to be done."

Victor and Girard exchanged a look. An obsession was what this girl had, not just a belief, but a true passion. It made them both respect her, even though she looked little older than a child. Her hair was tangled into knots and she hadn't washed her clothes for weeks.

"First, you have to do something about your hair," Victor said.

Ettie scowled and threw him a dark look. "What difference does that make?"

"Oh, it makes a difference," he assured her.

"I can fix it," Dr. Girard said. "It's not so different from surgery."

While Victor went to unpack the car, Girard asked Ettie to sit in a chair meant for patients. She faced an old desk strewn with books, along with a blood pressure cuff and a black doctor's bag. On the walls were posters of the digestive system and a chart of the ventricles of the heart along with his framed degrees.

"What kind of doctor are you?" Ettie had noticed a pile of freshly laundered white smocks reserved for patients' examinations.

"Whatever is necessary. A country doctor is a specialist in nothing and an expert in everything."

"So why do you put yourself at risk in working with us?" she asked. "You're not Jewish."

"That's my business," he faltered. "I can only say, I have my reasons."

From his tone, Ettie could tell the topic of their conversation stung. The doctor brought out one of the white smocks to toss around Ettie's narrow shoulders. He held a pair of small sharp scissors. "I'll tell you what I tell my surgery patients. Don't move."

Ettie ran a hand over her hair before he began. "What difference does it make how I look?"

"Well you certainly can't tell you're beautiful when you hide it like this."

Ettie threw him an indignant look.

"I'm stating an empirical truth." He took up the scissors and began to even out her choppy tresses. She shivered but sat still when he told her to stop fiddling. "Have you ever looked at yourself in a mirror?" he asked.

"No. I was a rabbi's daughter. I was taught such things are nonsense."

"Well, you may have to forget some of what you've been taught. You may have to go directly against everything you were taught. Especially if you are a rabbi's daughter."

Ettie made a face, but she thought of Esther, how she had used her beauty, as though it were a weapon. Some people believed she should be shamed for winning over a king with her wiles, but she had been responsible for the deliverance of her people.

The doctor was studying his handiwork approvingly. He was the sort of man who inspired confidence. He had held the hands of those who were dying, he had removed tumors, set broken bones, welcomed lives into the world.

"So tell me," Ettie said. "What do I need to forget?"

The doctor put one hand on her shoulder. "Thou shalt not kill."

Ettie nodded, her chin out. "I'm already aware of that."

The doctor handed her a mirror. "And you may have to occasionally look at yourself."

She did so and was surprised. She had mysteriously turned into the other person, the girl Nicole who she pretended to be.

"I know you want vengeance," the doctor said. "But remember, this is also about the future of others."

The doctor fixed them a meal that was simple, but good. An omelet with mushrooms, some brown bread and butter, white wine, which they insisted she drink. People might ply her with alcohol and what then? Would she remain sober or give herself away? She nodded and drank, and came to appreciate the taste by the end of her second glass.

There was a room in the barn where Ettie would stay. It had been built for a groom, but there were no horses now. Victor said good night, ready to return to the farm. He'd be back when he knew more of his mission.

"Which we won't discuss with anyone. It's between us."

"For which I had to cut my hair."

"I'll cut mine, too, if that makes you happier."

"It will." Ettie grinned.

"Then it will be done." He went out the door, calling over his shoulder, "I was planning on cutting it anyway."

Ettie was tipsy as she walked out in the chilly dark toward an old chair outside the barn. She sat to breathe in the mountain air. She was finally here, in the place where she had found a future. Still, night after night, the past was with her. When she closed her eyes, her sister was beside her, as she would always be.

CHAPTER EIGHTEEN

THE SILVER ROSE

RHÔNE VALLEY, NOVEMBER 1942

WHEN THE MOTHER SUPERIOR WAS A GIRL OF EIGHT, AND HER name was still Madeleine de Masson, her mother and father were killed in an auto accident and no one told her. Suddenly, her parents weren't there. Her mother did not come to kiss her good night, and there was such great sorrow attached to that loss, the mother superior still could not put her emotions into words. She understood why the girls at her school wept for their mothers at night.

The scent of Madeleine's mother's perfume vanished, and soon it seemed as if she had only been a dream, not a real flesh-and-blood person. Madeleine was rushed about by the governess and not allowed to see her grandfather, a very old man who lived in the attic. His name was Raoul Salomon, and he had sometimes joined the family for dinner; otherwise he was up-stairs, in bed, with his books. He was nearly ninety, and anyone could tell he had been a dashing, handsome man. He was six foot three, so very tall, even though he stooped, and Madeleine had been frightened of him; he still had a mane of beautiful hair, black when he was young, snow white as he aged. He was guarded and rarely looked anyone in the eye. People had disappointed him. His expression was tragic, but as a child Madeleine had merely thought he had stomachaches, something with which she occasionally suffered, so she was well aware of the pain they could cause. Her grandfather was so very old, and all by himself, speaking to almost no one other than the maid who brought him his meals on a tarnished silver tray.

When she tried to climb the stairs to see him after her parents' funeral, the governess had locked her in her room. A few weeks later her aunt, her father's sister, along with her entire family, moved in. Madeleine then knew something was terribly wrong. The dogs were all given away. She was told it was best for her not to see her grandfather. She would only be annoying him and, anyway, he didn't like children.

But she'd had a dream about him, and in her dream her grandfather was sitting beside an angel and he could speak the angel's language, something no other mortal could do. She went to see her grandfather despite the governess's smacks, sneaking up to the third floor when everyone else was at dinner, which was formal, so that thankfully little girls weren't invited. She had some sugar cookies in her pocket she intended to give him as a gift, but once she'd opened the door she found she was unable to say anything. They had never spoken directly. The old man was in a chair and he stared at her as she approached. He recognized her but he didn't quite remember her name. She introduced herself. "Ah, Masson," the old man said thoughtfully. Madeleine's father's family had come from Algeria just as the old man had, but they'd arrived two hundred years earlier, and had changed their name from Hasson, a Jewish name they did not wish to have associated with them.

He took the cookies and ate them all without offering any to her. "I came from Algeria," he told her.

She had no idea where that was, but she nodded.

"I'll go for a walk with you tomorrow," he told her. "Bring my coat."

The next afternoon they went to the garden. He used a cane but still had to lean on her when there was a stair. He hadn't been outside in over a year, but he wished to speak to her privately. He told her that he had made his money in diamonds, smuggled to France in his stomach.

"That's impossible," Madeleine remembered saying. She knew a thing or two about stomachaches. Swallowing things that were hard, like rocks, was not humanly possible. Even too many cakes eaten too quickly could make you sick. "They'd have to cut you open to get them and you'd be dead."

"You know very little," her grandfather told her. "Things go into your body and things go out."

That sounded distressing, but Madeleine thought it over.

There was a frog in a garden bed near a clutch of blue bellflowers. Monsieur Salomon reached down and caught it. Before Madeleine could blink he swallowed it whole.

Madeleine nearly fell down.

"You can train yourself to eat almost anything if you must," her grandfather said to the shocked little girl. She had never been as surprised in all her life, but there was more to come. Her grandfather proceeded to burp up the frog, whole and alive and equally stunned. He laughed, then plopped the creature back into the dirt.

He did his best to explain her parents' deaths. He told her that love was everlasting and that her mother was now with the angels. Her father, who was so stern and loved his horses more than anything, was there with her. This should have brought Madeleine some peace of mind, but it didn't.

Madeleine's grandfather told her a list of reasons not to be a Jew. Though he didn't care for her father's family, he understood why they had converted. Whatever happened, he told her, people would blame their kind, they would say Jews had secret societies, ran the world, were thieves, wanted to take their houses from them, were the reason they led miserable lives. That was why he had at last converted as well, for the sake of his children. Both Madeleine and her mother had been born Catholic, to ensure that they would not be persecuted. Now her grandfather wanted to see how good a Catholic she was. He wondered if she would recite the Lord's Prayer, and she was proud to do as he asked.

Our Father, Who art in Heaven, hallowed be Thy name. Thy kingdom come, Thy will be done, on earth as it is in Heaven.

After he praised her, her grandfather surprised her by reciting a prayer in a strange language.

Modeh ani l'fanecha, melech chai v'kayam schehechezarta bi nishmati b'chemla raba emunatecha.

I offer thanks to You, living and eternal King, for You have mercifully restored my soul within me: Your faithfulness is great.

Baruch ata Adonai, Eloheynu melech HaOlam, asher kidishanu b'mitzvotav v'tzivanu.

Blessed are You, Lord our God, King of the Universe, who has sanctified us with His commandments.

"They have the same meaning," she said to the old man.

"Yes, they are the same, and a world apart. Say one, and you are applauded. Say the other and you're condemned."

Madeleine was confused, especially when she asked the governess what a Jew was. She was curious after her conversation with her grandfather, for she had never heard the term *Jew* before. The usually docile governess struck her face so hard her cheek had stung for days afterward. "You have no need to know about what is wrong with the world and all the evil it contains," her governess scolded. "Don't mention that word again."

Madeleine heard her aunt speak of her grandfather as *the old Jew in the attic*. She wished to be rid of him, but it was his house, and they could not throw him out. At least not yet. A lawyer came to tell them so. They would have to wait for him to die.

No one could stop them from walking in the garden, so Madeleine and her grandfather began to meet on a daily basis. Madeleine always asked him if he would eat a frog again, but he always shook his head and refused. One day, while he drowsed in the sun on the bench, she went to the pond, which was stocked with fish and rife with yellow and magenta water lilies. It was a beautiful sunny day. She had a bucket and she managed to catch five frogs, and had gotten her petticoat good and muddy in the process, which she knew she would pay for later when the governess spanked her with a hairbrush. She ran over to her beloved grandfather and presented him with her catch. He woke from dozing and looked at her, resigned, but with a glow of pride in his eyes.

"You're a very smart girl. This is exactly the weight of the diamonds I carried to this country from Algeria." He reached for the pail, which he set on his knee, and then, to Madeleine's great shock, he proceeded to swallow all five frogs, one after the other. Madeleine scarcely breathed as she watched. He wasn't a monster, but now she was convinced he knew magic. "If you cannot protect yourself, you are at their mercy," her grandfather said. He burped up all five frogs, each alive and perfect, then he returned the bucket to Madeleine so that she could replace the creatures into the mud at the edge of the pond. As they went back to the house, they held hands. Each felt fortunate to be in the company of the other. The rest of the world and its cruelties didn't matter as much when they were together.

Everything was covered with ice that winter and the last time Madeleine saw her grandfather he couldn't get out of bed. He hadn't eaten for weeks, though Madeleine had brought him sugar cookies every day. She sat beside him, pale and unassuming, her face pinched with worry.

"I think I made a mistake," he told her one day when they were together. The old man found Madeleine quietly endearing. He patted her head, for he had come to care deeply for her, and he knew that she cared for him in return; he had also come to see his past quite differently and had regrets that he hadn't expected to have. He wondered why it was only when you were at the end of your life that it was possible to view it with honesty and truth. "You cannot hide who you are without doing great damage. Just remember that you're my granddaughter. Think about others before you think of yourself."

They said the wrong prayers when he was buried, but he would likely not have minded. The meaning was the same.

God our Father, Your power brings us to birth, Your providence guides our lives, and by Your command we return to dust.

He left Madeleine everything, but because she was a minor, her aunt took charge and sent her to a convent school. She was sad at first, for she was in mourning, but she soon came to love the rigor of her classes. She studied Latin and Greek and was a natural student, a favorite of the sisters. She was told early on that she should consider joining the order, and it had always given her great pleasure to succeed as a teacher who was known for her kind heart and her extraordinary patience, learned, perhaps, from the time she had spent with her grandfather.

She had been thinking of him more often of late, now that the world seemed as heartless as he'd warned it might be. She could have sworn her grandfather was there on the iron bench, in his fine clothes, with his beautiful head of hair, his one true vanity. In her own time she had studied Hebrew, which she could read perfectly so that she could know the prayers her grandfather had known as a boy in Algeria. She closed her eyes and prayed for his soul and then she said the Kaddish, the Jewish mourning prayer, which he had taught her so that when he died there would be someone to mourn properly.

Yitgadal v'yitkadash sh'mei raba b'alma di v'ra chirutei.

May His great name be exalted and sanctified in the world which He created according to His will.

When the baker, Monsieur Favre, arrived at the convent, the mother superior was waiting for him in the garden. He had always believed she thought she was too good to deal with him, but now she went so far as to invite him into her office.

"Is there a problem, Sister?" he asked as they walked inside. His hands were sweating. Once before there had been weevils in the wheat and it had nearly ruined him. "The wheat is not what you expected?"

"No, no, it's fine," the mother superior said. She was still thinking of frogs. She thought she had spied one in the garden and the memory now brought a smile to her face.

The baker had heard that Sister Marie came from a noble family north of Paris. Perhaps they were Jews, one never knew. He had been told that the Jews controlled the banks and the newspapers, and for all he knew they had bought this position for Sister Marie. There was gossip about her in the village, for the students she took in were often dark with foreign accents. Now she looked worried, and she leaned forward as if to confide in her wheat supplier. He sat back in his chair, suspicious. He had never trusted nuns; the way they all lived together with no men around, how they seemed to put themselves above all others, taking such pride in their education and dedication to God. Who were they to claim that the heart of Jesus belonged to them? Now that German troops had come to Vichy, such people would pay for their vanity.

"I was wondering if we could pay you half this month and the second half next month," the sister said.

Monsieur Favre stared at her, openmouthed. Now she was crying poor.

"It's just the current situation," she explained. "The finances."

He noted that her office was very well appointed. There was a hand-knotted rug on the floor, dyed with vegetable dyes in the old-fashioned manner. There were several paintings of the saints on the wall. On her desk was a crystal vase filled with cut roses that were a strange pale metallic color, among the last of the season, although they often bloomed until the first snowfall. There was a silver pen and pencil set on her desk. A lone bee hit against the window glass, trying to get in, for the weather was changing. Favre felt something changing between them as well. Her eyes were lowered. His were not.

"If we could have a little more time," she asked him.

"No," he said. He gazed at the rug and the marquetry floor. She was probably used to getting everything she wanted and took all of these luxuries for granted. He wondered if her family was even French. "That will not be possible."

"I see," the sister said. She went to her desk and drew out her checkbook.

"Cash," he said. When she looked at him blankly, he shrugged. "The bank has closed."

"Has it?" Her mouth tightened. "Has it really?" Her grandfather had always told her to trust no one but herself. But the truth was, she had trusted the old man completely.

The baker was convinced that a woman like the sister had her head in the clouds and knew nothing, not even the price of wheat, so he charged her a bit more this time.

"What unusual roses," he said as she looked through her drawer for francs. The flowers were silver, which made sense, why would she have plain pink blooms?

"Yes," she said, barely listening. The financial situation was horrible. Perhaps she could go to the doctor who had helped her in the past.

"Would you mind if I cut some flowers to bring to my wife?" Favre asked. Why shouldn't his wife have something so beautiful? "My wife cooks in the café and has no time for things that bring her pleasure."

He was told there were shears in the garden and that he was free to cut flowers to take home to his wife, so he said goodbye, his money in his pocket. He went down the corridor paved with polished bluestone, then into the courtyard. The gate to the garden was wrought iron, and he pushed through into the sunlight. His shadow fell before him. Two girls sat on a bench near the silver roses, one blond and one dark and small with a foreigner's features, both so intent in conversation they did not look up. Such strange flowers, these roses, looking as if they had dropped down from the moon, with their silver sheen and black, leathery leaves. Most of the other flowers were long past their bloom, and he thought these might be the sorts of roses that Jews grew; perhaps they were fed with the blood of children and that had caused their unusual color, for since medieval times Jews were thought to be magicians, suspected of sorcery. He had no idea that the flowers were a strain of roses created by a woman more than three hundred years earlier whose husband was so jealous of her beauty he wouldn't allow her to leave their house. She could only go as far as her garden, and often she sneaked out while he was asleep so that she might work in the moonlight. She wanted a bloom the color of the moon, a hybrid between a white Bourbon and a black climbing rose. After years of cross-pollinating and covering the plants with white burlap bags so the bees would not play havoc with her plans, she at last completed her task. When her husband found her with her silver roses, he locked her in the house, commanding her maid to dig up the rosebushes. They were given the name la Lumière Volée, stolen light.

The maid couldn't bring herself to do as she was told. She

kept two specimens in her own garden, and when the husband died she returned them to their rightful place. From these plants six more grew, and then another six, and then six more, so that an entire section of the garden looked silver at certain times of day.

There was a pair of green-tinged iron shears left on a stone table. Monsieur Favre could hear the girls speaking now, and after a moment he realized the brunette with the hawk nose spoke German. The few words in French that she said were guttural, a crime against the language. The pretty blond one spoke German as well. They were both dressed in blue convent dresses, wearing black stockings and laced shoes. The blond was so pretty she caught Favre's eye and his dark imagination. She was perhaps fourteen or fifteen, nearly a woman. He would never guess she was thinking about murder as she sat there in the lemony light. How to kill someone in the least painful way possible was on her mind. Would it be drowning or poison? The way to destroy Ava seemed painless enough according to her mother's instructions. She was to remove the aleph in the word *emet* drawn on Ava's arm, a single letter that turned *emet* into *met*, truth into death.

"What are you thinking about?" Rachel asked when she saw the faraway look in Lea's eyes. They had become quite close, and although both were too wary to have a friend, they had formed a bond. She could tell when Lea was preoccupied.

"Would you kill someone if you were asked to?"

Rachel shrugged. "It would depend on who they were and what they'd done to deserve it."

Rachel looked up to see the man observing them. She stopped talking and tugged on Lea's dress. Perhaps she could guess what he assumed by the way he was staring at them, with a dark, wary expression.

He saw a Jew right here, right in front of his eyes, one who ate bread made with his flour at every meal. She had the nerve to raise her eyes, as if she were better than he.

The girls often broke away from the other students so they might converse in German, which made them feel as if they were back home. At first they had both wept at night, longing for their mothers, but they had become accustomed to their situation. Most hours were accounted for, and that gave them less time to mourn what they had lost.

"Act naturally," Lea said in a hushed voice. She hoped they hadn't given themselves away as refugees. "Can I help you?" she called to the fat man glaring at them.

"I'd like to ask your friend a question," he said, gesturing to the brunette.

"I'm so sorry, but she has a sore throat and cannot speak." Lea spoke brightly. Her French was excellent. By now there was not the slightest German inflection.

Monsieur Favre considered the blond girl. He felt sure that she was telling a blatant lie, but one so well spoken that for a moment he almost believed her. It was the look of terror on the other girl's face that gave them away.

"You were speaking German."

"We're studying it in class so that we can read our texts in the language in which they were written." He was still staring at her. "Perhaps I can help you?" the pretty liar said cheerfully.

"I'm here for the flowers," Favre told her. He sounded unfriendly, even to himself, not that it mattered. He knew what was going on here. Just what the rumors implied.

The girls watched him cut far too many of the blooms, leaving a gash in the rosebush. They had grown to love this garden, and all of the girls without parents felt a special connection with the beauty of this place. Favre left the shears splayed open on the white gravel path. When he was gone, Lea and Rachel ran to the mother superior's office and told her that they feared a man in the garden had overheard them speaking German. They wanted her to say it was nothing to fret about, very likely he hadn't heard them at all, and what if he had? Everything would remain the same, as it always did in this convent.

When she heard about how Monsieur Favre had questioned them, the mother superior went to the window, frowning as she watched him walking to his old van. She thought of all the reasons her grandfather had told her not to be Jewish, but the truth was there was only one. The way people let themselves fill with hate. Some of the flowers he had taken were falling apart in his grasp, petals strewn on the walkway. He was careless and he didn't mind leaving a path of ruined flowers. Still, the petals seemed to glow. He stopped and regarded the convent, and the mother superior knew that look, she had seen it on other men's faces. It was greed.

The nun turned back to the girls. "Go upstairs and tell the others. You must leave today."

As there was no time to bake bread and no one to make breakfast, the mother superior joined Ava in the kitchen while the other sisters were packing up the girls' belongings, as well as their own. It was too dangerous for anyone to stay on.

The mother superior put up water for tea, then found a large pot in which to make porridge. Fortunately, Ava soon took over so the children would have a decent meal before leaving. They could always count on Ava. She was a wonder today as she was every day. Lea and Rachel were sitting together, knowing they would have to say goodbye. It had already been decided that Rachel would go with Sister Félicité. Lea would leave with Ava. The mother superior suggested they go to Le Chambon-sur-Lignon, a town on a high plateau in the Haute-Loire known for its tolerance and acceptance of refugees. There was a school of several stone buildings at the end of a road that was impassable in winter and difficult to find in all other seasons. When the time came to leave, Rachel embraced Lea. Just this once, she said, and they both laughed, although there were tears in their eyes.

The mother superior hoped decent people would prevail and the convent's paintings, along with the silver and the rugs, would still be here when they returned. Still, she had faith that they would someday resume their work here even if all their worldly possessions disappeared. She sat in the rose garden and thought of the years when she was Madeleine de Masson. She had been left a great deal of money when her grandfather died, some of which her aunt had appropriated, the rest of which she had given to the church when she entered the convent. She did so to be true to her faith and give back to the world. She wondered now how she had been so sure of herself at such a young age.

Yitgadal v'yitkadash sh'mei raba b'alma di v'ra chirutei.

May His great name be exalted and sanctified in the world which He created according to His will.

It was the end of something. She was certain of it. She wrote a note to the monsignor, thanking him for his kindness and good deeds, not daring to say more in case the note was intercepted after it was posted. When the sisters went to say prayers in the chapel, it was the last time they would do so. The mother superior was not with them; instead she was at work in the kitchen, and much to their surprise she presented them with breakfast at the appropriate hour. Ava had taught her to add goat's milk to the pot to stretch the porridge. Students and teachers ate standing up, for there was no time to get comfortable, and they all had their suitcases with them. Ava, always a hard worker, washed and dried the plates and pots, although it was possible they wouldn't be used again.

When all had gone, the mother superior waited for the soldiers. She looked back fondly on the fact that the sisters had never questioned her when she brought the girls to the school. They had done their work in good faith. And when it was over, and she said they must leave, even the reluctant ones took off their black habits and dressed in the clothes they had collected for the poor before going across the field toward the woods. Sister Félicité escorted the Jewish girls she watched over to a convent near Annecy. Even the heron that had nested in the chimney for so long took flight on that day. Sister Marie wished her grandfather were beside her, for his presence had always given her comfort. She saw the frog in the garden once more and thought perhaps this was a sign that her grandfather was watching over her. She had locked away some of the more important things: a very old Bible that was said to have come from Jerusalem. The silver chalice in the chapel. The book that each novice signed when she entered the convent. But such things would be stolen, most likely, and they were not what mattered most.

They came that afternoon, throwing open the gate, walking with muddy boots through the halls and up the stone stairs. The soldier who interrogated her called her by her given name, Madeleine Salomon Hasson. She was a Jew. The police had never noticed before, but it was right there in front of them. After Favre's report, the Germans had researched her family; they were very thorough after all, and they knew things about her grandfather that she herself didn't know. She would think of this in the camp they took her to after she was arrested, how little she knew about the person she loved most in this world. He had been twenty-four when he came from Algeria with his wife, Milah, and when she died he had donated a large bequest to the Jardin du Luxembourg, where roses were planted in his wife's name. He had made donations to many schools and synagogues and began a fund for the poor who were newly arrived from Algeria. These facts were read aloud, as if they were criminal acts, but they were simply the small truths that allowed the mother superior to understand why she had come to this place to teach and to accept girls no one else would take on, and why she had loved this rose garden so well, for it was in her lineage to favor beauty and knowledge, as it was to have regrets, now, at the end of her life.

CHAPTER NINETEEN

IN THE FOREST

ARDÈCHE, NOVEMBER 1942

THEY SLEPT IN THE TREES OR BENEATH BOWERS OF THE TALL, plumy underbrush, waking with leaves in their hair. The air was crisp and fragrant, the moon a silver slip that grew fatter and more orange every night. Sometimes they spied other people in the woods, living as best they could, Jews and refugees and young French men escaping from forced labor. Ava gave away half their food to starving families who had nowhere to go but the caves. When these refugees saw a tall woman followed by a huge heron, they were astonished and hopeful. It was a wonder, a message that all things were possible, even in this cruel world.

When they were alone in the mountains, they might have been a million miles away from Paris. The pastures were turning brown and the leaves were yellow, as if the stars had fallen from the sky. As long as they stayed away from cities and towns, the world felt as it had for hundreds of years, pure and elemental. The rivers and streams went along beds of stone and granite, the water a pale blue-gray.

Night after night, in the trees or in the grass, Lea dreamed of her mother. She heard Hanni's voice in the wind, in birdsong, in falling leaves.

I was with you when the roses bloomed with silver petals, when you saw Paris for the first time, when that boy looked at you, when you learned prayers in the convent, when you ran through the woods.

Every time Ava took your hand, it was my hand you held.

They were protected and hidden, while all across the continent there was the Shoah, an attempt at the total destruction of the Jews, as had been recorded time and again in the Torah. *That day is a day of wrath, a day of trouble and distress, a day of Shoah and desolation, a day of darkness and gloominess, a day of clouds and thick darkness.* By now millions of Jews had been murdered. They had been sent to the death camps; buried deep in the forests of Poland, body upon body, fragile and naked, twisted and torn. There were souls that had turned black with horror who now perched in the trees, trembling and stunned by what some men were capable of, unable to move on from the spot where they had been murdered, incapable of entering the World to Come. They had been tortured, separated from those they loved, made to dig their own graves, castrated, humiliated, with the gold removed from their teeth, gassed at a rate of six thousand a day in Auschwitz. The Destruction hung across the world in darkness, in a cloud. When Lea dreamed of her mother, Hanni was shoeless, her hair shorn. But her eyes were shining. Like Rachel in the Torah, who wept with grief over the loss of her children,

Hanni wept in these dreams. She was without words, without a mouth, without a body, beneath the dirt, none of which stopped her love.

You were with me when we discovered we were not hunters, but wolves, when the world was taken away from us, when they believed we were worthless, when we were sent away on trains, when the souls of our brothers and sisters rose with no place to go. You were with me every minute. You are my triumph, the one thing they could never take away.

What mattered in the forest was simple, and had nothing to do with the cruel perversions of men. A rock, a leaf, a star, a dream. Time stood still here. When a leaf fell it took forever until it landed on the forest floor. Winter would come, but not now, not yet, not in this place where if you fell asleep you dreamed for weeks. Wildflowers grew out of season; angels walked through the yellow grass and left their footprints for men to follow if they cared to see what was right in front of them, the path of the righteous, the forgiving, the faithful. Sometimes, at night, Lea would awake to see Ava dancing with the heron. He was staying later than he should. Sweeps of birds had left for warmer climates, but every day he was there, and every night they danced. Lea watched, entranced, well aware that she was seeing magic being made. Ava looked luminous as she danced barefoot, and sometimes she threw her head back and laughed with delight.

If a golem was made of clay, how was it possible for her to feel? Lea soon devised a test. She went out and gathered thorny branches and placed them on the ground beneath the bushes where they slept to see if Ava could feel pain. That night Ava curled up among the sharp branches and she didn't cry out once.

The next night, Lea took a glass bottle, broke it, then spread the shards in the grass. That night Ava danced as if nothing was wrong.

On the third night Lea left a heap of biting red ants in Ava's garments, but when Ava dressed she had no reaction, not an itch or a cry, nothing at all.

These tests proved that Ava felt nothing, and yet there was that look on her face when the heron bowed to her in the moment before the dance began. It was the gaze of someone who loved you, the same look Lea had seen when her mother kissed her good night, when her father was at home and there was laughter in the kitchen, when her grandmother told her stories. Once upon a time something happened that you never could have imagined, a spell was broken, a girl was saved, a rose grew out of a tooth buried deep in the ground, love was everywhere, and people who had been taken away continued to walk with you, in dreams and in the waking world.

They were so well hidden that Ava allowed Lea the freedom to wander. She was going for water from the nearby stream when she saw a wolf, just as Bobeshi had when she was a girl, not much older than Lea was now. At first Lea thought it was a dream she had never woken from and she was likely still sleeping, curled up under the bushes. But she reached down and pinched herself, and the pinch stung and she knew she was awake, and then she was certain that what had happened to Bobeshi was now happening to her. The wolf was black with yellow eyes. It was said such creatures had been hunted to extinction in this region, that they had been shot and hung on posts, murdered one by one by royal hunting parties. But some things cannot be destroyed so easily.

Lea lifted her eyes to look into his. He had been so quiet she hadn't heard him approach, though she should have known. There were no birds singing. The leaves refused to fall. She thought of Julien. Even if no one else believed her, he would.

She had to stay alive. She had made a promise. How to do so was the question.

Don't run, her grandmother had told her. *Do not be afraid. Be who you are, and know that he will be who he is.*

How many wolves were left? Three or four? Half a dozen? Or was it just this single wolf watching her from the edge of the stream, ready to leap if she was the sort of human who had a gun, or a knife, or an eye for murder? Soon enough he saw that she was just a girl sitting by the stream. They were themselves and they knew each other and they could feel one another's loneliness. When you are a wolf, no place is safe, no one can be trusted. Unless they are what you are. Hunted.

Lea was not as afraid as she had been in the alley. Her heart had stopped then and every breath hurt. She remembered how it felt to bite the soldier, how she had struggled with him and would have done anything to be free of him. But the wolf seemed more reasonable than the soldier.

"Hello," Lea said. Her voice sounded hollow and pure.

The wolf came toward her.

We were wolves in the forest, chased until there was nowhere to go. When you are not considered human, you learn how to run.

He was bigger than a dog, and ragged. Lea was motionless. When he came close his breath was warm and he smelled like grass, a sweet, deep, dark scent of the woods. He was not young, and he was weary, for he had seen enough of men to last him a lifetime.

Bobeshi had been carrying a pail of water when the wolf came to her. She could have thrown it at him, instead, she had stood unmoving as Lea stood here now. Bobeshi had taken a deep breath and spoken the truth to the creature in the woods.

Brother Wolf, I am not your enemy. You are not the beast that I fear. I fear men and their bloodshed, I fear soldiers with guns, I fear those who hate for no reason, those who leave bodies behind them like fallen leaves, in the grass, in the earth, on the streets of cities that were filled with life, but are empty now. We can walk through those cities together in silence, leaving no footprints, looking for the teeth they pulled from our mouths so that we can plant them in the earth and we can grow up from the dirt despite what they did to us, hanging us by the feet until the blood runs out of our mouths, taking us into alleys, shearing our hair, leaving us naked in the rain.

Lea put her hand out and the wolf came near. She placed her palm on him and felt how alive he was. She did not shake as she had in the alleyway, and time didn't move forward or back. It stayed exactly where it was. They were here together, at the same moment.

And then the birds began to call, and the leaves fell, and time moved, and the wolf leapt across the stream and left her standing there alone. He had disappeared into the dark woods, but she could still feel how alive he was. She was alive as well. When she walked, Bobeshi walked with her. When she made her way through the forest, her mother was by her side. She had once heard the ancient story from the Torah of how Rachel heard her son's grief when he came to her grave, for her love for him had never died. If you are loved, you never lose the person who loved you. You carry them with you all your life. They were with her as she ran.

Remember when I loved you above all others and you loved me in return.

Lea stopped setting out tests for Ava. Doing so had served no purpose, and she had found her answer without them. She knew when she saw Ava with the heron on the day he left. Not even magic could stop time completely. One morning there was frost on the ground and the yellow leaves were crisscrossed with ice. The frost faded in the shine of the morning sun, all the same it was autumn. They were in a tree, speaking to one another in the beautiful language of birds, in which heartbreak sounded like a song.

Once he was gone it was only the two of them. Lea had dreaded the fall as much as Ava had, for its arrival meant it was impossible for her to send or receive messages.

"If only time could move more quickly," Lea said. They had built a bonfire to burn away the chill of the night.

"Time is uncontrollable. It does as it pleases."

They had both huddled near to watch the fire.

"You can go if you want to," Lea said. When Ava gave her a look, Lea shrugged and made herself clear. "You can follow him."

All she had to do was go south until she reached the beach of black sand where a thousand herons all took flight at once to block out the sky to make the world their own. Of course she could find him. She had no need of maps or guides. The world was open to her. But instead, she made Hardship Soup for them to eat for supper. And when the fire had burned to ash, she took the thorns from her bedding, cleared the shards of glass from the grass, and shook the ants out of her dress.

Even if she could fly away, she had no intention of doing so.

PART TWO

1943–44

CHAPTER TWENTY

THE OLD MAN

HAUTE-LOIRE, AUTUMN 1943

JULIEN HAD BEEN AT THE FARM FOR OVER A YEAR. DURING this time he and Lea exchanged messages for the six months the heron was with them, but in winter there was no way for them to communicate. It was almost the time for the messages to end when the heron arrived on the hillside, standing there as if he were a thin, elegant man in a pale gray coat. Julien climbed the hill to meet him, his heart hitting against the cage of his ribs.

"Hello," Julien said, always in awe of the creature and half-expecting him to speak. The heron merely stared into his eyes, interested, but removed. Julien knelt to slip the tube from the heron's leg, then withdrew the message. It was the highlight of every month during the bright half of the year, and what he missed most during the dark winter months.

I'm still here.

I'm keeping my promise. Please, keep yours.

Julien crouched down in the shade. He had not seen Lea for nearly two years. They had been cast into the far sides of a maze, blindfolded, with no walls or trees or bread crumbs to guide them. What they needed was a map; then they would not have to depend on the heron's messages. Julien took out a pencil he carried with him for sketching, and got to work. He remembered his trip here backward, the way he would if he were spiraling out from the heart of a labyrinth. One could approach from over the mountains or from the village to discover Beehive House, set in the fields, with its barn and its beehives. He was precise in his rendering, even though his hands shook. The heron was still as Julien replaced the message. Time was moving in a blur. It was getting away from him. If he had no hope of finding Lea, perhaps she could find him. He stood with his hand over his eyes watching the heron fly away. It was then he saw Monsieur Félix on the porch with his rifle, pointing up. Julien ran as fast as he could, shouting for the old man to stop, waving his hands like a madman, startling Monsieur Félix so badly that he put down his gun. When he reached the porch, breathless, Julien grabbed it away from him.

"What's wrong with you?" Monsieur Félix said, aggravated by the interruption. "I won't have another chance. He's flying south. Herons bring good luck if you cook them."

"Don't ever do that," Julien said darkly.

"All right," Félix said, taken aback. Julien was surprisingly fierce when he was in a fit of anger. He was not such a kid, really. And he had a temper it seemed.

"It is not good luck to eat them," he told the old man. "It's a crime."

Monsieur Félix shrugged. "There are many crimes committed in this world, but this isn't one of them."

Bluebell had come to see what the commotion was.

"Really? Would you eat Bluebell?" Julien asked.

"I *know* Bluebell," the old man responded.

"Well I know that heron."

They stared at each other, and Monsieur Félix backed down. "You should have said so."

Julien managed to smile then. "I did." He handed the old man his gun.

"Then we understand each other," Monsieur Félix said.

Every day after, Julien went back to the hill to scan the sky for the heron. But Monsieur Félix was right, it was the season of migration. One drowsy afternoon, Julien fell asleep in the grass and stayed away longer than he'd planned. He awoke disoriented and chilled to the bone. He started back, and as he approached the farm he knew something was wrong. He shielded his eyes from the sun and immediately spied the imprints of truck treads in the muddy drive. Monsieur Félix did not own a truck, only a cart without a donkey or horse to pull it. The cart was over by the barn, the wood rotting. Victor was nowhere in sight, and, anyway, he preferred cars to trucks, the faster the better. Julien felt a warning bell ring inside of him.

He crouched behind the hedges. Blackbirds were in the yellow stalks of tall grass, but when they sensed his presence they arose all at once in a swirl of life. He looked up, holding his hands over his ears. The ringing was so bad, like church bells inside his head. In the farthest field there were the stalks of sunflowers, all the flowers cut down for the seeds that were drying in the barn in wire baskets. He hoped Victor had returned with a truck, or perhaps Marianne had come back from the border. But he realized it was too quiet. Beneath the ringing in his head, there was no sound of Monsieur Félix at work, not at the well or in the garden or in the small barn. Only the blackbirds taking flight.

Julien waited until the dark began to sift down, then he came out from behind the hedge. There was already snow in the high mountains, and a chill in the air even here. He went up to the house and stood at the door listening. Nothing, so he pushed the door open, slowly, with the caution he'd learned over the last few years. The front room looked unexceptional, except when he raised his eyes he saw Monsieur Félix hanging dead from a rope thrown over the old wooden beam that crossed the ceiling. Julien covered his mouth and nose with his hand because of the smell. He was paralyzed, and for a moment the ringing in his ears overcame him. He thought he might faint. More than anything he wished Victor were with him. His brother would have known what to do. Now he had no choice but to pull himself together and go on through the house.

You are in a dream. And there are rules even then. In a dream you walk softly, you keep your eyes open, you're ready to run, or do what you must. You stay alive.

The kitchen had been ransacked and was in wild disarray, the floor littered with powdery flour and dried beans. The Germans had been alerted to this place; perhaps the postman had been caught and interrogated, for they had clearly been searching for something. Julien did his best to find the papers, as he thought Monsieur Félix would wish him to. He tried to think as the old man might have, opening drawers, searching the pantry, daring to look through the front room, where the body was, avoiding glancing at it as best he could. He felt the weight of death, the deepness of it, the realness of it, how human people were, even in the throes of death, for the old man had soiled himself.

When Julien reached the top of the stairs, his chest was so tight he could hardly breathe. He went onward, opening the door to Monsieur Félix's bedchamber, even though he was rattled down to his core, with the desire to run taking hold. Still, he went forward. He expected to see a murdered woman, or face a soldier who had been left behind, and he burst into wild laughter when at last he spied what was in the room. There was Bluebell, the farmer's little goat, tied to the bedpost, kept out of the way to ensure she wouldn't come to harm. She must have been silent, perhaps sleeping, when the soldiers had come. Now she was restless, confused as to why she'd been kept in the house for so long.

"Well, you're definitely alive," Julien said. He untied her, and the little goat leaned her head against him. She had green eyes and was very quiet. Perhaps she knew what had befallen her owner.

He led the goat downstairs by the rope coiled around her neck and took her out to the barn, where there was hay for her to eat. He thought of Monsieur Félix, who had helped to save so many lives of fleeing Jews and was now hanging from a rafter. There were flies in the barn, too many of them. Julien took an old jacket that was hung on a peg. Monsieur Félix was dead, and therefore taking the jacket wasn't technically stealing. One owed a man like Monsieur Félix a debt of gratitude; because of this, once the sun had risen Julien grabbed a shovel and went out behind the barn and dug a grave. It took a while and the sun was surprisingly hot for the season.

Julien went back into the house, to search the kitchen for a sharp knife, then cut down Monsieur Félix. The body was heavy as it collapsed against him. It smelled like the moss on the trees in the woods, like bitter weeds. Julien folded the corpse onto a blanket, then pulled the blanket along, out the door and down the porch steps, dragging the dead man behind the barn. He kept the knife tucked in his waistband.

"I'm so sorry I don't know your prayers," Julien said after he had placed the farmer in the grave. His face was wet with tears. Still, he did the best he could, reciting the Kaddish, the Jewish prayer for the dead.

Blessed is He, beyond any blessing and song, praise and consolation that are uttered in the world.

Amen.

Afterward he covered the body with hard, cold earth, sweating more than before, for he was wearing the old man's jacket. The last of the bees were buzzing around him; it was the end of their season and they were wild. Julien had to bat them away. The sun was bright, with silvery light spilling over the fields. When he was done Julien went into the barn, where he drank water from the goat's bucket. She nudged him, and he realized there was something in the pocket of the jacket that had belonged to the farmer, a beekeeper's mask of cheesecloth, with the eyes cut out. A bee sat on his arm, so he stayed steady until it lifted and flew away.

He began to consider what a thousand soldiers could look at a thousand times and never think anything might be hidden there. He knew there was a rational manner in which to approach this problem. Mathematics had been his first language, after all. He cut the farm into sections in his mind, as if it were a pie. The house was in one section, the barn in another, the vegetable garden in another, the field in still another, and then there were the woods beyond. He thought about each of those sections, and where the papers might be, but all of the possibilities seemed too obvious. What would a thousand soldiers ignore?

He walked into the field. It was the least likely place. There wasn't much there. Cabbages, leeks, the large sunflower stalks leaning over like dead men in the chill air, an overturned wheelbarrow. The bees were clustered in the hive, keeping each other warm, but a few that had been guarding the entrance flitted out and surrounded him, so many their buzzing rang in his ears. He had no fear at all, only curiosity. The hives were at the edge of the far woods. It was possible to see the mountains from here, with their crags of gray volcanic rock. The sky was so blue, but inside that blue there were a hundred shades. There were bees buzzing around him. The old man had once told him he had no fear of God's creatures, and in turn the creatures knew this and respected him.

Julien stopped in his tracks. The least likely place was right in front of him.

He slipped on the mask he had found in the jacket pocket. As he approached a hive, he was covered with bees. He slid his hand inside the wooden box and reached up. The buzzing was more like a throbbing now, but he was used to noise inside his head and this was better than the dreadful ringing he alone could hear.

More bees rushed out into the air. At the top of the hive, his fingers hit against what felt like a piece of metal. He pulled at whatever it was, then used the knife he'd taken from the kitchen to work it free, and it soon dislodged. When he took it out he saw that it was a flat tin covered in honey. He was stung several times, and the feeling burned through him so that he didn't notice the other stings that followed. His arms and neck were dotted with red welts, but it didn't matter. He loped back to the barn, the bees following him until a gust of wind came up. They scattered and he laughed because they forgot about him and went back to their work in the hive and he felt lucky, which seemed such a far-fetched thing to feel, and yet it was there, making him grin with the joy of his discovery.

He sat down in the cool barn, beside the goat, who nudged him, curious.

"This is not for you," he told Bluebell.

He scraped the honey from the tin and devoured it. It was so delicious he didn't think of the stingers in his hands and neck. Then, when he had eaten his fill, he began to feel the sharp pain of the stings. He pulled the stingers out as best he could, then dunked his head in a bucket of water, shivering with the cold. He had figured out the puzzle and found what a thousand soldiers would have never come across, not if they searched for a thousand days. He went inside, and in a kitchen drawer he left the identity papers and a note telling Marianne where her father's remains had been laid to rest. He scrawled a brief message for his brother as well.

I'm not sure it's safe to stay. I'll go to the church. I'm sorry.

He thought it best to leave Monsieur Félix's farm quickly, in case the soldiers should return. He left Bluebell tied up in the barn with plenty of feed and water. He cleaned off the knife on the grass, and kept it with him. Just in case. He hated to think of Marianne finding the house in such terrible disorder. She would read the note he had left, then go out and stand beside the turned earth where her father lay. He hoped Victor would be there with her. As for himself, Julien was grateful for the air and the sun and for the strength of his own legs. He had kept his one and only promise to Lea. He was alive.

CHAPTER TWENTY-ONE

BELIEVER

VIENNE, AUTUMN 1943

JULIEN FOUND HIS WAY BACK TO VIENNE THROUGH THE MAZE of forests and towns by following the *L*'s he had carved into trees. He lodged at the church for three days and nights, the limit of anyone's stay. A stranger's presence became too noticeable after that, and one never knew when the authorities might come by.

On the fourth day, he had no choice but to leave. He passed the Roman ruins that had once been the temple of Augustus and Livia, and frankly didn't know where to go next. By now, there were starving people everywhere. The Germans took whatever they wanted from shopkeepers and farmers until there was nothing left. It wasn't safe to be in the street, so Julien retreated into someone's garden, his presence camouflaged by the surrounding bushes after he had cut down some branches with his knife. He had no way to contact his brother, and the best he could do was to occasionally check in with Father Varnier, so here he was, sleeping beneath the rhododendrons with their flat, shiny evergreen leaves.

In the morning it seemed he hadn't been as well hidden as he'd hoped. The elderly couple that lived in the house peered out at him from their window. Starving, he went to knock on the back door to ask if they might need household work done in exchange for a meal.

"You're a carpenter?" the old gentleman who answered the door asked.

"More or less," Julien said.

It was a lie but he supposed he could learn. He was hired for the price of a meal, which he wolfed down before the work had even begun. There was a hole in the roof, and although the old gentleman could still climb up the ladder that was propped against the house, he needed a helper to carry the heavy gray slate made of local rock and the bucket of tar. They worked all that afternoon with the steamy tar, their shirts off in the bright sun.

"I won't know if we've done it right until it rains," said the old man, who introduced himself as Monsieur Bisset.

They had dinner in the kitchen, where Madame Bisset set an extra plate, asking no questions, pleased that her ceiling would no longer leak. Their son, Alain Bisset, only twenty-two, was among those who had been lost in the Battle of France. They had lit a candle in the church, and had Father Varnier say the prayers for the dead. Perhaps this was the reason the couple allowed Julien to stay through the fall in their garden shed, where he slept among the rakes and brooms, quickly learning to ignore the mice who scuttled about at night, grateful they were mice and nothing more. He wore Alain's winter coat, and his boots, and he sat at his place at the table. Sometimes, Madame let out a gasp when she came into the room and saw him there. With his long dark hair, and lean body, he looked like her son. But he was not, and Madame Bisset knew it. All the same, they were happy to let him stay, to let one young man live and watch him emerge into the blue morning to knock at the door, ready to attend to the chores on his list.

Madame Bisset became ill in November; it was her son's birthday month, and most likely she was sick with despair over his fate. There was no body to bury and no one to mourn, and she went into a decline, refusing to rise from bed or cook or even to speak. Julien and Monsieur were halfway through plastering the old crumbling walls in the house when Monsieur Bisset told Julien he was sorry, but Julien would have to go. There were no explanations, but Julien understood. It was dangerous to have him in their house and they had been through enough pain and sorrow. But in truth it was more, when Madame saw a young man working in her parlor she was overcome with longing for her son.

On his last day with the couple, Julien found an old recipe book on a kitchen shelf and quickly set to work baking an apple cake, with fruit plucked from the spindly tree in the garden. He wondered what Ava would say if she could see him now. He'd been a spoiled boy in her eyes, and he had realized that had been true. But now he'd been forced to learn many skills: how to fix a roof, how to cook, how to steal, how to say goodbye.

When it was time for Julien to leave, Monsieur Bisset gave

him a sack of food that he could hardly spare. Bread, cheese, crackers, apples, all luxuries.

"Do you know why we helped you?" the old man asked.

The two had become quite close, working together as they did. The house was in far better shape now than it had been when Julien first arrived.

Monsieur lowered his voice, as if the Germans were right outside his door. "Because we hate them."

Julien would miss the scent of mint that grew in the patchy garden. He would miss lying on his back in the shed, where he would talk to Lea as if she were beside him. She alone understood him, and there were times when he missed her so badly he felt twisted with emotion. *Stay alive.* He was a flame when he thought of the words she had whispered to him. He did not intend to disappoint her.

The weather was still fine, and Julien could camp in the woods outside the city, like so many other boys and young men who were in hiding. He ran into them sometimes, groups from La Sixième and the French Resistance who were loyal to de Gaulle, the true leader of France, though he was in exile. One evening, Julien came upon two sisters, feral creatures of eight and ten years old who had been lost for weeks after their parents were arrested. Actually, the sisters had found him. He'd made a campsite and was eating the last of Monsieur Bisset's food, which he'd been doling out to himself in small portions. When he looked up he saw the girls staring, their eyes on his food. They had dark hair and big, glassy eyes, and they appeared to be starving. Their parents had been sent to the terrifying Montluc

Prison, where more than two thousand five hundred Jews were imprisoned by the Germans, with thousands deported and eight hundred murdered, dying from torture and neglect. Through a crack in the cupboard door they had seen the soldiers beat their father and do something to their mother that had made her scream. After their parents' arrest, the girls had hidden in their house with nothing to eat but the peeling paint on the walls. At last, they had climbed out the window and fled into the woods. They trusted no one, but they were starving, so there they were, watching him, not saying a word.

Julien shared his food with them as the girls crouched close by, but not too near. They wolfed down the bread. Julien had saved a crumb, which he kept in his hand. A sparrow swooped down from the tree, then lit in the palm of his hand to take the bread, eating it, unafraid. The girls laughed, shocked that they could do anything other than cry.

Julien brought them to the Bissets' late that night. Monsieur stared at him when he came to the back door, but when he saw the girls he understood. He summoned his wife from her bed, and when she saw how ragged and underfed the children were, she quickly gestured, willing to take them in. She let them bathe in the big old tub and had them wear her son's childhood clothing until she could find something more suitable. It was the first time in weeks that Madame had left her bed.

"She needed children," Monsieur said, to explain why the girls could stay while Julien had been made to leave. They had gone out to have a smoke in the garden. It was a habit Julien had picked up from Victor. "We can take them. We'll say they're our own, and after a while they will be."

Julien nodded and watched the smoke rise into the night

sky. Lea would be furious if she knew he was smoking. She'd told him her father had been a doctor, and said smoking was bad for the lungs.

"My brother has a farm," the old man said. "It's a little more than three kilometers outside town. Maybe he can use the help."

They went there together, Monsieur driving, Julien in the space between the front and backseats, beneath a blanket. It was a small farm, and Monsieur Bisset's brother was a brusque widower who had fields but no one to work them. Julien would stay in a borrowed canvas tent in the woods beyond the pasture until the snows came, and be given two meals each day, as long as he worked without complaint, for the hours were long, and the labor backbreaking. Julien shook hands with the first Monsieur Bisset and they wished each other luck. The food was not as good here, it was simple fare, mostly bread and eggs and cheese, but it was filling, and Julien didn't mind living outside.

This is what it feels like to be alone, he would have written to Lea if he could. *You hear more and see more. You're a part of the world around you.* Ants under the leaves, the clouds moving by. He had begun to divide the world into sections, as his father had taught him to do; everything was a piece of the whole, he understood that now. He had no difficulty finding his way to his campsite in the dark; he did so by touching the trees as though they were a map through a forest maze. The weather grew colder and he could feel how close winter was. At night he looked into the sky and remembered the names of the constellations. There was Orion, the hunter who appears in the winter sky with his bow and his dogs, so that he could be remembered by those who loved him during his time on earth. Julien imagined that his father lay on the ground beside him, looking upward. *Dear father,* he said aloud.

The nesting birds scattered at the sound of his voice. The vines had grown over his tent so quickly he sometimes thought he would disappear. Snow would fall, ice would cover the canvas, and one day Monsieur Bisset's brother would come looking for him and be unable to find him in the woods.

Find me, he would have written to Lea if he could.

Find me before I disappear.

CHAPTER TWENTY-TWO

THE DOCTOR'S HOUSE

ARDÈCHE, WINTER 1943

AT NIGHT, ETTIE WALKED OUT THROUGH THE DARK TREES TO have dinner with the doctor, nothing fancy, usually a shared omelet and some potatoes or stewed tomatoes. Dr. Girard, who was considered a fine chess player, had patiently taught her the game, and, as it turned out, she had a real talent for it. There was little else to do while she waited for Victor's return, although she had begun to act as Girard's nurse when he was called upon by the Resistance, always unexpectedly, often in the middle of the night. His telephone would ring and they would go off together in his car, a beat-up Renault that groaned when it took the hills as the doctor found his way to a safe house where a patient was waiting. In only a few months Ettie had learned quite a bit, how to clean and bind a wound, how to stitch flesh with a needle and surgical thread, how to calm a distraught man or woman who was in the throes of pain. *This will only take a minute, then you'll be fine, lie still, count to one hundred.* Sometimes they would be driven through the night to a remote field, then be blindfolded and led to the injured. Ettie never wavered; she was firm and calm with the patients, and the doctor had been impressed with her courage.

"You're a surprise," he said, pleased to have found a worthy opponent at chess and an even worthier assistant in the field.

"My mother used to deliver babies on our kitchen table," Ettie told him. "I suppose I learned a thing or two from her."

Still, Ettie felt uncomfortable whenever she was alone with Dr. Girard. She was accustomed to the world of women and had only known the boys in her community, all of whom she seemed able to outthink and talk rings around. She had no experience with men, or maybe it was more than her lack of experience. She had tender feelings toward the doctor, especially after watching his work with wounded Resistance members and refugees. He was such a good man, measured and deliberate, allaying his patients' fears. When their work was done, and their clothes bloodied, he would guide her back to the car with his fingers against her back, and the heat of his touch had both comforted her and enflamed her.

Tonight, after their chess game, the doctor had unexpectedly suggested they go upstairs. Ettie had immediately felt nervous. She had fleeting thoughts of all the men who had approached her, the fellow who ran the laundry, the owner of the café. She avoided the doctor's gaze, and had a moment of doubt as to what a man such as himself would want from her.

All the same, she followed him to the second floor, and as it turned out Dr. Girard wasn't after anything inappropriate. He simply went to the closet and opened the door, then turned to Ettie and motioned her forward. There were his wife Sarah's clothes, neatly displayed on wooden hangers. She had been gone for several years, lost to cancer. The fact that her disease had been incurable was a personal affront. He was meant to cure, and could do nothing at all. Girard often imagined that Sarah was in the kitchen, making coffee or reading a book at the table as sunlight came through the window, waiting for him at the end of the day. *Darling,* she would say when he walked in, *I've missed you.*

He could not save her, he could only watch her die, and so he rarely opened the closet where her clothes were still stored, for he was reminded of all he was incapable of accomplishing each time he saw anything that had belonged to her. But since Ettie's arrival he had been thinking what a waste it was to have Sarah's belongings locked away, when Ettie had nothing. He stood back, so that Ettie could get a good look. She had never seen more beautiful clothing. There were linen summer dresses and silk evening clothes, along with piles of sweaters in jeweled colors. At the rear of the closet there was a black coat with a fur collar.

"My wife liked beautiful things," Girard told Ettie. "She worked for a designer in Paris long ago. Try some of it on," he suggested. "It's not doing anyone any good in a closet."

Ettie reached for a simple shift. The soft fabric rustled in her hand.

"No," the doctor said. "Take something that you find to be truly beautiful."

So she chose a pale blue taffeta dress the color of an afternoon sky that Madame Girard had worn in Paris to an engagement party for one of the doctor's cousins. It was chic and fashionable without being too much. The doctor left the room so Ettie could try it on. She stared at herself in the full-length mirror. She was no longer the rabbi's daughter, but even in this glorious dress she was still the sister of a girl who had died in a yellow field. That was the one true part of her that remained. Nothing could hide that.

She went to the hallway, where the doctor was waiting, nervous again. He was slightly taken aback by her sudden intense beauty, but he smiled when she spun around. He remembered that night in Paris with Sarah. How cold it had been as they walked to the party, how he'd kept his arm under her coat so that he could feel her heart beating.

"It's perfect," Ettie said.

"One thing is missing."

They went back into the bedroom and Girard took out a pair of black heels. Ettie, however, had taken note of a pair of red shoes at the rear of the closet. They were exquisite, highly polished leather. "Perhaps these."

"Ah." The doctor nodded. "Her favorites."

The shoes were tight at the toes, but they would do. Ettie practiced walking in them out in the barn until, at last, she didn't stumble.

All the rest of the night, the doctor thought about the red shoes. He couldn't sleep, and sat up thinking about Sarah. He had felt her tumor when he held her breast, but he told himself he was wrong. He had been wrong before, so why not now? But in truth he was a good diagnostician, and he had gone outside to be alone that night after his wife fell asleep. He walked in the woods and wept. He knew he was right, and yet he, who had told patients the state of their health time and time again, even when the news was bad, couldn't bring himself to tell her.

In the end she was the one to come to him. She had felt the lump while bathing.

"It's like a stone," she told him.

He brought her to the hospital in Lyon, where they removed her breast and a good deal of tissue surrounding it, down to her ribs. Sarah was in terrible pain after the surgery, but said nothing. She wouldn't look at him after that, or let him see her. She locked herself in the bedroom, filled with shame. He had been her husband for nearly fifteen years, but there were things that were impossible to share with a husband, even after all that time. Her savaged beautiful body was now kept secret from him.

There were rumbles of the war during her illness, but he didn't hear them, he only heard her crying. She made him sleep on the couch because she couldn't bear to have him near and not be intimate. He was a doctor, he had seen the worst wounds, the most horrible tumors, but this was different. He made up a bed on the couch in the library, but he didn't sleep. He continued to see patients for a while, but he couldn't stand to hear their complaints, and in time, he sent them away, to another doctor in Lyon, though it was farther for his neighbors who had so relied upon him. He could not focus and he feared his preoccupation with Sarah's illness might cause him to make some terrible error in handling their care. He would not be able to live with himself if he made a mistake because he was more concerned with his wife than with any of them, men, women, and children alike. All the same, people from the village brought cakes and bread and stews. They left the covered platters of homemade food on the doorstep. They came at dusk so he wouldn't see them and feel he must politely engage them. It was clear they felt there was no need for him to thank them. That was when he understood that his wife was dying.

Finally, Sarah gave in and let him come back to their bedroom to sleep beside her. When he held her in the dark, he could feel another lump in her other breast, and another under her arm. He didn't have to tell her. She knew. That was why she had allowed him back. Nothing mattered anymore, not how she looked or how frail she had become. This was the only time they had, this and nothing more.

"I'm filled with stones," she told him, and it was true. Often a patient knew more than her doctor, especially when the doctor didn't wish to know. When he brought her back to Lyon, her surgeon X-rayed her and discovered the cancer was in many other places, her lungs, her liver, her spine. This doctor was a younger man, and he thought because he was dealing with another doctor there was no need to mince words. "A few months at most," he said to Girard.

She was still his beloved wife, but she was already leaving him. Sometimes when she slept he could see an illumination, as if the light was seeping out of her. He felt worthless and helpless. The reason he became a doctor was to possess the ability to change a person's fate, as he'd seen his father do with his patients. He wanted to heal, not to idly sit at her bedside with cups of tea and stories to read to her. Even books, which he'd always loved, seemed like silly, unimportant things. There was only one thing that mattered now. The single moment they were in.

As a boy he had often gone to see patients with his father.

At first he had been made to sit outside, but as time went on he'd been allowed into sickrooms. By the age of fourteen he'd seen more than most medical students would see in their first year. He had observed his father as he cared for those who were dying with great kindness and compassion, and afterward they would go out walking the steep paths in the Ardèche, where the air was thin and clear.

We're shepherds, the older man had told his son. *All we can do is tend to them.*

The doctor couldn't believe he was losing his wife, and yet every day he had more of an understanding of what she meant to him. They'd been fortunate to have had many years when they hadn't thought about time at all, and had just greedily and happily lived their lives, having breakfast, walking in the woods, working, quarreling over inconsequential things, making love in their old bed, which had belonged to his parents. And then time was blown up altogether. Her disease was incurable, so he put away the clocks and removed his wristwatch, which he left in the night table drawer. They had six months, and then three months, and then, suddenly, a single day. A single day to look at her so that he would never forget the smallest details. The mole on her neck, the way she bit her lip when she was in pain, for she never complained.

Now, the Germans forced every Jewish woman to use the name Sarah after her own name on every official document. Girard was unwilling to let another woman die if he could save her. Each person who had slept in his barn, each he had given refuge, each Resistance worker he had helped, was for Sarah. It was always her, she was with him still, as if she were waiting in the kitchen, ready to embrace him as soon as he walked in the door.

CHAPTER TWENTY-THREE

HIDDEN

IZIEU, APRIL 1944

JULIEN ENTERED THE CHURCH TO SEE A FAMILIAR MAN IN THE pew nearest the altar. At last, his brother. He went to join Victor, and though it was a joyous occasion, they were cautious, unsure of who else might enter the building. They both looked straight ahead, as if they didn't know one another, but it was a great relief for each to know the other was alive.

"I'm sorry I wasn't there when they came for the old man," Victor said.

"I'm glad you weren't. How is Marianne?" Fortunately, she hadn't seen the horror of her father's death.

"She's strong. All the same, it's a terrible blow. He was a good man. It probably took ten of them to kill him. They didn't see you, I assume?"

How could they? He was out on a mountain, daydreaming, waiting for the heron. In some ways, it was an embarrassment to still be alive. "By the time I got back, it was too late."

"They shot him?" Victor asked.

"You really want to know?"

"No. Don't tell me. If I know I'll have to tell her." He gave his brother a look. "And she should never know."

Julien agreed. He wished he himself didn't know, that he hadn't had to cut the old man down and drag him out of the house and down the stairs. He didn't like to think of it even now.

"It should have been me," he told Victor.

"It wasn't your time. Be thankful. But the thing about saving yourself is that once you do, you have to live with it."

Victor had a car parked around the corner.

"Yours?" Julien asked.

"Sure. Once I stole it."

Victor explained that he could not bring Julien back to the farm. Marianne was often gone now, taking as many children across the border as possible, and Victor had plans as well, ones he couldn't speak about. He drove even faster than usual on the steep and winding roads, on his way to one of the last safe places for Jewish children. Maison d'Izieu, deep in the countryside, more than 50 miles from Lyon, had a beautiful view of the chain of mountains in the Rhône Valley, and it had recently been granted protection by the Vichy government. A huge stone château with an enormous fountain outside the front door, it was a safe haven where children could have a good night's sleep, see to their studies, and breathe in the clean country air. In the hilly garden there were vegetables and a small orchard. Perhaps those in residence could forget some of what they had seen. Perhaps not. By now, hundreds of children had been in châteaus such as this, and Izieu was one of many OSE sanctuaries that would go on to rescue thousands of Jewish children. OSE schools were allowed by law to keep children of Jewish parents who had been deported. There was a standard of who could be arrested and murdered and who was allowed to stay in France. If you were under sixteen you were allowed to live.

When they arrived, Victor got out of the car to embrace Julien. "Eventually we'll meet at the farm, but for now, just stay here," he said. "You'll be safe."

"What if I don't see you again?" Julien wanted to know.

"Then you'll know you were my favorite brother." Victor shrugged, a smile on his face. Despite everything that had happened, he still had hope for the future.

"Was I?"

Victor threw him a look. "Were you what?"

"Your favorite?"

"Idiot! Of course. And my only one."

They clapped each other on the back. "Don't worry so much," Victor advised. "You'll turn out to be older than me if you do."

Julien watched the car disappear down the mountain road.

I'm still here, he wished he could write to Lea. *I don't understand how or why anymore.*

The air was cool and fresh, and there was the scent of lily of the valley. Time was moving so quickly, perhaps all he had to do was hold on and wait and this would all be over and he would have his life back, or whatever was left of it.

If I don't see you again, I have faith that you knew me.

He thought he might be turned away from Izieu due to his

age; he was now sixteen, the age when all Jews were sent on the trains, but the teachers were interested when they heard his father had been a professor of mathematics and that he was quite advanced in that field. They told him they were in need of teachers, and invited him to stay.

The forty-four children at Izieu, aged three to sixteen, boys and girls, came out on the terrace to greet him. Most of them had lived in several places in the past few months, and all had been moved to the free zone by the OSE. Their parents were in hiding or had been detained or were members of the Resistance. So far the government had allowed the children to have the dream that they were French; the OSE had an agreement with the French police to overlook the châteaus, and all of the children had paperwork that allowed them to be at Izieu.

Julien shook hands with as many as he could on his way inside the front hall. He was especially pleased to find there was a dog on the grounds, a friendly wolfish creature named Lex, who took an immediate liking to Julien. A young man named Max, who had been a medical student in Paris and now taught biology to the older children, showed Julien around. He would be a counselor, living in a dormitory room and overseeing some of the younger boys. He would be in charge of math lessons for the younger boys in the morning, and teach more advanced lessons in geometry, logic, and number theory to the older, more talented students in the afternoon. A few high-spirited ten-year-olds rushed past to get their mail as Julien was on his tour. The children wrote home faithfully, and mail call was the most exciting event of the day. Those who received packages shared with those whose parents were unable to send treats. There was no discussion about where missing parents might be, for there was a deep belief that they would return. No one wished to crush the idea of that possibility.

Exhausted from his travels, Julien lay down on his metal bed and slept through dinner right into the night. Lex had been tracking rabbits on the lawn, but he soon found Julien and woke him by licking his hand. The hour was late, and Julien sprang from his bed, confused as to where he was. He had been dreaming about the garden of his parents' house. Lea was there, but she was disappearing in front of his eyes. *Don't let me go*, she'd said to him, and he'd been panic-stricken, not knowing what to do.

Julien watched the huddled forms of the boys who had crept into their beds so as not to wake him and now slept soundly. Gazing at them, he felt old. Three years had passed since he'd been in school himself, and fought with his closest school friend, and realized the world had changed before they knew what was happening.

"We teach them to live in the woods," Max told Julien the following day about the expeditions with the children. "It's fun and games, but someday they may need to survive on their own."

Julien was polite, but he kept to himself. At night he often sat on the large patio, thinking of his last days in Paris, doing his best to remember details of that time. Sitting in the kitchen watching Lea and Ava prepare Hardship Soup on the day they arrived, his mother in the garden watering the tomato plants, his father in his study, sure that there was logic to the universe, the night they'd buried the few treasures they had left and Lea had looked at him, knowing it took everything inside him not to embarrass himself and cry.

Max came out to find Julien alone, gazing at the dark mountains. When they began to speak of their former lives, it turned out they hadn't lived far from one another in Paris. Both had gone to the same school. Max was the same age as Victor and knew him from their classes.

"Not that he was the best student."

"When the school wouldn't let us continue any longer Victor said that at least we had one thing to be thankful for. Freedom."

They both laughed. School was once important to them, but now they saw Victor as wise beyond his years.

"Let's drink to Victor," Max suggested.

"How do we manage that?" Julien asked.

Max motioned to him, and together they headed to the rear of the property. There was a sweeping view of the lawn, and in the distance the inky outline of the mountains, formed by layers of volcanic rock. The roof and steps at the château were made of this same rough rock, and the top of the roof was fashioned from planks of stone, an old pagan tradition, set there for fertility and joy and happiness.

At the edge of the garden was a wooden shed where supplies were stored. It was here Max kept a hidden bottle of Cointreau. He grinned when he saw the surprise on Julien's face. "You never know when you'll need it for medicinal purposes," he said. Julien took a swallow, then the two handed the bottle back and forth. Julien found himself speaking of his despair. He felt lost, he admitted. Most mornings when he woke, he had no idea where he was and he sprang from his bed confused. He didn't mention the old man, or Lea, or his parents. "I wish I had lived in another time," he said gloomily.

"We can only think about this day, and do the same tomorrow," Max said. "It's the only way to get through it."

Julien nodded. Max was right. If he thought too much, he might give up, and he wasn't about to do that. The following day he began to teach math. The children were good students, and one boy in particular, a cheerful fellow named Teddy, who was not more than eight, could do complicated sums in his head. Julien had been much the same as a student; he'd had difficulty showing his work, for it was all done in his head, and one of his teachers had accused him of cheating before it was explained that he was the son of the professor and therefore a natural at mathematics. When Julien questioned Teddy, it turned out that his father was a mathematician and an engineer. The boy was proud of his father, and when he received a package of sweets, sent by his parents, members of the Resistance who were in hiding in Nice, he shared the gift with his friends and presented Julien with a bar of chocolate. It was the first Julien had tasted since leaving Paris, and he found he could only eat a few bites. It was too rich for him now.

In the afternoons, while the children played outside and worked in the garden, Julien graded their papers. In his free time, he would lie on his bed and read whatever books he could find in the library, preferring Kafka above all others. He'd told Lea to read *The Castle,* and they'd talked about the book for days. In Kafka's work, the world made no sense, fates were cast for no reason, men were beasts or insects or they were simply lost, wandering through corridors that led nowhere, beset by those who followed orders no matter how foolish those orders might be. This was not a world in which a person could trust anyone. He'd learned his lesson at the farm and planned never to be defenseless again. He slept with Monsieur Félix's knife under his pillow, and in the mornings, when he dressed, he kept it tucked into the waistband of his trousers. His philosophy had been formed by his experience. *Trust no one, make your own future, love with all your heart.*

An apple tree grew outside the window, and below that there was some shrubbery where birds nested. Dozens of swifts were nesting at this time of year, and Julien lay in bed in the early mornings, listening to the birds. The heron had never returned. Julien often felt a wave of despair at this hour, but when he closed his eyes and imagined Lea, he realized this was the way to survive. If he imagined her, he had not lost her.

He became used to his role at Izieu. The teaching itself was fine; and he was good at it, and in many ways it was a relief to be once again immersed in mathematics. He felt close to his father, and to the person he himself had been. Students who were refugees from Germany and Hungary seemed to prefer his class to all others, for the language of math created an equal playing field even for those who fumbled with their French. The couple that ran the school told him he was a natural teacher, and clearly math was his field. And yet, to Julien, making sense out of numbers seemed a false construct. Mathematics was a man-made puzzle that was tugged at and pulled apart until it fit inside a logical mind. Those mysteries his father had spoken of, grand endless numbers that explained the universe, problems thought to be worthy of spending a lifetime studying, seemed preposterous to him.

He wandered down the hall one morning after his own class and happened to glance into another classroom. The session was taught by one of the older women, a local teacher who gave her time freely. Today, she was having the children draw and paint. The creations were pictures to be sent to parents, even though they might never be heard from in return. Julien opened the door and gestured to the teacher that he would like to join them. She nodded as she continued instructing the children in her class, most of whom were between five and ten.

"You can show your parents what you are doing now, and what you hope to be doing in the future," the teacher suggested.

Julien stood behind Teddy, his best math student. The boy was coloring a drawing of himself, his mother, and his father. The three were in a rocket ship, all waving. Julien sat down at the table and took a piece of paper for himself.

"Will you send yours to your parents?" Teddy asked.

Julien drew the outlines of a face. "If I could, I would send it to my girlfriend."

Teddy wrinkled his nose with distaste. "You have a girl-friend?"

Julien laughed as he sketched. She was not yet a girlfriend, not truly, and yet she was more. In a few instants Lea's image surfaced as if he'd conjured her.

"She's pretty," the boy granted.

"Actually she's *much* prettier than this." Julien folded up the paper and slipped it into his pocket.

That evening he went to the garden and gathered onions to bring to the kitchen to boil so he could use the residue as a wash of color over his sketch. When he painted the wash on the portrait, Lea seemed alive, as if the white paper had turned to flesh. From then on he joined the class every day, greeting the teacher, Madame Rey, then slipping into the room. He always sat beside Teddy, who grinned whenever he saw his new friend. In time, the teacher had managed to get some watercolors. It was a pleasure and a joy to have real paints, rather than washes and inks made of berries or grass or onion skin. Julien created his memory of the garden of his parents' house, before his mother removed the roses and the peonies so she could replace the ornamental plants with vegetables for their meals. There was the tree he and Lea had climbed so they could be alone, and the gate she had walked through when Ava had rightly insisted they must leave, and the sky that was so bright on the day the police came for his family.

Madame Rey came to watch, standing behind him. She made him nervous, so he put down the brush. "I don't know what I'm doing," Julien said, feeling a fool.

"No, you're very good at this," the teacher encouraged him. "You're an artist."

"I told him he was," Teddy agreed. "I want him to make a painting for my mother." Teddy was at work on a colorful picture of himself with Lex, who often slept in the classrooms, stretched out beneath the desks.

"I'm sure your parents would prefer your own work," Madame told Teddy. She patted his head and moved on. She already knew they were dead. A note had been received a few weeks ago; both mother and father had been apprehended in Nice for their Resistance work, sent east by train to a camp where they were murdered.

It had been decided that life in the château was difficult enough and that children who had lost their parents would be spared the news until their circumstances were more settled. For some of the children the château felt much like summer camp, a city child's dream of the countryside, and in the brilliance of the afternoons they played on the lawn with dozens of new pals. At first, many of the city children were frightened by the countryside, and others could not speak the language and missed their parents terribly. But soon they settled in. The overnights in the woods were the greatest fun, especially for those who didn't realize such excursions constituted training in case they ever needed to flee into the mountains. Sabine Zlatin, a French Red Cross nurse who had begun the home, was traveling, already looking for a safer place to move the children, for no matter how remote the château was, the situation was growing more dangerous by the day, and old agreements were being overturned by the Nazi regime. These nights in the woods were lessons that were more important than any learned in a classroom. How to catch a fish in your hand, how to tell if water was fit to drink, how to hide beneath a pile of leaves so that it seemed no one was there.

One afternoon the children were brought to a nearby waterfall. It was good practice to hide behind the falls. Children under sixteen were still protected, but what were rules in the hands of the Germans? It was best to be prepared. The children played a game in which they must make themselves invisible when a whistle was blown. Then, when the whistle sounded again, they were to show themselves. Julien's duty was to make sure none of the children fell into the water as they pretended to be explorers who held the key to invisibility.

He had quickly become a great favorite at the school, especially with the boys. He wasn't quite old enough to be a strict teacher, and he seemed more like a brother. The sun was out on the day of their waterfall holiday; it was April already. His memories of his own childhood in Paris had begun to fade, although those few memories he retained often included his brother. Today Julien told the children a story about a time when he and Victor had jumped into the Seine, which their mother had strictly forbidden. It had been a broiling hot summer day, and they had dared each other, and then, before they'd thought it through, there they were, splashing water at one another. Their mother had been furious when she found their sopping wet clothes in the kitchen. But, as usual, Marianne had been their salvation. She'd vowed she'd done the washing and had forgotten the sodden pile of laundry on the floor.

Excited by Julien's tale of disobedience, the boys dared him to jump from the rocky ledge into the pool of cold green water at the base of the waterfall.

"Don't be a fool," Max advised. "You don't want to get pneumonia."

All the same, Julien grinned and took off his boots and his shirt. He challenged Max to make the dive with him, but unlike Victor, who always rose to a dare, Max was more cautious. He shook his head, sure of himself. "You go, and don't say I didn't warn you."

The children came round to clap and chant *Jump* as Julien prepared to leap. A hush fell when the blade he always carried clattered onto a rock. Julien gave it to Max for safekeeping.

"Seriously?" Max said. "A knife?"

The boys gathering around were thrilled to discover that Julien carried a weapon. He was becoming a hero, he could see it in their eyes. They thought he was something he wished to be, and so there was no backing down. It was nearly impossible to hear anything but the roar of the water, so if Max continued his warnings, Julien no longer had to listen. It was so beautiful in this woodland spot he could forget nearly everything he had witnessed. It seemed he was a boy again. Let the children see that anything was possible, that daring was the only thing that mattered, that no one could keep a person earthbound when he decided to dive off a cliff. Let them not know that he wept at night, that he hated himself for his good fortune when he thought of the fate of his parents and friends. Let them see him leap as if he were fearless.

The cold was a shock that went right through him, sharp and quick, right down to the bone. But it didn't matter. Not one bit. He felt alive. Everything stung, his heart, his lungs, his head. In the depths of the water there were bursts of light. It was so moving to see beauty all around him, the wash of blue, the yellow shadows, the dark green flicker of a fish. He felt as if he never wanted to rise, but his lungs told him otherwise. He splashed his way to the surface, gasping, having turned quite blue in the frigid pool.

Julien pulled himself out, drenched, and shivering, to see that his audience of boys was stupefied and impressed, eyes wide. He stood and bowed and there was a burst of wild applause.

Max shook his head and clapped Julien on the back. "You're a crazy man."

He might be, but he was also alive, something he hadn't felt in a long time. He enjoyed the acclaim, even though he was a hero for something as silly as leaping into a waterfall. All through dinner people were talking about him and there was a sense of cheer in the dining room. But that night Julien began to cough. He felt a tightness in his chest, as if he were still underwater.

"You've gotten yourself sick," Max told him gloomily. "This is what happens when you take stupid chances. I hate to say it, but I told you so."

Julien did feel a fool then, a boy in a man's body trying to astound a band of ten-year-olds. To ensure that he wouldn't infect the children, he was relegated to a lone room in the attic overlooking the orchard. He was sleeping there, with Lex on the floor beside his bed, on the morning of April 6. He indeed had pneumonia, and he still felt as though he were drowning, for there was liquid in his lungs. In his sleep the sound of mayhem filtered into a dream of being in a yellow field with Lea. When Lex began to bark, Julien was brought fully awake in a matter of seconds. He rose from bed, in a fever, but conscious enough to quickly take in what was transpiring. It was a little after nine. There were German army trucks pulled up around the large stone fountain in the courtyard. The children had already been ushered from the house and were being thrown into the trucks as if they were bales of hay. Their shouts were muffled, but some of their cries rose into the air like doves. The teachers had been dragged out as well and stood helpless on the steps. There was wailing from within the trucks, and adults were arguing with the officers. Before he could be stopped, the dog ran from the room growling, even though Julien called for him to stay.

Julien let out a string of curses, then went to the window

overlooking the garden, three floors down. He was torn. Should he try to stop the arrests? Run into the fray and do his best to grab the children? Or should he escape into the garden? If he confronted the soldiers, the best he could do was kill one or possibly two with his knife before he was killed himself. His rational mind prevailed. Perhaps it was panic, or self-preservation, or perhaps cowardice drove him. Later he would come to believe his reaction had been mere survival, not a decision made due to thought or logic but a gut response, pure instinct. *All you have to do is stay alive,* Lea had told him.

As he had risen from the pool below the waterfall, he now felt the need to run. He was shivering and wheezing as he pulled on his pants and shirt and shoved his feet into his boots. He could hear soldiers stalking through the first floor, going from room to room. He could hear his own breathing rattling against his ribs. He did not think at all. He was far beyond such things. He went to the window and leapt.

When he jumped his heart was beating so hard he thought it might break. He closed his eyes and imagined the waterfall, his head filled with noise, the pool below him. This time his fall was broken not by water but by thorny shrubbery. He was so stunned it took an instant before he could begin to disentangle himself from the branches. He might have broken his leg; he felt a shooting pain, which he was forced to ignore. He hadn't time to make a run for the woods—he could hear the soldiers coming around to search the garden, then he heard barking. Lex had slowed down the soldiers and given Julien time to race to the lower garden and duck into the shed where he and Max had shared a drink. He locked the door, fitting himself between some old panes of glass and a pile of metal bed frames.

Then he crouched there, breathing hard, sweating through his clothes. The soldiers in the yard were laughing, pissing on the garden where the children had spent hours planting beans and herbs and tomatoes. He thought of the boys who had gathered round him at the waterfall and he began to shake, rattling the bed frames, his movements uncontrolled. He reached for the hidden bottle of Cointreau and took several deep swallows. If he was to die, he might as well be drunk. He drank until he felt dizzy, then he lay quietly, melding into the wood, disappearing. It was possible to become invisible if you were desperate enough. He slowed his breathing, and his blood barely ran in his veins. He waited for the door of the shed to open, half expecting to be spied, but in fact he was well hidden, and after a while the garden grew quiet. He fell, facedown on the floor, his heavy lidded eyes closing. The trucks were already gone, down the winding road that overlooked the blue mountains. The great *milan royal* kites were soaring above the fields.

When Julien awoke, sober and aching, he pushed open the door of the shed and peered outside. Nothing but shadows. No soldiers anywhere. He was soon passing across the lawn, as if he was nothing more than a shadow himself. His teeth were chattering, for his fever had risen to 104. The dog's body was beneath the hedges. Julien stopped to see if perhaps he were still alive. The grass was slick with blood as he crouched down to stroke Lex, whose body was rigid and cold. Julien could barely breathe in the damp night air. A sharp pain shot up his leg. There was the faint trilling of frogs in the garden, but otherwise not a sound could be heard. It was over. The school had opened on April 10, 1943, and now, a year later, everyone was gone. The French government had made a new proclamation declaring it was a *kindness* to send children to be with their parents in Auschwitz. This despicable edict must now be enforced by the French police in collaboration with the Germans. The forty-two children currently in residence were taken to Montluc Prison. The following day all were sent to Auschwitz. Not a single one survived. Six adults, educators and nurses, were arrested and murdered as well.

He went round to the front door, dazed and limping. He did not understand why he was here and not with the others. He could not make sense of anything, certainly not his own life. Strewn about the fountain were toys and clothes, as if a storm had come through. Inside, the rooms were deserted and dark, yet he could see the white sheen of windblown piles of letters, not yet handed out to the children, scattered across the floor. In the art room the air was heavy. All of the chairs were neatly in a row. Julien left, taking only some colored pencils and the drawing Teddy had made to send to his parents. A rocket ship with three people on board, a father and mother and son. They were in a blue horizon surrounded by clouds. *I love you a million times* had been written across a sky strewn with *x*'s, a million kisses given.

CHAPTER TWENTY-FOUR

THE OTHER SIDE

LE CHAMBON-SUR-LIGNON, APRIL 1944

IN THE VILLAGE OF LE CHAMBON-SUR-LIGNON WINTER AL-
ways fell hard and stayed for a very long time. When spring came
it was a joyous event, a miracle fashioned of blue and green,
slowly unfolding, even when the snow was still in the shadows.
It was a small town with a train station and long, sloping streets
that were treacherous in winter. A deep forest of pines ringed
the village of gray stone houses and shops. As soon as there was
a snowfall, local boys took their sleds to the top of the hill and
sledded all the way to the bottom, red-faced, shouting with joy.
Now the sleds were put away; trees were greening and the birds
were returning in huge flocks that nearly blacked out the sky.
This was the heart of the Protestant stronghold, almost completely cut off from the rest of the world, a place known for tak-

ing in refugees, beginning with those who had been displaced in the Spanish Civil War. In houses and farms there were Jews hidden with families who had never before met someone of their faith.

The children's home where Ava worked was made of a group of stone buildings in town with a school at the end of a steep road. She had gone directly to the kitchen, knocked on the door, and told them the only payment she needed was a place for her and Lea to stay. She had become a master baker and had no fear when the cook gave her a test. There was a stone baker's house that hadn't been used for some time where the stove was heated by logs. Ava was made to collect wood and fire up the old stove. Then she must bake ten *tartes* out of paltry ingredients: four cups of flour, ten bitter apples, sixteen chestnuts, unroasted and plucked from nearby trees. The results were stupendous and mouthwatering. The cook herself ate half a *tarte* in one sitting. Lea attended the school, but they were placed in the home of a local couple, as were many Jews who were hidden in town until they could be given false identification or taken to Switzerland. In all, somewhere between three and five thousand souls were saved by the village. The house they were brought to wasn't far from the train station, on a lane off Rue Neuve.

All through the winter, they had shared an attic with an artist who'd also been taken in, a Jew from Belgium, Ahron Weitz. The couple who owned the house were Adele and Daniel. They owned a fabric shop and rarely spoke to their guests; the less they knew about one another the better in case the Milice, a paramilitary organization instituted by the Vichy regime to assist the Germans, came to question them. Ava often brought home baguettes from the school's oven to share with their hosts, along with fruit pastries, tart due to the lack of sugar, but delicious all the same. The attic was well hidden, up two flights of winding stairs, more than ten cubits above the earth, which meant that Ava had no power at that height. She could not see into the future or hear the voices of angels or speak the language of birds while in that place. When she took a withered apple in her hand it remained so. Magic escaped her, and even when she tried to listen in to Lea's dreams she was met by silence. She was almost an ordinary woman in this attic, one whose feet hurt at the end of the day, who was chilled by drafts and needed to pull on a sweater, who told Lea to sleep tight, and who, herself, slept for the first time, deeply and without dreams.

The painter was an older gentleman, a landscape artist, once quite famous in Belgium. Though known for his oil paintings, he now had little choice but to use watercolors, ones he made himself from crushed plants and berries mixed with a bit of oil in a cooking pot. He had been an animated, successful, rather wealthy man. His situation had so radically changed that he did not even recognize himself when he walked past a mirror. He was in his mid-sixties, but his back had been broken when a gang of Nazi sympathizers set upon him one day as he left his studio, and he now walked with a limp. What little hair he had had turned white when his son was sent to a death camp. He wasn't sure if he had a reason to live, but some fellow artists had helped in his escape, and he felt he must stay alive in a show of gratitude. All of his paintings that had been left behind in his studio in Brussels had been stolen or burned. He knew he would not be remembered, not his work or his name, and that freed him to now do as he pleased. The attic walls were filled with small landscapes, luminous images painted in mysterious hues on plain white paper. A sky could be vermilion or crimson or indigo, an unexpected choice, yet true to nature.

The painter offered to give Lea his small bed, but she insisted she would be comfortable on the floor along with Ava. They were quiet, and didn't bother one another, and soon enough became used to each other. Ava and Lea knew Monsieur Weitz woke up at six and made tea on the hot plate set on a bureau where they could cook, and he knew they left for the school by seven. They had dinner together, often leftovers Ava brought home from the school's kitchen. The winter had passed in a dream, and before they knew it spring had arrived; the fields were greening and wild cabbages grew up through the frozen ground. There was soon mud everywhere, and people wore clogs or boots. They'd worn winter coats one day and shirt-sleeves the next. It was the time of year when the birds began to return, clouds of greenfinches and goldfinches, pigeons and turtledoves and swifts. Each day Ava looked out with a hand over her eyes, waiting for the heron. She walked in the mountains that surrounded the village in the evenings. At last she saw him, in the distance, at dusk. Though it was April, there were still patches of snow in the forest, yet he had come back to her, returning a month before most of his kind would begin to leave their southern homes. Ava threw her arms around him and felt his beating heart against her chest. He told her where he had been, to beaches where the sand was black, where the heat turned the sun red, and the shells were as big as a human hand. Everywhere he went, he dreamed of dancing with her in the grass. They did so now, as if enchanted, as if no other time or place existed.

At last she noticed the message attached to his leg. He had

carried it through the winter, to all of those faraway places. Lately, Ava had been trying to make time stop, but it was impossible to do, even for the angels. The border was a few days' hike away, yet she had remained here, hidden in the attic. All because of time. When the locket had opened, she had seen the message; she knew what her fate was to be once she brought Lea to safety. And so she had stayed in this village, in this attic. She told herself it was because it was winter, it was because she was waiting for the heron, but now he was here, and she still wanted to stay. She had lived too long, and as golems were said to do, she had begun to make her own decisions. She wanted to change her fate.

She knew the message the heron carried was for Lea, but she took it anyway. It was slick with salt and sand, diverted by the heron's migration. Ava unfolded the paper to find the hand-drawn blue map that led to Beehive House. She began to weep, and the heron held his wings around her. The map would lead her closer to the end of her existence. She was made to fulfill her obligation to Hanni, but how could she let go of this world?

She told the heron he must hide, so she alone could see him, then she folded the map into her pocket. She brought Julien's message to the attic, but rather than deliver it to its rightful owner, she hid it in a bureau drawer.

Once the weather was fine, Weitz ventured into the fields on Sundays to paint out in the air. Lea often accompanied him, after promising Ava they would not go too far. On their painting days it felt to Lea that Julien was with them. She said his name sometimes as they walked along, just to hear the way it sounded in the deep forest. She and Weitz took their lunch at the edge of the woods, usually an apple or a slice of bread cut from the loaf Ava had sent along. Then Weitz painted, and Lea lay in the grass in the sun, one hand thrown over her eyes. Through the weeks the two had grown close. People said the war would soon be ending, that they would soon be safe, and that crossing the border was easier with fewer guards to protect the crossings. Lea often thought about what her mother had commanded her to do. *All things must end.*

"Would you kill someone if you had to?" she asked the old man one Sunday.

He glanced at her, before returning to his painting. It was the time of year when huge migrations of birds were crossing over the mountains from the south. "What wrong did this person I'm to murder do to me?" he asked. "Did they kill my son?"

Lea turned to him, propping herself up on one elbow to study the old man. She should probably not have asked his opinion. He was painting the clouds from the inside out.

"Did they kill my wife?" he asked.

"You don't know the reason," Lea admitted. "You are just to do as you're told."

"Then I'd be a fool or a lunatic," Weitz said.

Or simply a girl honoring her mother.

"Would you do it if I asked you?" she wanted to know.

He glanced at her again. Talking about murder was a reasonable conversation in the world in which they lived.

"No," he said.

Lea sat up. The sunlight was thin, perhaps that was why she shivered so. She wished she were far away from here, in some far-flung land, on some hot beach where the sand was like sugar.

Ava said the heron went there when the weather changed; that he couldn't last through winter. So far he hadn't returned with a message from Julien, and she had no way to ask him the sorts of questions she now asked Weitz.

"What if your son asked you to do it?"

Weitz was finished for the day, out of precious homemade paint. He would mix more in the morning from the berries he'd had Lea gather earlier in the day. He began to pack up the brushes he had smuggled out of Belgium, his canvas seat, and what was left of their lunch. He couldn't yet speak to answer Lea's question. His son had been dragged off the street. He'd been a promising young artist who had joined the underground in 1941, when Flemish fascist collaborators burned down the house of the chief rabbi in Antwerp. Twenty-five thousand Belgian Jews were taken onto the trains the following year, Weitz's son among them. There would be no one to remember him or his art once Weitz was gone.

They walked side by side through the dusk. They always waited for this hour to return to the house, the time when they could slip through shadows on the steep streets of the village. There was some talk of Ava being Lea's cousin, but on one of their outings Lea had said she had no family left. Weitz felt his heart go out to her. If she asked this question she must have her reasons.

"Yes," he admitted. "I would do it."

Lea did her best not to cry, and Weitz did his best not to notice her distress.

"What color is the sky?" he asked her as they walked on, past the train station, past the town hall, past the shuttered shops. She had slowed her pace to suit his limp.

275

"Black," she answered with certainty. "With stars."

"So people say," Weitz said sadly. Dozens of colors were there, a hundred perhaps for those who could see underneath the darkness. "You should look more carefully." When they reached the house, Weitz stood outside for a while longer before he went in to paint the real colors of the night.

CHAPTER TWENTY-FIVE

THE LABYRINTH

IZIEU, APRIL 1944

THE MILICE SEARCHED EVERY HOUSE IN THE VILLAGES NEAR Izieu, rounding up Jews, refugees, and Resistance members. When they found Julien in a shed, he was deeply asleep, exhausted and freezing. He'd broken in and had been living on jars of fruit preserves that had long ago been stored on the shelves. A milicien kicked him in his injured leg, still badly bruised. Roughly awakened, he let out a shout as he rose up from a pile of hay where he'd fallen into a deep, dreamless sleep. He didn't argue when he was told to follow the policeman, but instead merely held up his hands and did as he was told, his mind racing. He had not survived Izieu to be picked up and led away like a mule.

He was marched out to the road, where he was stunned to

see a line of other prisoners, all of whom had been forced to drop their pants so the police could tell whether or not they had been circumcised. Those who had been marked as Jews were sent to one line, those in the French Resistance to another. Only a few of the men in line bothered to look when Julien showed himself, but the embarrassment he suffered made him seethe with fury. With a gesture, one of the officers sent him to the longer line.

"What difference does it make if we're in one line or the other?" Julien asked the fellow in front of him. They were all going to Montluc Prison in Lyon after all, that notorious place where the beast in charge was known to torture people for days.

"Their line is sent to a forced labor camp when they leave the prison, we go to a death camp."

"We should run," Julien said firmly.

His companion glared at him as though he was an utter fool as he muttered under his breath. "Don't draw attention to yourself. They'd be happy to beat you if you do."

But Julien was already devising a plan. His studies with his father had made him into an individual who could solve abstract problems, and his current situation was such a problem. He ignored his emotions and refused to give in to the panic that had set in. A man in their line was silently crying. Julien looked away from him and counted odd numbers to calm himself. The sky was gray, filled with mottled clouds. April could feel like winter when the wind came up, as it did now. After a while, Julien was able to think clearly. When he narrowed his eyes he saw the slit in the universe through which light shone through the darkness. He again thought of his father's theory of how the night sky could be broken into segments. Then he took it a step farther. Everything could be divided into pieces, a street, an hour, a life, a death march.

Close your eyes and see, his father had always told him at the Château de Villandry. A blindfold never hindered him. He could feel the space around him, the objects near and far. It took practice, but after a while there was never a time when he couldn't find his way.

He would treat this escape as if he were caught in another maze. Everything he had ever learned from his father as he sat in his study, annoyed and disinterested, came back to him. If he looked at his current situation as a mathematical equation, taking into account that there were fifteen men and boys in one line, twelve in the other, it was clear that it was best to be at the end of the longer line, an uneven number the police might fail to factor into their accounts. If nothing more, being last gave Julien more time to think of how to escape, and it made his presence less noticeable.

They walked all that day, without food or water or protection from the elements. In the afternoon it rained buckets and they slogged through a field where the mud was past their ankles. Julien continued to think of the maze. He closed his eyes as they walked. He saw the world inside of his head, at the backs of his eyes, in a lace of logic where everything was made up of numbers and everything made sense.

It was dusk when they reached a village. The night was cold and the prisoners were shivering. By then Julien's clothes were soaked from the rain, and mud-splattered, and his bad leg was throbbing. Still, he was focused. Time was growing short. The lines of men would be herded into the town hall ahead of them and locked inside for the night. He was lagging behind by now, using his leg as an excuse, when a police officer came to shout at him.

"Keep up," the milicien demanded.

"Of course." Julien was warily polite. "No problem."

It was dark and therefore difficult for anyone to see when he once again slowed his pace. As they entered the village, Julien leaned down to scoop up a handful of rocks. It was a trick often used when navigating a maze. He dropped the rocks as they walked on, marking the path so that he could retrace it or avoid it, depending on what was best in order to escape. When they reached the center of the village, tiny cobbled streets led out in all directions, like the petals of a flower. Julien grinned and felt his heart lift. The village was clearly a maze, and that was something he could manage. He mustn't overthink, he had to act quickly and leap into the labyrinth as if throwing himself into a well. He made certain to fall back on his heels as soon as the soldiers threw open the doors to the town hall. Right then, without taking a breath, he dashed into the closest alley. It was narrow in the alleyway, and pitch black, so he used another trick of running a maze; he kept his right hand on the walls of the buildings to lead him forward. He heard a shout behind him and a shot fired, but he continued to navigate the alleyway, faster now, as fast as he could go, as if his leg was perfect and no longer throbbed with pain.

The village was circular; many of these mountain villages were built to surround a château, in this case one built in the twelfth century. Julien dodged off as fast as he could. He felt a surge of nerves as he heard more shots. To calm himself, he imagined his father waiting for him. He had always been there at the end of the maze in the gardens at the Château de Villandry, where he'd been blindfolded, forging on when he heard his father call his name.

Finally, he came to the last street in the village. He slipped past a tumbledown house, then jumped over a low stone wall. His leg didn't matter. He was unwilling to think about it or feel any pain. He was flying now. He had left the village of stones, where everything was made of the local gray granite, all of the houses, and the stairs that led from one tiny street to another, the maze he had been through. He had not come upon a single stone that he had left to mark his path into the village. Here was the solution to his problem right in front of him. There was a stretch of woods, and he dove into the trees in the pitch black, cutting his face and hands on some thorny branches, and not giving a damn. He was glad there was no moon. That was a bit of luck. He ran even though breathing was coming so hard it hurt his chest. The forest was a maze as well, but he saw the North Star and knew to follow it and all the while he did, he heard his father call his name.

When he stumbled upon a stream, he stripped off his clothes and dove in, grateful to wash away the mud that coated him and gulp mouthfuls of water. He hadn't had anything to drink all day and his thirst had taken a toll. Now he was truly shaking, and the panic that had disappeared when he was so focused returned. He thought of the man in line who had been crying. If anyone took a count and discovered he was missing, all the men would be treated even more harshly. Either way, their journey would end at Montluc Prison, while he was here, gulping down cold mountain water, shivering so badly his bones hurt. He had escaped the arrests in Paris, and at Izieu, and now he was free again. Why was it that he hated himself for being so? He was pricked by guilt. He floated in the stream though the water was freezing cold, made of melting snow. He must be a monster. Why else would he still be alive? Or was it his promise?

Stay alive, Lea had told him. He heard that, too. Her voice was with him, inside his head. Now here he was, alive as could be, his leg throbbing, pulling his filthy clothes back over his wet body, his posture bent as he shivered so violently he could hardly stand up straight.

In the pitch dark he made out the form of a small stone farmhouse. There were clothes hanging on the line, and he grabbed a shirt and trousers. Both too big. He had lost weight, but what was left of him was all muscle and energy. His heart was pounding. He wondered if it would ever beat in a natural rhythm again. In the barn there were some boots, and he took those as well. He offered a silent apology to those he had stolen from as he took four eggs from the chicken coop; he broke them into his mouth and ate them raw. Eating those eggs, he knew he was alive.

He slept in the woods, in a ditch near a river. He curled up and rested for a few hours, and when he woke the sky seemed too big. He watched the pink turn to a deep blue violet and was grateful that he had lived to see it. The fields were filled with the yellow field flowers called *genêts*. All at once, he remembered things he thought he had forgotten. His brother teaching him to play soccer. His mother at the table on Friday night, lighting the candles. The garden as it was, before they tore out the flowers to plant vegetables. Marianne laughing as they helped her hang laundry on a windy day. Lea sitting on a bench in the hallway, her gaze meeting his. But more than anything, he remembered his father, who had studied how the universe was expanding, intent on statistical analysis to measure the speed of distant galaxies receding from Earth. The professor had believed in the miracle of an ever-expanding universe, but in the end, he felt his studies were no longer useful, for the rational order he found in mathematics and in the natural world was nowhere to be seen in the world all around them. If Julien could see him now, if his father could walk through these woods in his good suit to lie down beside his son in the grass, if he could step out of the grave in Auschwitz that he shared with thousands of others, if he came to Julien now, Julien would have told him that mathematics had saved him. When he'd heard the professor in his study, approaching the mysteries of the universe, he would pause outside his door. He had always feared disappointing him, but he thought his father might be proud of him. He had loved his father and had been in awe of him, but he had never felt as close to him as he did right now. *You are the man I admired most of all*, Julien would say to him if he could, if they were lying side by side watching the universe expand all around them.

CHAPTER TWENTY-SIX

THE RED SHOES

HAUTE-LOIRE, SUMMER 1944

THEY DROVE ACROSS THE MOUNTAINS, LEAVING THE CAR HID-
den under branches a few miles from their target, using the doctor's compass to aid them when they hiked to a wooded hillside
where they were protected from sight, yet could still see the
house and the gardens. Everything was in bloom, and the yellow fields of *genêts* were dazzling, but in front of them everything
was dark, a black cloud of chaos. The end of the war would soon
be upon them, and it was their duty to dispose of the evil that
continued to send men and women and children to their deaths,
more and more all the time, as if the Nazi regime was trying to
beat the clock that was running down by murdering as many as
possible.

Victor and Ettie had come here several times before to observe the habits of their target, a captain in the Milice who resided in a beautiful château he had appropriated. He was a thief and a monster and a beast, but he looked like a small, ordinary man with pale blue eyes. It was said that no one was allowed to utter the name of the rightful owner of the house in the captain's presence; he was simply called The Jew, or sometimes The Rich Jew. The previous resident's family had lived in the area for hundreds of years, and Dr. Girard had known them well, and had seen them through several illnesses; he had brought their children into the world.

There was no one to care for the garden, and by now most of the flowering trees were dead. Many plants had been crushed by soldiers who didn't bother to use the gravel paths, but walked through the flower beds instead. Nothing mattered here. There was blood in the soil, and teeth in the ground. Resistance members were brought here and tortured beside the fountain, in which there was no longer water, only black mud. The captain now in residence was a fierce anti-Semite, a ruthless local citizen who had profited greatly from his association with the Germans. Ettie and Victor had kept his identity secret from the doctor, but had Girard known, he would have been pleased by the choice.

The Jewish family who had lived in the house had been taken in for questioning two years earlier, had been sent immediately to Drancy, then to an extermination camp in the East. Between that time and 1944, more than 75,000 Jews had been deported from France to killing camps. The captain himself had been the one to have this family arrested, for he had grown up in the village and had greatly admired their house. As far as he was concerned, the Jews had always thought they were above the law, better than everyone else, for the husband was a lawyer and the wife came from a wealthy family. Her hair had shone black as she walked through the village in a pale cream-colored coat, and he had always watched her, wanting to have her and wanting to destroy her. Now he had done both.

On the first night the captain resided at the château, he began to burn the books in the library. There were so many, it took three full days to complete the task, and soldiers had to take over the job. There were sparks floating in the air all that week and people in the village complained of cinders flying into their eyes. The air stank; the sky was black. Everything that had belonged to the family now belonged to the captain. He wore the Jew's signet ring on his finger. He slept on his sheets. He looked through the bureau containing the wife's undergarments and spilled his seed on the silk and lace.

To show his loyalty to the Nazi regime, he continued to do his best to find hidden Jews, and had been honored by the Vichy government for his success in this matter. Several families had been discovered in safe houses, then sent east, with their French helpers arrested and taken to Montluc Prison. Anyone who had ever crossed him, or who feared him, had left the village, and fathers had begun to lock their daughters up at night in cellars and attics, hiding the girls under the floorboards or in the woods, hoping this beast would never catch sight of them.

Ettie and Victor kept watch, using the doctor's binoculars, trying to chart a way to get to the captain. The house was too protected for them to make a move against him here. There were members of the Milice stationed at the front and back exits; guards roamed the garden with little to do, idly destroying anything nearby, breaking the branches off the trees, using stone walls for target practice, pissing in the herb garden, where there had once been rosemary plants as big as the children who had lived here, boys of three and five, who had often been sent out for sprigs of herbs while their mother was cooking dinner. These children had been murdered in a camp in Poland, but one of the policemen on guard often thought he saw two little boys crouched down in reedy stalks of what was left of the rosemary. In time, he asked to be sent elsewhere, anywhere else would do, but even then, when he was stationed outside the prison, he heard crying whenever the wind picked up.

Each day, women were brought here for the captain's use. They were women from the village who had no choice but to do as they were told when the miliciens came to their doors. Some were married, and would never tell their husbands, for fear their husbands would come to avenge them and be murdered here in this garden, where there was now a pile of bones. One hot afternoon a woman left her son when she went in, and the boy sat by the door, unnoticed and uncared for. Ettie could barely sit still. She wondered how Queen Esther had restrained herself, dressed in her silken clothes in the harem where she was kept, one among many wives, biding her time, knowing that her people were about to be sacrificed.

"The more we wait, the more damage he does," she seethed.

"We're here to study him, nothing more. For now."

The goal was to rid the earth of him, but for that they needed patience. Still, that day neither of them spoke much, and the boy was still there on the step when Victor and Ettie left to make their way to the hidden car. They walked through the dark across fields of what was called the Plateau, the huge expanse of flat land between the mountain ranges. It was a beautiful summer night.

"You're sure you're ready for what we will do?" Victor asked, worried by how upset Ettie was.

"Are you sure you are?" Ettie responded, her tone dark.

Victor was quick to take offense. "Meaning?"

She wasn't questioning his courage, rather his willingness to throw away his life. "You probably have something to live for. Some woman."

Victor shrugged, but of course, it was true.

"I have no one," Ettie told him. "Therefore I'm more ready."

Victor grinned then. Ettie amused him. She liked to win every argument, and was especially scrappy with men, perhaps to prove she could be fiercer and more willing to do battle. Still, Victor was hesitant to bring her into a mission where the object was murder. And now he cautiously let her know that there might be certain circumstances where she would have to allow the captain to do as he liked.

"You think I didn't understand why my hair was cut? Why I was given beautiful clothes to wear? I know I'm not pretty, but you made me so. I understand I may have to draw him to us. So now, go ahead, make me hate him."

"You hate him already," Victor said.

"I want to hate him more."

So he told her more of what he knew, that their target liked torture as much as he loathed Jews.

"How so?"

The captain had ingratiated himself with the Nazi commanders, including the commander and chief of the secret police, Klaus Barbie, who had sent two thousand five hundred Jews to extermination camps and had executed eight hundred others, personally torturing and murdering them. When Jews were picked up and taken to the prison in Lyon, Barbie allowed the captain to stand outside their cells, built for two, but often packed with fifty people or more, men, women, and children, so that he could delight in their misery. The captain was known to carry a Star of David made from the flesh of a Jew in his pocket, a gift from Barbie.

Ettie shot Victor a look of disbelief.

"What?" he said. "You don't believe in evil?"

"Oh, I do. But now you've done your job and I hate him more. That will help."

She thought of her sister holding her hand as they leapt from the train, her face focused on Ettie with absolute trust. How could her beautiful sister exist in the same world as this monster they were to kill? There in the woods, Ettie began to recite a section of the Amidah, the standing prayer that is to be recited three times a day by Orthodox men. It was the twelfth benediction, which deals with the fight against enemies. *May all evil be destroyed in an instant.*

"May you be abundantly manifest as one who breaks enemies and humbles deliberate sinners," Ettie recited.

"You're Orthodox," Victor said, surprised. He himself had not been bar mitzvah and had never learned Hebrew.

"Not anymore. By now, I've offended God in every way possible. I'm amazed I'm not dead already."

Victor grinned. "What could a girl like you do that would be so terrible?"

She understood that he really didn't know her at all. He regarded her as a slight girl that he was instructing in the art of rebellion and murder, and had no idea of what she might be capable of. She had brought inanimate matter to life, she had forsaken her faith and her family, she had lost her sister, she had changed her name, she was willing to give up everything to rid the earth of a monster. When she didn't answer, Victor was wise enough to let it go. He, too, had committed acts he never wished to speak of. The bombings had taken lives, some by accident, and he could not put back together that which had been destroyed, nor would he have wanted to, for he had missions that must be completed for the greater good, for the good of all. He would not speak of such things, just as Ettie would not speak of the golem she had created, the affront to God that she had to bear. Had her father known what she'd done, he would have wept and torn out his hair. He would never have spoken to her again.

Now, riding through the dark, she wondered what had happened to the creature who had no choice but to do as she was commanded. She wondered if she should have kept the golem so that her duty was to watch over not one woman's daughter but all children: the brothers who crouched down in the rosemary before they were arrested, the boy left weeping at the door while his mother was brought to the captain's bedroom, the children separated from their parents who had been sent on the trains to the East. Perhaps she should have created a hundred golems, perhaps a thousand, an army to fight on their behalf, each one stronger than a hundred horsemen, all with the mission of saving their people. Perhaps her father regretted the very same thing, when it was already too late, when he was on the train and a sin such as the one she was responsible for no longer mattered.

Victor delivered Ettie to the doctor's house, assuring her that he would be back as soon as he had the materials he needed. She was surprised to feel a wave of sadness about his departure; she had come to think of him as a brother.

"If anything happens, what would you miss most in this world?" she asked.

"Nothing will happen." His expression was set. Doubt was something neither of them could afford.

"You must have it. The one thing you live for."

He flushed and looked annoyed. "You want me to look like a fool," he said.

"No, not at all. I don't know the answer for myself. But you're different than I am. Surely there must be something."

She looked so vulnerable in the dark, her nervous, chalky face flecked with freckles, so unlike her usual fierce self. Because of this Victor was moved to tell her the truth, whether or not he seemed a fool.

"Marianne," he answered. "Nothing else matters."

People said love was the antidote to hate, that it could mend what was most broken, and give hope in the most hopeless of times. That time was now. They had watched the captain enough to know that on Friday nights he went to the café in town to look for women and girls. This was why fathers hid their daughters and wives, why women no longer walked through the streets. But Ettie would be waiting for him. She would be wearing the red shoes.

She thought over her situation, and by the following day she'd come to a decision. She had never been with a man, and if things went wrong, she didn't wish the captain to be the first man who touched her. She went to Dr. Girard's study, where he was reading a book and having a glass of wine, doing his best not to think about the past, the same routine he had every night, disrupted only by chess games with Ettie. When he saw Ettie, he assumed she had come for a game, but she was barefoot and her expression was troubled. He knew her mission with Victor was approaching, and he wondered if she was backing out.

"Have you come for chess?" he asked.

In her old life, Ettie would not have been allowed to be alone in the same room with a man who was not a member of her family, but now she went to him, and because it was so difficult to ask for what she wanted, she came to sit on his lap. He was startled and confused by her unexpected action.

"There, there," he said as if she were a girl, perhaps one of his patients who feared being ill. "You're not getting frightened, are you? You have to be sure, Ettie. If this isn't for you, speak up now before you endanger yourself and the others."

"That isn't the problem. I want to be with you before I go," she told the doctor.

The doctor drew her off his lap, depositing her on the chair across from him. He was flattered, but not interested. He had not been with a woman since Sarah's death, and he didn't intend to be with one again. "Let's play chess instead," he suggested patiently, as if speaking to a child.

Ettie stood up and unbuttoned her dress. It was an ill-fitting frock, unlike any of the clothes in his wife's closet. Girard thought perhaps it had belonged to the housekeeper.

Ettie could only coax him by telling him the truth. "The first one can't be him," she explained.

Dr. Girard shook his head. "It's wrong."

"No it isn't," Ettie insisted. "It has to be you. I trust you."

He poured them both a glass of wine, then took the chessboard and placed it on the table between them. "Whoever wins decides."

He assumed there was no chance of his losing, but she was better than he thought, and, he supposed, he had been a good teacher. Ettie was a smart girl, smart enough to win.

They went upstairs, not to his room—he could not have taken her to the bed he had shared with his wife—but to a guest chamber where friends from Paris had often stayed in the time when people could travel freely. Many of their past visitors were already dead. No friends had visited for many years. Now the only guests he had stayed in the barn.

Ettie removed her dress and undergarments and folded them onto a chair, then slipped into bed. The doctor hesitated, watching her with concern. He noticed the scar on her arm in the shape of a letter.

"It's in memory of my sister," Ettie said when she caught him staring.

Girard thought this might be madness, for the two of them to be in this bedroom together; surely it was unethical. But when she motioned to him to join her, she looked fragile, and he didn't know which would wound her more, responding to her suggestion or turning away. He took off his jacket and folded it onto a chair, then undressed and sat on the edge of the bed. He ran his hand over her hair.

"Don't treat me as if I were your patient," Ettie scolded, taking offense. She leaned up to kiss him, and he kissed her in return. "That's better," she said.

He folded himself into bed with her, and they both forgot who they were and what had brought them together. But Ettie didn't forget that he was a kind, decent man, and he didn't forget she was a girl of twenty who might not live to be twenty-one. Because of this what transpired between them was something they hadn't expected, it was almost as if they had fallen in love in a world where anything could happen and nothing was impossible.

CHAPTER TWENTY-SEVEN

BEEHIVE HOUSE

HAUTE-LOIRE, JULY 1944

MARIANNE CAME FROM THE BORDER WITH BRAMBLES threaded through her hair. It was hot, with the white sun beating down on the hillsides. She was exhausted and looking forward to sleeping in her own bed after weeks in the woods. More children than ever were being taken over the border. Everyone knew the war would soon be ending, still there would be chaos for some time. Economies had been ruined; neighbors had turned against neighbors. The Royal Air Force had already dropped tons of bombs on Berlin. In June, Allied forces heavily bombed targets in France, invading Normandy on June sixth. Most of the Nazi efforts were now on the Russian front, and German soldiers in France were taking the opportunity to run away, doing their best to escape before their defeat. Local people often saw them in the woods, lost and panicked, willing to shoot anyone who came near. There were still German soldiers who did their best to find the last of the hidden Jews or members of the Resistance as they fled. They left bodies on doorsteps in the villages they passed through and mass graves in the woods. Every now and then a crow would soar past with a gold ring or coat button in its beak, a shiny souvenir of murder.

Marianne was thinking of Victor, as she so often did. She had to stop herself, or she would think of nothing else. She'd taken three young children across a few nights earlier, along with a woman of twenty, who was without any family or friends and still wept for her mother and father at night. Crossings were a bit easier in some sections, for the Italian guards at the border often looked the other way throughout the war; they were far from home, and many had no idea what they were fighting for. When they shot at fleeing figures, they had often shot into the air. The Nazis had recently withdrawn from Sicily, and Italy would surrender to the Allies in September.

She remembered every child she had brought across, not their names, which were often false anyway, but their faces. They would cross the Wolf's Plain in the dark, holding hands, shivering no matter the weather. She always told them they were not to stop for any reason. Even if their hands stung and bled when they climbed over the barbed wire, even if a shot was fired. *Think of a cup of hot chocolate waiting for you,* she would tell them. *And a very warm soft bed. Think of dinner on the table, and new shoes. Think forward, not back.*

She did her best to think forward as well. She was convinced that what had happened between herself and Victor was meant to be, and everything she had ever done had led her to him. But who could depend on fate? She had loved him while she worked in his parents' house, first as a sister or friend might, and then in the months before she'd left as something much more. It had happened slowly, and then, shockingly, she knew she had fallen in love with him. Perhaps that was part of the reason she'd gone without any goodbyes. Back then, Victor was nearly eighteen and she was twenty-three and the five years that separated them was not so much. Although lately, when she looked in a mirror, she saw that she looked older than her age; she was weathered, her skin damaged from so much time spent outside, especially in winter. Not that it mattered. She paid little attention to her looks, simply braiding her hair or piling it atop her head to keep it out of the way. She had never worn lipstick or mascara or high heels, though in Paris she had sometimes envied the women who did, but it was not in her nature to do so. She had been born plain and had remained that way. Yet Victor had told her she was the most beautiful woman in the world. She had laughed, but she saw in his eyes that he believed this, and later, when they were apart, she'd wept, grateful to know he thought so.

Her father, a traditional, old-fashioned man, would not have been happy to know she slept with Victor here in his house, and that she did so with fierce abandon, even though they were unmarried. There was never enough time. She could count how often they had been together, twelve times, that was all. But twelve occasions could be a world.

It was strange to be at Beehive House now that her father was gone, and even stranger when she was here with Victor, and stranger still to be so happy whenever she was with him. In this terrible time they had managed to find joy. They had made a pact that each would live life without fearing for the other while they were in the Resistance; each had their work to do, and that meant being away from the farm and one another. Yet secretly Marianne worried. Victor was young and brash and fearless, an unpredictable combination.

Still, she would never tell him how to live his life. She hadn't when he was a boy, and she wasn't about to do so now. What they both did was dangerous, but living was dangerous. Her father had been at his own farm, taking care of his bees, breathing in the blue air, when they'd come to murder him. All Marianne could do was live her life, and let Victor live his.

She took note that in her absence, the flowers in the wreath she had left on her father's grave had dried into husks that had blown away in the wind. She decided she would spend the following day working on a new one. The fields were rife with clouds of Queen Anne's lace, which would make a billowy wreath. Her father had always said there were people who saw Queen Anne's lace as a weed, and those who considered it a flower, and he belonged to the latter group.

If you think it's beautiful, it is, he had told her.

She smiled to think the same was true of her. She was both plain and beautiful, a simple woman with a complicated heart. Marianne went into the barn to leave her boots. They were caked with mud and she never wore them inside the house. Victor was already at the farm and he'd caught sight of her through the window. He came out to the barn, shouting her name, delighted to see her.

He had been to Lyon and gathered the material he needed, all in a rucksack kept in the storm cellar a few yards from the house, a safe place where Marianne stored preserves and canned goods. He'd been at the farm for two days, and had seen to all her chores. He was no longer the boy from Paris, but was instead a bearded man dressed in the rough clothing of a farmer who liked to get his hands dirty and forget about the war for a few days.

Once they were in the barn together, Victor pulled the old door shut. He took her in his arms and loved her fiercely. He was so young, and he wanted her so. They realized Bluebell was watching their lovemaking and they laughed as Victor chased the goat away. When they were through, and had pulled on the clothes they'd cast into the straw, Victor went off through the field to see to the beehives. He did so in honor of Monsieur Félix, who would not have wanted the bees to go uncared for. It was a perfect evening, and Marianne stood in the doorway of the barn, picking bits of straw from her hair. *Go forward*, she told herself. *Let yourself love him completely no matter where it leads.*

Victor was beside the beehive when he noticed the lupines blooming. Marianne's favorite flower. He picked a handful, and yellow pollen dusted his hands. He turned to wave the bunch of flowers in the air. When he called to Marianne a bee flew into his mouth. A single sting inside a person's throat could kill him in an instant. Victor seemed to be choking, his arms waving above his head. Marianne ran to him, terrified. She pounded him on the back, and thankfully the bee flew out. They watched it rise into the sky, relieved and somewhat mystified. Was this what fate was? An instant in which you could lose everything or walk away unscathed? Victor let out a joyful shout, as if he was indestructible, but Marianne ran to the house to cry. People were so breakable and so easy to lose, especially now.

Victor came to her and kissed her, asking if his kisses tasted sweeter now that he'd had a honeybee in his mouth. He made a joke of it, but death had been close, an instant away. She wished he weren't so young, maybe then it could last. They rarely discussed what would happen after the war, although Victor had spoken about plans to live on a kibbutz in Eretz Israel with his friends. He was excited about a new country and a new homeland. *Imagine me with a camel,* he'd said in a fit of laughter. He had asked her to go with him, but she had told him no, she could never leave this place. Now, in bed, he told her he had changed his mind about Israel. Instead, he would live with her here when the war was over, and help her with the farm. It was a dream, she knew, and she kissed him, again and again, not wanting to hear any more of what might or might not be. She knew what was between them was different for her than it was for him. He was *in love* with her, but she *loved* him, and that was more. Love was the thing that lasted, no matter where fate would take them.

In the morning, before he set off, he showed her how to shoot her father's rifle. It came as no surprise to him that she was an excellent shot.

"A natural," he declared. "You're good at everything." He kissed her for a long time. "Especially this."

When it came time for their goodbyes, Marianne had a sinking feeling. She didn't want to let him go, and that wasn't like her. She had never wanted to hold him back, but now here she was, with her arms around him, reluctant to let him leave. He promised he would take on this one last mission and then he would be done. Why was she so worried? The war would be over before they knew it. Had she no faith in him? He reminded her, laughing, that he was the best driver in all of France. He'd be gone only a few weeks. Afterward he would come back to take care of her. Then, he swore, he would never leave again.

CHAPTER TWENTY-EIGHT

THE MAP

LE CHAMBON-SUR-LIGNON, JULY 1944

AT SCHOOL LEA KEPT TO HERSELF. THE GIRLS WERE FRIENDLY enough; still she was an outsider, the tall fair-haired girl in the gray dress. When she stood outside her gaze followed the birds swooping through the sky as though she was trying to summon one, but she always walked away disappointed, brooding. The message she was waiting for had yet to come.

By now she was sixteen. She didn't want to grow any older. The farther she was from the age she had been when she left Berlin, the more she feared she would forget her past. Who had taught her how to read, who had sewn her clothes, who had told her stories about the wolves she sometimes heard up in the craggy mountains. People said none were left, that they had been hunted to extinction, but some had survived, up where the altitude was so great and the air so thin not even the birds could fly. Who would know you when you were the last one left of your kind? If she could no longer remember her mother and grandmother, would she forget that she had once been loved?

But time was moving forward, and everything changed. Even in this tiny, isolated village, people had heard about the attack on German forces in Normandy. News was carried by members of the Resistance, and there was a wild conviction that the war had turned. Anything might be possible now, and it seemed that fate might not be set out before them in a straight, unwavering path, but might instead be a curving line marked by chance and choice, infinite in its possible destinations.

Lea decided she would write a note, to be ready when the heron returned. He was late this year. She imagined Julien waiting to hear from her, one hand thrown up to block the bright light as he scanned the sky, just as she did. One afternoon, as Weitz was out smoking one of his precious cigarettes, which he cut in half, so they would last longer, and Ava was in the yard hanging the laundry, Lea opened the bureau drawer in search of a pad of paper and a pen. She did not expect what she found, and her chest immediately felt hollow. There was a note, folded over itself, tucked away. She steadied herself and took it in her hands. She recognized his handwriting right away.

Come here as soon as you can.

She turned over the paper, her heart pounding.

There was the map. He'd sketched Beehive House, and the winding rutted road, and the pastures filled with flowering *genêts*. In her hands was the barn and the stone house with its tilted chimney and white shutters, the goat named Bluebell,

and the beehives in the field. It had been here in this drawer
for months.

Lea waited until after dinner, when Weitz went outside to paint
in the yard in the last of the day's light. Then she put the map
on the table.

"When did this arrive?"

Ava glanced at the map. She felt a wave of shame and confusion, emotions she was not supposed to have.

"You decided to hide it from me?" Lea said.

"The heron came back just after winter, but the time wasn't
right." The lie burned her tongue and she flushed, something
she had never done before.

"The heron has been back all this time!" Lea's mouth tightened. "It's not winter now, and still you kept a message that was
meant for me. You stole it!"

Ava had often regretted asking the heron to carry Lea's and
Julien's messages. She'd thought there would be no harm in it,
but she was wrong. "You may not understand everything I do."

"I understand perfectly. You want to keep me away from Julien, because I'll leave with him, and you don't want me to cross
the border."

"But I do," Ava insisted. "I promised your mother I would
get you to safety."

"And yet we're still here." Lea held Ava in her gaze. "You and
I know why. You don't want to do what you promised my mother
because you know what happens once I'm safe." Every word
Lea spoke was brittle, a sharp broken hook. "You've known all
along. You know what she wants me to do."

"I want the best for you." Ava felt something sharp inside of her. By now she knew that people always lost what they loved most.

"I don't care," Lea cried. "I'm leaving here. I'm following the map."

She went to get her suitcase. Let Ava try to stop her. She would scream her head off if need be. She was nearly as tall as Ava and she wasn't a girl of twelve anymore. She would never be a child again, and she didn't have to listen to anyone.

Watching her, Ava felt as if she were breaking. It was all true. She might have taken Lea to the border a hundred times, but she had done as she'd pleased; she had her own mind and her own desires. She had wanted to remain in this glorious world, despite how wicked those who inhabited it might be. She had let her desire for life affect her vow.

She had betrayed her maker.

"You can't go alone," Ava said now. She reached for the suit-case. "I'll go with you. Let me pack."

Lea scowled. "I don't need you."

They both took hold of the suitcase, and when they tugged, it flew open. Before their eyes, the lining split in the place where Hanni had sewn a thousand miraculous stitches. Inside the torn lining, hidden there on the day they left Berlin, was a blue dress, perfectly made. *Mein Schatz*, her mother had written on the note tacked to one sleeve. *Für dich.*

My darling, for you when you reach safety.

Lea sank to the floor, the dress in her arms, her face hot with tears.

Heart of my heart, love of my life, the one loss I will never survive.

As for Ava, she was sick with shame. Her emotions were so

raw she could feel herself melting, and a pool of muddy water gathered around her on the floor. That was when she decided, they would leave that night.

Ahron Weitz gave Lea one of his paintings, the night sky filled with stars. She embraced him, but not for too long. They would likely never see each other again, and so there were no good-byes. Weitz stayed at the window and watched them go. They had thanked their hosts, but thanks could never be enough for people who were willing to risk such danger for complete strangers. Lea said a blessing Bobeshi had taught her at their door, the Hashkiveinu, a petition for safety through the night.

Lay us down, our God, in peace, and raise us up our King, to life. Spread your shelter of peace over us, and over all of Israel and Jerusalem.

It was dark, a good night for traveling, for cutting across fields, and finding the twisting road that had been sketched in blue, the same color as the sky when they reached Monsieur Félix's farm in the pale morning light, for they had been walking all night. There was Beehive House, exactly as Julien had drawn it before Monsieur Félix was murdered, before he worked as the Bissets' carpenter, before he went to Izieu. The farm was deserted except for a small goat that had been tied to a post in the stable, a creature so delighted to see them that it jumped into Lea's arms when it was freed.

The door to the house was locked, so Ava shoved open a window and climbed in. She could smell death, and she called for Lea to wait on the porch. When she placed her hands on the tabletop she could see the image of a body hanging from the beam. She went outside and could see past the barn to Monsieur Félix's grave. There in the tree was Azriel. The angel usually departed once his work was done, and the fact that he was still hovering nearby was troublesome.

They had a dinner of potatoes and onions, fried and made delicious in Ava's experienced hands. She was long past Hardship Soup. She could make a meal out of anything and nothing. She washed the dishes, then made up the bed in the small upstairs bedroom.

Lea was sitting on the porch in the dark. Things had not turned out as she had wished. The deserted farm had been a huge disappointment, but the fury she had felt at Ava had faded. Why would anyone want to give up life on earth? They both knew where fate led once Lea was safe, and what a sacrifice Ava was expected to make. It was an act of love that only a mother would do for a child, and her companion did not owe her that.

Ava had come to stand in the doorway. She wasn't certain this was a safe place. If it was up to her, they would leave right now.

"He'll be here," Lea told her.

Julien would keep his promise. He would stay alive and walk down the dirt road and when he saw her he would know her and she would know him in return.

Ava didn't argue. She knew that Lea's mind was made up. She came to sit beside her on one of the old chairs Monsieur Félix had made long ago, when his daughter was small, when people kept their doors unlocked and had no fear of their neighbors or of the police. The view was dusky in the fading light. Lea had grown taller and thinner. She hadn't been a child for quite some time. She looked like the woman she would soon be, and she had a woman's certainty. She intended to wait for as long as she must.

CHAPTER TWENTY-NINE

THE LAST ANGEL

HAUTE-LOIRE, JULY 1944

MONSIEUR CAZALES DROVE FROM A NEIGHBORING FARM TO deliver Bluebell, now in the back of the truck, for she had wandered over to his property, as she often did. He'd already heard from his wife that odd things were going on at the Félix place and had been ever since Marianne had returned. As he pulled up, two strangers, a girl and a woman, came out onto the porch, as curious about him as he was about them.

"The old man's not here?" Cazales said. "Or his daughter?"

"No one was here when we arrived," Lea told him.

"And who are you?" Cazales asked, not that it was any of his business. Still, old Félix had been his neighbor for a long time. He supposed he had a right to know. The dark woman was oddly silent and the girl was not someone he'd seen before. His wife had gossiped that the daughter, Marianne, was involved with some young fellow who came and went as he pleased, speeding down the road in some rattletrap car that was likely stolen, scaring the cows in their pasture.

"We're friends of the family," Lea said.

Cazales shrugged. Maybe this was true, maybe it wasn't. But they weren't German soldiers, and how much damage could they do even if they were thieves? Perhaps they were simply homeless, making their way to the border. He wasn't that interested in other people's personal lives. If Marianne had a boyfriend, for instance, who was he to care? Let her have a hundred of them for all it mattered to him. People here were entitled to their privacy. Still, there were some things that were quite concerning, the coming storm, for instance. He had already rounded up his cows and shut them in his barn. "Take my advice, tie up the goat so she doesn't go running off and get lost in the storm. It will be here by dark." He could tell from the way the wind was rising, from the upturned leaves on the trees.

They did as he suggested, keeping the little goat in the barn, though she complained about her confinement. It was a good thing she was tied up because the storm that arose suddenly that night was vicious, a swirl of black in the sky that gave way to a drenching rain, and then sudden hail, so that it seemed stones were being thrown on the roof. The wind was dreadful; it shook the house and the trees. Branches broke, haystacks went flying into the air, sunflowers were pulled up by their roots. Anything not tied down rose into the whirlwind before dropping to the ground with a crash.

Lea curled up and slept through most of the storm, but Ava was more restless than usual. She looked out the window to see the darkening sky. She was thinking about running away. She had been thinking about it ever since they'd come to the farm.

Erase the e *and turn* emet *into* met, *truth into death.*

But what would happen then? Would she melt into clay or water, or would she die with all of the pain and agony of a mortal death? She should be satisfied merely to obey her maker's will, but that had changed. She had awoken to her life, and she didn't wish to give it up. She had become attached to this world, to fields and trees, to the heron and the sky, to feeling her heart beat, for she had one, she was sure of it now, even if it had begun as clay. She could hear the birds in the trees, telling her to run as far as she could from the world of men. Creatures such as herself were not made to have a soul, they were made to do the bidding of their makers, but she had already lived for too long, just as the rabbis warned, she was stronger now, uncontrollable, making her own decisions, defying what she had been told to do.

In the morning, the storm was over and the air was heavy and still. Ava went out into the yard. She began to walk. She thought about the moment when she opened her eyes, and the first time she felt sunlight on her skin, and of Paris when they got off the train, and the Seine at night, and the heron dancing in the garden. She was walking faster by now. She was thinking for herself. The world, however cruel it might be, was too glorious to give up. She had no rights to it, she wasn't human, but neither was the heron, and he had rights no human had, the rights of flight and sight. She stopped at the crest of a hill and turned to gaze back at the farm. There were the fields, and the barn, and in the distance the neighbor's cow pastures and orchards. Lea came through the door still in her nightgown, her feet bare. Ava felt a catch in her throat to think of how the girl might feel when she realized she was alone. But she was no longer a child, and when Julien arrived they could make their way to the border.

Ava might have walked over the mountain and vanished, but when she turned she saw that Lea had left the house. As the girl proceeded toward the barn, Ava spied Azriel in the tree beside the beehives, glimmering in the leaves. The wooden hives had smashed open when the wind threw them over and now honey was leaking into the ground. Azriel had been reading from his book of names, but as soon as Lea came near, he gazed up.

Ava was stricken as the angel moved from branch to branch. It was only at that moment that she realized she could gasp, like any ordinary woman. Her breath came out hot and fevered, burning her throat. Lea was headed toward the barn, a pan of crusts for the goat in her hands. Was it possible that Lea saw the angel? She put one hand over her eyes and stared into the tree, confused. You could not see him unless he came for you, unless he was ready to take you in his embrace, and then you could see him so clearly the rest of the world disappeared in the blink of an eye.

Ava ran down the hill through the pine forest, her head pounding.

By then Lea had gone into the barn to let the goat off her rope. Bluebell, intoxicated with freedom after the terror of the storm, dashed out before she could be caught, racing through the field.

"Come here!" Lea called, chasing after the goat, regretting that she had not slipped on her shoes as she ran over the rough sunflower stalks littering the ground, near the broken beehives.

She observed a strange shadow moving through the trees. It seemed to be a handsome man in a black suit. All at once she felt she'd lost her hearing. He had long dark hair and he seemed to know her. Could it be that he was saying her name? The air was alive with a deafening buzzing. The bees were maddened from the storm, in a fury ever since their hives had been destroyed. In an instant they began to swarm over Lea. They were on her arms and legs and lips and all over her scalp, in the strands of her hair. She was numb at first, and then she was on fire. She did her best to escape, running through the field to a small green stream that was cold as ice, but she was running with the buzzing cloud; they were flying together, so fast that the world was a blur. The angel was above her in the air, his long dark hair loose, his beautiful dark eyes focused on her alone. There was a light inside of him and Lea had to squint to see him, but as he came near she saw him more clearly. He was so beautiful she found she couldn't speak.

When she collapsed she was lost inside the swarm, so hidden from sight that when Ava came upon her all she saw was a thousand bees. Ava had all but flown through the field and the uprooted sunflowers. The storm had left the air fresh and sharp, and hawks circled in the sky. The noise of the swarm was terrible and fierce, but Ava could understand it. She spoke to the bees in their language, and when they heard her voice they were comforted, and dispersed in a cloud.

There was Lea, motionless in the new grass. There was the angel, in the tree.

"You can't have her," Ava told Azriel.

The angel couldn't see her. She was neither human, nor animal, nor spirit, but some oddity, and none of his concern. Lea, however, was his concern. He was God's messenger, known to some as *malakh ha-mavet*. He plummeted from the trees and stood over Lea, and his light embraced her. Ava went to him and took hold of his coat. He felt her grasp and was annoyed. At last he looked at her, and it was terrifying to be held in his gaze, still she held tight. Azriel wondered why he had never seen her before, and then he knew. God had not created her.

"If you want to fight me for her, do so," he commanded. "Otherwise step away."

He was so beautiful, he was a light before her eyes, but she refused to bow to him. She was stronger than a hundred horsemen, but she couldn't win against Azriel unless she could find a remedy. She knew the cure for beestings; the purest clay must cover every sting. Solomon himself was said to have battled honeybees, coating their hive with clay, for clay was protection both for the bees and for their victims.

Ava lifted Lea in her arms. She was heavy as lead, light as a feather, and she had an unearthly pallor. She was already losing consciousness, and her swollen tongue could no longer fit inside her mouth. Her pulse was weakening, and a red rash had begun to rise in circles over her pale skin. Ava caused the stingers to drop away with a single command. She undressed Lea, then unlatched the locket, which she stored in her pocket. She must cover every inch of the afflicted skin with clay, but there was none to be had; the nearby stream had only a stony granite bank. Ava hastened to unbutton her dress. She knew what she must do, and she quickly reached down and grabbed the flesh covering her hip. She did not flinch as she tugged and pulled. At last it came off in her hands. Once taken from her body it appeared to be ordinary flesh, a bloody portion of it, but when she mixed it with water the flesh once again became the clay it had first been.

The mystical number for beestings was 348, therefore Ava mixed the water and clay 348 times before she applied it, coating Lea's face and throat and body, taking more handfuls of her own flesh to use for the balm. Beestings could cause blindness, or asthma, or death, and Lea was motionless. Azriel had followed them and was crouching on the bank of the stream.

There was a huge gash in Ava's side, and once the clay became flesh once more she was shocked to see she still bled, like an ordinary woman. That was impossible, and for a moment her fear burned hot inside her; perhaps she had unmade herself. But when she took her scarf and bound herself with it, she stanched the flow. She was missing a piece of herself and there was a deep indentation over her hip. Her eyes were hot and she ached with some unfamiliar pain, but she could not give in. She must do more to fight the angel. She was made to do more. She knew that honey could cure beestings as well, and that what wounded you could also cure you. She went to the hive, took fistfuls of the honey, then grabbed a dozen bees and crushed them in her palm. She did away with the stingers, and trickled the mixture of honey and crushed bees into Lea's mouth, then used the rest as a seal over the clay.

She had a single task, to keep Lea safe, and that was what she planned to do. She could not run over the mountain, or escape into the forest. They must flee from Azriel. She went to the neighbor's house, where she pounded on the door, crying out for help. Monsieur Cazales was shocked when he saw what he believed to be a desperate mother with her limp, unconscious child in her arms, the same two he'd seen at the Félix farm. Clearly some calamity had occurred: the girl's clothes were in disarray and her breath was shallow.

"Come with me," Monsieur Cazales told the woman. "We'll go to the doctor."

Ava lifted Lea into the bed of the truck, where Cazales kept a blanket for his sheepdog. They went across the mountain on the old roads, sometimes cutting across fields, as Cazales knew the shortest route. He'd had a daughter who'd had measles, and one dark night many years ago, he'd driven this same route in a panic, desperate for the doctor's help. When they reached the château, Cazales leaned his arm on the horn, and the sound broke through the deep silence and had Girard running for the door. At first he thought the police had come for the guest in his barn, then he saw the old farmer.

"Come," Dr. Girard called to Ava, who carried the girl inside. He thought perhaps the girl had a head injury, but then he noticed the stings and knew she'd had a severe allergic reaction.

"Do you need me, Doctor?" Cazales wanted to know, but Girard shouted out his thanks and told him to go. Before he turned to care for the girl, he was relieved to spy a glimpse of a figure in the barn.

Once inside the office, Girard switched on the lights. "Put her right on the couch," he told Ava. He went to get a dose of precious epinephrine, hard to get in these times, which made the unconscious girl gasp and open her eyes for a moment, shuddering from the power of the drug. The angel was outside the window; he had followed, but he came no closer. Ava had turned and had shaken her fist at Azriel. "No," she said aloud, in a voice that emerged from deep inside of her.

316

The doctor knew this angel and understood the seriousness of his appearance. He gave Lea another dose of the drug, and they had to hold her down, Ava taking her legs, the doctor her arms, to help control her seizure. After a moment, Lea calmed down and they could let go.

"That's right," Girard said to the listless girl. "Breathe deep."

He took out some *apis* that a patient had given to him in lieu of payment, a mixture made from honeybees and alcohol with the venom of the bee extracted. He placed a few drops under Lea's tongue. Perhaps it was an old wives' tale to battle a disease with a measure of that illness, but he'd seen it help before. There was truth in the locals' homeopathic remedies, ones they had used for generations, and this girl needed all the help she could get. Lea slipped back into a deep dark sleep, and Girard was pleased that her pulse was now stronger. He had noticed the covering of clay and honey on the girl; the poison had been stopped and therefore had not reached her heart, or kidneys, or lungs, but had stayed pooled beneath her skin.

"You acted wisely," he told Ava. "Your daughter's alive because of it."

Ava didn't bother to correct him. Her hands still burned from taking hold of Azriel's coat. It was her fault; she had done what was forbidden. She had left the girl and thought of her own needs. "She's too pale," Ava told the doctor, her voice unsteady. "Her breathing isn't right."

"She'll be more stable in the morning," the doctor promised. "Rest is the best medicine."

He'd noticed letters on the woman's arm that he recognized to be Hebrew. When she caught him staring, Ava quickly pulled down her sleeve. Still, it was in his nature, as it is in every doctor's nature, to be curious. He had not asked many questions about who they were. He assumed they were Jews from Berlin, for in her delirium Lea had murmured *Wo ist meine Mutter?*

Where is my mother?

Later that evening Girard took a Hebrew book that had belonged to Sarah from the volumes he had hidden in his filing cabinet, for any books relating to Jews were no longer legal to own. He thumbed through the alphabet, writing down the letters he'd seen. They spelled out *truth*. He sat at his desk, pleased.

He could not imagine a more beautiful word for a woman to carry.

That evening, Girard offered Ava his room, but she declined, insisting she would prefer to keep vigil from the bedroom chair. She wasn't about to let the girl out of her sight, especially after the doctor said there was another guest in the barn.

In the early hours of the morning, Lea became conscious. When she opened her eyes she thought she was in a bird's nest. She had spied the heron out in the orchard. He'd managed to find them. He always did, and that comforted Lea. The casing of clay and honey she had been covered with had fallen away, leaving a gray and yellow powder on the sheets. Now that the light had broken, Ava was stunned to see how the girl had changed. Overnight, her hair had turned white as snow. Such things could happen when mortals saw Azriel yet continued to live, when they had come so close to the World to Come that he had become visible in all of his blinding brilliance.

It was shock that had caused it, Dr. Girard told Ava when he came in to check on Lea's progress. It was possible for a person's hair to turn white overnight after a traumatic event, certainly he'd heard of such cases. But it was a small price to pay for what had been accomplished. Another girl would not have survived the bees' attack. Ava took Lea's hand in hers. Human lives were like quicksilver; let go and they vanished. But not this time. Not now.

"More rest," the doctor declared. "That's all she needs. Together we've brought her to life."

CHAPTER THIRTY

THE MAKER AND THE MADE

ARDÈCHE, JULY 1944

SHE MIGHT NOT HAVE RECOGNIZED AVA IF NOT FOR HER FAther's boots. Those she would never forget, for the morning after the golem was created the rabbi noticed they were missing from the wardrobe. He had the children search the house, but it was a pointless pursuit and Ettie hadn't bothered to look. She knew she was leaving that night so she ignored her father's shouts. Had there been a thief in the house? Had someone borrowed his boots without asking? Ettie had stood in the kitchen and memorized it all, down to the spoons and the forks. She'd memorized his voice and the voices of her brothers and sisters.

"Are you too good to look for your father's boots?" her mother had said when she found Ettie dreaming in the kitchen. She'd been shocked when in response Ettie threw her arms around her and held her tight. Their family did not do such things. Raw emotion was ignored and love went unspoken, and sometimes unknown.

"I was your worst child," Ettie said thoughtfully, as if she was already gone.

Her mother could not bring herself to say anything. Whether or not that was true there was one thing that was certain. Ettie was her favorite child.

All this time later, the boots looked no worse for wear. Perhaps they had been enchanted, or perhaps the rabbi had chosen the strongest leather available. But Ava had changed. She now resembled a woman more than she did a creature made of clay. Her black hair shone, and she lacked the pallor she'd had when she was made, and now possessed a rosy complexion. More than anything, what was different was the expression in her eyes. If Ettie wasn't mistaken they had changed color. She remembered them as gray as stone, but now they glinted with light.

They walked toward one another, each measuring the other.

"Do not get to your knees," Ettie warned the golem when they met.

Ava smiled. She hadn't intended to. She was not the same foolish creature she had been on the train. "I can still thank you."

"For bringing you into this wretched place?" Ettie felt a wave of guilt for her selfish actions in creating life in exchange for a price. "I should get on my knees and beg you to forgive me."

It was a heartless world, but there were the swifts, soaring above them in the half-light.

"No. I'm grateful to you," Ava said.

"You realize that you were born to do our bidding? To serve us and nothing more?"

Ava knew that her maker was wrong. She was born to walk through the reeds and dance with the heron, she was made to watch Lea sleep safely through the night and to feel the sun on her skin and to stand here in the rabbi's boots beneath a bower of green leaves.

"And what were you born to do?" she asked her maker.

Ettie grimaced. She knew the truth about herself. "I was born to fight."

They sat in the wooden chairs where the doctor's wife had spent early mornings in the last weeks of her life in order to watch the sun rise. Azriel had often kept Sarah Girard company; he had appreciated the long view through the trees, across to the mountains, and now he had returned to sit at Ettie's feet. He could unleash flames and fire if he wished to do so, he could open the earth to send a plague of snakes and frogs. Instead, he leaned against Ettie's legs, so that she thought a breeze had come up.

"If you fight," Ava told her, "you will die." She could glimpse the future, not for herself, but certainly for her maker. She saw a field and she knew that Ettie wished she had never let go of her sister's hand.

"We all die," Ettie responded. "Except for you. Until the girl gets rid of you."

Lea was in the house, asleep, or sleeping as best she could. She had bad dreams of bees and of those she had lost, dreams that had turned her hair white.

"We had no right to make you and she has no right to un-make you," Ettie said.

323

Ava saw Azriel's eyes flicker over her maker. "If I don't stop you, you will die."

She was strong enough, she could do so if she wished.

Ettie nodded. "And if I don't stop you, you will."

They exchanged a gaze, aware that they would leave each other to their own fates.

"You have fulfilled your part of the bargain," Ettie assured her creation. "A mother could not ask for more. As soon as the girl is safe, don't think twice. Run away."

But the vow Ava had made was no longer a burden. It was a choice. She might have run if the bees had not changed her fate, but now she would stay. She had been wrong to try to gain more time on earth. That was not why she had been made, but perhaps the first human trait a creature such as herself would acquire was to be selfish. She was renouncing that now. She sat with her maker and they both wept because they would not see each other again. What had been created was alive. Ettie did not see clay before her, but rather a woman who had been made by women, brought to life by their blood and needs and desires.

Later, as the sun was breaking, after Ettie had gone inside, Ava made her way through the woods until she reached the bare reeds. The river was only a trickle now, splashing over the rocks. The fish were singing with their silver voices. It was a perfect summer day, despite the cruelty of the world. When the heron came, Ava bowed to him, then asked for one last favor.

Find him if you can.

CHAPTER THIRTY-ONE

THE BEAST

HAUTE-LOIRE, AUGUST 1944

ETTIE SLEPT MORE FITFULLY AS THE DAY DREW CLOSER. IT was hard to sleep after you had heard a prophecy, harder still when you believed it. Once Victor came for her, time moved in a rush, as if they had stepped inside a rocket ship that was rattling through the Milky Way, a journey that, once begun, could not be undone. She would be lingering on the road when the captain drove to a café, as he did every Friday. She was to convince him to let her into the car. Victor would be waiting for her, and if anyone could quickly get them away from the scene it was he. She knew what might happen with the captain. Victor had mentioned how she might hold the captain's attention while the bomb was set in place in the tailpipe of his car, not quite able to meet her eyes as he spoke. She was then to escape from the car and run back to where Victor was parked.

Ettie brushed her glossy red hair, then chose the doctor's wife's black dress and slipped on the lucky red shoes. She hadn't said goodbye to him. It was better this way. Instead she went to stand near a clutch of snowy white phlox Sarah Girard had planted in the last year of her life that were scattered beneath the trees. They had become a field of light. She closed her eyes and recited a section of the Amidah.

We hope all evil will be lost on earth.

The dusk was falling in ashy waves and the white flowers were turning blue when Ava came to stand beside her.

"You should leave," Ettie told her. "You don't have to be anyone's slave." She took Ava's hand and shook her head. "You should listen to me, but you won't."

"You should listen to me," Ava responded sadly.

They both knew that when Ettie left she would never return to this place. But she was not really here anyway, she was in the field with her sister.

She'd been there all along.

Victor dropped her off on the road and she stood there in the gloaming. They'd both had a case of nerves on the ride, which was not a bad thing, even though Ettie's stomach was lurching so violently she had to stop so she could get out and be sick in a nearby jumble of marshy weeds. All the same, their nerves would serve to make them cautious, so fewer mistakes would be made.

Victor felt a stab of guilt once he'd let Ettie out on the road.

He waited in the field, parked in the tall grass, ready to follow once the Milice captain had picked her up. Everyone had doubt at a moment like this, everyone had a stab of fear, but by then the captain's car was headed toward the village and Ettie was standing in the road waving and there was no time for doubt. The car, a Delage sports car, with black and red paint and red leather seats, had belonged to the previous owner of the house. It pulled over and idled. To Victor, from the darkness of the field where he crouched behind the wheel of his stolen car, the sports car looked like a lizard. Ettie went over to talk to the driver. She was shaky on the high heels, but she quickly regained her balance. She walked around to the passenger seat and then it began. Victor's hands were sweating as he followed the speeding car. He had a rifle and more explosives in the backseat and the detonator on his lap, wrapped in a cloth so nothing would jog it before it was time.

The captain had suggested to Ettie that they go back to his house. The Jew's house where the gardens were in ruins and there were still piles of ash from all of the books he had burned. He told her she'd never been in a house like it and would be stunned by its beauty when he led her up to the bedroom where there were silk sheets. She convinced him to pull into a field. Why should they wait? For weeks, Victor had been teaching her to flirt, and she understood she must keep a smile on her face, even though she knew the captain had been responsible for forty souls that had been deported to Auschwitz. Victor had been funny and charming as he pretended to be a girl seducing an old man. *You're so handsome,* he had crooned about their ugly, old target. *I'm so lucky I met you. Come closer. Closer.* They'd laughed over it, but now she felt sick to her stomach again.

As soon as they pulled off the road, the captain kissed her.

She thought about the way she'd run when she'd left her sister behind. She had forced herself to go forward, even though it had become impossible to spy Marta when she looked back. Just the hem of her dress, her boots, her newly cut hair. Ettie twisted away now so she could whisper in the captain's ear. *Turn the car off, we will be here for a while.* This was her reason to be alive, this was the reason she'd run into the woods.

By then Victor had crept near. The ignition was turned off, and as soon as the tailpipe cooled, he shoved the bomb in. His hands were dusted with gunpowder. This was it, the moment they had planned for.

The captain was pulling down her dress. He kissed her roughly as he ran his hands over her. He had her now, she belonged to him, but she didn't feel any of it. She thought about the doctor's guest room, where everything was in its proper place. A comb and brush on the bureau, a glass of water on the night table, a silk rug on the floor. She thought of his kindness when he leaned down to speak to his patients, the way he stood at the door and looked into the dark, the way he kissed her, as if she were precious, as if she might break.

"Wait," Ettie told the captain. She smiled of course, as she'd been taught to do. "I have to get ready." She wanted to step out to relieve herself. He told her to hurry, and she said she would. She wished she could stay and look into his eyes as he was dying, but that wasn't the plan.

"I will," she promised.

She got out and didn't look back. She raced through the dark. Victor was gesturing to her to be faster; a police car had gone by, and he had a funny feeling when it slowed down after passing. Unused to the high heels, Ettie tripped as she ran. She fell, then got back on her feet, kicking off the shoes. She knew this was her fate, she was running into a field of grass, she was half-bird half-girl, flying.

Victor spied the police car in his mirror, so he didn't delay. He hit the detonator the moment Ettie was in the car. When the sports car blew up, a rain of fire and smoke shot by them. The car windows flew out, scattering glass, and a black cloud rose up. The passenger door of Victor's car was blown off, so that Ettie nearly fell out when Victor stepped on the gas. He went through a pasture flying over the hilly land, surrounded by orchards, whose branches smashed against the windshield.

The police car was behind them, and soon a second car approached at top speed, the wail of sirens tearing through the still night. A trail of smoke followed them and filled up the car. Ettie covered her mouth with her hand so she wouldn't choke. Victor was going so fast she felt they were in a whirlwind. She remembered flying once before with her sister. She remembered that moment. It was happening again. She thought of Ava, that brilliant creature she'd made with her own hands who could see the future. It had happened even though Victor was known to his friends to be the best driver in France. He shouted for Ettie to hold on, but his tire blew out and they went round and round on the slick grass until they were dizzy and shaking. They skidded in a circle, crashing into a tree. The police cars pulled up on either side. Steam had begun to rise from the engine, and little flares of sparks flamed from beneath the hood.

"Get out of the car," Victor urged. She must jump before the explosives in the backseat caught. "Ettie, go now!"

She knew it was too late as she watched Victor make the leap. He was taken down by two members of the Milice. One of the officers sat on his back, a knee to his spine, crushing his ribs, as he cursed himself and the damned car that hadn't been fast enough. He'd made a promise to Marianne, and she wouldn't know if he was taken to Montluc Prison. He fought, but it did him no good. They slipped handcuffs on him and pulled him onto his feet. There were sparks everywhere. The car was already on fire, and the police officers backed away, pulling Victor with them. The explosives could be set off at any moment. It didn't matter to Ettie. She knew the future and the past. She might appear to be in the car, but she was already running through the forest with her sister. She had seen what no human could see until her last moments. There beside her was the Angel of Death, more brilliant than any of his luminous brothers, so compassionate and so bright that she couldn't look away. He was too beautiful, more beautiful than anything on earth.

She had created life, she had been with a good man, she had battled a beast. She could hear the policemen shouting in the field. She had seen Victor being beaten until he couldn't fight back. She knew that there was fire in the sky. Everything was black and red and burning. Everything was so loud it was as if the world was beginning or ending. When the angel finally took her, she was grateful. In his arms, she forgot everything, except for the grass in the fields when they jumped from the train, her sister's hand in hers.

CHAPTER THIRTY-TWO

THE WAY HOME

VIENNE, AUGUST 1944

JULIEN DARED TO RETURN TO THE CHURCH IN VIENNE. HE
went to Father Varnier's room and knocked at the door, hoping
for news of his brother. It was late, but the priest was awake.
Neither he nor Julien could find sleep easily. Varnier worried
over the souls of his parishioners, and Julien saw the faces of
the children at Izieu whenever he closed his eyes. He looked
exhausted as he explained that he had not seen his brother for
several months and he worried more each day. Usually Varnier
was brusque, he had little time for personal complaints, but this
time he invited Julien in.

"Perhaps I should stay out in the hall," Julien suggested.

His clothes were filthy and caked with mud. He had been

eating regularly and had put on some of the weight he had lost in the past few years. He was muscular now, nearly six feet tall. But he didn't bathe regularly and he labored outside and so he was embarrassed by his condition. All the same, the priest insisted he sit down in a leather chair. Julien ran a hand through his long hair, self-conscious. When he thought of the boy who had stood in the hallway in Paris on the day Lea arrived, it was as if he were imagining a younger brother, someone who was forever lost to him, a boy with little experience and too much confidence, who could fall in love in the blink of an eye.

Father Varnier sat back in his chair and asked if Julien believed in heaven, and Julien answered truthfully. He wasn't sure if he believed in anything anymore. The priest poured them both glasses of cognac, though it was all of ten A.M. When the father offered him a drink, Julien knew something was wrong. He waved his hand no to the drink and leaned forward in his chair.

"We can't know God's reasons for what we mortals must endure," Father Varnier told him. "We can only be grateful for our lives and for his love."

Julien was then told that his brother had been arrested. There had been a bombing in which a captain of the Milice had been killed, along with a Resistance worker, and the news had gotten back to Varnier. Victor had been taken to Montluc Prison in Lyon, and even though the end of the war was near, and Lyon would soon be liberated, he had been on the last train to Auschwitz on August 11. The Germans were retreating but the deportation was personally overseen by Klaus Barbie. One hundred and thirty-one Jews had been gassed upon arrival, Victor among them. Lyon was to be liberated thirteen days after the convoy was sent east.

Julien stopped listening. He refused to hear any more. Not how the prisoners were chained two by two, Jews on one side, Resistance members on the other, not how the prison was being emptied, with as many as possible killed so there would be no human evidence when the British and Americans arrived. Julien stood and shook Father Varnier's hand, then walked out without another word, past the flickering candle he had lit for Monsieur Bisset's son, past the pew where he had slept when his brother had come to take him to Izieu. He didn't let himself feel anything until he was on the road. Then he called out to God, his shouts shook the sky and he, himself, was made deaf by his own wailing. He fell to his knees, and tore his clothes in a wild fit of mourning, and he did his best not to curse himself for being the only one in his family who had managed to stay alive.

When Marianne came home she was shocked by the damage from the storm and especially saddened to see the beehives were destroyed and, by now, deserted. She went to search for the key, tucked between two stones behind the wall near the old pump. She kept the house locked now, and only she and Victor knew where the key was hidden. She unhooked the latch and pushed the door open, breathing in the musty, damp scent of the house. She had been away for nearly a week. They were trying to get as many children over the border as possible. The closer they came to the end of the war, the more the Germans wanted to rid the countryside of all Resistance workers and Jews. Everything was moving so fast, spinning closer to the end. At the border there were places where the Italians had left and it was possible to walk right into Switzerland, and other places the Germans shot whoever moved in the dark. Marianne had been very lucky. She'd lost no one. She was quite famous, really; everyone wanted to cross the border with her. Some people called her Saint Marianne, they said she wore armor under her dress, that she could walk through fire, that she was invisible to the Germans.

But these were the imaginings of children who still believed in such things. The children would throw their meager belongings over the fence, then crawl beneath the wire that Marianne often held up so they could fit under. She told them to be brave, because when they crossed over the Swiss Border Guard would place each child under arrest, then give him over to the Corps des gardes-frontière, where a military officer would question the child yet again and draw up the formal arrest. *Do not break,* she told them. *They are only questions. Make your statement when asked. Tell them, I crossed to escape the Germans' actions toward the Jews. Think forward, not back.*

She tried to do the same, but when she opened the door, she had a feeling of dread. Someone had been in her house. Perhaps they had climbed in through the kitchen window, which had never closed properly. The intruder had been neat and tidy, and nothing was out of place. Some potatoes and onions had been eaten, but the dishes and the frying pan had been washed and set on the drainboard. Upstairs, the beds had been made. Someone had left some lupines in a glass jar on the long dining room table.

Marianne stood by the sink and drank her tea once it had steeped. For some silly reason her hands shook when she lifted the cup. She was bone tired, of course, but it was more. She felt a wave of panic. In the following days, she went about her business, taking care of the farm, seeing to the damage caused by the wind, but all the while she had the same sinking feeling. The weather was hot and dry and the rows of vegetables needed to be watered. When all of her other chores were done, she saw to the watering, using a bucket to bring water up from a small nearby stream. By afternoon she was sweating through her dress, a bit dazed, suffering through a case of nerves. She was usually calm, and was known among the other *passeurs* for her patience and easy nature, but when she finished working in the field, she went in and took a bath and sobbed in the soapy tub, staying until the water was ice cold, which frankly felt good in the heat and in her feverish state of mind.

She dressed and went downstairs and told herself to look forward, as she told the children at the border. And sure enough, when she looked out the window she saw Victor coming down the road, on foot, which was unusual. He was never without a car. She felt a thrill go through her. She'd been crazy to worry. She ran outside to the porch, calling as she went to meet him. There were crows in the fields she had watered, drinking from the puddles. The closer Victor got the more puzzled Marianne was, even though he lifted both arms to wave. And then she saw it was not Victor at all, but Julien who was approaching, who began to run toward her now, even though he had been walking for three days, not bothering to eat or sleep.

"Victor will be so relieved," Marianne said as they embraced. "He's been worried sick ever since they took everyone from Maison d'Izieu. Where on earth have you been all this time?"

When she let go of Julien and took a step back, she saw that he had intentionally torn his clothes. She looked at him, puz-

zled. That surely had some meaning, but she didn't fully understand what.

"Julien?" she said.

He shook his head. What words could there be now? So he
said only one, his brother's name, and that word was so sad, so
tragic, so beloved, that he needn't say more for her to know that
Victor was gone. Not that she believed it.

"No, no," she insisted. Already, she felt turned inside out.
"He's coming back at the end of the week. He's going to stay
here, with me. We decided that."

She turned from him so he wouldn't see her cry.

"He never loved anyone but you. He told me he didn't care
what my mother would have thought."

She laughed at that, through her tears.

"I know exactly what she would have thought," she managed to say.

Marianne's laughter became a sob, and she sank to the ground.
Julien knelt beside her, his arms around her. She cried for a very
long time, and then she nodded and said he was surely starving,
which he was. They went inside and he sat at the table below the
beam where Monsieur Félix had been hanged, and he wolfed
down an omelet and toast with jam. Marianne stood by the window and looked out. She could not believe Victor would never
walk up the road again, that he would never shout with joy, or tell
her she was beautiful, or come upstairs with her to bed.

After Julien slept for a while in the parlor, she asked him to
tell her everything, and he told her all that he knew. Victor had
been on the last train to Auschwitz, where everyone had been
gassed to destroy the evidence that they had ever existed. But
here were two people who knew Victor had existed. They lit a

336

candle and Julien recited what he could remember of the Kaddish, the prayer for the dead. *Blessed and praised, glorified and exalted, extolled and honored, adored and lauded be the name of the Holy One, blessed be He, beyond all the blessings and hymns, praises and consolations that are ever spoken in the world.*

After supper, during which they said very little, Julien went out to hike along the hillside, mostly to give Marianne some time alone. He went up to the place where he'd been when Monsieur Félix was murdered, a beautiful spot where he could see for miles. Though it was nearly nine, the sky was still light. There were clouds above the mountains, but here it was clear, and Julien threw himself on his back in the tall grass. He was so tall and strong that his body often seemed to belong to a stranger. He closed one eye and squinted at the fading sun. If Lea was beside him in the grass she would surely know what he felt, a longing for something he could never have again. A normal life, a family. He spied a cloud coming close and then closer. It was the heron. Julien stood up to greet the bird, and as he did he realized he was crying, and that he couldn't stop, and that anything which gave him hope of any sort was overwhelming.

He slipped the message out of the tube, hands shaking, but before he could read the note or respond, the heron departed. The bird had an awkward gait at first, but when he leapt into the sky he was a marvel. Julien called for him to wait. He shook his arms at the sky. How would he ever write back to Lea? He turned to the message, but when he unfolded the paper, he saw it had not been written in Lea's familiar script.

She's waiting for you here.

There was a small intricate map, as if seen from a bird's-eye view.

Ava, he thought.

He went back to the house and waited for Marianne to come down from her room, anxious, tapping his long fingers on the tabletop. He wished he had a cigarette, a habit he knew he would have to quit.

When Marianne finally came downstairs she said she had been sleeping, but her eyes were red and her face puffy. Her hair had come undone, and for the first time Julien saw that she was, indeed, beautiful, just as his brother had always vowed.

Marianne offered to help him cross the border, but he told her there was somewhere he must go. He placed the map on the table. "Here."

"It's the doctor's house," Marianne said after a quick glance. "A day's walk. An hour or two if Monsieur Cazales next door will take you in his truck."

She sent Julien with two golden jars of honey to bring to Cazales in return for the favor of a ride. He wouldn't need the map. Everyone knew where the doctor lived.

"You'll be all right here?" Julien asked. She certainly didn't look all right, but she nodded, and he remembered what his brother had told him. Marianne was strong.

She went outside to see him off. She hugged him and told him she would say a prayer for him at her church. They would likely never see one another again, but they had both loved Victor and they always would. Julien had no belongings, but Marianne packed a bag of Victor's clothes that had been left behind. It made sense for someone to get some use out of them.

"What will you remember most?" Julien asked Marianne.

Everything, she thought, but she couldn't bring herself to say it aloud.

"Remember when he jumped off the roof?" Julien said.

They remembered the house in Paris, and the laundry being hung in the yard on Tuesdays. Long before Victor had become a fighter, or planted bombs, or taken Marianne to bed, he used to run through the fresh white linens, insisting he was a ghost. Marianne embraced Julien for a long time. He was so tall she had to stand on tiptoes to kiss his cheek. They wished each other good luck, for they both believed in luck now, good and bad, a fate cast for no reason, where some would live and others would die. Julien headed to the neighboring farm, just over the hillside, setting off on the path Marianne had always taken when she brought their cows home from the pasture in the dark.

Remember when I was his favorite brother, when he sulked whenever he didn't get his way, how bad his temper was, how deeply he could love someone, how fast he drove, how bees didn't frighten him in the least, how he was always convinced he was the best at whatever he tried, from explosives to kissing, how he filled up a room, how he would never follow his mother's rules, how convinced he was that a plain woman was beautiful, how he always saw her that way, how he had promised he would never leave again.

When Julien reached the farmhouse he introduced himself to the neighbors and presented the gift of honey from Marianne, then asked for a ride over the mountains to the doctor's house.

Monsieur and Madame Cazales muttered between themselves, wondering if this was the young man who drove too fast.

"No," Julien said, having overheard them. "That's not me. That was my brother."

Monsieur Cazales recognized the look on Julien's face. There

339

was no need to say more. The people in this village knew sorrow when they saw it. Cazales got the keys to his truck and told his wife he'd be back late, for these were roads that were difficult to navigate even for the best drivers, those who had lived here all their lives and would continue to do so no matter the circumstances.

Marianne's stomach was churning, and once Julien was gone, she knelt to be sick in the low bushes on the path where she used to walk at night to find the cows. The cows were white and their flanks had gleamed in the dark; when she had sounded a low whistle they would always follow her back to the barn. She could not go inside the house. It would be much too empty. That night she slept out near the hedges where there were migrating birds, little flickering golden things that darted through the dark.

In the morning, she decided she would make a wreath for Victor to lay beside the one she'd woven for her father. As she walked through the fields of Queen Anne's lace, she was deeply aware of Victor's absence. How selfish he could be sometimes, how sure of himself, how easy to love. She imagined him everywhere. She sat in the grass, barefoot, gathering the flowers she would use to festoon his wreath, with tiny white roses and wild poppies to decorate the Queen Anne's lace. Once, in Paris, not long before she'd left, he had come up to her in the corridor and put his hands on her waist. She had firmly said *no*. She had said it was impossible, but he'd said nothing was impossible and she should know that by now. She was glad Julien hadn't told her any more than he had. Not the details. That would have been too much. *He's alive to us.* That was all she'd wanted to hear.

She went beyond the field early the next morning, out to where the wildflowers were blooming in a riot of color. The bees had all left, in search of empty logs and old trees to begin new hives. It was quiet and she felt her aloneness here now, just as she had felt alone while she was growing up. It was likely the reason she had left for Paris in the first place. It hurt to be so alone. She could move into the village, or go to a city and find work, not Paris, she couldn't go there, but perhaps Lyon, someplace where she would see people whenever she walked out her door, where the wind would not remind her she was alone. And yet her father had lived here all his life, and had been completely by himself during the years Marianne was gone. He said there was not a more glorious place on earth. In that, she believed he was right. He said that a person could get used to being alone, and perhaps she would discover he was right about that, too.

She sat on the porch all that afternoon, the wildflowers collected in her skirt, and by the time the wreath was done, she had decided to stay. She would eventually get some cows and more goats. She would go to a neighbor on the other side of the village who had many beehives and ask for his help restarting one in the field. Monsieur Cazales would likely be willing to help her in the fields until she could pay someone to work for her. It would be a beginning. She would walk the old paths and look at stars. She hadn't lost the ability to find her way in the dark. She would be here alone, and as time passed, she would find that she enjoyed it, just as her father had. She would soon bring out a rocking chair so she could sit outside on clear nights. There was little need to go any farther than the village, or the neighbor's. The world was right here. She had brought more than sixty children to freedom; she'd held down fences, her coat covering the barbed wire, and she would always have small gashes in the palms of her hands to remind her of this. She'd had her heart broken, she'd been in love, she had lived her life, she'd done something worthwhile, and wasn't that what she had wished for most of all when she left the farm and continued walking, when she went to Paris and was so happy that she had no regrets about what she had done? She was especially glad that she had slept with Victor the last time, when the bee flew in his mouth, when she feared she would lose him and they spent all night together in her bed.

It would be May of the following year when the baby arrived, that green time of the year when the bees are working so hard in the fields. By then, the war in France would be over. She would name the baby after Victor, and when the pastor came to call he would understand why she would not wish to have the child baptized in a church, since he was his father's son. Instead, they would bring the baby to a stream beyond the field on his naming day and Marianne would hold him in her arms while the pastor recited Jacob's blessing.

May the angel who delivered me from all harm bless this boy.

CHAPTER THIRTY-THREE

THE WEIGHT OF A SOUL

ARDÈCHE, AUGUST 1944

Ava found the bones in the field. The captain's car had been towed away, but the burned-out skeleton of Victor's car was left, blackened and smoldering. It was a hot day and the sun struck her skin as she made her way through the grass. She first came upon the shoes, then the bits of charred, blackened bone. She carried what was left of her maker into the woods. The place she chose was deeply green and silent. She dug the grave with her hands. Her fingernails broke, but they would grow back. The scent of earth stung the back of her throat. If she cried there was no one there to witness her tears, other than the birds that came to watch, in silence.

She was without a maker. She was herself. She walked back to the doctor's house, though it was a long way. When he saw her with the red shoes he came out to meet her, and they mourned together in the orchard. She had a solemn expression as she asked if, in his opinion as a doctor, he had come to the conclusion that all living things had souls. Creation began when God commanded, *Let the earth bring forth living souls according to their kinds, domestic animals and creeping animals and wild animals.* *Ruach* applied to spirit, the invisible force of a spark that animated all living creatures. If a soul was formed by meaning and purpose, did not every blade of grass have a soul, for each had a purpose. If this was true, Ava believed she might have one as well, just as her maker did.

It was an unexpected question.

"Perhaps," he answered.

Ava was clearly unsatisfied with his remark. "A dove feels sorrow when she loses her fledgling, does she not?"

"I believe so," he agreed, both to please her and because he had seen animals mourn one another.

"And a cow separated from its mother, does it not cry and wail?"

"Yes. True. The difficulty is, we can't know if such responses are merely nature, ingrained to continue the species."

"So you're saying no. That beasts are sparked with life, but not a soul."

Girard rubbed his eyes and thought this over. That conclusion didn't seem right. He thought back to the dog he'd had when he was a boy, a long-legged hound. Once he'd been lost and the dog had tracked him for over ten hours. His parents had sobbed, assuming they would soon be planning a funeral, but

344

the dog did not give up. When at last he tracked Henri into the woods and they saw each other, it was difficult to know who was more overjoyed. So now he asked himself, was the dog merely a beast trained to search for a missing child, or was he doing so out of his own desire, because his soul would not let him rest until he found his beloved master? It was a complicated matter, one he did not feel qualified to answer.

"I'm a doctor," he said. "I deal with flesh, not spirit."

"But you *do* deal with spirit. You speak to the dying. You're with those who are being born. This is an honor not many humans have." Ava was very serious. "Have you seen the World to Come?"

He supposed she meant heaven. "Why do you ask?" Perhaps she was more religious than she appeared to be; all of this talk of spirit seemed to point to it.

She wanted to know what she herself was, but she merely shrugged and said, "Isn't it natural to wish to know such things?"

"Actually, in my experience, it seems most people try their best *not* to think of such things. They avoid doing so at all costs."

"But you do." She seemed very sure of this. "You think about these matters every day."

In order to continue his work in the best way possible, he did not dwell on such matters. And yet, he had an inkling of what she was speaking about. There was often an illumination around the dead, and those being born seemed touched by a similar light. Sometimes it lasted for no longer than the time it took to blink, but there were other times when the light continued to hover, so that a room might be filled with sparks for an hour or more after someone had passed away. He'd never spoken of this to anyone, it seemed pompous, perhaps mad to suggest that he was in some way doing God's work. Yet there were times when the doorway into the next world seemed to have been flung open and all he could do was get down on his knees and look with awe upon the gift of life. It was the same with death, how strong an adversary death was, how all encompassing, how its arrival could be a gift or a tragedy.

When he thought about the matter of the spirit, Girard was forced to think of his wife as she truly was, not as sitting in the kitchen or parlor waiting for him, as he liked to imagine, but as mere bones, cold and in her grave. Now he must think of Ettie in the same way, when only days before she had been so alive, filled with spirit. He wondered what he might have done to change the fate of the two women he had loved in this world.

He had lost his faith on a night when Sarah asked him to lie beside her. He took off his shoes and did so. She was so thin in his embrace, it broke his heart. He knew the way the ending of a life occurred, and was well acquainted with the simple facts of death—how the kidneys stopped functioning, how the breathing became labored and the body could no longer maintain heat and was cool to the touch. Girard knew it was impossible to stop what was happening, yet begged her to stay. She stroked his hair and Henri sobbed, as if he were the one who was dying. Sarah had already given up on the world they were in, the beautiful blue world where it was possible to fall in love at first sight. "I've done everything I wanted to," she told him. They had never been able to have children, and instead of that lack being a burden, it had served to make them closer. It was fate, she always said, insisting she wasn't disappointed. There was no one else to love, only one another.

He kissed her, as if his breath could bring her back. He was not like other people, he was a doctor, and because of this he could see the Angel of Death. He knew him well. *Look for the shadow*, his father had told him when he was a boy and they visited the homes of the dying. *And do what you can to defeat him.* When he finished his medical studies his father reminded him to keep watch for the last angel. He'd thought the old man was joking with this Angel of Death nonsense, but his father's expression was serious. *He will surprise you and you'll think you're going mad sometimes, seeing all manner of things. But he'll be there at the moment life ends. He's always there.*

Since that time Girard had spied the angel as he threw open a window and stepped inside a house. He had seen him in the fields, moving through the sunflowers, and in hospital surgery wards. Now he had appeared in their bedroom. Henri was not about to give in to him. He had planned for this moment, and quickly shifted Sarah to his side of the bed, then positioned himself in her place.

"Are you expecting me to take you instead?" the angel asked.

Henri had been awake for three nights in a row and he knew he might be imagining the angel, but he remembered what his father had said. *It will be him, there in the room.*

Azriel listed the names of everyone who would not be rescued by the doctor if he should die on this night. Since that time, Henri had kept a small leather notebook in which he later wrote down the names, at least the ones he could remember, and every time he met one of the people he crossed their name off the list, even though he had not been the one to decide to save them, so he took no credit. He wanted his wife, and no one else, but it was not his will to decide such things.

He could not claim to know what a soul was, or who possessed it. But he knew that a dove mourned its young, and a dog yearned for its master, and a man who lost his wife never truly recovered, and love that was given was never thrown away. He went to the closet in his bedroom and carefully stored the red shoes. Then he went to the guest bedroom, where he found Ava sitting in the chair. He put a hand on her shoulder, and when she looked up at him there were tears in her eyes.

When the moon was high, Ava went out onto the lawn, where the heron was waiting. She had danced with him a hundred times before, and they danced again on this night. Girard could see them from the window. He'd heard a call that he'd thought was a person wailing, but when he looked outside he saw the bird. He realized how little he knew of this world, but he knew this: If you could love someone, you possessed a soul.

CHAPTER THIRTY-FOUR

WEST OF THE MOON

THE WOLF'S PLAIN, AUGUST 20, 1944

HE STOOD IN THE ORCHARD. SHE KNEW HIM EVEN THOUGH everything had changed. He was a young man with long dark hair, handsome, six feet tall, well muscled but too thin, a troubled look on his face. There was a halo of darkness around him that hadn't been there before, yet when he saw her, his eyes filled with light. She came through the back door without bothering to pull on shoes, in a hurry, her hair much paler than he remembered, ash white, shimmering, but it was her, the reason he'd stayed alive.

"You," she called out, her hands on her hips. "Julien Lévi from Paris."

She knew him still, despite everything that had changed. He came to her slowly. He didn't wish to rush, even though it had been such a long time. He wanted to see her standing there by the door and remember everything about it, the dress she wore, her pale bare feet, the flame of sunlight across her face, a stray curl of her hair that she brushed away.

"What are you waiting for?" she cried.

They weren't children now, and maybe they hadn't been then. Nearly four years had passed. She was sixteen, and he would soon be eighteen.

"Are you certain I'm who you think I am?" he said, grinning.

She didn't bother to answer, or to wait any longer, but instead came to throw her arms around him. He had kept his promise. They broke away from each other and sank to the grass, near enough for their hips and shoulders to touch.

They took in each other's differences, and liked what they saw. Neither wished to be anywhere other than where they were, in the doctor's orchard at this exact moment in time. They could have told each other everything, but they wanted to go forward, not backward, and so after years of wanting nothing more than to talk, they sat in silence, their fingers laced.

This is how it ends, Julien thought.

This is how it begins, Lea knew.

Ava watched from the window, then pulled down the shade.

This is how it was always meant to be.

She baked her last loaves of rosemary bread for supper, somber. This was what Hanni had wished for, this was their covenant, this was all the time she was allowed.

The doctor came to stand in the doorway. He had been introduced to the young man who'd come for Lea. He was a well-mannered fellow who shook the doctor's hand, thanking him for his hospitality. The haunted look in his eyes left only when he gazed at Lea. The doctor recognized him; he resembled his brother, the same handsome dark features, but with more reserve, intelligent, but wary.

"I knew Victor," Girard said. "I knew him very well."

"Did you?" There was that haunted look.

"And the girl he worked with. I knew her." He had gone to the spot of the accident with a handful of white phlox to leave in Ettie's memory. "They were extremely brave."

It was hard to talk after that, no one wanted details, how tall the grass was in the place where Victor was arrested, how there in the field the doctor had found a perfect white tooth.

When she saw how Julien brooded when his brother was mentioned, Lea took his hand and challenged him to a chess game, which lightened his mood. Each insisted they would easily win. Ava and the doctor could hear them laughing and teasing one another in the parlor.

"Will you leave tonight?" Dr. Girard asked.

"Yes. I'll see them to the border."

Girard had given the boy a compass, in honor of his brother and Ettie. Now he poured himself a drink, and offered Ava one as well, but she declined. He had two women to mourn now, and perhaps he drank a little more than he should in the evenings.

"You could stay here," he said casually.

Ava gave him a hard look. "If you're searching for a housekeeper you should look elsewhere."

"That's not what I want, Ava. You're a healer. I saw it myself. I could use your help. When the war is over, there will be so many wounded from the prison alone, we won't have enough hands."

"I have no training."

"I'll train you, or more likely you'll train me."

But Ava knew what would happen when they came near the border. Lea would honor her mother, and Ava would allow her to do what was meant to be.

"If life was different." She shrugged.

The doctor remembered how she had dared to shake her fist at the angel at the window; he'd been stunned that she had such nerve, but by the next day the angel was gone.

"I know you've seen the man in the black coat. I have as well, outside of sickrooms, in hospitals, in my own home. There aren't many of us who have encountered him and are still here to talk about it, you know. You sent him away."

"But how do I defeat him so that he won't return?" She wished to be ready should he come again.

"There's only one way. You have to trick him. And you must be willing to change places with the person he's come for."

"You've done so?"

"I tried. And failed. The other person has to agree to let you take her place." He leaned forward, the memory burning hot inside of him. "My wife would not agree."

He was fairly certain Ettie would not have agreed either. This is what happened with stubborn, principled people and so it was impossible to claim death's attention. "To do so you have to accept a sacrifice."

Ava understood completely. To make such a trade you had to be willing to forsake your life.

It was dusk when they left and the air was eggshell thin. The world was so green it swallowed every shadow. Before long a cold moon would rise into the sky. Julien walked ahead of them, his eyes on the compass the doctor had given him. There was enough starlight pricking through the sky so they would be able to see. Ava and Lea had Julien lead the way, even though Ava saw the world as a map. It was the last time she and Lea would be together and so they walked side by side, as they always had, their strides evenly matched.

Julien turned and waved at Lea, a grin on his face. Lea waved back. Inside of him was the boy she had known, but she was the only one who could see him.

"What will happen to him?" she asked Ava. She had worried about him for so long it was difficult to stop. No person should know what fortune would bring, but the nuns at the convent had gossiped, insisting that Ava could read the future, and all Lea wanted to know was whether Julien would continue to keep his promise to her.

Lea and Ava both gazed at the young man ahead of them, the one who had given them plums on their first day in Paris, who had listened outside Lea's door when she wept for her mother and grandmother, who had lost every member of his family.

"He'll be the man you trust."

That was all Ava would say, no matter how Lea begged for more, but in the end, it was enough.

They planned to cross near midnight, when it was most difficult to see shapes moving through the woods, when invisibility was a virtue and a gift. Once they went across they would be arrested, then officially questioned by the Swiss guards before being turned over to the Red Cross. There was only one answer to any of the guards' questions: *I fled because I feared for my life.*

Lea wore the blue dress her mother had sewn. She felt naked without the locket she had lost before she reached the doctor's house. She had nothing to take across with her except for Ahron Weitz's painting of the sky. She had shown it to Julien. By then, he had realized he would not be a painter; he was a mathematician and had always been so. At night, when he regarded the stars, he often felt his father beside him. He viewed the world in shapes, for indeed, the universe was made up of pieces of a puzzle. He remembered his lessons in the library. His father had said there was a logic to the natural world and to life itself, it was simply that the plan hadn't yet been understood.

He and Lea had decided they would go to New York, where anything was possible. They wanted a new world, one where the future could be made by anyone who wished to do so, a country made by immigrants.

"What if they separate us?" Lea asked.

"That won't happen. We go together."

They would cross the border at the Wolf's Plain. They knew who they had been, but not who they would become. They would find that out as they lived the rest of their lives. The sky was black, but Lea could see what was inside of it now, and she wished she could tell Ahron Weitz that she finally understood how much more complicated things were than she'd ever imagined. Julien pointed out the constellations his father had named when they stood in their garden, and Lea leaned back to see the thousands of stars in the sky. When they crossed over they would carry everyone they had ever known or loved with them. They would close their eyes and still see it all.

I remember when my mother would do anything for me, when we discovered we were not hunters, but wolves, when the world was taken away from us, when we hid in an attic, when the roses bloomed with silver petals, when a bird danced like a man, when I saw Paris for the first time, when I saw your face in the hallway as you turned to me, when they believed we were worth nothing, when we were sent away on trains, when my father bought my freedom, when the souls of our brothers and sisters rose into the trees, when we ran through the woods, when I loved you above all others and you loved me in return.

"What of Ava?" Julien whispered. Ava had made a campfire. She'd brought along a cast-iron pan and was frying mushrooms she'd plucked in the woods so they would have a proper meal before crossing over. Her black hair shone in the firelight. "What happens to her?"

"She'll do as she pleases for once."

"Without you? All she knows is how to watch over you."

Lea stared at the golem. "She'll learn. She'll live her own life."

"She seems different than she was in Paris," Julien noted.

"Does she?"

"Well, for one thing she doesn't hate me."

They laughed, remembering her initial reaction to him.

"She didn't trust me for a minute."

"Well, neither did I. At first."

"Why would you? I was intolerable."

She grinned. "Not all of the time. Anyway, she trusts you now."

Julien shook his head, in disbelief.

"She told me so herself," Lea told him.

His eyes were so dark. Those gold flecks were gone. Lea ran a hand through his long hair. She wanted to cry whenever she looked at him. She wanted to thank him for keeping his promise.

"You never told me what she was," Julien said. "You said you would."

"I will." As Lea watched Ava she felt a catch in her throat. "But someday," she said to Julien. "Not today."

Ava felt the angel in the heat of the firelight before she spied him. He had come to them again as she had feared he would. She had cheated him out of his rightful prize and now he had come for Lea once more. But he hadn't taken her when the bees had swarmed and Ava most certainly would not allow him to take her now. That was when she knew. She would not take her maker's advice. She would not run.

Since their last encounter, Azriel could see her even though he was meant to only see mortals. Perhaps it was because she had grabbed hold of him and he now recognized her essence. Whatever the reason, he knew her and he knew what he wanted. She could not persuade him to change the course of what was meant to be, but she remembered what the doctor had told her. There was a trick mortals played, and now she would do the same.

You must be willing to change places.

She was willing.

She called for Lea to follow her.

Lea must be willing as well.

If it was possible to trick an angel, it was possible to do the same to a mortal girl.

"What could she want?" Julien asked.

"Whatever it is, I owe it to her."

They went to a cave used by wolves when the mountains belonged to them.

"Don't ask any questions," Ava said. "One last time, do exactly as I say."

They exchanged clothes. There was no reason for Ava to tell Lea why she now donned the blue dress and Lea wore the gray dress Hanni had made for the golem when she first decided she must send her daughter away. Ava wrapped a black scarf around her head to ensure that her even blacker hair didn't show. She pulled off the rabbi's boots and gave them to Lea, then slipped on Lea's shoes even though they were two sizes too small.

"Don't leave this cave until you can no longer see me. Do you hear me? Then, once I'm gone, go to the border with Julien. He'll find the way."

There was something unexpected in Ava's tone. A sort of terror was folded inside the words.

"Where will you be?" Lea asked, feeling Ava's terror.

"I will be doing what I was made to do," Ava told her.

When she led the angel away, he would assume he was following Lea into the dark woods, and by the time he realized his mistake, it would be too late. The moment to take her would have passed.

Before Ava left, she and Lea threw their arms around each other. They didn't need to speak.

I beg you for one thing. Love her as if she were your own.

This was how it had begun, and how it would end.

Ava set out in mortal guise, the angel following. She made certain not to be too fast and went at a mortal's pace. She forced herself to think like a mortal. This way or that? Over this rock or around it? Mortals hesitated. They stumbled. There he was, at her heels, in his black coat, carrying his book, ready to open its pages. She was so concentrated on the Angel of Death that she made a very human mistake. She could see a distance of a hundred miles and could inhale the sparks of fires burning in Paris, for the city was in chaos, and would be liberated in a matter of days. But she didn't spy the shadow of a man lying in wait. A German soldier on his own was camped nearby. He had killed too many people to count or remember. He had one thing in mind, how to go on living. He spied Ava long before she took note of him, and when she was almost upon him, he lifted his rifle.

Ava stopped in her tracks. In a way she was relieved. If meeting with the soldier was meant to have caused Lea's death, it was a death she would have gladly taken on. But he would find out she wasn't mortal soon enough. She would trick him as she'd tricked death.

"Come here," the soldier told her in German. "Do as I say and I won't shoot."

He had no idea that a single letter was more lethal to her than any weapon, and so she went to him and lowered her eyes so he wouldn't know she had no fear of him.

"What are you doing here?" he wanted to know.

Not wishing the Angel of Death to hear her voice, she didn't answer.

"Can't you speak?"

She pointed to her throat and shook her head.

"So you're dumb?" A smile curled at the young man's lips.

Ava felt the heat of compassion that radiated from Azriel as he sat above them. He was preparing himself. He was ready to take a mortal life into his arms.

The soldier nudged her with his rifle. "Do you know the way to the border? Can you take me there?"

She nodded. By now, Lea and Julien would be on their way. By now the stars were shining. The night was clear and cold. How strange that when one was pretending to be mortal, it was possible to shiver.

"Good," the soldier said. "You'll take me there."

They ventured on, with Ava slowing her gait so he could keep pace with her. She led him around aimlessly, something he didn't realize until they stumbled upon the place where he had made camp.

"What sort of trick is this?" the soldier cried, hitting her with his rifle.

She ignored his attack, horrified by what she saw. There was a makeshift tent and a fire pit. Beside them he'd set up traps to catch his dinner. There above them hanging from a rope was the heron, shot, with blood on his breast, gray feathers littering the forest floor. A howl escaped from her throat.

"This miserable thing." The soldier shrugged. "Not worth eating."

Ava's fury burned hot inside her, her loss was immeasurable.

This world that could be so heartless had stung her through and through. When she turned on the soldier it was as if the wind had caused his fall. Once he was on the ground, she climbed on top of him. Did he believe she was a mere woman? She was a monster, wasn't she? She was made for witchery. She called to the angels of destruction and could hear them gathering above her. The wind drew near, summoned by her cries, and the birds above set up a racket of mourning that could be heard for miles. In their struggle Ava was so focused that she did not see another hidden trap, there under the leaves, carefully set to catch the first creature that passed by.

Her foot was seized by the rope, which caught and held on, as if it were a snake. There was only one way to end her existence, to remove a single letter, and only one way to defeat her in battle. Once she was held ten cubits above the ground, her powers would cease.

Before she could slip out of the rope, she was flung upward, exactly ten cubits above the earth. She had been fearless. She had been unbreakable. Until now.

The soldier laughed and said he would not do her the favor of killing her. Instead, he would leave her there to die. It was impossible for her to get back to the ground no matter how she struggled; in the air she was only as strong as a woman, and could face a woman's death. Azriel surely knew her for who she was now. Her scarf had fallen to reveal her black hair. Yet he was there in the tree. Still waiting for the mortal he'd been sent to claim.

She pleaded with the soldier as a woman might, begging for mercy.

"Oh, so now you can talk?" The soldier laughed, pleased

with himself. He was laughing when Lea came up behind him. She was a thread of shadow that fit into the falling dusk. She was the wolf in the woods. She was the flower on a branch filled with thorns. She was the daughter of a woman who would defend whomever she loved.

She had done as Ava said, and was about to leave with Julien, when she found the necklace in the pocket of Ava's dress. She had Julien close the clasp around her throat. She spoke to her mother in the realm of the World to Come. Surely she would understand that you owe a debt to those who protect you.

When I join you in that other world, where we are free of terror and pain, and you embrace me, know that I acted as you would have done, with love and compassion and loyalty.

Reluctantly, she left Julien.

Reluctantly, he let her go.

To help her make her way through the deep overgrown forest, she took hold of a fallen branch, a perfect walking stick. It was what she used to strike the soldier. He cried out when he fell, but she hit him again. She didn't stop because she could not stop. She thought of her mother, who had saved her life, and of those who had been herded onto trains, and of the wolves that had been hunted in these mountains, and of the golem in the blue dress hanging from the tree who would follow her to the end of the earth, and of the heron who would never fly again. She could hear a wailing come from within her that she had heard only once before, from behind the door of their apartment in Berlin when her mother sent her away.

She had taken Julien's knife, and now the point hit its mark.

As it did the soldier's spirit left in a single breath of air, caught by the angel in the trees who had come to collect him. This was the death he had been waiting for. In the blue dusk, Lea saw Azriel. She was grateful to have seen him twice and to still be alive. All the same, she was shaking. She climbed the tree to cut the rope, sawing until her hands were bloody. Ava landed on the ground easily, in her bare feet, then took the knife from Lea and cut the second rope so that she might bring the heron to the ground.

She sobbed as she buried him. She was not made to mourn and cry. She was clay and water, a creature called into being in a cellar, so how could it be that she appeared to be a woman in tears? Still, she wept, with Lea beside her, their arms entwined. She continued to cry as she marked the heron's grave with seven black stones. When she was done, she told Lea to shed her bloody clothes. It was bad fortune to wear another's death. Ava gave her the blue dress, the one with ten thousand miraculous stitches, sewn in Berlin, in the light of a yellow lamp before the darkness fell. It was close to midnight, and Lea and Julien would have to hurry now.

"You shouldn't have saved me," she told Lea. "You should already be on your way."

Lea had come to realize that she'd had a mother not once, but twice. This had been her mother's gift and her blessing.

"Do one thing for me before we part," Ava asked.

"Of course. Anything."

Ava refused to let this girl commit a sin for her. She must honor her mother and their covenant. "You are commanded to put an end to me. It will not be murder."

Lea took a step back, her face ashen. "It will be!"

Ava's arms were bare. It was easy enough to erase a single letter. She lay down in the grassy clearing. When she gazed into the trees she saw how alive they were. She felt her eyes burning. She felt a rush of emotions that were impossible for her to have, and yet there they were, tangled inside of her.

"Do as you were told."

"My mother didn't understand," Lea protested.

"It doesn't matter. You know what I am. My kind are always destroyed."

"So are mine!"

"But your life is in the hands of fate. My life is in your hands. And you must take it."

Lea let out a soft sob when she heard this. For all these years she had been unsure of what she would do, but now that the time had come she knew the answer. Her mother hadn't told her that not only would Ava love her but she would love Ava in return, and that it would be a blessing, until it was a curse.

"You must do as your mother instructed," Ava told her.

There was darkness pooling all around them. It was still a good hour to cross the border, but light came early in the mountains, and soon enough the sky would crack open.

"It was meant to be," Ava urged, her voice gentle. "Do what you must."

Even though she was water and clay, she was between worlds, more than her maker ever imagined she would be. Perhaps love had done this to her; she ached with love and was torn apart by it. She did not know what was logical, only what love made her do.

"Do it because I love you," she told the girl. "Because I value your life over mine. I cannot let you carry a sin."

Lea nodded, ignoring the tears running down her face. It was the end of something. She got down on her knees. She would never be a child again. She could not go back in time and put the pieces together of what had been broken. But it was the beginning of something. "You must close your eyes," Lea whispered. "You can't see what I do."

Ava did so, knowing she was to give up this world. She could hear the wind and the sound of the grass growing. She could hear the ants in the earth and the birds above them. Time passed and Lea was already crossing the border at the Wolf's Plain, walking out of the forest with Julien. When she turned back, Lea saw everything that had happened in the years since she had been sent away, the door closing in Berlin, the train to Paris, the boy in the hallway, the heron in the trees, the village where snow lasted until April, the bees all around her, Ava.

Birds scattered overhead. Ava let go of all that she was and all she had ever been. She was ready, even if there was no World to Come for her, even if she had no soul. She was willing, but after several hours, she was still in the world. She could hear her own heart beating, a thud that shook her to her core, a sound she had never before heard. Perhaps she was not broken, a monster made of clay. Her pulse beat thickly, sounding in her ears. She was more than she should ever be, made by women to be a woman. But that made her less as well, for there is an ending to all mortal life and all life is damage. The bruise left by the soldier bloomed like a dark flower on her now delicate skin. Her breath came hot and fast. She had thought she would never know why humans fought so hard to stay alive, but now she understood. It was love everlasting. It was the thing that could never be erased. She had been made flesh by Lea's love for her. She ached and bled and felt tired in her bones.

When she opened her eyes, the word *emet* was still on her arm.

This is what it was to be human, to be at the will of fate. This is what it felt like to lose a child you loved who had loved you in return. She was awake and brought to life. Being human came to her unbidden, it took hold of her, and changed her. She was helpless against time, the owner of a fragile heart. She felt her pulse and the human blood in her veins. This is what love did. It was a miracle and a sacrifice.

She went to the heron's grave and lay down beside him. This is what grief was, she understood that now. It was never-ending and you carried it with you. You could not stop it or regret it, you could only keep it close to your heart. She could no longer speak the langauge of birds, or hear the fish in the streams, or speak to the angels, but she could heal the sick and she could find her way even though she was alone. The world was no longer a map, it was the place she walked through. She had no idea whether or not she would still see the angel when she tended to the sick and the broken. Perhaps he would look through the window or walk through the door, or perhaps she would not see him again until she took comfort in his arms. Either way, it was morning and she knew where she was going.

She arose from the grass in the first light of day, alive.

ACKNOWLEDGMENTS

There are many people to whom I owe a deep debt of gratitude, most especially Amanda Urban, for her wise counsel, and Marysue Rucci, for her generosity and faith.

Thank you to Ron Bernstein for so many years of friendship and loving support.

Thank you to everyone at Simon & Schuster who championed my work, especially Carolyn Reidy and Jonathan Karp.

Much gratitude to Zack Knoll, Anne Tate Pearce, Elizabeth Breeden, Richard Rhorer, Cary Goldstein, Wendy Sheanin, Mia Crowley-Hald, Carly Loman, Lauren Peters Collaer, and Jackie Seow.

Thank you to Suzanne Baboneau at Simon & Schuster UK for support for many books over many years.

I am indebted to Madison Wolters for historical research and literary insights, including an astounding ability to see this world with fresh eyes at every reading, with patience, enthusiasm, and a deep understanding of the story.

A most special thank-you to my beloved friend Jill Karp and my wonderful and invaluable assistant, Katherine Painter, for traveling to France with me on an unforgettable journey. And gratitude to Jill for introducing me to Facing History and Ourselves, and to Judi Bohn for introducing me to survivors in Boston.

Gratitude to Deborah Thompson for her continuing assistance with historical and religious research and her ability to get to the truth. I am indebted to the Visiting Scholars Program at the Women's Studies Research Center at Brandeis University for bringing us together many years ago.

Thank you to Deborah Revzin for jumping into this book wholeheartedly.

Thank you to my brother, Dr. Ross Hoffman, for his mathematical expertise. And many thanks to the Hoffman-Nichols family from Paris and Vienna for German and French translations. Thank you Mindy Givon for visiting Yad Vashem in Jerusalem with me.

All historical errors are mine alone, but I was fortunate enough to discuss much of this history with experts, as well as with those who had lived through this dark time. I was privileged to travel through France with Pierre-Jérôme Biscarat, historian and educational coordinator of Yahad-In Unum who has researched Maison d'Izieu and the fate of Jewish children in France for the past seventeen years. I am so grateful to have had his insights as a French citizen, a historian, and a man of compassion. Thank you to Adrien Allier, in charge of development of the Mémorial National de la Prison de Montluc, for guiding me through the prison and its history.

Gratitude to Susan Rubin Suleiman, scholar and writer, the C. Douglas Dillon Research Professor of the Civilization of France and Research Professor of Comparative Literature, Harvard University, for her friendship, her careful reading of the manuscript, and her invaluable comments.

Through Facing History and Ourselves, an organization dedicated to the education and remembrance of the Holocaust and all genocides with the hope of confronting hate in the future, I was introduced to many child survivors, now in their eighties and nineties, who generously shared their stories. Some had not spoken in detail about their childhood circumstances before but now wished to speak, some spoke often, especially to young students, and some had written valuable memoirs. I am so grateful to all who raised their voices. I am in awe of your courage.

I extend my heartfelt thanks to the Gossels family: filmmaker Lisa Gossels; artist and writer Nancy Gossels; and most especially to Peter Gossels, a child survivor and an extraordinary man who spoke to me at length about his childhood in France. I'm grateful to the many survivors who were so generous in sharing their stories with me, including Sarah Miller, for her kindness and insights, and Eveline Weyl in Boston and her family in France, Henri and Claudine Moos, for sharing their histories. Thank you to Christian de Monbrison for traveling back in time with me to Le Chambon-sur-Lignon and for speaking so eloquently about a truly amazing life. Thank you to everyone at Maison d'Izieu and to the generous current residents of Saint-Julien-de-Coppel for allowing me to visit and greeting me with such warmth and generosity, and to everyone who was so gracious and welcoming at the Centre Culturel Jules Isaac in Clermont-Ferrand. Thank you also to my guide who was rebuilding the Château de Chabannes and took the time to open every door.

To my dear and beloved friends, thanks will never be enough. To Pamela Painter, writer and Professor at Emerson College for her early reading of the manuscript and her thoughtful comments. To Laura Zigman for always being willing to run away to write. To Diane Ackerman for sharing fictional worlds by the sea. To Professor Sue Standing, for her friendship and devotion to literature.

ACKNOWLEDGMENTS

I will always be grateful to my beloved teacher Professor Albert Guerard, in whose office I write every day, and to Maclin Bocock Guerard, my dear friend.

I am so grateful to my readers for years of support and loving kindness.

Love and gratitude to my grandmother, Lillie, for telling me my first stories.

To my mother, Sherry Hoffman, I will miss you forever.

FURTHER READING

For those who wish to know more about the history explored in *The World That We Knew*.

Alter, Robert. *The Hebrew Bible: A Translation with Commentary. Volume 1, The Five Books of Moses*. W. W. Norton & Company, 2019.

—"No sojourner shall you oppress, for you know the sojourner's heart, since you were sojourners in the land of Egypt."—Exodus 23:9

Bailly, Danielle, ed. *The Hidden Children of France, 1940–1945: Stories of Survival*. State University of New York Press, 2010.

Berg, Rav P. S. *The Essential Zohar: The Source of Kabbalistic Wisdom*. Three Rivers Press, 2002.

Cretzmeyer, Stacy, Klarsfeld, Beate, and Hartz, Ruth Kapp. *Your Name is Renée: Ruth Kapp Hartz's Story as a Hidden Child in Nazi-Occupied France*. Oxford University Press, 1999.

Gilbert, Martin. *The Righteous: The Unsung Heroes of the Holocaust*. Holt Paperbacks, 2004.

Klarsfeld, Serge. *Remembering Georgy: Letters from The House of Izieu*. New York Aperture, 2001.

Klarsfeld, Serge. *The Children of Izieu: A Human Tragedy*. Harry N. Abrams, 1985.

Lang, Andrew, ed. *The Blue Fairy Book*. Dover Publications, 1965.

Lefenfeld, Nancy. *The Fate of Others: Rescuing Jewish Children on the French-Swiss Border.* Timbrel Press, 2013.

Marrus, Michael R., and Paxton, Robert O. *Vichy France and the Jews.* 2nd. ed. Stanford University Press, 2019.

Matt, Daniel C. *The Essential Kabbalah: The Heart of Jewish Mysticism.* HarperOne, 2009.

Miller, Sarah Lew, and Lazarus, Joyce B. *Hiding in Plain Sight: Eluding the Nazis in Occupied France.* Academy Chicago Publishers, 2012.

Sigward, Daniel. *Holocaust and Human Behavior.* Facing History and Ourselves, 2017.

Suleiman, Susan Rubin. *Crisis of Memory and the Second World War.* Harvard University Press, 2006.

ABOUT THE AUTHOR

ALICE HOFFMAN is the author of more than thirty works of fiction, including *The Rules of Magic, Practical Magic,* the Oprah's Book Club selection *Here on Earth, The Red Garden, The Dovekeepers, The Museum of Extraordinary Things, The Marriage of Opposites,* and *Faithful.* She lives near Boston.